*She was a governess,
about to tame London's most
notorious nobleman…*

Praise For
New York Times bestselling author

LIZ CARLYLE

and her fiery romances

"Carlyle writes with a unique voice that
makes each book memorable."
USA Today

"Liz Carlyle weaves passion and intrigue
with a master's touch."
Karen Robards

"Intriguing . . . engaging . . .
an illicit delight."
Stephanie Laurens

"Carlyle delivers a fast-paced pleasure."
Christie Ridgway for *BookPage*

"Sizzling love scenes are tastefully
written, revealing the allure of love, not
merely lust . . . suspense and romance
entwine to create an engaging read."
Publishers Weekly

By Liz Carlyle

THE EARL'S MISTRESS
IN LOVE WITH A WICKED MAN
A BRIDE BY MOONLIGHT
THE BRIDE WORE PEARLS
THE BRIDE WORE SCARLET
ONE TOUCH OF SCANDAL

Liz Carlyle

The Earl's Mistress

AVON

An Imprint of HarperCollinsPublishers

This is a work of fiction. Names, characters, places, and incidents are products of the author's imagination or are used fictitiously and are not to be construed as real. Any resemblance to actual events, locales, organizations, or persons, living or dead, is entirely coincidental.

AVON BOOKS
An Imprint of HarperCollins*Publishers*
195 Broadway
New York, New York 10007

Copyright © 2014 by Susan Woodhouse
ISBN 978-0-06-210030-6
www.avonromance.com

First Avon Books mass market printing: September 2014

Avon Trademark Reg. U.S. Pat. Off. and in Other Countries, Marca Registrada, Hecho en U.S.A.
HarperCollins® is a registered trademark of HarperCollins Publishers.

Printed in the U.S.A.

10 9 8 7 6 5 4 3 2 1

The Earl's
Mistress

CHAPTER 1

England

1856

Misery for one man can feel like slow absolution to another, and the misery that came to Northumbria in February could have absolved a man of capital murder. The Earl of Hepplewood had never committed capital murder—well, not *quite*. But the incessant, bone-chilling cold and the spatter of ice that periodically hailed across his windowpanes felt deservedly isolating just the same.

Yet if isolation it was, it was a splendid one. Bejeweled by its elegant, perfectly proportioned Palladian mansion set amongst eighty acres of rolling parkland, the estate of Loughford was a showcase of ornamental follies, fountains, and footpaths, the whole of it possessing a beauty even the wickedest weather could not dim.

Moreover, all that elegance had been burnished by a grand infusion of new money—specifically, his late father-in-law's mill money—until the house was now the finest gentleman's seat within two hundred miles.

Hepplewood reclined with feigned leisure in what was commonly referred to as his grandfather's study, for though the sixth earl was thirty years dead, the house might as well have been still his. Hepplewood's father had cared nothing for Loughford; he had lived and breathed politics and had let the place run to ruin.

Hepplewood, on the other hand, lived and breathed sin.

There was no better venue for either pursuit than London.

He could not possibly return there soon enough, the earl decided, tossing aside the letter he'd just read. He lifted a pair of ice-blue eyes to meet his secretary's gaze.

"So our new governess brings us a reference from the Marchioness of Petershaw?" he remarked, his mouth twisting. "How's that for irony, Jervis? A letter of character from *La Séductrice,* the most notorious lady in London."

Jervis cleared his throat delicately. "One cannot always choose one's employers based upon their moral character, my lord."

"No, I gather not." The earl's mouth twisted further. "Otherwise, you would not likely be working for me."

Jervis's pale face infused with color. As if to obscure the accuracy of his employer's point, he gestured at the desk's pile of paperwork. "The young woman has also brought a glowing recommendation from some country vicar in Sussex."

"And quite a moralizing bore he sounds, too," said the earl, rising languidly to circle round the massive desk. "Well. Let us hope our Miss Aldridge is not as bland, demure, and well-churched as the last one, for we're fresh out of curates for them to marry. Send her in."

Jervis bowed himself from the room.

An instant later, Hepplewood's breath caught.

Isabella Aldridge was anything but bland.

She was instead a dark, fragile beauty; perhaps the most beautiful creature he'd ever beheld, with a face pale as porcelain and thick, inky tresses that the most severe of arrangements could not disguise. She was tall, too, he realized, as she swept her gray skirts through the door, yet far too thin for his liking.

He exhaled slowly, and with no small measure of relief.

She stopped some distance from the desk and dropped into a curtsy that was at once graceful and subservient, her hems puddling like quicksilver upon his bloodred carpet.

"Your lordship," she murmured, flicking a glance up at him as she rose.

"Good morning." Hepplewood's words were cool and clipped as he tossed aside her paperwork. "Miss Aldridge, I believe?"

She gave a nod that held something less than agreement. "Actually, it is *Mrs.*, my lord," she said, in a quiet, throaty voice, "Mrs. Aldridge. I am a widow."

"Without children, I trust?" he said a little harshly.

Her gaze faltered and dropped again to the carpet. "I was never so blessed," she replied. "It was the briefest of marriages. In my youth."

Mrs. Aldridge did not look, however, as if her youth was much past her.

Hepplewood stared her boldly up and down, willing himself to be unaffected as he motioned her to take the chair before him. Despite her dull attire and quiet demeanor, Mrs. Aldridge could not be much past five-and-twenty by his assessment—and Hepplewood was known to be a keen judge of female flesh.

He suppressed a bitter smile. Hers had doubtless been a short and tragic union, then. What a coincidence.

But Mrs. Aldridge's marriage had likely been made of more honorable stuff than his had been. She had wed a soldier, perhaps? Or an older gentleman?

But the latter sort of alliance was made only for money—and if Mrs. Aldridge had possessed two shillings to rub together, she would not be here.

She must surely know who and what he was.

Lady Petershaw, to be certain, could have told her plainly enough. They ran in the same social circle, he and the marchioness; a circle that was, if not the very rim of Polite Society, then certainly its thinning edge.

And society, the poor, collective idiots, scarcely knew the half of what Hepplewood was up to, no matter the scandalous gossip they might titter over. He had learnt early on to hide his darker habits—usually in a small country house or a Parisian brothel.

No, surely Mrs. Aldridge hadn't been fool enough to reply to his agent, then make no further enquiries into his character?

But having settled into his chair, the woman was still looking up at him through her wide-set and striking eyes. They were haunting, those eyes; a sort of violet blue rimmed with thick, black lashes that held no hint of judgment or even of fear.

No, it was resignation. She looked as if she'd come into his house believing it the portal to Hades and prepared to endure it.

All hope abandon, ye who enter here.

Well. She would make for easy pickings, then.

Hepplewood realized at once the train of his thoughts and derailed it.

He'd no interest in harboring any temptations here at Loughford. He still possessed enough discernment, he hoped, to indulge his baser inclinations well away from his family home.

Well away from Lissie.

The woman surprised him by speaking. "M-may I ask, my lord—what is the child's name and age? Your employment agent, Mr. Gossing, was not very specific."

"Lady Felicity Chalfont," he said, the words clipped. "She's five years of age."

"Felicity," she repeated, mouthing the word as if it were new to her. "What a lovely name."

"I did not choose it," he said abruptly. "She is called Lissie. Felicity is her mother—or, that is to say, it was her mother's name. My in-laws wished it used."

Now why the devil had he said that?

Mrs. Aldridge could not possibly care. Moreover, it was none of her business.

To dispel the awkwardness, he snatched up her paperwork again and let his gaze run blindly over it. There was no point, for he didn't give a damn what it said. He'd no intention of hiring Mrs. Aldridge.

He still sat with one hip propped upon his desk. It was a position of neither authority nor gentlemanly formality; he wished merely to study her. Perhaps, even, to agitate her ever so slightly. He felt the devil stirring inside him again. What would it take to bring a flush of color to those lovely, if perhaps faintly hollow, cheeks?

Her face was otherwise perfection, with a delicate nose, high but gentle cheekbones, and those wide, curiously colored eyes that he'd somehow expected would be brown. And that hair—yes, *that,* he imagined, was her glory. It would tumble down like a dark, lustrous waterfall when pulled free of that punishing array of braids, and slide through a man's fingers like—

She cleared her throat sharply. "Was there . . . anything you wished to ask me, sir? About my qualifications, I mean?"

"Yes," he lied. "You were last employed, I see, by Lady Petershaw. Did she hire you? Yes, I suppose Lord Petershaw was long dead."

"Sadly, he was."

That, perhaps, explained the infamous lady's willingness to employ such a beauty. But what of Lady Petershaw's pack of panting admirers? Had she locked Mrs. Aldridge in a turret in order to keep her from sight? Or had she made some use of the girl?

Given Lady Petershaw's proclivities, another beautiful woman to hand mightn't have gone amiss.

He cleared his throat. "Petershaw left only sons, as I recall."

"I'm quite capable of tutoring a young lady, I do assure you." She stiffened perceptibly. "Indeed, I should prefer it."

And Hepplewood thought *he* would prefer to tutor Mrs. Aldridge. He had a subject in mind, too, though it did him no credit. Very little ever did. Still, he could almost envision her strapped up in black leather, inky hair spilling over her bare breasts, her beautiful wrists caught fast against his headboard.

But she was too thin. Too fragile. And her eyes, he thought, were far too wise.

He tossed the paper down. "So the lads have gone on to the greater glory of Eton."

"Yes," she said. "They are bright boys."

"And did you enjoy your work in Lady Petershaw's entourage, Mrs. Aldridge?" he asked, dropping his voice an octave. "Did you find it in every way . . . *satisfying*?"

Her color heightened ever so slightly. "I enjoyed the children, sir," she said a little tartly. "Yes, I enjoyed being with them."

"I see," he said more blandly. "And it was your first and only post, I gather?"

"Yes, but I was with Lady Petershaw six years." There was a hint of irritation in her voice now. "Is there some question, my lord, as to my qualifications? Mr. Gossing implied that this post was to be mine were I but willing to—"

"Willing to what?" he interjected a little suggestively.

"Willing, sir, to travel so far north," she snapped, "in the dead of a wicked winter."

And there it was. As if he'd set spark to tinder, her eyes were blazing now—burning with a dark, amethyst fire. He had sensed it, that depth of suppressed emotion inside her, and found himself oddly pleased.

Alas, it was time to put an end to this charade. A man had to know how to pick his battles, and he had the distinctly uncomfortable feeling that the beautiful Mrs. Aldridge was a battle best not fought. A battle that might leave a man scarred, and by something a bit more painful than just her nails raking down his backside.

Yes, sometimes a man just knew.

Hepplewood sighed and picked up her papers, drawing them between two fingers and creasing them to a knife's edge.

"I thank you for coming, Mrs. Aldridge," he said, "but I fear you will not do."

She stiffened, her gaze flying to his.

He seized the brass bell on his desk and gave it an abrupt clang.

Mrs. Aldridge's eyes had narrowed. "I beg your pardon?" she replied, coming out of her chair. "What do you mean, *I will not do*?"

"I mean you are not what I need in a governess," he replied, tossing the papers aside, "though it was a pleasure meeting you. Ah, Jervis. There you are. Kindly show Mrs. Aldridge back to the village and arrange train fare back to Town. First class, of course, to thank her for her trouble."

"No." The lady had the audacity to spin around and throw up a staying hand at Jervis. "No, I will have another moment, Mr. Jervis, if you please."

To Hepplewood's surprise, his secretary blanched, bowed, and backed out of the room, shutting the door again.

The woman turned to face Hepplewood. He returned the gaze, a smile twisting upon his face. "Well, madam?"

She marched a step nearer. "What do you mean," she again demanded, "by saying I will not do? I have come all the way from London, sir, at your agent's behest—in *February*."

Hepplewood felt his own eyes flash at that. "I think you forget, my dear, your place," he said warningly.

A flush crept up her cheeks. "I am not *your dear*," she countered. "And you . . . why, you have not even interviewed me! How can you possibly know what I'm capable of? How can you know if I will or will not suit?"

At that, his emotional tether snapped. Hepplewood leaned very near and caught her chin in his hand. "Let me be blunt, my dear," he said, tightening his grip when she tried to draw back. "You would *suit me* very well indeed. But you are not the sort of pretty distraction a wise man wants running loose in his house, and had Petershaw not been dead in his grave, his wife would never have employed you, either. Surely you must know it."

Acknowledgement flickered in her eyes. Ah. It was not the first time she'd heard this—or suspected it, at the very least.

He released her chin and forced his hand to drop, but by God, it was harder than it should have been.

Mrs. Aldridge drew a deep, shuddering breath, her hands fisting, then slowly unclenching at her sides. "*Please*, your lordship," she said hoarsely.

He leaned in a little. "Please what?"

"Please just . . . just give me a chance." Her gaze dropped again to his Turkish carpet. "I've come such a frightfully long way. And I . . . I need this post, sir. I need it very desperately."

"I shall, of course, cover all the expenses of your return to London," he said.

"But I wish to *work*," she said more emphatically. "I am a *good* governess, Lord Hepplewood. I am possessed of a lady's education. I paint and sew and keep accounts with the greatest of skill. I speak three languages and even have a flair for mathematics, should you wish it taught."

"Ah, both beauty and brains," he murmured.

"Surely you, of all people, know that beauty can be a curse," she said sharply. "But I will take excellent care of Lady Felicity, and love her as if she were my own. And I shan't be underfoot. I *swear* it. Indeed, you need never see me. We may . . . why, we may communicate in writing."

He gave a snort of suppressed laughter. "You realize, of course, how ludicrous that sounds?" he suggested.

"No." Her long, lovely throat worked up and down. "No. Indeed, I think it might work admirably. You are not even here that often. I mean, *are* you? Please, sir, I beg you."

He did laugh then. "While I never tire of hearing a beautiful woman beg," he said, dropping his voice, "I strongly advise you to take yourself back to London, Mrs. Aldridge. Put on a stone or two, then find yourself a husband or—more practically—a rich protector." He let his gaze settle on a promising pair of breasts, presently flattened beneath layers of gray worsted. "With your assets, it won't prove difficult."

"But I am here *to work*," she repeated, her hands fisting again. "Why, I have brought my trunks and all my books! Mr. Gossing ordered me to come prepared to start at once. He *told* me this job was to be *mine*."

Hepplewood was not accustomed to argument—or to restraining his desires. "Then I fear Gossing, too, forgot his place," he returned.

Her eyes widened to round, almost amethyst pools as he backed her nearly into his bookcase. "I . . . I beg your pardon?"

Irrationally tempted, he lifted his hand and drew his thumb slowly over the sweet, trembling swell of her bottom lip.

Ah, God. How he wanted her. Her entire body seemed aquiver to his touch.

"Alas, Mrs. Aldridge," he murmured, dropping his eyes half shut, "there's only one position I could offer to a woman of your looks—and that position, my dear, would be under me, in my bed."

On a gasp, she tried to shove him away. "Why, how dare you!"

"I dare because to my undying frustration," he replied, seizing her shoulders, "I desire you. I prefer bedding women with a little fire. Indeed, you may assume your new position at once." He lowered his mouth until it hovered over hers. "Right here, in fact, since you've so high-handedly dismissed my secretary and left us alone. What, will you have it? Do please say yes, for I begin to find myself quite uncomfortably arou—"

He did not finish the sentence.

Mrs. Aldridge did not say yes.

Instead, she drew back her hand and struck him a cracking good blow across the face.

Startled, Hepplewood stepped back, one hand going gingerly to the corner of his mouth. The little wildcat hit like a man, by God.

"Why, how *dare* you!" Mrs. Aldridge's eyes blazed with outrage as she scooted away from him. "How dare you, sir, shove me up against a wall and speak so vilely! Indeed, you are every bit as bad as they say!"

Lust thrumming through him now, Hepplewood glanced at the blood on the back of his hand. "Ordinarily, Mrs. Aldridge, I'd put a woman over my knee for what you just did, and spank her bare bottom," he said. "But the way your lashes just dropped half shut? The way your lips so delicately parted? Oh, be glad, my dear—be *very* glad—I'm not hiring you, because the fire that flared just now would scorch us both."

"You *cad*," she hissed.

"I don't deny it," he acknowledged, "but I also know a woman's invitation when I see it, my dear, and you were well on your way to my bed. One of your hands, by the way, had already slid beneath my coat and was halfway up my back—not, alas, the one you just slapped me with."

"You are utterly depraved." She strode past him to snatch her paperwork from his desk. "Kindly forget, Lord Hepplewood, that you ever laid eyes on me."

"I take that to be a no, then?" he murmured. "How frightfully awkward. Still, I console myself with the knowledge that you were fully aware of my less-than-sterling reputation when you walked in here."

Mrs. Aldridge was shaking all over now. "How very much you must despise yourself, Lord Hepplewood, to behave with such lechery," she declared, one hand seizing his doorknob.

"Spoken like a true governess, Mrs. Aldridge," he said mordantly. "Perhaps you might like to take *me* upstairs for punishment? Sauce for the gander, *hmm*?"

A sneer sketched across her beautiful face. "You may go to the devil, Lord Hepplewood, and be served a proper punishment," she replied, yanking open the door. "It would have to be a cold day in hell before any respectable woman would lie with the likes of you."

At that the door swung wide; so wide the hinges shrieked and the brass knob cracked against the oak paneling behind.

As to the lady, she plunged into the shadows and vanished.

Lord Hepplewood sat back down and wondered vaguely if he'd gone mad.

How very much he must despise himself!

Oh, the woman really had no clue. . . .

And now he was supposed to forget he'd ever laid eyes on Mrs. Aldridge and her softly parted lips? Well, be damned to her, then, the purple-eyed bitch.

He would do precisely that.

Hepplewood got up again and kicked his chair halfway across the room.

CHAPTER 2

Isabella's tears had run dry by the time she reached King's Cross two days later. Indeed, they had dried before she'd left Northumbria, since she'd been obliged to put up another night at the damp coaching inn near Loughford in order to be hauled rather gracelessly in a farm cart down to Morpeth to catch the morning train.

So much for Lord Hepplewood's *noblesse oblige*, she thought bitterly. The man was a cad and a bully.

But he was not quite a liar, was he?

Isabella could still hear his rich, deep laughter ringing in her ears. Dear God, *would* she have kissed him?

The truth was, she did not perfectly remember the moment when he'd seized her and lowered his mouth to hers. She could remember only the overwhelming strength of his grip and his warm scent drowning her. The sensation of her knees buckling beneath a wave of sudden longing. The shiver of his muscles as her hand went skating up his back.

Stupid, stupid, stupid woman!

Until that moment, she could have saved the situation.

She was *sure* she could have done, for she'd needed that job so desperately.

But then the man had tried to kiss her, and rather than hold the course, her bloody brain had gone to mush! She had proven his very point—that she'd no business anywhere near him—and lost her opportunity. And all for what? The heat of a man's touch?

Isabella swallowed hard and closed her eyes. Good Lord, had she no pride?

But pride always went before a fall, did it not? That was what her old vicar had been ever fond of saying. Moreover, during that long, sleepless night beneath the Rose and Crown's moldering bedcovers, she'd had much time to consider—and cry over—what her pride had brought her to.

Had she been overly proud? Did she deserve this fall? A fall that was destined to lay her so low she might never rise again—this time taking those she loved down with her?

Dear God. How had it come to this?

As the fringes of London appeared, Isabella stared out the train's window and pondered the question. She had been foolish, certainly, in her youth. She had made an impetuous marriage in a moment of desperation, and as it was with most such marriages, she'd been left to rue the day.

But prideful? She prayed not. She had tried to step cautiously, and after Richard's death, to choose wisely and work hard. To think about those people who now depended on her, rather than those on whom she'd once depended. Her father. Her stepmother. Richard, so very briefly.

And somehow, she had managed.

But as the cramped and malodorous third-class carriage went clackity-clacking back into King's Cross Station, Isabella was seized by the fearful certainty that she was no longer managing; that she had just run out of options. Almost nauseous with dread now, she drew her landlord's last missive from her bag and, to further torture herself, reread it for about the twentieth time. No, this time, he would not be forestalled. The licentious Lord Hepplewood had been her very last hope.

And yes, she had known precisely what he was. A wastrel and a womanizer. Lord Hepplewood was infamous in certain circles.

Yet she had gone to take the job anyway, for such was her desperation.

The train ground slowly to a halt beneath the vaulted roof in a steaming clatter, porters darting along the platforms to throw open the doors to the first-class compartments. The man on the long bench beside Isabella—a cobbler from Newcastle—rose before her and elbowed open the door himself. From the bench behind her, someone hefted a squawking hen in a wicker cage over Isabella's head. A boy with a knobby burlap sack that smelled of damp earth and parsnips pushed past.

The odor made Isabella want suddenly to wretch. Settling a hand over her stomach, she hung back until everyone else had clambered out and onto the platform. Then she stood and hefted down her valise, wondering if she could spare enough of Lord Hepplewood's leftover fare money to hire a conveyance to haul her trunks back down to Munster Lane.

She was still standing on the platform, pawing through her reticule to count her coins, when she felt the hair rise on the back of her neck. A shadow drifted past—uneasily near—and when she looked up it was to see her aunt, Lady Meredith, studying her from beneath the brim of a hat perched at a jaunty angle atop a pile of unnaturally pale curls.

Isabella bit back a quiet curse and tried to smile.

"Isabella, my dear." Lady Meredith touched a bit of darning on Isabella's sleeve with feigned concern. "Good heavens, child. You look a disheveled fright."

Isabella dropped her hand, sending her reticule swinging from the cord on her elbow. "My lady," she murmured, bobbing the stiffest of curtsies. "How do you do?"

"Better than you, I fear," declared her aunt. "Indeed, it troubles me to see those dark smudges beneath your eyes. Isabella, are you losing weight again?"

"I don't think so," Isabella lied, noting a little bitterly that Lady Meredith did not look in the least troubled. "Please, ma'am, don't miss your train on my account."

Her aunt gave a dismissive wave. "We've plenty of time," she said. "What of yourself? Are you departing? Or arriving?"

"Arriving," she said, praying her aunt did not ask for details.

But Lady Meredith had begun to glance up and down the platform. "You will wish, of course, to pay your respects to your cousin Everett," she said a little stiffly.

Isabella felt a cold chill settle over her. "I don't see him."

"He went back to fetch my portmanteau." Her aunt flashed a self-satisfied smile. "We are just on our way down to Thornhill. As I'm sure you know, the manor house is so very cozy this time of year."

"It's lovely, yes," said Isabella.

But there wasn't a corner of England one could charitably call cozy at this time of year, and they both knew it. Cousin Everett, however, was now Lord Tafford of Thornhill—Isabella's father's former seat—and Lady Meredith loved to wield that fact like a weapon.

As to her cousin, he simply loved to wield control—over anyone smaller and weaker than himself.

Isabella was not weaker.

And once upon a time, she had proven it—but at a terrible cost.

Lady Meredith had never forgiven her. "I wish you'd had time to return my letters, Isabella," she said, tugging absently at her gloves as if to neaten them. "I have been thinking how desperately you must miss the old family pile."

"I do miss it," Isabella admitted, for what was the point in denying it?

But her aunt's face held no real sympathy. "I could lie, Isabella, and say I pity you, but I think you know that I do not," she said with some asperity. "This is what comes of thinking too well of oneself. Still, I hope no one has ever called me unforgiving or unchristian. Perhaps I might ask Everett to have you and the children down to Thornhill for a day or two, if you would find it a comfort?"

"To Thornhill?" Isabella echoed. "With Everett?"

"Yes, he still speaks of you—and lately of Jemima, too. We saw her in the park last week. What a beauty the child is becoming! Perhaps I might agree to bring her out, too, when the time comes."

"Bring . . . *Jemima* out?" The chill became like a knife in Isabella's heart.

"Oh, pray do not thank me yet!" cautioned her aunt, throwing up a limp hand. "I must ponder it. But I *will* have Everett bring the three of you for a visit."

"Thank you," Isabella managed, "but the girls have school."

Her aunt wrinkled her nose. "Is that what you call it?" she said, dropping her voice to an admonishing whisper. "Really, Isabella, I cannot think it seemly that the late Lord Tafford's daughter—or even his stepdaughter—should be reduced to rubbing elbows with charity waifs. Everett, I do not mind to tell you, is appalled. And before you turn up your nose at that, kindly recall your father appointed him trustee."

"A moot point, I imagine," said Isabella dryly, "since Papa had nothing left to entrust—nothing that was not entailed to the estate for Everett. Moreover, the Bolton School is not a charity. One pays according to one's means, and they take only the brightest children in Kensington."

"Along with the spawn of every second-rate actor and starving artist in a two-mile radius," her aunt countered. "Oh, Isabella! It pains me to think how unnecessary all this is!"

"I thank you, Aunt, for your concern, but—"

"Oh, never mind that, here is Everett now." Her aunt brightened. "And he has found Viscount Aberthwood. They have become great friends, you know, so he's going down to Thornhill with us."

The gentlemen drew up, both attired in the height of fashion. The viscount looked younger than Everett's twenty-seven years, but otherwise the pair appeared to be peas in an aristocratic pod. Her cousin had managed to shoehorn himself into the highest echelons of society, it seemed.

"Bella, old thing," Everett oozed, bowing over her hand. "Aberthwood, do you know Mrs. Aldridge?"

"Your cousin, isn't she, Tafford?" The gentleman looked Isabella up and down, as if taking in her plain gray coat and worn boots before finally acquiescing to lift his hat a fraction. "How do you do, ma'am?"

"Quite well, thank you."

Just then, a porter pushed out Isabella's trunks and looked at her enquiringly. "Out to the curb, miss?" he asked.

"Yes, thank you," said Isabella. "And might you help me hire a cart of some sort?"

Lady Meredith tossed her hand dismissively. "Oh, just

run back, Everett, and catch our coachman," she ordered. "Brooks has nothing better to do. He can take Isabella and her trunks down to Fulham."

It was on the tip of Isabella's tongue to refuse and suggest her aunt go to the devil with Cousin Everett riding on her coattails, but she wisely bit back the words. She had already consigned the vile Lord Hepplewood to hell, and while she had no wish to be further beholden to her aunt, what was left of Hepplewood's first-class train fare would pay for several days' worth of heat. Assuming they weren't turned out before the coal-monger came round.

So she accepted Lady Meredith's charity and allowed Everett to escort her from the station and out onto the street, though she refused to take his arm.

On the curb beyond the crowd, however, he stopped and turned with a smile that did not reach his eyes.

"Isabella." He lifted his hand and set his fingers to her cheek for the briefest instant. "Oh, my dear girl, how you do try my patience."

"I am not trying anything, Everett," she said wearily. "Do not start with me."

Something ugly twisted his almost effeminately handsome face. "Come, Bella, we both know how this ends," he replied. "Look at yourself. Look what you've been reduced to. Think what your father would say. Think of the girls. Come home to Thornhill. You have only to say yes."

But Isabella *was* thinking of the girls. "Everett, I've already said no," she reminded him, "repeatedly. And if you really gave a tuppence about the children, you wouldn't wait for me to marry you. You would do something to help them."

"What, and sacrifice that ace I've been keeping up my sleeve all these years?" He laughed. "Look, Bella, you aren't getting any younger. And I'm not getting any more patient."

"Then we've reached an impasse, it would seem," she said calmly. "Look, there is Brooks."

"So it is."

Fury darkened his eyes, but he would not lower himself to berate her in front of her father's old servants. With one last bow to Isabella, Everett snapped out orders to the coachman, then tipped his hat and calmly walked away.

Yes, pride did indeed go before a fall, she thought as her trunks were hefted up. In fact, Isabella had begun to wonder if she had any pride left at all, for Lord Hepplewood's advice had been ringing in her ears all the way down from Morpeth.

Go back to London, he had suggested, *and find yourself a husband or a protector.*

Well, she had already found herself one husband, and given how that had turned out, she was not apt to find another. Not unless she was willing to humble herself and accept Everett's oft-repeated proposal—which made starving to death look like a viable option.

And the other choice—a protector; dear God, it churned her stomach just to think of it! But the truth was, women were faced with that hard choice every day. The knowledge had wrenched at her heart during the interminable ride back to London.

Isabella fleetingly shut her eyes and swallowed hard. She was a widow of poor but noble descent, not some dashing high-flyer. But she had a measure of grace—and beauty, she was often told. And though she had made some foolish choices, she was not stupid. Such assets might provide a way, she acknowledged, of paying the proverbial rent. Some women flourished from such arrangements; a few even grew wealthy.

Isabella felt tears threaten again. It felt as if Lord Hepplewood had been her last honest hope—and he'd been her ninth interview since leaving Lady Petershaw's employment. She truly had not imagined it would be so hard to find a post.

She had believed, she supposed, that her employment with the scandalous *La Séductrice* would be overshadowed by the fact that she had been governess to the young Marquess of Petershaw. She had believed, too, that her father's good name would still carry some weight. Worse, in her naiveté, she'd imagined her reckless marriage and abrupt widowhood would be long forgotten.

But memory of her father had not long survived the grave, and Lady Petershaw was as notorious as ever. As to Richard's death, his ghost still clung to her like a shroud, and she was not apt to ever cast it off. Between Richard's vindictive father and her scheming aunt, one of them would surely make certain of it.

The porter was hefting the last of her trunks onto Everett's coach. Brooks, her father's old coachman, was holding open the door with sadness in his eyes.

"Fulham, is it, Miss Bella?" he gently pressed.

"Yes, Munster Lane," she said. "And thank you, Brooks. It is lovely to see a dear, old face."

"Thornhill is not the same, ma'am, without you," he said as she climbed in.

Her cottage in Fulham was well beyond the elegant environs of Belgravia, where her aunt and cousin lived, and so small the great hall at Thornhill could have swallowed it. But it was her home now—for as long as she could pay the rent, which was already three months behind.

As was the butcher's bill, the greengrocer's bill, and every other account Isabella owed. Jemima's shoes were worn nearly paper thin. Georgina was in Jemima's hand-me-downs. Mrs. Barbour hadn't been paid in months, though the woman never whispered a word of complaint. But the rent—dear heaven, to lose the very roof over their heads? How would they survive?

The last time Isabella had gone to beg mercy from Mr. Greeley, her landlord, he'd stopped picking his teeth with his penknife long enough to offer her an easy payment option—one which had involved Isabella on her knees and Mr. Greeley getting his *"knob polished reg'lar-like."* Following this offer of Christian charity, the man had fumbled beneath his ponderous belly with a gesture sufficient to get his point across, even to one so dim-witted as Isabella.

A shudder ran through her at the memory, but just then, the porter circled back around.

"That'd be the last of it, gov'ner," he shouted at Brooks. "Off the curb, if you please."

On impulse, Isabella set a hand on the door. "Wait, Brooks." She hesitated and crooked her head out. "Have you nothing pressing to do just now? Truly?"

A smile split his warm face. "Well, you know what they do say, miss," he said, winking at her. "Whilst the old cat's away, the mice may play. Can I do you some service?"

The familiar teasing in his voice was very nearly her undoing. Isabella blinked back the hot press of tears. "Will you take me round to Lady Petershaw's first? I might be a while."

"I've all the time in the world, Miss Bella," he said.

CHAPTER 3

The Marchioness of Petershaw resided in an ivory palace along the west side of Park Square, preferring, as she liked to put it, to always situate just uphill of the very best shopping.

And shop the lady certainly did. Isabella looked about the pink withdrawing room —not to be confused with the blue or the gold withdrawing rooms—and let her gaze take in the sparkling new garniture of ormolu and magenta marble, its center clock soaring four feet off the mantelpiece. Near it sat a new ottoman of tufted pink velvet that, in the East End, might have slept a family of four in comfort.

There were also new porcelains, new lamps, a new Axminster carpet woven of pink, cream, and burgundy, along with six pairs of sweeping, deep-rose draperies that had replaced the pale lilac ones Isabella had seen a mere month earlier.

Returning her gaze to the door, she neatened her gray skirts and tried not to think how much all of it must have cost.

As usual, the marchioness kept her waiting.

La Séductrice made it a policy to keep everyone waiting—especially her gentlemen callers. *After all, my dear Mrs. Aldridge,* she had often said, *salivation is good for the soul,* oui?

The marchioness admired all things French—words, wine, couture, and décor—despite the fact that her father had been a cooper from Margate, and the closest her mother ever got to Paris was selling *pastilles de Vichy* to the well-bred drunks staggering up St. James after their clubs closed.

But one somehow forgave the marchioness her pretense. She was rich, charming, and beautiful. And even the *grande dames* of society who professed to loathe her would likely have cut off their best strand of pearls just to be Lady Petershaw for one day.

Or perhaps for one *night*?

The notion made Isabella smile.

After half an hour, the double doors opened, flung dramatically inward by a brace of identical footmen in the marchioness's white and gold livery.

It was at this moment that Isabella always expected a blast of tasseled trumpets and a run of red carpet flung down the center of the room. But there were no trumpets, just a litter of toy poodles, barking and nipping at Lady Petershaw's heels as she floated across the carpet, arms outstretched in greeting.

"My dear Mrs. Aldridge!" she declared, as if her most heartfelt wish had just been granted. "To what do I owe this inestimable pleasure?"

Isabella had risen to make a graceful curtsy, mentally steeling herself. "My lady, I hope I did not disturb you," she said.

"No, for I was entertaining a gentleman who had become

overconfident," she said, eyes sparkling with humor. "A snub will remind him, perhaps, of the value of my affections. But those shadows beneath your eyes, they *do* disturb me." Here, the lady laid a finger to her lips. "Ah, I recall you've but recently ventured north. It was not, I collect, all you might have hoped?"

"It was not," said Isabella, her heart sinking anew. "It was . . . frightful, really. I came straight here from King's Cross."

Her frown deepening, the marchioness bade Isabella be seated and sent one of the matching footmen trotting off for tea. Then, after settling one of the poodles in her lap, she began to pry from Isabella the details of her trip to Northumbria.

Reluctantly, Isabella supplied them—without mentioning Lord Hepplewood's name.

He was, in fact, just the sort of man who danced attendance on the marchioness, for despite her charm, the lady had a taste for lovers who were mad, bad, and dangerous to know—and she could drive them to an inch.

At the age of thirteen, it was rumored, Lady Petershaw had been sold off the street by her bonbon-hawking mother to a duke reputed to be a devotee of the carnal arts. The price had been two hundred guineas and no questions asked. Lady Petershaw's mother had hung up her wooden vendor's tray, never to be seen again.

It was said the wicked nobleman tutored his young mistress diligently, both in and out of the bedchamber. So pleased was the duke with his pupil's progress that he began keeping her in a grand and increasingly public fashion, showering her with jewels and delighting in the envy of his friends, until one day he obligingly keeled over and fell off the bed from exhaustion—a victim, one might say, of his own tutelage.

La Séductrice had gone on to a succession of wealthy protectors, throwing them off when they bored her, the legend of her sensual prowess growing by leaps and bounds, until, at the age of five-and-twenty, she became with child by the elderly Marquess of Petershaw. Or so the rumors had it.

Whatever his reason, the widowed Petershaw married his young mistress, and together they embarked on a two-year tour of the Continent that gave birth to Lady Petershaw's lifelong love of unrestrained shopping and Lord Petershaw's long-awaited heir. Further, as if to forestall any protests from Petershaw's grumbling nephews, the new marchioness came home two months' pregnant. Thus possessed of an heir with a spare on the way, Petershaw popped off to his great reward, leaving his rich widow to return to her sensual and retail pursuits.

The marchioness sighed dramatically. "And so, this wicked gentleman," she said, pensively tapping her cheek, "what reason did he give for such abysmal behavior?"

At this point in the narrative, Isabella blushed. "He merely said I did not meet his qualifications."

The marchioness lifted both eyebrows. "Indeed? And these rarified qualifications included what, *précisément*?"

Fleetingly, Isabella hesitated. "I gather he wished me to be a little more . . . more . . ."

"Out with it," she ordered.

Isabella sighed. "Ugly?" she suggested. "Old? Wart-riddled?"

But the marchioness had begun to laugh. "Ah, now we reach the truth of the matter!" she said. "His wife's doing, depend on it."

"He is a widower," Isabella blurted.

"Indeed?" The finely arched brows elevated again. "And what is this paragon of restraint's name, I wonder?"

"I should rather not say, ma'am."

"Then I commend your discretion," the marchioness said, nodding sagely. "It is a woman's most valuable asset. Still, did I not always say, my dear Mrs. Aldridge, that it would eventually come to this? You are too exotic—and far too beautiful—to make a suitable governess."

She had said it, but in the gentlest, most roundabout of ways. Still, Isabella was not a fool. She had grasped at once just what the marchioness was warning her of—then put it from her mind.

La Séductrice was something to be envied and perhaps even feared by other women, yes. But wasn't the impoverished, overeducated, and painfully naive daughter of a rural baron another thing altogether?

Apparently not.

Her face a mask of sympathy, Lady Petershaw was still studying Isabella across the tea tray, which Isabella had not even noticed being brought in.

"My dear girl," said the marchioness solemnly, "you have no future in this career. Trust me when I say that men will always want from you something else entirely. It is both your gift, you see, and your curse."

"But you hired me," Isabella countered. "Was I not an excellent governess?"

"Exemplary," the marchioness agreed, grinning. "But *La Séductrice* fears no competition."

Isabella's eyes must have widened, for the marchioness burst into laughter again.

"Oh, my dear Mrs. Aldridge!" she said. "Do you think I don't know what they call me? I hired you because I wished the very best for my boys. And in time, yes, you *might* find another such employer. But time, perhaps, is not on your side?"

Isabella caught her lip between her teeth. "I never dreamt

it would be so hard to secure another post," she murmured, dropping her head.

"And your straits, I fear, are fast becoming dire," said the marchioness matter-of-factly. "You have your sisters to care for, yes? And children are expensive. Indeed, coal and bread and rent are expensive. I am not so far removed from my humble origins, Mrs. Aldridge, that I do not comprehend this. How may I help?"

Isabella lifted her gaze from her lap. "It is so difficult to ask," she said quietly.

"May I make you a loan?" suggested the marchioness. "It would be my honor to do so."

Isabella licked her lips uneasily. She had almost expected the offer—and she was terribly tempted. Not for herself but for the children.

"Thank you for such kindness," she finally said. "But in the long run, what would it solve? Georgina is but six, and Jemima twelve. If I cannot find gainful employment, you'll be making me a lifetime of loans."

The marchioness frowned. "Yes, I understand," she grumbled, "but what was Lord Tafford thinking to leave the three of you impoverished?"

Isabella gave a weary shrug. "Father never could grasp accounts," she murmured. "I suppose he believed Cousin Everett would do the right thing. Or that the girls' maternal uncle would—but Sir Charlton has always been a coldhearted miser. Moreover, so far as I go, most people would say it was my husband's duty to provide for me, not my father's."

"Bah, a penniless poet?" said Lady Petershaw. "A younger son cut off by his father, only to drink himself to death in despair? Richard Aldridge, if you'll pardon my saying, was a romantic fribble who possessed not an ounce of grit."

But he had possessed a head full of thick brown curls, Isabella recalled, along with brilliant brown eyes and the face of an angel. At first he'd been utterly glittering; filled with life and joy and an excitement she'd found infectious. He'd also been able to spout pure poetry—his own words, not someone else's.

In short, Richard Aldridge had been in love with life. He had only imagined himself in love with Isabella, declaring himself eternally smitten as he'd tripped off sonnets and odes in praise of her beauty. And that beauty had been her undoing.

After their impetuous wedding, Richard's father, the hardfisted Earl of Fenster, had not relented, as Richard had glibly insisted he would. Instead, he cut them off without a farthing. His son had been ordered to marry money, and an alliance with a pretty little piece of rural gentry was unacceptable.

Richard, Lord Fenster declared, had always been a dreamer and a fribble, and the earl had decided that life must teach the fool what the father, apparently, could not.

Life had taught Richard quickly. He'd fallen to pieces before Isabella's eyes, slipping into a lethargy so deep he could bestir himself only to drink.

Isabella had had a little money—a very little, by Richard's definition—provided by her maternal grandfather to serve as her dowry, and it had been sent out of guilt, she was sure, for her mother had long been estranged from her family. But that small sum had scarcely covered Richard's existing debts.

Nearly insolvent, they had returned to Thornhill to beg her father's charity. And when Richard died there before the year was out, Lord Fenster was driven by grief and guilt to lay the blame at Isabella's door; to claim to all who would listen that she'd poured the spirits down Richard's throat. Or worse, married him for his money, then simply poisoned him to escape a life of poverty.

Lord Tafford's solicitor had recommended a suit for defamation, and Fenster's family had finally managed to hush him up. It had been a tremendous relief. The cost of a suit had been beyond Lord Tafford's means, for he had honorably paid the rest of Richard's bills—yet another drain on the estate's modest coffers.

When the scandal was over, Isabella's name was badly tarnished. Indeed, it was tarnished still.

She lifted a bleak gaze to Lady Petershaw's. "I made a terrible mistake," she said quietly, "in marrying young. I was barely seventeen, ma'am, and the worst sort of country mouse."

The marchioness shrugged. "And what good, in any case, is a man without money or grit—or, truth be told, stamina," she said, flashing a sly smile. "I fear there is nothing else for it, my dear Mrs. Aldridge. You must find a man with a firm hand and a fat purse, and remarry."

Isabella sucked in her breath. "Remarry?" she said. "Good Lord! Whom?"

"Well, not that vile cousin of yours," declared the marchioness. "You would not allow desperation to drive you to *that,* my dear, would you? Pray reassure me."

"But you hardly know him," said Isabella.

The marchioness fell oddly silent for a moment. "My dear, I can only say that the circles in which I travel give me insight, oftentimes, into the . . . er, moral inclinations of certain men," she said. "I fear your cousin is rumored to possess tastes which render him unfit to—"

Isabella threw up a hand. "Ma'am, you need say no more," she said quietly. "I am painfully aware of Everett's predilections, having shared his roof during my come-out."

"Ah, I see," the marchioness said, carefully folding her hands over the poodle. "I feared, my dear Mrs. Aldridge, you mightn't understand the depths of his depravity."

"I'm not *that* naive," said Isabella darkly. "I wouldn't allow the ugliest scullery maid to live under my cousin's hand, let alone a pretty child like Jemima or Georgina. But Lady Petershaw, I've no intention of marrying again."

The marchioness opened her hands expansively. "But I cannot see, my dear Mrs. Aldridge, as you've much choice."

"Very little, it's true." Isabella looked at the floor. "But you must know there were rumors I had a hand in Richard's death."

"Bah!" The marchioness dropped her hands. "Entirely disproven. No, outright *lies*. I rooted them out before employing you."

"What if Lord Fenster should stir them up again?" said Isabella quietly. "The few gentlemen who remember me do look at me a little strangely, ma'am, when they pass me on the street."

"It has been a long time," the marchioness countered.

"But has it been long enough?" Isabella jerked her gaze up. "Tell me honestly, Lady Petershaw. *Has* it? What man of wealth would take to wife an impoverished widow however faintly blackened by rumor? Particularly when she has two children in tow? I cannot even secure a governess's post. How will I make a decent marriage?"

"Well, some gentleman might—"

"But will that gentleman be *sane*?" Isabella interjected stridently. "Will he be sober and decent—and will he remain that way? Will he be kind to my sisters? And will he leave me provided for, or will I be doing this again in five years' time? No, Lady Petershaw, I will never trust another man to look after me. I *won't*. A husband—oh, a husband would *own me*. You know as well as I what the law says."

Lady Petershaw fell quiet for a moment. "I never did take you, Mrs. Aldridge, for a fool," she finally said. "Yes, it is far better to use men for what *they* can give *you* than to surrender yourself to their use permanently."

"I have often marveled you married Petershaw at all," Isabella confessed.

"Two barren wives will make a nobleman shockingly eager," said the lady dryly. "And I was not such a fool, my dear, as to enter that union without a good solicitor and an ironclad understanding. You, however . . . alas, you simply have no leverage. You've only your looks, which, while prodigious, will get a decent woman only so far."

"But what if I were not so decent?" Isabella blurted the words, her gaze fixed upon the dogs drowsing at their feet. "What if I did not marry but instead struck . . . a sort of bargain?"

"A bargain?" Curiosity laced the marchioness's voice.

Isabella forced her gaze up; forced herself to own her next words.

"What if I were a courtesan, Lady Petershaw?" she asked, her voice surprisingly strong. "No, more of a mistress—one of those beautiful women that rich men keep tucked quietly aside for their pleasure? You . . . why, you know people who live that life—and people who broker such arrangements. *Don't* you?"

"Well . . . yes." For once, Lady Petershaw looked nonplused. "But what is the difference, my dear, in that life and the one your Northumbrian gentleman just offered you?"

"He threatened to seduce his governess." . . . *and nearly got away with it, too,* she silently added. "No, I'm talking about a . . . a private understanding—one in which I have some say—with a discreet gentleman, away from prying eyes. Many men purchase country cottages for their mistresses, do they not?"

"Yes, commonly." Lady Petershaw's eyes were still round with disbelief. "But these are not the high-flyers of Town who are captured like prizes by the highest bidder—or, in some cases, the most skilled lover. Most gentlemen merely want beauty, companionship, and sexual pleasure, discreetly provided. And for that, yes, they prefer widows or fallen ladies who have been forced to the fringes of society."

"Lady Petershaw, I fear you just described me," Isabella pointed out. "I have been reduced to working for my crust and keeping my sisters in a farm cottage in Fulham, where our nearest neighbor is a pigsty. I dress them in hand-me-downs, and they must walk two miles to a—yes, *to a charity school.* We are barely hanging on to the fringe."

This last was said, to Isabella's shame, a little tearfully. But Lady Petershaw did her the kindness of ignoring it and merely said, "Have you considered how this might affect the children?"

Isabella sniffed. "It will do them less harm than starvation, I daresay," she replied bitterly. "But yes, privacy is my paramount consideration. I must avoid exposure—if I can."

"Ordinarily when a lady finds herself in this position, a less reputable friend—myself, for example—lets it discreetly be known that the lady has fallen upon difficulties and wishes to make the acquaintance of a generous protector. If the lady is beautiful and flirtatious, it never fails to work. But it also never fails to tarnish the lady's reputation."

"Precisely why I must be away from London," said Isabella, who'd had a long train journey during which to consider it. "I wish for a brokered arrangement. With an unmarried man, or a man whose wife will not grieve should she suspect. But yes, a rich, even-tempered widower, ideally."

"Oh, you will not be able to choose so nicely," the marchioness warned in a dark tone. "There are people who make such arrangements for gentlemen—*introductions,* they are politely called—and yes, they can be lucrative in the long term. But a courtesan must prove her mettle, my dear. It is not a career for the faint of heart."

In this, at least, Isabella felt confident. "I am not faint of heart," she said. "I have survived much these past eight years. Now I wish to make an alliance with a wealthy—no, a *rich*—man. *Disgustingly* rich."

"Do you, indeed?" The marchioness smiled.

"Indeed," said Isabella more determinedly. "Actually, he needn't even be a gentleman. A banker or merchant or a sea captain will do nicely. And I wish to be away from London. And to begin *immediately.* My trunks are downstairs, already loaded onto Lady Meredith's carriage."

"My, you do not wish for much, do you?" But the marchioness was looking at Isabella with a new sort of respect.

"I can't go home with nothing," said Isabella. "I *cannot.* The children think I've taken a post in Northumbria. They think . . . they think everything is going to be all right. Because I *promised* them it would be. Can you understand, ma'am? I *promised.* Jemima is old enough now to comprehend our circumstances—and to fret herself ill."

"Very well!" As if in surrender, Lady Petershaw threw up her hands. "But if I'm to help you in this, Mrs. Aldridge, I shall tell you right now that nothing in your trunks will be of service," she warned. "You must dress and act the part. And pray do not imagine some sweet, rose-covered cottage and a quick pump in the dark, my dear. A wife is required to do *that* much. Shall I tell you just how it will be?"

Isabella opened her mouth, then shut it again. "Yes," she finally said. "Yes, I daresay you ought."

"You must learn to loosen your hair and lower your bodice," said the marchioness firmly. "You must learn to flutter your lashes, flirt dangerously, and convince this man to whom you are introduced that you burn to writhe beneath him—even if you both know, in your hearts, that it's nothing but a charade. Once the deal is struck, you must bend yourself to his will in bed and out, and pray that he is not cruel or depraved. It is what's *expected*. It is what a mistress must do that a wife need not. Shall I be more blunt?"

Isabella looked away, swallowing hard. "Yes," she whispered.

"Very well, then," said the marchioness. "If the man is terribly cruel—if you fear for your life—then you must return his gifts and leave him. If he is only a *little* depraved, you must learn to tolerate it—and learn to become whatever he most desires, be it dominating or utterly shattered and submissive. Some men will wish you to struggle, then allow yourself to be taken. The odder ones will wish to braid your hair, dress you in white lace, then put you across their knee. And they will want you to beg for it—which you will do, my dear Mrs. Aldridge. You must, in short, become *a whore*. There, I have said it."

Isabella felt her color draining. "That is indeed a harsh word."

"And I use it for a reason." The marchioness set her head assessingly to one side, eyes narrowing. "Yes, my dear, a high-class and well-kept whore—but you'll be one nonetheless. And if you are caught at it, you will be called a whore, probably to your face. You might have to cut your connection to your sisters, or risk dragging them into society's abyss with you."

"I've thought of that," Isabella admitted. "But their standing is already precarious."

"Still, these are morally rigid times in which we live," the marchioness warned. "No one who receives you now is apt to do so if you're caught. Not unless you have the rare good fortune to be redeemed by an extraordinary marriage—and even then your redemption will have its limits. Trust me. I know."

"Yes," Isabella quietly admitted. "I understand."

"Well," the marchioness went on, "have you the stomach for it?"

"Is there security to be gained from it?" Isabella lifted her chin.

The marchioness eyed her. "With your looks?" she said. "Yes, buckets, though it will probably come in the form of what will tactfully be called *gifts*—jewelry and an annuity first; later a pair of carriage horses or tuition, perhaps, for the girls. Though you are, if I may say so, a tad too thin just now."

She *was* thin; thin for a painfully good reason, too. Food was dear, and children had to eat. And lately, truth to tell, her appetite was waning anyway.

The marchioness said no more for a moment, holding Isabella's gaze. "My dear, is there absolutely no one in your family whom you can call upon?"

Isabella shook her head. "My cousin wishes only to punish me for spurning him," she whispered. "The children have only their mother's brother, Sir Charlton, who lives near Thornhill. But he's a wicked pinch-penny and has refused my every plea since Father died. Worse, he has of late become friends with Cousin Everett."

Frustration sketched across the marchioness's face.

Then, as if resolved in her decision, she nodded, rose, and rang the bell.

"Fetch my maid," she ordered the footman who answered. "Then unload Mrs. Aldridge's trunks. Carry them up to my suite, and send round for my barouche."

The footman bowed and scurried off.

"But what are we doing?" asked Isabella breathlessly.

Lady Petershaw whirled around. "You are going home to the bosom of your family," she said. "Tell them . . . something. That you have engaged an even better post. I'm going down to Covent Garden to make certain enquiries of an old acquaintance—let us politely call her a matchmaker. My maid is going to take your measurements, then sort out the undoubtedly dismal contents of your baggage."

"Th-thank you," Isabella managed, rising. "But why?"

"We are of a height," said Lady Petershaw, going to her rosewood writing desk by the windows to unlock a drawer. "I have a few gowns that can be taken in. Tomorrow you will take this"—she turned and handed Isabella a roll of banknotes—"and go down to Madame Foucher's in Oxford Street. Purchase yourself an assortment of undergarments and nightclothes. I trust I need not tell you what sort?"

Numbly, Isabella took it. "N-no, ma'am," she replied. "But I cannot take your money."

"Nonsense," said the marchioness tartly. "You may pay me back if you insist. There is enough there, I trust, to settle your rent 'til next quarter day and fill the larder before you go off in whatever direction this takes you."

Isabella glanced at the note. "Yes, ma'am, quite."

"Very well, I will call on you by week's end," she said. "Be prepared to leave that instant should an opportunity have arisen."

Isabella folded the paper in half, then pressed it between her palms. "Thank you," she whispered. "*Thank* you, my lady. I shall be forever grateful."

The marchioness sighed and shut the desk.

"Then why is it, my dear Mrs. Aldridge," she said grimly, "that I feel as if I am sending my lamb to the slaughter?"

JUST A FEW short days later, and only a mile and a half away in Clarges Street, a less innocent sort of sheep found himself being led to slaughter, and by a far less tender shepherdess. Anne, Lady Keaton, practically had the rope round her cousin's neck before his lordship apprehended that the sanctity of his home had been invaded.

With a wary eye, Hepplewood watched her sweep into his study in a whirl of teal-colored silk, her dainty heels fairly snapping across the marble floor.

Fording, his butler, shot him a withering look before bowing low and shutting the door.

The lady was nothing if not sly; Hepplewood had slunk back into London little more than two days earlier, and save for one small matter of personal business—*very* personal business—he'd laid low, calling upon no one.

Still, he believed a man ought to be gracious in defeat.

"Good morning, my love," he said, rising. "You are in radiant good looks."

"Stubble it, Tony," said Lady Keaton, shrugging off her shawl. "You've a nasty little bruise beneath that eye. Dare I hope your latest mistress put you in your place?"

"Actually, I fell," said Hepplewood, "against her fist. And alas, she's not my mistress—though I will confess, my dear, to having given it a good go."

"Ha! She refused you!" Lady Keaton flung the shawl over his leather sofa, and her reticule after it. "A rare event, I daresay. But one of these days, my boy, you'll get your heart royally trod upon, or some lover scorned will stab you in the back. I wonder, honestly, how you sleep at night."

"Oh, cowards die many times before their deaths, but the valiant taste of death but once," said Hepplewood, studying his manicure as his cousin plopped herself into his favorite chair. "But I trust, Anne, you've not come to inquire into my affairs of the heart?"

Lady Keaton had the audacity to point at an especially private place. "Is that where you're packing your heart nowadays, Tony?" she said on a laugh. "No? I thought not. So no, I have not come to discuss your affairs—and you are no Caesar, by the way."

Hepplewood smiled and settled himself on the sofa. He glanced again at Louisa Litner's missive lying open on his desk, and the strangest shiver of desire ran through him.

Anne was right, of course. He hadn't an ounce of judgment when it came to women.

"Tea?" he said. "Or coffee?"

"No, and no. Thank you."

"Gin? Scotch whisky?"

"It's barely half past one," said Lady Keaton on a sigh. "Now pay attention, Tony. I've come about Lissie."

"Lord, Anne, not again!" Hepplewood got up and poured himself a whisky. He was going to need it.

"You are drinking too much," said Lady Keaton, watching him. "I blame it on your mother's death."

"Why? It was sudden, and it was merciful." Hepplewood rammed the crystal stopper back in and returned to his chair. "Still, it's as good an excuse as any, I daresay. Well, out with it, my girl. What's the daily diatribe?"

"Lissie should not be left alone at Loughford now that Aunt Hepplewood is gone," said his cousin. "She is only six."

"Five," said Hepplewood.

"*Nearly* six," said Lady Keaton. "She needs to be with family. With you. Or with Mrs. Willet. Or with me—or even with Gwen and Mrs. Jansen at the Dower House. But she should not be left to freeze to death alone in the wilds of Northumbria."

"Actually, I rebuilt all the chimneys at Loughford," said Hepplewood dryly, "with her filthy-rich grandfather's money. And you do apprehend, Anne, that your sister and Mrs. Jansen are—well, how shall I put this?—devotees of Sappho?"

"Oh, good Lord!" Lady Keaton rolled her eyes. "How it galls me that you, of all people, should question a devoted and monogamous relationship—friendship—arrangement—*whatever.* They adore Lissie."

"I know," he said more gently, "but Lissie is perfectly warm, Loughford is staffed to the teeth, and I'm searching for a new governess even as we speak."

"No, you are drinking whisky in your wrapper at one in the afternoon," said his cousin hotly. "You will send for her, Tony, or by heaven, I shall! Harry and Bertie could do with a playmate. She may take her lessons with them."

Hepplewood slammed his whisky down, all pretense gone. "By God, don't you dare suggest, Anne, that I give up my child," he said, stabbing a finger at her. "I will never surrender her; no, not even to you. Indeed, you and Mrs. Willet are two of a kind, I begin to think—the damned old vulture."

"Mrs. Willet is not wrong," said Lady Keaton hotly. "She's Lissie's *grandmother,* for God's sake. Let one of us raise her, Tony, if you will not."

"Mind your own business, Anne," he snapped. "Doesn't Sir Philip have an election to rig or a reform to push? Can you not occupy yourself in being his wife, rather than running up here to bedevil me? If I'd wanted to put up with a lifelong harangue, by God, I would have married you instead of Felicity."

"Oh, I knew you too well, Tony, to have you," said Anne grimly, "and Felicity simply did not."

"Oh, *thank you,* Anne, for pointing out the obvious!" he said bitterly. "But in the end, my dear, Felicity did know, didn't she? It was simply too late."

"And that," declared Anne hotly, "was Mr. Willet's fault. He could have let Felicity break your betrothal. *He could have.* Indeed, she begged him. I *know.* I was there—and you were not."

Hepplewood felt his anger burn down to futility as swiftly as it had come. "I was not there," he said, shrugging, "because she did not want me there. And it was a bloody good thing in the end old Willet forced our hands. Felicity paid a price, did she not, for her one brief moment of folly?"

Anne fell silent, staring into the fire. After a long moment, she heaved a great sigh. "Shall I tell you what your problem is?"

"Have I an option?" He felt his mouth twitch. "Experience suggests not."

"Your problem is that you cannot bear to look at that child. Lissie is pining away for her family, and you are down here whoring yourself blind."

"*Whoring*—?" He forced a wicked grin because it was expected. "My, Anne, how the pristine have fallen! And raging promiscuity, by the way, does not actually *cause* blindness. That's just one of Uncle Duncaster's old saws."

"Tony, you are the very devil." Leaping up, Anne snatched up the reticule and shawl she'd tossed aside. "I *loved* Felicity. She was *my friend.* And I owe her daughter this—so I'll tell you how it's going to be. Philip and I are going up to Loughford to fetch her and take her down to Burlingame—and if you try to stop me, I will go straight to Grandpapa, do you hear me? I *will,* I swear to God."

"Duncaster's a hundred years old and house-bound," said Hepplewood dryly. "What's he going to do? Come down here and strop me?"

"He has certainly done it before!" Anne was trembling now, her reticule clutched to her chest, her shawl straggling off her elbow. "And I would not try him, Tony! I really would not! Grandpapa might just—*just—*"

Hepplewood realized then that he had pushed her too far; that Anne was not aggravated, she was on the verge of tears. Suddenly, she flung her things to the floor and clapped her hands over her eyes.

"No, you're right," she sobbed. "He *w-won't, w-will he*?"

"Well, damn it all," he muttered, going to her and putting his arms about her shoulders.

"I hate you, Tony! I hate you!" Anne set her forehead to his shoulder and sniffled miserably. "Why are you always such an ass? Until you were s-seized with good looks and charm, you were so n-nice! And I l-loved you quite utterly!"

She did cry then, sobbing into his loosely tied cravat like a little child, and clutching at both his lapels. He set a hand awkwardly between her shoulder blades and made soothing circles, his mind tallying up the clues; her old arguments dredged up anew, the irrational tears, her flowing dress—and the belly she was pressing rather high against his waistcoat.

"Anne, my love," he finally murmured, setting his lips to the top of her head, "are you by chance expecting again?"

"*Y-yes!*" she sobbed. "Is-is-isn't it *w-wonderful*? But Grandpapa is going to d-die, isn't he? He will not live to see another child born, will he? He is going to die with only

Harry and Bertie and Rob and Barbara and Lissie and *th-the twins—!*"

It would have done no good at all to remind Anne that Lord Duncaster was one of the richest, meanest, most self-satisfied men in Christendom, and that to have lived to the great age of ninety-odd years with a more or less happy family and an entire cricket team of nieces, nephews, and great-grandchildren was far from a tragedy.

But there was nothing else for it; she would not be reasoned with. Most of the time, Anne was the sweetest soul he knew, but she could turn into a raging lunatic during those early months of expecting.

More worrisome still, she might not be wrong.

About anything.

So he made another little circle, gave her a couple of neat pats, and said, when she lifted her head to look at him, "Do you know, Anne, I think you might be right."

"I'm always right," she snuffled. "Philip s-says so!"

"I'm sure he does," said Hepplewood, straight-faced. "Go fetch Lissie for a visit. Take her straight to your grandpapa's, if you wish. Uncle Duncaster isn't especially well, and it will do them both a world of good."

"Well, all right, then," she said in a conciliatory tone. "Won't you come up, too?"

He hesitated. "I can't, Anne," he said. "Not for a few weeks. I have business in the country."

She pushed herself away from his chest. "I won't bother to ask what sort," she said darkly.

"I must look in on one of my properties." He glanced again at Louisa's letter and felt his blood stir dangerously. "But I promise to meet you back in London, *hmm?* In a month's time, or thereabouts. That will give Lissie a long visit with you and Duncaster."

"And then we will talk about her future?" said Anne.

Hepplewood gritted his teeth. He did not know, precisely, how to raise a little girl, but he damned well meant to manage. And no, he wasn't doing an especially good job of bringing up Lissie—he did not need Anne to point that out.

He told himself with every passing year that the next year he would snap out of this god-awful rut. But Anne, he feared, was right. Lissie was almost six, and he was out of time. His mother was dead, and the child required more than swaddling and coddling now; she required a family.

Moreover, Anne was still looking at him expectantly.

"And then we will talk about her future," he managed, "if that is what you think best, my dear."

"Oh, thank you, Tony!" Lady Keaton stepped back, her face brightening. "Aren't you just the best thing!" she added, dashing a fist beneath her eyes. "Don't I always say so? And oh, what a watering pot I am. Look, why don't you get dressed and walk me down to the arcade? You can buy me a new pair of gloves."

Hepplewood glanced at the longcase clock and sighed.

Then, resigned to his fate, he yanked the bell and sent Fording off in search of his valet.

CHAPTER 4

The morning light cut across the wintry fields of Fulham, casting a faint sheen upon Georgina's hair as Isabella swiftly braided. Above the glare on the window, she could see a rime of frost melting inside the glass, dripping inexorably into the cracked caulk and rotting wood.

Isabella looked away. She could not afford to have the glazier in, and with the rent barely out of arrears, her landlord would be less than sympathetic to complaints.

An old wool blanket tossed round her shoulders, Jemima sat perched on the end of the girls' bed, her face a little anxious. Isabella knew too well the look, and it troubled her.

"Jemma, darling, what's wrong?"

"Must you go so quickly, Bella?" she asked. "Lady Petershaw's friend must be in a frightful rush."

Forcing a smile, Isabella picked up Georgina's hair ribbon and tied off the blonde plait. "Wealthy gentlemen are always in a rush," she said, her motions deft. "Mr. Mowbrey's library is vast, I'm told, and will take weeks to catalog."

Georgina twisted around on her dressing stool. "And

there won't be *any* little boys at this house?" she said again, her little brow furrowing. "Or any little girls? At *all*?"

"No, my only little girl is right here." Isabella crooked her head to set her lips to Georgina's temple. "And I will long for her madly—and for my big girl, too. Still, I did enjoy telling you funny stories about Lord Petershaw and his brother."

"They were so *wicked*," Georgina giggled. "Remember, Bella, when they put the mouse in the chalk tin?" The child flashed a grin that showed the gap where her bottom front teeth should have been.

The impossibly tiny teeth had been the first to appear, Isabella remembered wistfully, and now the first to go. Where would she be, Isabella wondered, when the rest of Georgina's teeth came out?

Most likely in the mysterious Mr. Mowbrey's bed, she thought bitterly, at least for the next two incisors. Beyond that, she might not hold his attention.

Still, that was how one remembered one's life, she supposed, when a child was the center of one's universe. Such memories became the milestones by which one measured happiness. The small triumphs and tragedies—like Jemima's first fall from her pony in the ring at Thornhill. Or the time Jemima cut off all Georgina's hair with the gardener's shears. Or the day she'd taught both girls to skip rope in Green Park.

Dear heaven, how she would miss them! For an instant, she shut her eyes, already struggling against the yearning.

When her father and stepmother still lived, Isabella had spent her holidays and every other Sunday at Thornhill. After their deaths, Lady Petershaw's mansion had been but a six-mile walk from this little cottage. Buckinghamshire seemed, by contrast, the backside of the moon. And yet she was fortunate, she knew, to be going no further;

lucky, really, that she wasn't stuck halfway to the Highlands with the wicked Earl of Hepplewood chasing her round the schoolroom trying to toss up her skirts.

Isabella drew the comb through the other side of Georgina's hair. "No, I shall have no little imps to manage this time," she said pensively. "Just books, mostly."

"And bones," added Jemima sullenly. "And dead bugs and stuffed birds and even dried lizard bits, I daresay."

Isabella glanced at the clock, hating the fib she'd told. "A natural philosopher might have any of those things, I suppose," she said, swiftly twitching the braid back and forth. "I will simply have to catalog them, Jemma, not carry them round in my pockets."

"Well, you don't look like a governess," said Jemima, "or a librarian, or whatever it is you're going to be."

The ugly word Lady Petershaw had used flashed through Isabella's mind.

But she must not think of that now. She must think only of all the back rent she had just paid, and of the monstrous goose Mrs. Barbour had just hung in the larder.

"Promise me, Georgie, that you will behave for Mrs. Barbour," Isabella said, reaching for the comb, "and for Jemma, too. I'm counting on you both. Help wash and clear after dinner, please, and clean your teeth without being asked."

"Yes, ma'am," said the girls in unison.

"I hope you will like Mr. Mowbrey," Jemima added more hopefully, "and that he'll give you lots of time to write home."

"Of course he will," said Isabella, "so long as I get the cataloging done."

But Isabella deeply disliked misleading the girls, and the notion that had seemed so tolerable a few days ago in Lady Petershaw's withdrawing room had begun to feel more like a trip to the gallows.

"Am I done?" Georgina craned her head back.

Isabella snatched the last ribbon and tied it. "Yes, off to school with you," she said, giving the girl a little scoot. "Quick, kiss me. Oh, have you your reader and copybook?"

"I left it in the kitchen." Hastily, the child gave Isabella one last peck on the cheek. "Love you, love you, love you, Bella!" she said, darting out and down the stairs, her tiny footsteps light.

But Jemima was still sitting on the edge of the bed, one coltish leg dangling. "I like your hat," she said in a voice that was uncomfortably grown-up. "That shade of aubergine becomes you."

"Thank you, Jemma." Isabella stood and smoothed her hands down her skirts. "I like it, too."

The carriage dress of aubergine velvet had come with Lady Petershaw's letter, along with a faintly frivolous velvet hat with a dramatically curling black feather. Isabella had recognized both as having belonged to the marchioness. And while the ensemble was by no means *outré*, it was the sort of thing Isabella had not worn in a very long while.

"You look glamorous, Bella, as you used to do at Thornhill," said Jemima quietly. "Before all the gray, when I was very little."

Isabella wanted to stroke the child's hair and tell her that she was *still* little. That she was a good, sweet child who deserved to be protected from the world's harsh realities. But the realities already told in Jemima's fraying cuffs and in the disquiet that shadowed her eyes.

"It is going to be all right, Jemma," said Isabella, bending over to tuck a loose lock of hair behind the girl's ear. "I promise. Things are looking up for us."

Just then there was a harsh tattoo upon the door. "She's come, Mrs. Aldridge," said Mrs. Barbour through the planks. "I daresay you'd best go down."

Isabella tipped up Jemima's chin. "I'm off, then, my love," she said. "I wish I did not have to ask you to look after your sister, but I do."

It was a dance they had done a score of times before. Jemima slid off the bed and silently hugged her.

"I can do it, Bella," she finally said.

"I know," Isabella whispered into the girl's hair. "I'm counting on you. And thank you."

There was little more to be said. After a moment, Isabella released her stepsister, blinking back an unexpected tear. "Well, then," she managed. "Don't be late for school."

Then, before she began to cry in earnest, Isabella turned and went out the door to find Mrs. Barbour still standing there.

"I shall say it again, miss," the elderly cook grumbled, handing her the marchioness's ivory calling card, "but I don't like the sound of this business."

"Oh, pray do not scold me, Barby," said Isabella as they went down the stairs. "It will be quite all right."

"And your aunt and cousin?" she said fretfully. "You've seen to them, ma'am?"

"Oh, yes! I wrote Lady Meredith yesterday," Isabella said over her shoulder, "and refused her invitation to Thornhill. Indeed, I told her as much in the train station eons ago. I begin to wonder if Everett is desperate? Now, do let Lady Petershaw know if I'm needed, and she will send for me straightaway."

"*Hmph*," said the old woman, jerking her head toward the parlor door. "Well, I've put her in there, miss. Now hug my old neck before you go tearing off again. Natural philosophy, indeed!"

Isabella did, then kissed the old woman's cheek. "What a dear thing you are," she said. "And what would have become of those poor children without you, I shudder to think."

"And I never thought I'd see the day you'd be so burdened," the old woman returned, starting down the kitchen stairs. "That Sir Charlton is Old Scratch himself, and your cousin Everett and his mother are worse. They could have spared you this."

But Isabella had long ago learnt there was no point in grieving over right and wrong. Sir Charlton had refused to support his sister's children, or even to bring them up—not that Isabella could have borne surrendering them.

Returning her attention to Lady Petershaw's plan, she turned, gathered her courage, then pushed open the parlor door, trying to look willing and properly grateful.

But the marchioness did not herself look willing. She turned from the windows that overlooked the lane, her beautiful face a mask of pique.

"Well, my dear, I am come as promised." She crossed the small room to hand Isabella a folded paper. "Here is the direction and Mrs. Litner's letter of introduction. But I shall tell you straight out, this leaves me a trifle uneasy."

"Does it? Why?" Isabella glanced down at the address, scarcely a three-hour drive away.

The marchioness's brow furrowed. "I cannot recall a Mr. William Mowbrey, and I know nearly everyone. I also didn't like the look I saw in Mrs. Litner's eyes yesterday." She made an airy, uncertain gesture, lace swinging from her cuff. "Oh, I cannot call it fear—no, it was not that—but it came an inch too near desperation for my comfort."

"What did she say about Mr. Mowbrey?"

Lady Petershaw snorted. "That he is thirty-something, handsome, widowed, and wildly rich, if that comforts you," she answered.

The vision of Lord Hepplewood's mouth hovering over hers went skittering through Isabella's mind. What would it be like, she wondered, to go to his bed? Would the mysterious Mr. Mowbrey be as handsome?

He could not possibly be as arrogant—or as dangerous.

"I suppose handsome and widowed is better than ugly and married," she said with a shrug.

"Very true." The marchioness smiled. "But she admits, too, that so far as she's seen, Mr. Mowbrey cannot be pleased; that you are the fourth or fifth young lady of grace and beauty to whom she has 'introduced' the gentleman— and if you will not do, she means to give up."

"So I'm her last-ditch effort?" Isabella lifted her gaze from the paper. "Is that why she didn't bother to meet me?"

"Count yourself fortunate," said Lady Petershaw with a sniff. "Louisa Litner is decidedly common."

"Then I wonder any gentleman acknowledges her?"

Lady Petershaw had paced back to the window to glance down at the waiting carriages. "I wonder a little, too," she said pensively, "so I've decided on an insurance plan."

"An insurance plan?" echoed Isabella.

"I'm sending you in my unmarked carriage," Lady Petershaw said, pointing at the plainer of two carriages parked on the grassy verge. "My under-coachman will drive you. Dillon's a clever lad. I've instructed him to remain nearby for a fortnight."

"Yes? To what end?"

"I'm of the opinion that Mowbrey is an assumed name,"

said the marchioness, "one taken merely for discretion's sake, I hope."

"An assumed name?"

The marchioness shrugged. "It's a common ruse when a well-known gentleman is scouting about for a new mistress," she said, "but it makes my scrutiny difficult. So if you find the gentleman acceptable, kindly hang a handkerchief out your window each evening. Just a few inches will do. It is but a small lodge in the countryside; there cannot be too many windows."

"I expect not," Isabella agreed. "But why?"

"If no handkerchief appears on a given night, Dillon will come to collect you the next morning," the marchioness answered evenly. "He's to say there's been a death in your family—we could do nicely without Lady Meredith, could we not?—and you're wanted immediately."

"How extraordinary," murmured Isabella.

"One cannot be too careful in such matters," said the marchioness knowingly. "If Dillon is given any nonsense, the next face Mr. Mowbrey will see shall be mine."

A silence fell across the shabby parlor, punctuated only by the clatter of bare branches beyond the window. "My lady," Isabella finally said, "why are you doing all this for me?"

The marchioness flashed a wincing smile. "If I do not help you establish yourself, you'll do it anyway, my dear, and make a hash of it," she said. "And yet, if I get you into it, I feel it falls to me to get you out again. Moreover, I deeply dislike seeing intelligent women forced into poverty through the vindictiveness of men."

"Lady Petershaw, my problems with Cousin Everett—the current Baron Tafford, I mean—are my own."

The lady shrugged, then patted Isabella's hand. "Now, you will write to me as soon as you have judged the man sane," she reminded her. "If I've had no letter in that first fortnight, I will assume the worst—handkerchief or no."

Isabella nodded. "In which case I can again expect my aunt's demise?"

"Followed by my visit if you don't turn up on my doorstep the next day," Lady Petershaw added.

"Thank you," said Isabella, bowing her head.

The marchioness flicked a glance at the clock on the mantelpiece. "I thought you should leave at once," she said, "before dread sets in. Your trunks are already loaded—the brown one was full of books—and I assume you've a portmanteau?"

Isabella did, now filled with garments of lace, and even a bottle of perfume she would otherwise never have dared purchase. But the tools of her trade were no longer books and chalk, Isabella considered, but something altogether different.

"There's little point burdening your horses with the brown trunk," she said quietly. "Where I go now, I shall scarcely need schoolbooks."

"No," said the marchioness a little somberly. "No, you will not."

Then she went to the front door, threw it open, and shouted at Dillon. "Bring in the brown one," she commanded, "and carry it upstairs."

Isabella gave a long, inward sigh.

Her journey into darkness had just begun.

CHAPTER 5

Mr. Mowbrey's rural lodge lay in a long, low wood a few miles northwest of Chesham, approached by means of a carriage drive lined by fieldstone walls to either side. Isabella looked about, disconcerted by how deep in the countryside they were.

Along the wall, the trees seemed to bow almost formally toward one another, forming a skeletal canopy of gray that would have been beautiful in the summer but now looked merely bleak. The lane was rutted, the center tufted with frostbitten grass, giving one the impression the road was rarely used. Isabella hung on to the strap, craning this way and that in hope of seeing some sign of civilization.

But there was nothing until, after some two miles, a clearing came suddenly into view and the lane simply ended. She looked out to see a pretty Georgian manor of red brick with an arbor arching over the front door.

The façade was nearly covered in creeper, now dormant, and the windows and doors were freshly painted white, yet the house still held an air of abandonment. The wide stone wall encircled the whole of it, separating the carriage drive from the house itself, as if visitors were being walled out.

Or as if the people inside were being walled in. . . .

With legs that shook, Isabella climbed down, told Dillon to stay put, then pushed open the wrought-iron gate and went up the path to the door. She could hear a hammer ringing in the back of the house, the sound like metal on stone, rhythmically cleaving the silence. She lifted the ornate brass knocker and knocked, but there was no response.

After a second attempt, Isabella simply lifted her skirts and waded into the garden, her footsteps crunching on the stubbled, almost frozen, grass. She wished desperately to get through these first awkward minutes and to reassure herself that Mr. Mowbrey was not a murderous ogre before Dillon abandoned her to her fate.

In the rear, another pretty gate gave onto a graveled yard with a coach house and stable block. Here, however, a section of wall had collapsed, leaving the gate listing drunkenly. A man was chipping away at a piece of fieldstone set on an old mounting block, swinging his arm with a rhythmic expertise and sending chunks of gray flying.

He was bare to the waist, Isabella realized, his leather braces having been slipped off his shoulders to hang loose about a pair of lean hips. A blindingly white shirt had been tossed over a nearby branch, and the man seemed intent upon his work, his muscles bunching thickly as he swung his hammer in cadent, cracking blows.

Despite the cool air and the late winter sun, the man's broad back was lightly sheened with sweat, and Isabella watched in mute discomposure for some seconds—long enough, apparently, for the man to finish his work. He laid the hammer aside with a grunt, then hefted up the stone and turned.

Recognition slammed into Isabella, seizing her breath.

It was the Earl of Hepplewood.

She froze, gaping at his tall, rangy form that no longer looked so elegant.

Indeed, absent the civilizing effects of a coat and neckcloth—not to mention a shirt—the man looked shockingly barbaric.

Then, to her acute discomfort, he smiled and set the rock back down.

"Mrs. Aldridge," he said, snatching his shirt from the branch. "Welcome to Greenwood Farm. You're a trifle early. I shall take it as a sign of eagerness."

Isabella stepped backward. "Eagerness?" she parroted, her eyes fixated upon a broad expanse of bare chest.

Hepplewood moved with a languid grace, shaking out his shirt as he came. "I was glad to learn you'd taken my good advice," he said, shoving an arm in a sleeve, "but the coincidence of the thing did take me aback—as it has you, too, I see."

But Isabella couldn't begin to make sense of it; her brain felt stuffed with wool and her lungs had ceased to work. Hepplewood dragged the shirt on, his chest wall rippling as he drew it down his lithe, smoothly muscled torso.

Somehow, she forced her gaze to his face, resisting the urge to run back to the carriage. "I beg your pardon," she said again, blinking slowly, "but *what* are you talking about?"

He propped one hand on the gatepost that still stood upright, his gaze sweeping her length. "My advice," he said with a faint smile, "to give up the dull business of governessing for an option that better suits your . . . well, let us call them your God-given attributes."

Indignation welled up inside Isabella. "How dare you," she said quietly. "I do not know, Lord Hepplewood, just what sort of deceit you employed to trick me here, but I will have—"

"Mrs. Aldridge," he interjected, his eyes flashing dangerously as he came around the gatepost. "I should very much like the two of us to get on, but *deceit* and *trickery* are not insults I'll tolerate." He set a large, very firm hand on her forearm. "Do we understand one another?"

But the word *coincidence* was slowly seeping into her consciousness.

"Surely you don't mean to claim—" Isabella cut off her words and tried to draw back. "Surely you aren't suggesting this is purely—"

"Accidental?" He gave an odd half smile. "Little in life is. I saw a woman I wished to bed, but alas, she declined. Still, women, to my mind, are very nearly interchangeable. It was no great inconvenience to ask the resourceful Mrs. Litner to find me another raven-haired, violet-eyed beauty willing to slake my lust. Imagine my surprise when she wrote that I should expect *you*."

"Dear God." Isabella tried to back away, but the hand on her arm did not relent. "I don't believe it."

"Mrs. Aldridge," he murmured, his eyes roaming over her face, "you approached Louisa Litner with every intention of marketing yourself in just the fashion I suggested. And she has sent you to—well, let's be blunt—to charm and to flirt and to almost certainly warm the bed of one Mr. William Mowbrey, a gentleman of very specific tastes. What can it possibly matter to you that I have turned out to be Mowbrey?"

"I . . . I don't know." Isabella tried to think. "It just does."

"Does it?" His voice dropped, his eyes suddenly heavy. "My dear, you intrigue me."

"I don't wish to intrigue you," she managed, setting a hand against his chest. "I want n-nothing to do with you."

But she knew it wasn't true; not entirely. More than once during the long drive from London, she had remembered their almost-kiss and wondered what this man next would be like. Would his eyes flash with fire? Would his touch singe her through her clothes?

Oh, yes. It would.

And she, apparently, was an idiot.

Hepplewood had caught her chin and was holding it none too gently. "No, Mrs. Aldridge, I was not mistaken in you," he murmured, his voice thickening. "You are a stunning creature—and very much in need, I think, of being tamed."

Isabella had the sense of slipping over a mossy cliff; as if she were falling, her stomach bottoming out. His mouth was nearly over hers, his intent plain, and she would not escape it a second time.

"Just a taste, my dear," the earl murmured, his lashes lowering. "Yes, merely that—for *now*."

Isabella knew she should run; that to kiss him would be surrendering something of herself. But her feet were frozen, his grip relentless.

Hepplewood pulled her hard against him, surrounding her in the scent of male sweat and something even more primitive. He settled his lips over hers, gently at first, and Isabella let escape a faint whimper.

The sound elicited a deep groan, and Hepplewood opened his mouth over hers, thrusting deep on the first stroke. Blood seemed to well up, roaring in her ears, and it was as if the garden and the world around them spun away.

His heat and the overpowering weight of his body surrounded Isabella. Sliding his tongue deep, the earl drew her firmly against him, one hand settling boldly on her hip, urging her against him as he thrust.

Isabella had been kissed, but she'd known nothing like this. It was raw and vulgar and wonderfully knee-weakening; a rush of hot desire that threatened to swamp her. His fingers, she dimly realized, no longer held her arm but had instead plunged into the hair at her nape, forcing her to hold still. His left hand was cupped beneath her hip, lifting her slightly against his groin as her will went weak with a longing that frightened her.

The tip of his tongue stroked the roof of her mouth in the lightest, most erotic of caresses. Inexplicably, the raw hunger it engendered jerked Isabella from her confusion. She wedged both hands flat against his chest and shoved.

To her shock, he stopped, lifting his lips an inch, his eyes still heavy with desire. His mouth, which she would have called thin and a little cruel, now looked soft, his bottom lip faintly swollen.

Something like lust went shivering through her.

"Isabella," he said huskily. "It's Isabella, yes—?"

She nodded.

"Isabella, I want you beneath me," he rasped. "In my bed."

"In your bed?" Isabella echoed witlessly.

"Or wherever you prefer," he amended, his voice dropping.

Isabella's eyes flew wide. "I cannot," she said, this time jerking free of his grip. "Not in Northumbria. And not here."

He did not follow her but watched her warily instead. He had wicked eyes that glittered like shards of blue ice.

"I'm sorry." She forced down a hard swallow and shook her head. "I've made a foolish, foolish mistake."

But her foolish mistake, Isabella knew, had more to do with what she did want than with what she did not.

She wanted him. A man who was dangerous, demanding, and, unless she missed her guess, a little cruel. And she wondered, fleetingly, if she had lost her mind. If something inside her was simply not . . . *normal*.

"Made a mistake, have you?" he murmured. "I certainly haven't. I find you more desirable now, my dear, than ever. And though you don't like me a great deal, you *do* want me."

"How very confident you are," she whispered.

"But not, I think, overconfident," he replied, studying her. "Your eyes are wide, your lips damp and slightly parted. Your gaze—and a moment ago, your hands—were drifting in directions that, strictly speaking, a lady's do not."

Isabella could only stare. She wanted to slap him again, but she had the most frightful realization that what he said was true; that her hands had slid down his shoulders and back, and that this time she'd even caressed—

Lord Hepplewood saved her the shame, for he was suddenly looking up at the wintry sky. "In any event, it will be dark by five," he said with annoying calm, "and quite likely wet. You came by carriage, I assume?"

Numbly, she nodded.

He jerked his head toward the back door. "Go inside," he said, not unkindly, "and pour yourself a brandy. The parlor is to the front. I'll see to the bags and carriage. You cannot possibly leave here tonight."

Fear must have flashed across her face. Lord Hepplewood caught both her arms in a strong grip. "I've never needed to force myself on a woman, Mrs. Aldridge—well, none save my wife—and I've no interest in forcing myself on you."

She gaped at him. "And how am I supposed to trust—"

But her words broke, her face flooding with heat, for Isabella wasn't sure which of them she trusted least.

Hepplewood knew it, too. He leaned into her again, his mouth low. This time, however, he did not quite kiss her.

Instead, he captured the swell of her bottom lip, drew it between his own, and lightly suckled until her most private places throbbed.

When at last he lifted his mouth, his eyes were hot and knowing. "Yes, my dear," he murmured, his gaze drifting over her face, "if you come to my bed, you will assuredly do it on *my* terms. And by God, you'll do my bidding whilst you're in it. But the choice to come?" He shrugged. "That will be entirely yours."

Then he let her go, turned on his boot heel, and strode around the house.

Fingertips flying to her bruised lips, Isabella watched him go, still trembling.

Good heavens, was ever a man so insolent?

But then, a nobleman could afford to be insolent—particularly to someone like her.

Attempting to gather her wits, she smoothed her hands down her dark purple dress as if she might sweep away the evidence of his kiss. She still stood in the back garden, though it seemed surreal now.

Beyond the fence, the carriage house and stable were unchanged, even though her world had just turned topsy-turvy. A pile of large, unwieldy fieldstone lay to one side of the mounting block, and to the other, a pile of smaller, more manageable pieces.

Hepplewood had been at it a while, exhausting his demons, perhaps, with a hammer and chisel. How very odd it seemed.

And how very much she needed that brandy.

Left with no better alternative and now cold to the bone, Isabella did as he had commanded and went inside the house. Both the parlor and the brandy were easily found, and with a hand that shook, Isabella sloshed out too much, tossed half of it back, and considered her prospects as the harsh, unfamiliar spirit burned through her chest.

Through her watering eyes, she watched as the earl helped Dillon heft down her trunk. She wanted to go to the door and order them to put it back. To say that she was going—and leaving Lord Hepplewood and his wicked, ice-blue gaze behind.

But Hepplewood was not wrong in what he said, was he?

What did it matter to her whose bed she warmed?

If she meant to do it as a means to an end—for security for herself and the children—why not bed a man who, at the very least, was physical perfection? She had seen that much, at least, out in the stable yard.

Moreover, what other choice was left to her? To return to London and Lady Petershaw? Yes, she might make an escape now and pass the night at one of the shabby inns back in Chesham. But what would the next gentleman be like? Better? Worse? *Cruel*?

That was the very trouble when one sold oneself, she thought, her mouth twisting. One lost much of the say in the transaction.

Lord Hepplewood wanted her in his bed—to do his bidding, he said. The very notion made her tremble again. But was that not the very thing Lady Petershaw had warned would be expected of her? That she must discern a man's most intimate desires and fulfill them?

There was a darkness and a force within Hepplewood that frightened her, but he was, after all, employing a mistress to slake his needs. Perhaps all such men held such a darkness within themselves?

Isabella did not know. Richard had been the gentlest of creatures, her father much the same.

Everett was a rapist and a despoiler of children.

And that was the sum total of her experience with men. Surely there was something in between?

Her canvas portmanteau now sat in the carriage drive, and to her surprise, Hepplewood had slid her trunk onto his shoulder. Dillon tugged at his hat brim, then climbed back onto the box.

Isabella stood transfixed. She did not walk out, climb in, and order Dillon to drive on. And she knew, even then, that it was a choice she would regret. But she did nothing because she had run out of options—and a bad one, she feared, was as good as it might get.

The bad option in question had now snared the handle of the portmanteau and was carrying both up the steps as if he were the footman rather than lord of the manor. Somehow he shouldered his way through the door. He seemed not to see her standing in the depths of the parlor and instead thundered past and up the stairs.

Suddenly, it struck her as odd. Were there no servants?

No, there were not.

The knowledge came to her on a rush of certainty, and with it an understanding of the house's odd air of abandonment. She was utterly alone here, she realized.

She was alone with the Earl of Hepplewood.

And Dillon was driving away.

Isabella threw back the rest of the brandy.

The house had back stairs, too, from the sound of it. Over the course of the next half hour, Isabella heard his heavy tread going up and down repeatedly somewhere in the depths of the house. Her hand shaking a little, she pulled the pin from her velvet hat with its saucy black feather and set both aside.

By the time the earl returned to the parlor, she'd almost finished another generous brandy—the second of her life, truth be told—and was feeling rather too warm.

"Did you order my coachman to leave?" she asked, still staring out the window.

He closed the distance between them, his expression darkening. "No, I did him the great insult of offering him accommodation," said the earl, "but he had the oddest notion of putting up in the village."

"Oh." Isabella suddenly remembered Lady Petershaw's instructions. "H-how far away is that?"

He laughed, but with little humor. "Back out the lane, turn right, and continue on another two miles," he said, "so do take a lamp, my dear, if you decide to bolt from my little den of iniquity."

"Kindly do not make a jest of me." She turned too swiftly and felt the floor sway.

He flicked an appraising glance at her. "You will sit down, Isabella," he ordered, snatching away her glass, "in that blue chair by the fire."

"You're very domineering," she remarked, watching the dregs of her brandy go.

He set her glass on the sideboard with a hard *thunk*.

"Quite domineering," he said, turning to cut her a dark look. "Are you going to have a problem with that? If so, I'll fetch that lamp now, Mrs. Aldridge, and you may head on back to Virtue-upon-Boredom, or whatever little village you came from."

Her breath caught at the unholy glint in his eyes. "No, it . . . it is your house," she managed, "and, as you've so clearly stated, your rules."

"Yes, I've found matters run more smoothly when a man is unwavering in his expectations."

"More smoothly for whom?"

"For the man giving the orders," he replied without rancor.

"Ah, and that would be Mr. William Mowbrey?"

The earl was pouring himself a brandy, his hand rock steady. He set the glass by one of the chairs, then squatted down to poke up the fire.

"I was christened Anthony Tarleton William Mowbrey Chalfont," he said, staring into the depths of the hearth, "if it somehow matters to you."

Strangely enough, it did. She watched as he stood with a leisurely grace and folded his rangy length into a matching chair opposite hers. His tousled gold-brown locks were damp, Isabella noticed, and he'd put on a fresh shirt, left open at the throat beneath a waistcoat of fine brocade. With his aquiline nose and harsh cheekbones, he was a shockingly handsome man—and all too aware of it, obviously.

Using one long, booted leg, Hepplewood kicked a footstool over in his direction, propped up his feet, then steepled his fingers to study her. It was a posture of utter repose, yet a commanding one all the same, leaving Isabella to wonder if everyone who came within the man's sphere was obliged to obey him.

"You haven't a drop of charm, have you?" she remarked.

He smiled faintly. "I used to have," he said, "but I found it a double-edged sword. Nowadays I find it more expedient to simply order what I want—and to pay for it when I must."

Isabella swallowed hard. "And what, exactly, do you want, Lord Hepplewood?"

"Exactly? To bend you over that chair, Mrs. Aldridge, and fuck you until you beg for mercy." He picked up his brandy with his long, elegant fingers. "But I'm willing to wait until you're more comfortable with the notion."

The alcohol must have numbed Isabella, for she did not blush. "Well," she murmured. "At least you're honest. And along with your lack of charm, I notice you've no servants."

"I haven't any servants *in the house*," he corrected.

"But there is . . . someone?" she said a little hopefully.

Again, he shrugged. "I've a caretaker in a cottage beyond the stable. Yardley sees to my horses and builds up the fires. His wife and daughter come in most afternoons to tidy up and take away the laundry. There are village girls when I need the house turned out."

"You do not eat?"

A smile twitched at his thin mouth. "Oh, I'm a man of appetites," he said. "Yes, I eat—and cook, too, when necessary. I enjoy a measure of self-sufficiency. But yes, the helpful Mrs. Yardley comes back and forth, and sometimes puts a joint on to roast."

Isabella was mystified. "Why do you live here?" she asked more softly.

"It is my home," he said simply. "I have others, of course. But Greenwood is private—a sort of sanctuary—and a place where I can indulge my less civilized habits away from public scrutiny."

"Like dressing fieldstone whilst half-naked?"

His mouth twitched again. "Amongst other things."

"It seems an odd occupation for a gentleman," she said.

He looked at her very directly and did not smile. "Tomorrow, my dear, perhaps you might like to watch me split firewood?" he suggested. "I assure you, I have near-inexhaustable stamina."

Isabella felt that curious, swamping sensation in the pit of her stomach again. She looked away, refusing to hold his gaze.

But the house's seclusion was, in fact, perfect for Isabella's purpose. She let her eyes roam about the room, which, like the other two rooms she'd passed through, was elegantly and comfortably furnished.

Had she not wished for exactly this? To be kept in a pretty, private house away from London? So why, then, did the isolation leave her uneasy?

Because there was not enough brandy in all England, she feared, to make her entirely comfortable with the Earl of Hepplewood. And yet she had the oddest feeling he did not mind her unease; that he took an almost perverse satisfaction from it.

"This is the perfect sort of place a man might hide his mistress," she said, almost to herself.

"I have done, yes."

At last, she looked at him. "Mrs. Litner says you are very hard to please."

"Without question." Again, Hepplewood's voice dropped to a darker tone. "But I'm quite confident, my dear, that you can be taught to please me."

"Taught?" Isabella blinked. "I am not witless, Lord Hepplewood. I understand what sex is."

"Oh, I very much doubt, my dear, that you do." Calmly, he picked up his brandy and sipped. "Tell me, Isabella, how many lovers have you had?"

She felt her face warm. "I—I was *married*," she said a little defensively.

He laughed. "Dear God!" he said. "*One*? And then you took to the nunnery, did you?"

"I became a governess, yes, if that's what you mean."

"And planned to live forevermore without sensual pleasure?" He was studying her across his glass. "Then it was a poor excuse for a marriage, my dear."

Isabella felt faintly awkward. "I don't know what you're suggesting."

He smiled without humor again. "I'm quite sure that you don't," he said. "Tell me, Isabella: Are you going to remain here with me and uphold your end of this devil's bargain? Or do you mean to turn tail and run back to London like the sexual coward you've thus far been?"

"I've never heard virtue called cowardice before," she retorted.

He shrugged, sipped again, then set the brandy aside. "I asked Mrs. Litner for an introduction to a particular sort of female," he said, "a service she has provided me for some years, with sadly declining success. But with you, Isabella—oh, with you, the good lady may have just redeemed herself for all time. Or she may have just suffered her last failure."

"And you suffer from a vast deal of presumption," said Isabella.

"No doubt," he said, "but tell me, my dear: If I ordered you right now to kneel between my legs, unbutton my trousers, and fellate me, would you?"

She did blush then, heat rushing to her face.

Hepplewood set his head to one side, eyes glittering wickedly in the firelight. "Is that a *no*, Isabella?" he softly pressed, "—or do you simply not know what I'm asking?"

She clasped her hands in her lap. "I do not know," she confessed.

Hepplewood scrubbed a hand around the dark stubble of his beard. "I'm not surprised," he said, "but perhaps naiveté will prove diverting. Yes, my dear, I think you'll suit. But you must decide if you wish to stay—and before you refuse, explain, if you will, why you approached Mrs. Litner in the first place?"

She felt her body stiffen. "Because I decided you were right," she said bitterly. "There, does that please you? *You were right.* No one is willing to hire me for the one talent I do have—the education of children. So I may as well cultivate another."

"You might try to remarry," he softly suggested.

"I should sooner whore myself," she snapped, "as I think my presence here proves."

"Dear God, and I thought I had a miserable marriage," said the earl. "And kindly don't use that word again. Not in relation to yourself."

"I can't think why I oughtn't."

"Because that is not what you are, Isabella, and not what you will become to me." His voice softened a little. "I merely seek a sort of companionship without emotional complications. A woman with beauty and grace and a wish to please me, and a wish to be pleasured in return."

"And I seek a way to pay the rent," she replied honestly. "I can pretend, my lord, to have other motivations, and perhaps, if you are very clever, you can charm me into thinking—"

"No, Mrs. Aldridge." He held up one hand. "I will not charm you or flirt with you—*ever.* So you'd best take that long walk to the village now if that's what's required to ease your *petit bourgeois* sensibilities."

"I beg your pardon?" Isabella drew herself up like a true scion of nobility. "You know nothing about me, sir, or my sensibilities— or the color of my blood, come to that."

He hesitated. "Quite so," he said stiffly. "Well. Let us merely agree, then, that you seek an arrangement with a gentleman. But you could easily find that without the aid of a predator like Louisa Litner. You would turn heads on the Town, you must surely know."

Isabella snared her lip, debating what to tell him. "I have a family, my lord."

"Good God, you have *what*?"

"A stepsister and a half sister who depend on me," she

clarified. "They are but children. I may have fallen far, Lord Hepplewood, but I've no wish to drag them down with me."

"Where are these children?" he demanded. "Who are they?"

She lifted her gaze to his very steadily. "They are private," she said. "They are my life. And they have nothing to do with this, or with what I do or don't become."

For an instant, he looked taken aback.

"Are you a gentleman, Lord Hepplewood?" she asked.

"A gentleman with more than a few vices," he acknowledged, "but no one has ever accused me of lying, or cheating, or breaking the sacred bond of my word."

"Then I ask for your word as a gentleman," she said, "that you will not pry into my private life, nor discuss our arrangement beyond the bounds of this house."

"Do you?" he murmured. "Fascinating."

"I wish to be a rich man's mistress," she said, "and I wish for utter privacy. If you can give me those things"—she dragged in a rough breath—"then yes, I will stay. For as long as it pleases you. I will learn to pleasure you. And to-to *fellate* you—whatever that is."

He observed her almost clinically for a moment. "And to receive pleasure, Bella?" he finally murmured. "Will you promise to learn to do that as well?"

"You may not call me that," she said.

He crooked one dark eyebrow. "I'm not sure you get to decide."

She fisted her hands on the chair arms. "I *do* decide, my lord," she said vehemently. "I will please you—yes, I will uphold my end of any bargain—but I am not *nothing*. I will not be ground beneath your boot heel. And I do not give you permission to call me that."

He was turning his brandy glass round in little circles on the tabletop. "May I ask why?"

"I prefer only the children use that name."

"Ah," he said, inclining his head almost regally. "Very well then, *Isabella*. Answer my question."

"W-what question?"

"Will you learn to take pleasure?" he asked, watching her very intently. "Will you learn to receive as well as give? Will you trust me to lead you on this exquisite path? And most importantly, my dear, will you be obedient?"

She nodded.

"I should very much like to hear you say it."

Isabella looked away. "I shall do as I'm told."

"And—?"

"I shall learn to do whatever you require," she managed, "and to give and receive pleasure. Is that what you want to hear?"

The earl sat without speaking for some moments, the utter silence broken by nothing but the crackle of the fire. After a while, Isabella looked up from her intense study of the carpet to realize the room had slowly gone almost dark.

Hepplewood sat at an angle to the flames, which now cast an almost satanic glow up one side of his face, emphasizing the lean plane of his cheek.

"We shall deal very well together, Isabella, you and I," he finally said. "Yes, I agree to your terms. And you agree to be my . . . my disciple, let us say. How shall we begin?"

"H-however you wish," she said.

"And that, my dear, is the precisely right answer," he said without a trace of sarcasm. "However *I* wish. Now, go to the sideboard and pour yourself a glass of sherry—*not* brandy, for I would not have you insensate. Then sit back down."

"I . . . I do not care for any, thank you."

"I did not ask," said the earl.

For an instant, she froze. Then, remembering Lady Pe-tershaw's instructions, she pushed herself from the chair and did as he had ordered.

"Excellent." The earl sat fully reclined in his chair, his feet still up, his brandy cradled low between his thighs. "Now, drink it, Isabella, then pull all the pins from your hair. I wish to see it down."

"Now?" she said incredulously.

He did not answer. She could feel his gaze drilling into her through the gloom. She was going to pay, she feared, for standing her ground. And once again, the ugly word came to mind.

Whore.

Isabella shut her eyes and pulled the first pin.

"Good God," he said thickly when all her hair was down. "Draw your fingers through it, Isabella. Yes, like that. Over and over. Does it feel good to be free of constraint?"

She did as he ordered. "Yes," she whispered, "it feels good."

He had steepled his fingers pensively together again. "Excellent," he said. "Now, Isabella—this might feel awkward, but I wish to see you touch yourself."

"T-touch myself?" she said.

"Yes, begin with your breasts," he said. "Just stroke them with your fingertips. Stroke them until your nipples become aroused."

Isabella felt a little ill. "I . . . I do not know how."

"Isabella," he said warningly. "In such things as this, I will not be gainsaid. Just do it."

Awkwardly, she did so. When he did not tell her she might stop, she continued. After a time, he braced his hands on his chair arms and rose. She stopped, watching warily as he crossed the room toward her.

He halted before her and flashed his strange, dark smile, his gaze hooded. "Isabella," he said quietly, reaching down to weigh her left breast in his hand, "you are beyond inept at this."

Somehow, the insult stung.

"I beg your pardon," she said, "but I was of the impression you wished to bed a woman of beauty and grace, not watch some twopenny tart prick-tease you."

At that, he threw back his head and laughed. "My dear, your vocabulary is impressive," he said, "and I'm finding ineptitude has its own allure."

At that, she pushed him back and stood. "You do not make a grain of sense, my lord," she said. "I still think you might be mad."

"Ah, Isabella." Lightly, he reached out to thumb her nipple, which, to her horror, went pebble-hard beneath her gown. "And so I might be—mad, that is. But in any case, here endeth the lesson, my dear. I have business in the village tonight."

"In the village?" Isabella felt a wave of relief mixed with disappointment. "Then shall I see you la—" She bit off the words and looked up at him.

He smiled thinly. "You mean, will I require your services tonight?" he said. "No. I expect to be late. Make yourself at home. Dinner is in the oven. Your room is adjacent to mine, with a bath and dressing room between. We've rudimentary plumbing upstairs, but I've carried up hot water from the kitchen for you. Ask me to do so at any time."

At last, he looked faintly apologetic.

"I assure you, I'm quite capable of hauling bathwater," she said. "Indeed, I should prefer it to—to . . ."

"The loss of privacy?" he murmured, tipping up her chin on one finger. "Then in that, my dear, we are agreed. It is amazing what a man will give up in order to have his way, and to have it in private."

When she did not reply, he looked hard into her eyes.

"Isabella?"

"Yes, my lord?"

"Will you be frightened here alone?"

She exhaled slowly. "No," she said honestly.

He dropped his hand and made her a slight bow. "Then I bid you goodnight," he said quietly, "and welcome."

With that, he was gone, his boot heels ringing down the passageway in the direction of the back door. There came the sound of a heavy coat being dragged on, the swish of what might have been a crop, followed by the slamming of the back door.

Isabella sank back down in her chair.

Perhaps ten minutes later, she heard the pounding of hooves rounding the side of the house. She looked out to see the earl vanishing into the gloom, the tails of a sweeping black duster flying out behind.

He was gone.

Exhausted and oddly dejected, Isabella rose and slowly climbed the stairs. It took but a moment to find the room in which her bags had been placed, though she spared it scarcely a glance. Instead, she went straight to one of the windows that overlooked the side garden and threw up the sash.

For a time, she simply stood there in a rush of damp and frigid wind, her loose hair lifting lightly, her hands braced wide on the sill as she leaned into the night. To an innocent passerby, Isabella considered, such a pose would give the impression of a woman bent on hurling herself out.

But Isabella had already thrown herself into the abyss—one from which even the Marchioness of Petershaw, she feared, would not be able to extract her, however much the lady might care.

And now the rain had begun to spatter down. On a sigh, Isabella withdrew from the window, extracted the white handkerchief from her skirt pocket, and carefully dropped the sash on it.

UNABLE TO SLEEP, Hepplewood went belowstairs in the cold, quiet hours before dawn, making his way across the flagstone floor in his slippers, wrapped in a silk banyan that was barely sufficient to the chill. But Yardley, God bless him, had been there before him to sweep and lay the upstairs hearths and leave the kitchen blazing.

He yawned, and caught the smell of something savory. Cracking the warming oven, he found a platter heaped with back bacon, and alongside it a large covered dish. Black pudding and eggs, he guessed.

Content with the simplicity of it, Hepplewood shut the oven and went about making his coffee. On mornings like this, when he rose in one of his grimmer moods, steeped in a sense of life's futility, he often wondered what his small staff thought of him; that he was both dissolute and eccentric, he supposed, or perhaps just Satan incarnate.

But however they might view his character and the goings-on under his roof, they were at least discreet and dependable. And he paid them well for it, too.

He wondered if he was going to be paying Isabella Aldridge well for it.

He certainly hoped so—hoped rather too much, perhaps. It was never wise to invest one's self too deeply when it came to women. He'd gotten much, much better at that over the years, slicing away at the artificial elements of every liaison until he had pared each one down to the clean, white bone of lust that lay beneath all the breathless sighs.

No, he'd no intention of allowing Isabella Aldridge to dull that well-stropped blade.

Instead, he put the coffee on and sat down at the ancient worktable to wait for it to boil. He expected he'd down an entire pot of the stuff before his houseguest rose.

Last night he'd passed a miserable evening at the Carpenter's Arms, sipping a dreadful stout in his damp boots, chin-wagging with a pair of local squires about the prospects for spring planting and when to expect the lambing to commence in earnest.

God knew he was no farmer, for all that he owned a dozen. But he'd feigned an interest because it was what any decent landowner did, however removed from it he might have felt. And perhaps because—once upon a time—he'd aspired to nothing more than a quiet life and the land beneath his feet.

But he'd stayed at the Arms to drink and natter on, primarily because he'd known better than to go home.

He had lied to Isabella about having business in the village. He almost never went there, and as soon as he'd arrived he'd longed to turn around and go home to his bed.

No, he had longed to go home to *her* bed.

But her bed was not home, and he'd damned well better not confuse the two concepts.

Yes, keeping Isabella as his plaything would be like playing with fire unless he kept sentiment from the process. And though he'd never really loved a woman in any romantic sense, Hepplewood still had sense enough to recognize an emotional sinkhole when he saw it.

To his chagrin, the woman had turned up earlier than he'd expected, and he had not been prepared. Not mentally, and not physiologically. Had he taken her last night, he would have expended all of about five minutes at it and pumped himself into her like some pimpled schoolboy.

He did not intend to let her off that easily.

No, he intended to savor the woman and break her gently. She would not slap him through the face again, by God. But that first, cracking blow she'd struck? It had definitely caught his attention—and merely hinted, he suspected, at the depths of heat and passion hidden beneath those layers of gray wool.

The soft shuffle of leather on stone stirred him from his reverie, and he looked up to see the object of his fascination perched like a tentative bird upon the last step, pushing a curl of loose hair off her face.

"Good morning," he said.

She was still blinking against the lamplight. He was inordinately glad she had not put her hair up but had merely fastened it over one shoulder.

"So this is the kitchen," she remarked, coming fully into the room.

She wore a morning dress of yellow silk and a shawl of paisley wool that looked warm but still elegant.

"Did you not come down last night?" he asked.

She shook her head. "I wanted a bath whilst the water was hot."

A little irritated, he had risen and gone to the dresser where the breakfast china was kept. "You need to eat," he said, taking down teacups. "You're too thin."

"Rethinking your boney little bargain?" she said dryly.

He turned and cocked one hip on the dresser's ledge. "By

no means," he said. "I'm merely remarking on the state of your health. Go upstairs to the dining room, Isabella. I've got coffee on. I'll serve you shortly."

She looked with what he imagined was longing at the battered table. "Might we just stay here?" she asked. "It's warm by the ovens."

"It seems somehow inappropriate, given you're my guest."

She laughed without humor. "You sound like my mother," she said. "I was never permitted in the kitchens as a child, even though our cook begged—"

Her words broke off, but he hardly noticed. Indeed, he was hardly listening. Instead he found himself again transfixed by her eyes. In the lamplight they appeared a deep, luminous purple—and filled with a barely veiled sorrow.

What had she just said? He tried to recall and failed.

Instead, he took the cups to the table and put them down. "I spend most mornings here when I haven't a guest," he said. "You may suit yourself."

He went about serving coffee and putting out the food. To his surprise, she ate ravenously. It made him wonder again at her weight. There was no way on God's earth a woman could eat like that, he decided, and look as she did.

Why had she not been eating? It troubled him.

Damn it, he did not wish to be troubled. He wanted to fuck her.

"Shall I clear?" she asked when they were finished.

"Mrs. Yardley will see to it later," he said, extracting a small velvet box from the pocket of his dressing gown.

He rose and went to stand behind her. Lifting her hair, he bent over and set his lips to the tender, silken spot where her pulse beat. He heard her breath catch. Need stirred in his loins with a speed that shocked him, and it began at once to throb through his veins.

Rein it back, old boy, he cautioned, *or it will be your master.*

He stood and blew out his breath slowly. "I wanted you to have this," he said, setting the package down before her, "by way of welcome."

Isabella did not turn her head to look at him but instead merely lifted the lid. The twenty-carat amethyst brooch glowed with purple fire, the wide fan of pavé diamonds surrounding it ablaze in the lamplight.

Tentatively, she touched one corner of the box. "But why?" she said.

"Because it put me in mind," he said, "of your eyes."

She did turn then, her brow furrowed. "But I haven't . . . done anything yet."

He smiled at her innocence. "You are going to be my lover," he said. "And it's customary for a gentleman to offer his lover gifts to show . . . well, in this case, anticipation."

The furrow did not clear. "And you just keep such baubles lying about, do you?"

He did not, but he wasn't about to confess it.

In fact, upon learning the identity of Louisa's latest acquisition, he'd sent Jervis to purchase the finest collection of amethysts money could buy, and to bring them at once for his careful perusal.

Even now, the rush of raw lust he'd felt reading Mrs. Litner's letter could make his breath catch. The possibility of having within his grasp the woman whose eyes had begun to haunt his nights kindled in him a level of rapaciousness he would have been loathe to confess.

It should have worried him.

It did worry him, a little.

But Hepplewood was a hardened case, and once he'd scratched that amethyst itch, his lust, his life, and his sleep patterns would, he was confident, simply return to normal.

"Thank you." Isabella shut the box without touching the stones. "You are beyond generous."

"As you will be, my dear," he murmured against her throat.

He let his lips slide down as he drew the tip of his tongue lightly along her skin. He felt her shiver and sunk his teeth into the soft flesh near her collarbone. She made a sound of surprise but tipped her head obediently, as if to grant him access.

"Isabella," he murmured, "it's time."

For an instant—just enough to make him doubt—she hesitated. Then, "Yes," she whispered.

He slipped a hand under her left breast, cupping it until it nearly spilled from his hand, then lightly thumbed her nipple until it budded.

"Go upstairs," he said, "and lie down upon the bed. I'll join you shortly."

"Yes," she said, rising at once. "And in which roo—"

"Yours," he firmly interjected. "Always."

"Of course," she said.

Isabella left without looking back. More tellingly, perhaps, she left the brooch lying on the table. Slipping it back in his pocket, Hepplewood went to the narrow staircase to watch the luscious sway of her backside as she made her way up. Impatience bit at him like a fly at the back of his neck.

Waiting last night hadn't tempered a damned thing, he realized. There was nothing else for it. Hepplewood went alone to his study, locked the door, and did the one thing he had not needed to do since the long, dreadful days of his marriage.

Opening his trousers, he closed his eyes and pleasured himself, jerking violently at his flesh and remembering the sharp sting of Isabella's hand across his face. And as he did so, he imagined what he meant to do to her in return. How he would twist his hands into that beautiful mane of hair and ride her until she begged—for mercy, for more, or for sweet release; he almost did not care. And when he came, it was in a spasm of pleasure that nearly drew him double.

On a guttural, choking sound, he jerked again, spilling himself into his own hand.

Afterward, when the shaking had drained away, he restored himself to order and went up the second flight of stairs to his suite of rooms, lust already stirring in his loins again.

In keeping with his orders, Isabella lay supine on her bed, looking rather like a candidate for martyrdom.

Watching her, he shucked off his robe and toed off his slippers.

"Get up," he said quietly, holding out his hand.

She pulled her knees round in an almost girlish fashion, then scrabbled to the end of the bed. He drew her to her feet and stroked the backs of his fingers down the hollow of her cheek. Her eyes dropped half shut, her nostrils flaring faintly.

Though Isabella likely did not know it, he mused, she was in the prime of her need. And he wanted very much to make her aware of that fact.

Dropping his hand, he began methodically to undress her. He did not expect much resistance. She seemed docile—and, he soon realized, appropriately dressed for the occasion.

He pushed the shawl from her shoulders and let it slither to the floor. Slipping his hand behind, he unbuttoned the yellow dress, then drew his thumbs around the neckline, pulling it down.

Beneath it she wore a gossamer chemise and a well-boned, strapless corset—one made, he was pleased to see, for a lover's eye, cut enticingly low to cup beneath her breasts and thrust them high. The attire surprised him, and he wondered, fleetingly, if her late husband had required her to wear such things.

And on the heels of that thought came a stab of jealousy, sudden and explosive. Angrily, he bit it back, breathed deep, and forced his attention to her nearly bare flesh. Isabella's gaze was uneasy, her embarrassment acute.

He ignored it; there was no cure for modesty save to push her ruthlessly past it.

Beneath the chemise, he could see her round, apricot-colored nipples, still unaroused. Thus challenged, Hepplewood set a firm hand between her shoulder blades and bent his head to suckle her. She drew in a sharp breath when his mouth closed over her, and a little tremble shuddered through her.

"Should . . . should I have worn less?" she murmured.

"Wear what you please," he whispered against her wet flesh, "unless I instruct you otherwise."

"Y-yes," she said.

"I like that word," he replied, cutting a glance up at her. "You're using it often, I notice."

"I wish to please you," she said softly. "I've given my word. You must tell me, my lord, if I do not give satisfaction."

He laughed and pressed his teeth hard into the tip of her nipple. When she cried out, he moved to the other breast, his hand roaming low to shape the swells of her buttocks. When the chemise was clinging wetly to both nipples, he deftly unhooked the bone busk and pushed her corset away.

The chemise followed, floating up and over her head and

sending her silken hair cascading back down, one long curl catching across her damp breast. They were small, and her ribs almost painfully apparent, but on the whole, she was still the most sensual creature he'd ever laid eyes upon.

"Isabella, the mere sight of you gives satisfaction," he said, yanking hard at the tie of her drawers. "But we have unfinished business, you and I."

"Unfinished business?" The beautiful brow furrowed again.

"Turn your back," he said. "Bend toward the bed, and roll down your stockings."

Her face was already pink with embarrassment, but to her credit, she did so.

His mouth went instantly dry, and he seemed unable to swallow. For all that Isabella was too thin, the creamy swell of her arse was the stuff of a man's fantasy. He allowed himself the luxury of setting both hands to it, weighing the plump globes in his palms, and slipping his fingertips into the sweet cleft between.

Shocked by the sudden intimacy, Isabella caught herself on the mattress, bracing her hands wide. "W-what are you doing?" she said over her shoulder.

For an instant, he hesitated, but the temptation was too much. "You struck me, Isabella," he said very softly. "That day at Loughford. Do you remember?"

"Y yes," she said, her voice very small. "I'm sorry."

"Are you?"

"Very." As if sensing what was about to happen, Isabella shifted nearer the bed.

Lashing an arm round her waist, he yanked her back a little roughly and smacked her hard across her buttocks. She cried out and half turned, eyes shying wildly.

"Don't move," he growled. "Did you like that, Isabella?"

Obediently, she turned back. "No," she said huskily, "but I . . . I deserved it, I suppose."

"Yes," he said, "and then some."

He turned his attention to his night tables. They were a matched pair set on delicately turned legs, the interiors bespeaking the hand of an exquisitely skilled French craftsman. Hepplewood gave the upper cabinet a little push. With a mechanical *snick!* it spun on its axis a quarter turn to reveal a drawer that opened from the hidden side.

He pushed a latch concealed in the satinwood banding, and the drawer slid open. Isabella watched warily, cutting a sidelong glance at the fitted velvet interior. Carefully he lifted out the few items he meant to use, then selected a slender leather crop.

She drew in a deep breath and opened her mouth as if to protest, but immediately shut it again. His hand, he noted, had drawn a pink rush of blood to her bottom.

"We have to get through this, Isabella, you and I." Hepplewood drew the tip of the leather between his fingers. "Don't ever raise your hand to me again. Not unless I tell you to."

"No, I-I won't," she choked. "And I *wouldn't have,* but you—"

He snapped the little crop across her backside, causing her to yelp and jerk upright.

"Set your palms back atop the mattress," he said calmly, "or I can bind you. Would you like that, Isabella?"

"I . . . I don't think so." Shaking a little now, she set her hands wide on the counterpane, bending forward at the waist to do so.

"You might be surprised, my pet." He trailed one fingertip down the delicate arch of her spine and felt her skin prickle. "I can teach you. Some women enjoy it vastly."

"I *wouldn't*," she whispered, "b-but if it's what you wi—"

He gave her another snap, making her jerk, the soft orbs of her arse trembling.

"That stung!" she said.

"It should," he said, striking her again. "You need to learn a lesson, Isabella. But it won't sting for long, I promise."

Then, tucking the crop under his arm, he stroked his hands soothingly down her buttocks, circled lightly, then urged them a little apart.

"Wh-what are you doing?" she whispered.

"*Deciding*," he said gruffly. "And don't ask a third time, my dear, or you mightn't like the result."

The truth was, he realized, he wanted suddenly to push himself inside; to work himself deep beyond that tight barrier to invade her in that most carnal of ways. It was not his general habit, but it was the safest way for a man to take his pleasure. And with an arse like that . . .

Still, Isabella was far from ready for that sort of erotic adventure. And he was not, he hoped, a cruel man.

Musing upon it, he extracted the crop and struck her twice more—just hard enough to pink the skin, not welt it. Isabella jumped, then sniffled a little pitifully.

"Would you like something to ease the sting?" he suggested, drawing one finger down her cleft. "You haven't yet learned to savor this, my darling. Shall I pour you a brandy?"

"I would like you to *stop*," Isabella gritted. "I don't know what you want. Do you want me to beg you? Is that it?"

He laid the crop down beside her hand and cupped his body around hers. Bending over her, his chest pressed to her shoulder blades, he set his lips to her ear.

"I would love you to beg," he said, drawing one finger through her thatch of curls, then probing deeper, "but only if you want this. Shall I make you *learn* to want it, Isabella?"

"I—I *don't know*!" she said, her chest falling.

Her hands were still splayed on her mattress, her head hanging. Lifting his knee, Hepplewood nudged her legs wider, giving his fingers access. He slipped one into her soft folds, gingerly probing.

Isabella was wet, but only a little. And perhaps a little too frightened. There were many women, he knew, who had no natural inclination for this sort of business. Some could be taught. Others not.

He reached out and dipped his fingers into the jar he'd taken from the table. But when his hand brushed her inner thigh, Isabella yelped.

"Shush, sweet," he crooned, slipping his slickened fingers into the softness. "Just relax, my dear, and urge yourself against my hand."

She made some feeble effort at compliance. Pressing his erection firmly along the cleft of her hips, Hepplewood forced her against his hand. Gently he stroked, running one finger round her swelling nub until a pearl of her own wetness leached out.

"Good girl," he whispered.

Again and again he circled, sliding the other hand up to stroke and pluck her nipple. Isabella made a sound; the faintest sigh, and at once he felt the need begin to bubble up inside her, awakening to his touch. He stopped, stepped away, and took the crop to her arse again.

She gasped, her breath seizing and her buttocks jiggling.

It was his turn to swallow hard.

"God Almighty, Isabella," he rasped, "but I am hard-pressed here."

"Hard-pressed to what?" She began to turn, then, thinking better of it, froze.

"You don't want to know," he managed. "Turn back to the bed. Give in to me, Isabella."

"Y-yes," she answered, but the word was feeble.

He resumed his position, trapping her between his cock and his fingers, rubbing and circling, this time probing her with one finger and then a second. But Isabella was as tight as a virgin, and for an instant, he wondered. . . .

But it did not matter. She was his now for the taking—and he burned for her in a way that felt altogether too dangerous. But he'd be damned if he'd turn back now.

This time as he stroked she began to breathe more rapidly, and he could feel the confusion stirring inside. He brought her a little nearer the edge, then stepped back and whipped her again. Just a smart snap across the cheeks.

"*Ohh,*" she moaned.

Again and again he repeated the process, edging her nearer pleasure's abyss, then steeling her to the rod with one swift stroke until she trembled. Until, on the twelfth blow, he surrendered to sheer weakness, his cock throbbing impatiently.

Turning Isabella, he pushed her back onto the bed. Still standing between her legs, he ripped free his buttons to release himself, shoving roughly at the tangle of fabric. Then, wisdom overcoming lust, he slicked one hand down his rigid cock, desperately glad he'd frigged himself.

Isabella was watching him beneath her fringe of black lashes, her eyes somnolent and glassy, her mouth slightly parted, one knee drawn up and tipped outward. It was a position of carnal surrender; the need to be taken. Her fear had faded, and the hunger was coming upon her in earnest.

Taking himself firmly in hand, Hepplewood pressed the head of his cock inside her. Despite the sweetness that flowed from her, it was no easy job. Hepplewood might whip a woman—into a sexual frenzy, or perhaps just as a reminder—but never had he willingly drawn blood. But Isabella was so tight, so *damned* tight, that he began to fear he might tear something.

"Good Lord," he rasped, "are you a virgin?"

"N-no," she whispered. "Just . . . not good at this."

"Oh, you are very good at this." Reassured, he pushed inside another fraction and felt her silken passage give, but only slightly.

"Isabella," he said, sliding one finger between her slick folds, "have you ever reached orgasm?"

She opened her eyes and looked at him blankly. Her inky hair was like a dark, silken waterfall across the white of the bedding, her breasts puckered into tiny knots.

She had answered his question, he realized.

He should not have been surprised; it was a common failing of husbands. But Isabella should have engendered a near-slavish devotion in any ordinary man. Indeed, he could feel a stirring of it himself—and he did not like it.

Drawing in his breath, he pushed himself deeper but did not drag himself fully over her. Instead, he stroked her sweet folds, then began to lightly circle her nub again, this time with the ball of his thumb, pushing his cock deeper only when she relaxed enough to permit it.

After a time, the pace of her breath shifted. Her tongue darted out, lightly touching the corner of her mouth. Over and over he stroked, until her hands went flat against the counterpane and her head tipped back. He began to thrust inside her slowly, ratcheting up her need as he kept up his delicate ministrations.

Suddenly Isabella's eyes closed and her hands clawed into the bedcovering, fisting up great knots of it as her belly went taut. *"Ah—ah—ah—"*

Her cries were more breath than sound, and he knew she

hung on that sweet, precarious edge. He thrust and thrust again, then watched as she collapsed into sensual bliss and slid down into a blinding release.

When he withdrew to shuck his remaining clothes and climb over her, Isabella was still shaking. So was he, truth be told.

Turning her onto her side, he cupped his body around hers and reached for the jar of unguent. She heaved a little sob; a sort of sigh, really—and out of gratitude, he prayed.

He kissed her lightly on the shoulder. "There, Isabella," he murmured, rubbing the soothing oils into her buttocks, "it's done, love."

Another rough sigh went shuddering through her.

"So beautiful," he murmured. "Such a good girl."

She had drawn her knees up a little and did not look at him. The pink marks were no longer visible across her bottom, and her breath had returned to normal. Still, he felt a little uneasy—but not enough to wilt his raging cockstand.

"Roll onto your belly, love," he whispered. "I'm not finished with you."

She nodded, her hair scrubbing the pillow. The morning sun was slanting through the window now, and as she turned, he caught something like a diamond glistening in her lashes. Not a tear, he thought—for was a tear truly a tear if it had not been shed?—and in the urgency of the moment, he did not question it.

Gently, he pushed a pillow under her hips, urged her legs apart, then knelt behind her.

"Up on your knees a little, love," he whispered.

Isabella rose, bracing herself on her hands, sensing instinctively what he wanted.

She was utterly open to him now as he pushed his throbbing cock back into her passage. He thrust hard and fast on that first stroke, intent upon finishing his business with what should have been practiced efficiency.

But it was not.

It was exquisite, and he did not want it to stop.

He felt himself slide deep on another long, perfect stroke, her womanly scent washing over him, and suddenly something altered. His pace hitched, then slowed. He looked down at her—not the woman who'd slapped him and tormented his dreams but Isabella, his lover.

He knew it was a romantic and silly notion even as he felt himself being drawn into her, drawn into that moment, melting into her. And strangely, he let the moment go. He watched her sweetly familiar profile and felt no need to hasten it. On and on it stretched as he slowly pumped himself into her, as though for him only Isabella existed, her head bowed in supplication, her body warm and purifying.

After a time he felt the quickening inside him, the unmistakable instant when release edged near. Then Isabella made a sound; a soft exhalation in the rain-washed light, and suddenly reality hung suspended. His vision seemed to blur and warm, as if those exquisite strokes had pushed him into a different sort of light, into a place where his past twirled like an ornament in the sunlight, throwing off glimpses of a memory resurrected.

Glimpses of her, a woman he hardly knew.

And yet he did know her. He knew Isabella in his bones.

He drew a deep, wracking breath and thrust harder and deeper. Then she *became* the light, surrounding him in a haze of joy as he convulsed, pumping his seed inside her. And when at last the ecstasy surged through him, it shifted and became something more, bringing with it a sense of completeness that melted through muscle and sinew, down to his bone, the pleasure so intense that his breath stopped.

So intense that the world as he knew it stopped.

Time and light ceased to exist, the moment spinning away. He could hear a distant heartbeat, dropping slower and slower, and knew it was his own.

Suddenly, his entire body seized. On a harsh cry, he collapsed, his face buried against Isabella's neck. He gasped for breath, then gasped again. He drank in air in deep gulps, even as he wished to return to that place of light and joy.

But the oxygen was flowing into his brain once more, bringing him back to life.

La petite mort.

This time, it had damn near killed him.

And for the first time, he understood what it meant.

He stirred long moments later to the sound of rain spattering on Isabella's windows. Water was gurgling down the drainpipes, edged with the sound of ice, but within it was as if the room cocooned them in warmth. Dimly, he realized he lay on his side again, spooned about her fragile body, one hand cupping her belly, awash in a sense of well-being that, had he been fully awake, would have worried him.

But he was not quite ready to wake yet; not quite ready to let go of the ephemeral pleasure. Burying his face between Isabella's shoulder blades, he kissed her, drawing in the scent of his own sweat mingled with the smell of her soap and her skin. The scent of purity and perfection. Then, through the sensual languor, he felt her stir a little, the stark flatness of her belly shifting beneath his hand.

She was rail thin, he mused, for all that she was beautiful. Perhaps later they might do something foolish—like toast cheese over the fire in their wrappers. And tomorrow—yes, tomorrow he would put extra butter on her bread, or feed her on strawberries and cream. Yes, tomorrow he would have Yardley see if hothouse berries might be had.

Still, he thought on a drowsy chuckle, he hoped it was not a telling gesture, the way he'd spread his fingers almost protectively over the flat of her belly.

Over her womb.

Then, on his next breath, he remembered what he had *not* done.

The haze of well-being lifted like a veil, and his blood ran cold.

"Isabella," he rasped. "Isabella, when did you last bleed?"

She lay silent for a moment. "Five days past?"

It was a question, not a statement. He cursed beneath his breath.

Damn it, what had he been thinking?

Was he so selfish—so caught up in his own depravity—he simply didn't care for her? He drew a deep breath and looked at her again, impassive and quiet beside him. Good God, she was innocent—or nearly so.

With a hand that shook a little, he tucked a loose curl behind her ear.

He had learned the hard way to be excruciatingly careful. To find ways of taking his pleasure that didn't involve such a risk.

Still, if she was right, they should—*should*—be safe. And yet, for all his experience in pleasuring women, their bodies were still a physiological mystery to him. He stroked one finger around the pink shell of her ear, still shaken.

"Next time I won't spill myself inside you." His voice was far steadier than he felt. "Please. Forgive me. I won't take that risk again. I swear it, Isabella."

"Thank you," she murmured, her voice distant. "Are we . . . finished?"

Something inside him froze; something uglier, even, than cold terror.

"For now, yes," he said, levering up onto his elbow.

She did not move, but he had the overarching sense she wished him to leave.

Women *never* wished him to leave. They always begged him to stay, sometimes literally on their knees. Of course, most of it was just artifice. Hepplewood did not delude himself; he knew what such women were.

But did he know what Isabella was?

Did she just not know how the game was played?

Clearly the woman had no real sexual experience. Clearly she wanted teaching. Indeed, he had begun it this morning; begun the process of hardening a new lover who would be able to take all that he could give, and who would perhaps tempt, at least for a little while, his jaded palate.

In that, however, would he be making of her what she was not?

It was a novel thought—particularly for a man who had long ago vowed to stop thinking.

But the chill was still stealing over him and deepening to something a little like fear. Isabella's face was still emotionless, her gaze fixed on the distant wall.

He had the most frightful sense of having misjudged. Of having pushed too far, too fast. Of having lost all capacity for true tenderness. He'd never had a virgin. Never had a woman who wasn't well experienced. Never had a woman he'd wanted with such . . . wrath and desperation.

Yes, that was a part of it. He wanted Isabella so desperately that it made him angry.

At himself.

The sick chill deepened. He shoved it away ruthlessly.

It would not do. He was what he was.

Isabella was still curled around the pillow he'd placed under her hips. He lowered his mouth and kissed her cheek.

"Isabella," he murmured, "how long have you been without a lover?"

She drew a shuddering breath. "Eight—no, nine years."

"Good Lord," he said. "Were you married from the cradle?"

"At seventeen," she said.

"Ah, a marriage of short duration, you'd said."

"Yes," she said. "A few months. Weeks, really."

Hepplewood waited, accustomed to more talkative females—females that ordinarily would never stop nattering at him, even when a man yearned for silence. But this was not, he sensed, a good sort of silence.

Damn it all, he did not mollycoddle women. He did not coax or cajole. He rolled onto his back and dragged an arm over his eyes. He had fucked himself blue and ought now be grateful for the opportunity to skulk off and go to sleep in his own bed.

That was another thing he did not do, he remembered as he drifted off again. He did not sleep with women. That could turn to intimacy, and in a damned quick hurry, too.

He dragged the arm away and turned back to her. "Isabella," he pressed, "what happened to your husband?"

"He died."

"May I ask of what?"

At last she rolled over to look at him. "You may do anything you please," she said, her eyes glistening. "I think we just established that."

Hepplewood looked at her and sighed. "Oh, Isabella," he said, reaching up to push his fingers through her hair. "Perhaps that's the sort of arrangement we have, yes. But I should like to please *you* in the process. And you seemed, in the end, to take pleasure in what we just did."

"Pleasure?" she said, her lips thinning. "It was like nothing I've ever felt before. Yes. It was a sort of pleasure."

"Did it feel . . . distasteful?" he asked, crooking his head. "Isabella, *did* it?"

"It felt frightening at first." She looked away. "What am I to say, my lord? I am your wh—I mean, your lover—and here to accommodate your wishes. Please, may we not have this discussion? It seems perilously near those things we vowed we would not discuss."

Hepplewood felt as if he'd just been shut out of something at once precious and yet deeply unpleasant. He did not like it one damned bit.

And what was far worse, he didn't like that he didn't like it. He much preferred to not give a damn. Yes, he was what he was, and he'd best remember it. Isabella's beauty and her goodness would never change him.

And perhaps he ought not change her.

"Can you be content here, Isabella, in my bed?" he said gruffly. "Will you wish to continue this arrangement?"

She was staring up at the ceiling now. "I am content enough," she said. "I agree to continue our arrangement. And I will give you satisfaction—and obedience—from here out."

Hepplewood felt a prick of raw anger. "Good," he snapped, "because that's damned well what I expect of you."

She drew another long, uneven breath. "My husband died of drinking," she said, her voice emotionless. *"Acute alcohol poisoning,* the coroner called it. He was young and romantic, and married, he'd once proclaimed, to the love of his life. And yet his life still turned out to be not what he'd wanted. So one day he took the cork out of a cheap bottle of gin, and washed that bottle down with another, and perhaps even a third, and that is all I know, my lord. Beyond that, his death is as much a mystery to me as it is to the next person. Now, have I given satisfaction with my answer?"

Hepplewood got the unpleasant feeling he'd just struck a nerve.

"You're right," he said, forcing down his ire. "I should not have asked you. But if it is of any comfort to you, my marriage was also short, and it ended just as miserably, trust me."

"How can anyone take comfort in another's misery?" Isabella murmured. "And you had *a child*. At least you got a child for your misery."

Her tone, husky, with the barest hint of longing, made him shiver. Was that what she wanted, deep down? A child, a husband, a family? The simplest of dreams? And if she did, why was she wasting her time and her beauty on him?

The question chafed at him. He did not wish to feel tenderness.

"Yes, I got a child because I seduced her," he snapped, since simple subtraction made it obvious. "She was rich, lovely, and green as grass, and I was charmingly irresistible. So I seduced her—*easily*—and by the time she climbed out of my bed and came to her senses, she had my babe in her belly and it was too damned late. So yes, I got a child. And she died bearing it—married to a man she despised."

Isabella folded her hands just below her breasts and studied the room's crown molding in excruciating detail. "Well," she deadpanned, "I'm glad we got those little formalities out of the way."

Hepplewood laid back down on the bed again, oddly exhausted. He knew he was not done with Isabella; no, not by half. Not in the physical sense. Ordinarily he would have permitted her to drowse a few moments before urging her on to the next step, then taking her again.

But this time the raging need had seemingly burned clean through him, and now his hunger for her lay more like a cold weight over his heart than that familiar, pooling warmth he would ordinarily be feeling in his groin.

Ah, God. He could feel what this was coming to.

"Isabella," he said quietly, "would you like me to leave you now?"

"If you are finished with me," she said with exquisite politeness, "then, yes, my lord, thank you."

If he was finished with her?

Was he finished?

Yes, *thank you,* he very much thought he was.

Certainly, he'd better be finished—for the sensual experience he'd so triumphantly anticipated upon reading Mrs. Litner's letter did not feel at all like the experience he'd just had.

It should have been just the raw, sexual release born of driving himself into a beautiful woman's body. Why, then, had there been nothing releasing about it?

He let out his breath in a long, pensive exhalation, still savoring the warmth of Isabella's body beside his. But their mingled warmth changed nothing. Nor did his anger. A wise man knew when to surrender and how to cut the ache of his losses before they were . . . well, *losses.* For if he did not, the ache he'd feel then might just eat him alive.

If you are finished with me. . . .

Well, be damned to her.

"Then I will leave you, Isabella, to rest," he said tightly.

And with that, Hepplewood rolled off the mattress, circled around the bed to snatch up his clothing, and went back down to his study, slamming the door behind.

He threw on his clothes, roughly yanking and buttoning and shoving things this way and that, steeping in his own wounded pride.

But once dressed and a little calmer, clarity dawned.

He had known she was a danger; known she was not

meant for him. Yes, he'd known it all the moment he'd first laid eyes on her, and the knowledge had both angered him and taunted him.

She really was an innocent, he realized. A sweet and beautiful innocent who wanted children, and an ordinary life, he supposed. And he . . . well, he had not been innocent in a very long time.

On a long sigh, he sat down at his desk and scratched out a few succinct lines. When he was done, he pushed the letter away, shut his eyes, and considered his alternatives.

It still felt as if he had none.

The truth was, he'd had none since that day at Loughford.

Had he been so bloody willing to shove his cock into a meat grinder, he should have simply seduced her then and there. He could simply have dusted off the foolproof Hepplewood charm that once had served him so well and had Isabella tipped back onto his desk in a mere trice, with her skirts tossed up to her waist.

She had been that vulnerable.

And he had nearly been that stupid.

His bitterness burning bright again, Hepplewood unlocked his bottom desk drawer. Then he lifted out all of Jervis's diligently gathered jewel boxes and simply heaped them atop the letter.

Well, all save one. The one he loved most; a ring set with a ten-carat diamond surrounded by dark, flawless amethysts.

To remember her by, he told himself.

CHAPTER 6

Attired in a fuchsia-colored gown and matching peignoir, her pink satin turban trimmed with magenta-colored ostrich tips, the Marchioness of Petershaw was sequestered in her private sitting room, hastily scratching out invitations to an especially intimate soiree, when Isabella was announced.

More than three weeks having passed since their last meeting, the marchioness had given standing orders that her former governess should be brought to her at once, at any time of day or night, should she happen to turn up. Thus, upon hearing Isabella's name announced, the lady immediately flung down her pen and, in a shocking breach of her usual decorum, actually rushed across the floor.

"Wicked girl!" she said, grasping both her hands in a reassuring squeeze. "You've left me all agog. The note Dillon brought me was so vague as to be unsettling. Sit down at once."

Isabella sunk into a chair by the desk, grateful to be received. "Thank you for allowing me time to collect my wits," she said. "You . . . you are not angry with me?"

The good lady drew back an inch. "Why should I be?"

she said evenly. "But are you, perhaps, angry with yourself? Come, child, you must tell me about this Mr. Mowbrey and what he did to make himself so intolerable."

Isabella caught her lip in her teeth. "Actually, ma'am, he sent me away," she said. "That's what I meant, you see, when I wrote that things didn't work out. And there was no Mr. Mowbrey. It was just as you said—a ruse."

Lady Petershaw's eyes widened. "And he did not find *you* acceptable? I don't believe it. Well! Did he at least give you his real name?"

"He didn't need to," she said quietly. "I knew him."

"Oh, dear." The marchioness leaned forward. "That sounds ominous."

"It was the Earl of Hepplewood," Isabella blurted, looking up from the floor. "The gentleman who interviewed me as governess. Th-the one who tried to seduce me, and said that I was better suited to—" Tears suddenly welling, she made an impotent little gesture with her hand. "—to nothing, it would appear. It seems he really cannot be pleased."

"*Hepplewood*?"

The marchioness was rarely shocked by anything, but this struck her speechless for a full half minute. "Well," she finally said on a rush of indignation, "of all the impertinence! Still, I cannot imagine how . . . I mean, Tony *is* clever, of that there's no doubt. But to manipulate Louisa into literally handing you over? It is unconscionable!"

Tony.

Was that his nickname? Isabella had lain in his bed and in his arms—and allowed him the most indecent intimacies imaginable—and yet she'd never asked what he preferred to be called. Indeed, she'd taken pains to learn nothing at all about the man.

Why, then, was she unable to put him from her mind?

Why did she keep remembering his touch—those moments of passion, and yes, even of tenderness? She felt her stomach twist into another knot and set a hand lightly over it.

"I don't think he tricked anyone, ma'am," she managed. "I think . . . I think he was just angry I refused him at Loughford. I collect he simply—good Lord, it's so mortifying—but I collect he simply wanted someone who *looked* like me. It was my eyes, I think. He seemed oddly obsessed with them."

Lady Petershaw trilled with laughter. "Heavens, where's the mortification in that, my dear?" she declared. "To get beneath a man's skin, and to do it in such a way that he cannot stop thinking of you? Now *that* is the stuff of which rich courtesans are made—sometimes even rich wives— and you'll allow that I've some experience in this regard."

Isabella sighed. "Well, I clearly had none," she said, opening her reticule. "He sent me away after one night— laughing, I do not doubt. And I scurried off like a rabbit. But here, ma'am, enough of that. I've come to repay your kindness—not that I ever can."

With a look of reluctance, Lady Petershaw took the money Isabella counted out. "He was generous with you, then?" she said, her lips thinning. "He damned well better have been. I have some notion of the tricks that cheeky devil gets up to. Tony has developed rather a twisted streak these last few years, if all I hear is true."

It was this discussion that Isabella had so dreaded. "I could not say, ma'am."

"Of course you could not," said the lady, nodding with approval. "No mistress worth her salt would. But I am glad, my dear—desperately glad—that Hepplewood let you go if he has become truly depraved. I mean— *that* sort of life with *that* sort of man—oh, my dear, it is a hard one. After all, one feels so desperately sorry for them."

"Sorry for *them*?" squeaked Isabella.

"Dear me, yes." The lady waved her hand again. "That sort of man is more wounded, and more angry with himself, than with any woman he might subjugate to his perversions."

"Wounded? Angry?" Isabella was incredulous. "I fear, ma'am, we are talking about two different sorts of men. The Earl of Hepplewood seemed the most arrogant, most cock-sure gentleman of my acquaintance."

"Oh, that's as may be," the marchioness said, "but his sort of wicked desires, once they rise beyond mere bed play, become self-loathing in its purest form. And a man like that, my dear . . . well, any woman who could want him would not be *worth* wanting, would she? That, you see, is the twisted way such men think. And so she must be punished. For being available to him. For being beautiful to him. And above all things, for being desirable to him."

Isabella shook her head, her mouth gaping. "You were quite right at the outset," she finally said. "I do not know how to go about this business."

At this, Lady Petershaw cast her a wary, assessing glance. "Is it at all possible, my dear, that you misunderstood?" she said. "*Was* it more than bed play? For Tony's not a bad man. Indeed, as a boy, he was a very sweet sort—so very charming and kind—and so *unflaggingly* devoted to his lovers, if you know what I mean."

Isabella felt color flood her face. "He doesn't seem sweet now. Yes, he seems angry at someone. Did marriage change him?"

Lady Petershaw laid a finger to her cheek. "It worsened things, perhaps, but he'd altered slightly even before that, I should have said. And I can't think as I laid eyes on the man during his marriage. He must have stayed in the country—he always did have rustic leanings—but he took up again in

Clarges Street after his wife died. Long before that, however, there was . . . some little scandal."

"Really? Of what sort?"

Lady Petershaw threw up a hand. "Hush, let me think, let me think," she said, shutting her eyes a long moment. "Tony had a cousin—a pretty girl named Anne. They were promised to one another, he once said, and he meant to have his fun whilst he could. But then she married elsewhere."

"Was his heart broken?"

"I fancy not," Lady Petershaw said, her brow furrowing, "for he turned his eye to her sister—or another cousin . . . well, some sort of relation—but that ship never sailed, either."

"Really?"

"Yes, but this girl's heart *was* broken, and I heard she went mad. And some years later, when he betrothed himself to Felicity Willet, this girl attacked Miss Willet in a fit of jealousy—all hush-hush, to be sure—but Miss Willet quit London and refused for a time to marry him."

"But she did," said Isabella, "eventually."

"As I recall, her father forced her to." Lady Petershaw's mouth twisted. "Then she died. Tragic, to be sure. And yes, after that, I think Tony's bad habits further hardened."

Isabella shrugged. "Well, in fairness, ma'am, I cannot say his habits much varied from those you warned me about. The worst ones, I mean."

"So he was . . . demanding?" The marchioness lifted one eyebrow. "Rough?"

"Yes," Isabella whispered. "He suggested it was to be enjoyed. But it . . . it merely frightened me. Well, at first."

Lady Petershaw made a sound of irritation. "Because you are practically a virgin!" she said. "And Tony is a damned fool. He's been running with a hard crowd so long he's forgotten what sweetness is. But I will say this, my dear—there is no harm in a little rough play amongst lovers who enjoy one another and want it. Do you understand?"

Did she understand? Isabella shook her head.

She understood Lord Hepplewood had frightened her, and that he'd taken great pleasure in bending her to his will. And yet, something inside her had thrilled to his touch. The feelings he'd sent coursing through her body defied all explanation. They had left her confused and desperately ashamed.

Lady Petershaw reached out and patted Isabella's arm. "My dear girl, if an otherwise skilled lover needs to put you over his knee," she said gently, "or lash you to his bedposts, little harm will come of it—and perhaps a good deal of pleasure. Men are curious creatures and like to think they're getting their way. One should simply play along—to a point—if one doesn't mind it."

"Really?"

"*If* one doesn't mind," repeated the marchioness. "Even wives do it—the wise ones, at any rate. And *their* husbands, my dear Mrs. Aldridge, do not frequent my salons or visit Louisa Litner."

Isabella was turning the subject over and over in her mind—as she had been for some days now. Lady Petershaw was speaking very bluntly indeed. How very strange the world was!

As if sensing her discomfort, the marchioness let the subject drop. "Well, has the man at least provided you enough to survive on for a time?" she asked. "Indeed, I will speak sharply to Louisa if he has not. She can hardly hold you accountable for Hepplewood's persnickety taste. She must find you a better place—an older, gentler man, perhaps."

"No." Isabella threw out a staying hand. "No, ma'am. I thank you. You were right. I haven't the mettle for this business. Moreover . . . something far more disturbing, even, than Lord Hepplewood's sexual proclivities has happened in Fulham. It requires my complete attention."

"My dear, what?" Brow furrowed, Lady Petershaw leaned intently forward in her chair. "You've turned perfectly white."

"My cousin—" Isabella's words broke away, her fingertips flying to her mouth. "It is dreadful—and yet it is nothing. Still, I feel most uneasy."

"Heavens, what has that vile scrap of humanity done now?"

"As I say, nothing." Isabella dropped her hand, but it trembled. "But he came to call whilst I was away—to check on the girls, he told Mrs. Barbour."

"And that fool servant let him in?"

Swiftly, Isabella shook her head. "No," she rasped. "Barby knows to lie, and to tell Everett no one is at home. But she was hanging the wash, so Jemima answered the door. He stayed for all of an hour, Lady Petershaw, and he . . . he coaxed Georgina onto his lap for sweets. And gave Jemima hair ribbons."

Lady Petershaw looked uneasy. "You have cause for concern," she said, "but at least no harm befell the girls."

Upon applying to the marchioness for employment almost seven years ago, Isabella had been compelled to explain her reasons for seeking work; specifically, that her father had remarried to a vacuous young widow who did not relish sharing her new home with a stepdaughter scarcely her junior—particularly one who'd already married and left home, only to return like a bad penny.

But she had not needed to tell the marchioness why she'd refused to marry her father's heir. She had merely hinted at the ugliness she'd witnessed whilst living beneath her aunt's roof—worlds ago now, it seemed, yet still seared into her brain.

No, the good lady knew too well the dark side of humanity. And sadly, there were better than a dozen brothels in greater London catering to gentlemen who preferred young girls—and boys, too, though that choice could get a man hanged were he caught.

But when such a man's prey was a girl? No matter her age, such travesties were met with little more than a snicker by society and the law.

Lady Petershaw suddenly shivered. "What a dreadful man," she declared. "I remember, my dear, after your father died, he began calling almost monthly in an attempt to see you."

"It was inappropriate," Isabella murmured, "and embarrassing."

"No, it was revealing," the marchioness corrected. "He does not like to have his wishes thwarted, that one. For my part, I wouldn't let Baron Tafford near any female under the age of twelve. But my dear, what *will* you do? If you will not take a rich lover, you must earn a living."

Isabella was twisting the ties of her reticule in her lap. "Well, it is the strangest thing, ma'am—like a small miracle, really—but Lord Hepplewood, you see, has given me the gift of time."

"How so?"

Isabella lifted her shoulders weakly. "When he left his letter telling me I should go, he left a great pile of jewelry atop it—amethysts—his parting gift to me, he said."

The marchioness sniffed disdainfully. "Amethysts? And not diamonds?"

"He said in his letter that amethysts reminded him of my eyes," she replied, "and most of the pieces were set with diamonds, too. His letter was . . . stilted, but not unkind. Of course I did not wish to take the jewelry, but then I remembered my sisters, and what you had said."

"And you remembered rightly!" said the marchioness. "Hepplewood owed you dearly if he used you ill. Oh, my poor child! You will not wish to keep his jewels. You must sell them straightaway."

"I have already done so," said Isabella. "The jeweler's name was labeled on each box—Garrard's, ma'am, the lot of it."

The marchioness lightly lifted her eyebrows. "Heavens!" she said. "What must the man have paid?"

Isabella shrugged. "Enough to permit me to catch up on my bills and set a little aside," she said, "and now I must think very carefully what I'm to do with it." Here, she paused, then drew a deep breath. "Given my cousin's recent behavior, it would be best if I had a way to both work *and* watch over the girls. So I am of a mind, ma'am, to open a shop—one we might live above, you see."

"A *shop*?" said the lady. "That is quite a social step down, my dear. And have you enough for that? And what sort of shop?"

"A bookshop," Isabella said, "specializing in scholastic materials and children's literature. A few educational toys, perhaps. I think I can do it—and London is desperately short of such establishments, you must admit."

"Heavens, I've not a clue," said the marchioness airily. "That is what governesses are for, you'll pardon my saying."

At last Isabella managed a smile—perhaps the first since her dreadful journey home. "In any case, I must thank Lord Hepplewood—in my heart, I mean, not in person, for I couldn't bear to see him again."

"Could you not?" The marchioness looked at her a little oddly. "Surely you do not fear him, my dear? Whatever his passions or his problems, I do believe Tony is a gentleman."

Isabella considered it. Once their bargain had been

struck, Lord Hepplewood had treated her with unerring courtesy—beyond those harsh moments in bed, of course. "No, he was . . . kind in his way," she answered. "It's just that I cannot stop thinking about him—I mean, about what happened. Between us. I mean—oh—it's just so very awkward!"

The marchioness threw up her hands. "Well, I've known the man since he began poking round Town at seventeen, and he's always had the devil in his eyes."

"Always? How old is he?"

"We are nearly of an age, so he's—oh, thirty-six, thereabouts," said the marchioness. "Certainly, the man has weathered beautifully. But there, you do not need to hear any of that."

"No." Slowly, Isabella rose. "Well, I must let you get back to your writing. Thank you again for—"

Her words were cut short by a sharp knock. Lady Petershaw's butler swept in, bearing an ivory card on a silver salver, cutting an apologetic glance at Isabella.

The lady took it and laughed.

"How long, ma'am," asked the butler, "shall I make this one wait?"

Lady Petershaw tucked the card into her ample bosom. "Oh, this one shan't wait an instant, Smithers," she declared. "In fact, this one I shall receive here in my dishabille. Quick, quick, Mrs. Aldridge, go into my water closet."

"Yes, ma'am." Like the governess she was, Isabella rose to obey unthinkingly, then stopped and turned. "But . . . why?"

"Just go," said the marchioness, shooing her with the back of her hand. "You shall see. And mind you leave the door cracked."

Mystified, Isabella went into the dark, windowless room and, not knowing what else to do, perched herself upon one arm of the wooden, chairlike frame. She had no more twitched the pleats of her skirts into place when she heard a shockingly familiar voice and nearly gasped aloud.

She peeked out to see Lord Hepplewood stride into the room to make a sweeping bow over Lady Petershaw's hand.

"*Enchanté,* Maria," he said, pressing his lips to her knuckles. "How good of you to see me."

"Tony, you handsome devil!" Lady Petershaw blushed like a maiden and waved him toward the chair Isabella had just left. "Where have you been keeping yourself?"

"Oh, here and there."

Hepplewood was dressed for riding in knee-high boots and breeches, his dark blue coat cut snugly to his lithe frame and wide shoulders. He sat, throwing one leg over the other in a pose that should have looked effeminate but instead looked faintly dangerous, and Isabella had a sudden vision—swift and unwelcome—of the man stripped naked to the waist, swinging his hammer, his back and shoulder muscles rippling powerfully beneath a sheen of sweat.

She drew a deep breath and forced the thought away—not, regrettably, for the first time since leaving him.

"Well, Maria, how have you been keeping?" he said. "Pink best becomes you, by the way."

"And *nothing* best becomes you, if I recall correctly," she teased, "though I confess to only glimpses. And what a coincidence this is! I was just penning invitations to a very private soiree. I wonder if you might join in?"

"As always, ma'am, you are too kind," he said in his deep, timbrous voice. "But I fear I cannot make it."

The marchioness laughed. "Darling, you haven't even heard the date!" she declared. "But there, I merely tease you. You did not come, I apprehend, to wheedle your way into my bed?"

"I would be undeserving of the honor," he said silkily. "No, you are right. I've come, actually, to inquire after a former employee of yours."

"Oh, never say that rascal Oscar has turned up in Clarges Street!" she declared. "No, Tony, one cannot need a footman badly enough to take on that clever fellow. He can diddle your housemaids with one extremity whilst pinching your silver with another."

Lord Hepplewood smiled, but his eyes were grim. "Now why do I get the feeling, Maria, that you deliberately misunderstand me?" he asked quietly. "I think you know that it's no footman I've come seeking."

"What, then, Mrs. Aldridge, is it?" she asked, a little less warmly. "That chatterbox Louisa sent you up here, didn't she? Well, don't look at me! I thought you had Mrs. Aldridge hidden away in Buckinghamshire."

Lord Hepplewood tapped a long, thin finger on the arm of his chair. "I did have," he said. "But we parted company after a time. Has she not been by here?"

Lady Petershaw widened her eyes ingenuously. "Well, I had a letter from her, but it was vague," she declared. "Heavens, my boy, you didn't let that prize slip your grasp, I hope? It wouldn't be at all like you."

But the charm had left Hepplewood's voice as swiftly as it had come, and he was looking less and less benign. "I wish you to give me her address," he said. "Louisa swears she doesn't have it."

Lady Petershaw lifted a shoulder almost insouciantly. "And do you believe everything Louisa Litner says? That woman will sell you mutton dressed as lamb, Tony, if you aren't careful."

"I am not looking for lamb," he said almost dangerously,

"or mutton. I am looking for Isabella Aldridge. Kindly write down her direction for me."

The marchioness drew a deep breath. "No," she said. "I don't think I shall."

"Damn it, Maria, do not thwart me in this," he demanded, setting his fist on the chair arm. "I will have her address—*now*."

"*Now*—?" Lady Petershaw echoed, drawing herself haughtily up in her chair. "Tony, I am not some submissive girl being paid to take your abuse and buggery. Mind your manners or get out. As to Mrs. Aldridge, I'll do as I damned well please, for I don't think you treated her well."

Something inside him seemed to give way then, the anger vanishing on a sigh. "Damn it all, Maria," he said, raking a hand through his gold-brown curls. "What was Louisa thinking to send a girl that green to me? What were *you* thinking, come to that?"

"I was thinking Mrs. Aldridge was beautiful, lonely, and unwilling to marry again," the marchioness retorted, "so why should she live without pleasure? Moreover, I knew nothing of your involvement, Tony. Louisa was not honest with me. And Isabella is not a girl. She is twenty-six, and capable of choosing her own lover. Indeed, it's remotely possible she's already gone on to bigger and better things than you, my boy."

At this, his breath seemed to hitch. "I beg your pardon?"

Lady Petershaw cast her gaze lower. "Well, probably not bigger, if my recollection is accurate," she conceded, "and perhaps not even better. But if you threw the lady off, Tony, what is it to you where she goes—or with whom?"

"I did not throw her off," he gritted. "At least—it wasn't quite like that."

"So she simply left you, did she?" Lady Petershaw narrowed one eye. "Were you cruel to her, Tony? Did you use her ill? Some women don't take well to that, you know. Isabella was brought up in a high style, and accustomed to giving orders, not taking them."

Hepplewood glared at her. "What in God's name, Maria, are you saying?"

The marchioness just shrugged. "That perhaps those blue-blooded girls won't bow down beneath your lordly hand as you're accustomed," she said. "Did you never think of that?"

"What blue blood?" he said. "She was your damned governess, Maria."

"And governesses are gently bred ladies, or something near it," replied the marchioness. "Isabella was Tafford of Thornhill's daughter."

"*Baron* Tafford?" His expression darkened, if such a thing were possible.

"Heavens, Tony! Could you not even be troubled to get to know the girl before you tossed up her skirts? In my day, we at least made a pretense of politesse. Anything less and—well, one simply hired a Covent Garden uprighter and saw to one's business in the nearest alleyway."

"Maria," he said wearily, "you are vulgar."

"*I'm* vulgar?" she declared. "Are you going to confess to me what you did to poor Mrs. Aldridge or not?"

His lips thinned angrily. "Fine, I had my wicked way with her—or started to," he said. "Wasn't that the plan? And now I wish to see her, damn it. Give me her direction."

"Why?"

"I just need to see her," he said. "I just . . . wish to reassure myself of something."

"Of what?" said the marchioness snidely. "Your place in

her affections? I think we can both assume it's running level with the pavement."

"Look here, damn it. I don't care what you and Louisa claim—that poor girl was naive," he said more determinedly. "A virgin, almost. So here is my concern—what if I've left her with child? That's all I wish to know. I mean her no harm; I just need to be sure. And I need to see her *myself*. And then I will be on my merry and dissolute way."

"Good Lord, Tony, hadn't you sense enough to exercise caution?" But Lady Petershaw's voice, Isabella noted, had gentled. "And what if she is with child? What then?"

"Then you *know* what," he said hollowly, "and God help us all. Maria, please. I'm begging you. Just tell me where to find her. For if you won't, I'll simply have Jervis run her to ground. Or I'll go down to Thornhill. Isabella is hiding out there, perhaps? The present baron must be a relation."

"Tony, *no*." The marchioness seized his wrist. "You will not. On no account will you go down to Thornhill or mention her to Lord Tafford. The trouble you might cause her then would pale to whatever you did to her in Buckinghamshire."

Hepplewood cursed beneath his breath, jerked back his hand, and dragged it through his hair again. "That's my very point, Maria," he said. "If Jervis starts poking about—or if I go down to Sussex—both are bound to stir up gossip. And searching takes time; time she mightn't have."

"Oh, dear. A moment, Tony, if you please." With an uncomfortable smile, the marchioness jerked from her chair. "I must be excused."

With that, the marchioness marched straight toward the water closet, flinging open the door, scarcely leaving Isabella time to leap into the shadows. Cutting her a grim glance, the marchioness slammed the door shut again, plunging them into a darkness so deep that Isabella could see nothing but the crack beneath the door.

"*Shh,*" breathed Lady Petershaw.

Then, after a long moment had passed, she apparently reached out and opened the valve. A great rush of water ensued, gurgling loudly down the trap.

"My dear, you will not avoid this one," the marchioness said beneath the racket, her mouth near Isabella's ear, "not for long. And his concern, frankly, is not misplaced. Do you still refuse to see him?"

Isabella said nothing. For what was there to say? Lady Petershaw was right; a man of Hepplewood's wealth and power would run her down like a rabbit.

"I . . . I will see him."

The hand fell away, the water ceased to gurgle, and in an instant, the door swung open again.

"Heavens!" said the marchioness, marching back into the blade of light. "I'm not as young as I used to be. Now, Tony, what was it you wanted? Oh, yes! Mrs. Aldridge's direction."

"*Now,* Maria, if you please," he ordered.

"Oh, very well," she said a little irritably. "And once you've settled your business with her, perhaps you'll come back and join my merry little band?"

"No," he said tightly, "I won't. Thank you."

"Careful, old boy," she cautioned. "All work and no play might make Jack—and all his tools—very dull indeed."

With that, the marchioness drew up her chair to her desk and made a great pretense of looking for her address book.

Lord Hepplewood jerked from his chair and began to pace the room.

In a moment, the marchioness lifted a piece of paper,

blew on the ink, and thrust it at him. "Fulham," she said. "Enjoy the drive."

"Maria," he rasped, seizing her hand to kiss it, "*thank* you."

"Well, don't thank me yet," said the marchioness peevishly. "You'll first have to get by that gorgon of a cook—so good luck with that, my boy."

"Her *cook*?"

"An elderly retainer, fallen on hard times. Cook. Nanny. Whatever. Mrs. Barbour guards Isabella's virtue like a mastiff." Here the lady paused to tap the side of her nose. "But the woman *does* go to evensong religiously on Wednesdays—no pun intended. *That,* old boy, would be your best bet if it's privacy you want."

"What?" said Hepplewood. "To go on Wednesdays?"

"And this Wednesday might be best," replied Lady Petershaw, "before Isabella is off on her next adventure. After all, if she's with child, you will wish to be sure it is yours, will you not? For once she's taken up with her new gentleman, it will all be the very devil to sort out."

Something ugly flashed in Hepplewood's eyes. "Oh, I will sort it all out, Maria," he snapped. "On that you may depend."

"Very wise!" Lady Petershaw reached out and squeezed his hand. "Well, off with you then, Tony. And remember— evensong generally starts at seven!"

CHAPTER 7

During her come-out Season at a very naive seventeen, Isabella had learned a great deal about the nature of men, and little of it bode favorably. Until that time, she hadn't understood that men married not for love but almost unilaterally for power or money, or that once given in marriage, a woman became legally subsumed in her husband, to the point of near invisibility.

Perhaps her ignorance was understandable; her father had been a sweet, dithering sort of man, while her mother had been brought up in the Canadian provinces amidst the harsh wildernesses of the timber trade. Both organized and energetic, Lady Tafford had managed hearth, home, and husband with a deft hand, and when she collapsed and died on Isabella's twelfth birthday, Lord Tafford had sunk into a swamp of perpetual bewilderment.

Isabella had sunk into a swamp of bad novels; novels that had—or so Lady Meredith claimed—stuffed her head with notions of love and romance, and left her ungrateful in the bargain.

The relict of Lord Tafford's younger brother, Lady Meredith had for some years occupied herself with climbing the Table of Precedence by wedding a succession of doddering old noblemen who had just enough money to keep her in silks.

The dowager was no favorite of society, a fact that did not deter the well-dressed vultures from swooping down on Isabella, who was stunned to find herself accounted the beauty of her London Season. Once cheerfully informed, however, by the dependable Lady Meredith that Isabella had no fortune to speak of, most of the vultures flapped away again in search of richer brides.

After a few tears had been shed and her heart had been if not precisely broken, then at least a little trod upon, Isabella had been blithely told not to fret herself; that in the end it would be best for everyone if she simply married her cousin Everett and spent the rest of her days at Thornhill.

Everett shrugged his agreement and declared Isabella might do as well as anyone.

Isabella, however, had already seen the dark side of her cousin and his pack of vile friends, and had no intention of marrying him. And then, when the worst of Lady Meredith's shrill accusations of ingratitude were being brought to bear, Isabella had been swept off her feet by Richard Aldridge, a poet and *bon vivant* just returned from Italy.

Richard was handsome, his father was rich, and Isabella was smitten to the point of idiocy. When Richard swore he would be unable to write without her beauty as his muse, Isabella had felt an almost moral obligation to run away with him to Thornhill, where it had been a simple business to press her father for approval, then call the banns in the parish church.

Within weeks of meeting one another, Richard and Isabella were wed and Lady Meredith was outraged. Cousin Everett, however, was too busy defiling the tweeny to notice Isabella was gone. And even now Isabella was left to wonder how much of her misjudgment of Richard had been driven by her outright fear of Everett.

Yes, most men were relentless when they wanted something—and if they were not relentless in getting it, then they were manipulative. Isabella sometimes wondered which was worse. But she did not once wonder if Lord Hepplewood would turn up on her doorstep come Wednesday.

Even from a few feet away, she had been unable to miss the ruthless set of his jaw as he'd hounded Lady Petershaw. And though the good lady had held her ground admirably, the earl was just the sort of man, Isabella felt sure, who got precisely what he wanted.

Yes, on Wednesday he would come.

So when Wednesday dawned bright and fair, Isabella took the precaution of sending Mrs. Barbour and the children down to Brighton, for she hadn't known what else to do. The children were all she had, a precious and very private part of her life. She did not want them tainted, and she did not know how to explain Hepplewood's presence to them. Worse, the unholy wrath she'd glimpsed in the earl's eyes had unsettled her just a little.

Still, a journey by train—even a modest one—was a luxury. But Mrs. Barbour had a much-loved niece in Brighton, and the girls had not enjoyed even the smallest treat since Isabella's savings had run out some months earlier. A leisurely visit and an afternoon in the clean, salt-washed air, she told herself, would do them good.

But as the day dragged on and the house grew ever emptier, Isabella began to wish she'd not been so alone. To distract herself, she started on the ironing, for they had let their washerwoman go months past. Until this business of investing in a shop was settled, Isabella feared to spend an extra shilling.

At five she went up to bathe and to dress. This presented a conundrum. She was under no obligation to array herself in any of the tempting gowns Lady Petershaw had given her—nor did she wish to. Yet she could not quite bring herself to put on one of her old gray ones.

Rifling through her wardrobe, Isabella tugged out the old rose-colored dress she'd had made up for Georgina's christening, only to find it hung off her frame like a sack. On a sigh, Isabella returned it to the wardrobe and drew out the least flamboyant of the marchioness's made-overs, a lavender silk day dress with a full, triple-flounced skirt and a fairly modest décolletage.

The bodice fit like a glove—a very soft, very elegant glove—and the wide skirts floated like a cloud over her layers of petticoats. The unusual color, she noticed, served to deepen the intensity of her eyes—the feature that had so fascinated Lord Hepplewood.

Good, she thought a little spitefully. *Let him look and see what he's missing.*

On her next breath, Isabella's hand flew to her mouth. She glanced at herself in the mirror again and wondered where such a thought had come from. Was she really so vain? She wished neither to tempt nor to punish the Earl of Hepplewood.

She wished never to see him again.

With a ruthless jerk, she pulled a gray serge gown from the wardrobe, determined to put it on.

But it was too late.

Suddenly she heard the jingling of harnesses and the sound of hoofbeats in the lane; the sound of a carriage, not a mere farm cart, which was the sort of conveyance usually seen in this part of Fulham.

The arrogant man was early. She might have guessed he would not wait but come at his own convenience. At least she had sent everyone away.

Flinging the dress aside, Isabella hastened down the narrow staircase and through the hall just as a harsh knock sounded on the door.

Her heart suddenly pounding, Isabella threw it open.

But it was not Lord Hepplewood who awaited her.

Everett stood on the top step, his expensive beaver hat tucked beneath one arm. He startled when he saw her but regained himself immediately.

"Bella, my girl," he said, his gaze sliding down her length. "Fancy catching you at home—and aren't you looking splendid, by the way."

"Everett," she said very coolly. "We did not expect you."

His gaze chilled at her words. "Nor did I expect you," he pointed out. "Thought you'd taken a post up in Bucks."

"And yet," she said quietly, "here I am. Which begs the question—why are you here?"

The cold smile warmed. "What, can't a fellow drop by to check on his wee cousins?" he said. "After all, I am at least a *little* responsible for their well-being, and you're always off in parts afar, leaving the poor mites to their own devices."

"Jemima is not your cousin," said Isabella, "for you share not one drop of her blood—"

"Nor do you," Everett interjected, "but your father wished—"

"—Moreover," she said, speaking over him, "they are not left to anyone's devices. They are left—*when* they are left—with Mrs. Barbour. And they are watched every minute of every day."

"Yes, yes, no doubt," said Everett, craning this way and that. "Where is the old dear, anyway?"

"She is at"— Isabella caught herself — "church. I expect her back any moment."

He looked her up and down again, his gaze warming. "Not going to invite me in?" he murmured. "I'm thinking whilst I'm here, perhaps you and I should have a little chat."

"An excellent notion." Isabella stepped out onto the narrow stoop, slamming the door behind her and forcing Everett back down a step. "Let's chat."

"Inside, Bella," he said gruffly. "Christ, it's freezing— and you haven't a shawl."

"I am warmed, Everett, by the fires of righteous indignation," she said. "Say your piece and then I shall say *mine*."

"Oh, Bella, so cruel!" he said. "Look, don't be bitter. I know life hasn't been kind to you, my dear, but I can and will take you away from this misery. I adore you, and my offer still stands. That's all I want to say."

"Your offer?" she said incredulously.

At this, he snatched up her hand and kissed it, his lips unpleasantly moist. "What do you say, Bella?" he asked softly, "Will you give it a go? I'm tired of being alone. Aren't you?"

Isabella drew an unsteady breath. "Everett, are you mad?"

"Yes, mad for you," he said. "And don't get your hackles up. Look at yourself. Look how you're living. Marry me and bring those girls down to Thornhill. We'll be a regular family."

"Everett, you frighten me," she said quietly. "I am not going to marry you. I am not going to marry you— *not ever*—and you know why."

The breath went out of him in a harsh, impatient exhalation. "Good God, not that old rag again!" His gaze darkened. "Do you mean to hold that against me until hell freezes over?"

"Your mother may call your act mere mischief if it comforts her, Everett," Isabella whispered, "but that girl was just *a child*. A little girl taken from her mother—taken far too soon—and put into service twenty miles from home, terrified."

"Someone has to break them in," said Everett, shrugging, "and you'd no business barging in, then turning snitch."

"She was *screaming*."

Everett winked. "Women do, sometimes," he said, "if a chap knows what he's about. I swear, Bella, you are such a goose. Girls like that—they know it's going to happen. Why do you think they call it being *in service*? She was pleased, I daresay, the master would deign to look at her."

"And was she pleased your chum Sir Harry looked at her, too?" Isabella snapped. "What about the other man—good God, I don't even remember his name—and I don't want to. Everett, you are cruel. She was twelve years old, and the three of you—"

"What can I say, Bella?" he interjected. "Fine, then, we oughtn't have done it! Is that what you need to hear? But the girl's long gone, so what does it matter? Besides, Mamma and I are agreed—if I had a wife, I would give up my diversions."

"She doesn't know your diversions still involve mere children, I'd wager," said Isabella. "Everett, why start this again? Why now? Just leave Georgina and Jemima alone."

"Why *now*?" he echoed sarcastically. "Look at yourself, Bella. You're just the downhill side of thirty, and so damned scrawny you'd be lucky to carry a child. You're starving yourself to feed those two brats, when you could have one of your own."

"Have . . . a child?" The thought of Everett fathering a child was beyond horrific.

Everett shifted his weight uneasily. "Well, I need an heir, don't I?" he muttered. "Mamma keeps saying as much, and she's right."

"Get out," said Isabella, jabbing a finger at the rusting garden gate. "Get away from this house, Everett! You are a cad and a despoiler of innocence and I have no idea what your mother's fascination is with me, but I have *never* been willing to marry you."

Something dark twisted his face. "Never? Quite sure, are you?"

"There is not enough depravation or starvation or any other sort of misery on this earth that would make me marry you. Good God, Everett, do you think people can't find out about your proclivities?"

"I've done nothing against the law," he said.

"Rape is not?" she challenged.

He laughed. "Find someone who will say I raped her," he retorted. "Go on, Bella, try it. And perhaps I shall try my luck, too."

Suddenly her blood ran cold. "What are you saying?"

"That those girls belong in their childhood home," he said, seizing her wrist. "You were never meant to take them away from Thornhill."

"What?" She gaped. "You never showed the slightest interest in having them—nor did your mother."

"And we are both ashamed of that," he said, "having seen what your life has come to. Do you think any reasonable judge would keep them in this hovel when they could go back to Thornhill? To live in their old home with Mamma and me?"

"A judge just might," she snapped, "when I tell him what I saw."

"And what better place for that conversation than the Court of Chancery?" he replied, backing her up against her own door. "Heavens, Bella, I wonder if your father-in-law would attend?"

"You *bastard*," she hissed.

Something like alarm sketched over his face then, and he relented a little. "Come now, Bella, threats are foolish on both our parts," he said. "We are cousins, and I have never done you the first harm. I adore you, and want only to marry you. My desperation makes me rash."

"Your desperation makes you an ass," she said. "And one more word from you or your mother about marriage and I swear, Everett, I shall take her up to that vile little house in Soho where you and your friends spend your evenings and make her look in the window for herself."

At that, Everett went white, his upper lip quivering. "You ungrateful bitch," he said, lunging.

Isabella jerked back so hard that she struck her head on the door.

Suddenly Everett was seized by a hand that clapped his shoulder and hauled him ruthlessly down the steps. Arms windmilling wildly, he tripped, collapsing backward onto the Earl of Hepplewood.

The earl stepped smoothly to the side and let Everett go sprawling across the moss-slick flagstone. "That third step looks a bit of a trick," he said in his quiet, rumbling voice. "Baron Tafford, I presume?"

CHAPTER 8

Everett jerked himself fully upright, yanking his coat back to order. "And who the devil are you to interfere in family business?"

Hepplewood flashed his dark half smile. "The devil who's about to haul you into that lane"—he pointed across the gate with his brass-knobbed walking stick—"and thrash you within an inch of your life for putting your hands on a lady."

"Don't I know you?" said Everett, narrowing one eye.

"No, but you are about to make my acquaintance," said Hepplewood quietly. "Isabella, you will go inside. *Now.*"

Isabella knew that tone. Scrabbling at the wood behind her, she found the latch, lifted it, and stepped backward into the house, slamming the door behind. If it came to an outright brawl, her money was on Hepplewood.

On the other hand, Everett was just the sort of man who might keep a blade to hand.

Her heart in her throat, Isabella flew into the parlor and looked out to see the earl, true to his word, dragging Everett through the garden gate—well, propelling him might be a better description.

On the other side, he threw Everett off, disgust plain on his face. Words were exchanged—hot and swift—but Isabella couldn't make them out. Then Everett turned and foolishly came at the earl. He got nothing but five hard fingers to the chest for his trouble, a shove that sent him hitching up against the door of his curricle.

Unfortunately for Everett, rather than regaining himself, he tripped one foot over the other and fell sideways into the mud.

Hepplewood extracted a silver case, flicked one of his thick ivory cards into Everett's lap, then turned and came back through the gate, his hat still in place, his stick tucked neatly under his arm.

Isabella opened the door, deeply grateful and yet uneasy all the same.

"Precisely what was that about?" said Hepplewood, coming briskly back up the steps.

"Nothing," Isabella said, shutting the door after him. "I'm very sorry, my lord. Are you all right?"

"Perfectly." He looked at her askance. "But you are not; you're white as a sheet, Isabella, and you are shaking."

She held out her hands to see that it was true. "My temper, nothing more."

"Nothing more?" His expression darkened. "Then what was all that shouting about marriage and your aunt? And a house in Soho?"

"Merely an old family quarrel," she said more firmly. "I beg you to let the matter go. My cousin is an ass."

For an instant, he hesitated. "Well, now the ass knows where to find me," he finally said, "should he wish to seek satisfaction."

"My cousin preys only upon those weaker than himself," she said, taking his stick and his hat, "so I think you're quite safe. Thank you for ridding me of him."

Though he still looked suspicious, the earl apparently decided to let his questions go. With neat, swift jerks, he tugged off his leather driving gloves, his gaze sliding down Isabella's length in a way that made her breath catch.

"You don't seem surprised to see me," he murmured, draping the gloves over his hat brim.

Isabella flashed a smile. "I'm not, actually," she admitted, setting the hat on the hall table. "Lady Petershaw told me you might call."

"Did she say why?" His voice was unerringly polite, perfectly calm.

"She did." Isabella felt her face flood with heat. "I assure you, sir, that you've no need for concern."

"No need?" he pressed, dipping his head to better see her. "None whatever? You are certain?"

"As certain as nature can make me," she assured him. "Yes, quite certain. May we leave it at that?"

Stiffly, he nodded. "May I sit down, Isabella?"

Her embarrassment deepened. "Yes, certainly." She motioned at the open parlor door. "Do go in."

He did so, his gaze sweeping the small and desperately ordinary room. But it was clean, and furnished with a few lovely things she'd been able to take before handing over Thornhill to Everett forever; things that had been her mother's, and thus not entailed to the estate. Her mother's will had been very specific in that regard; her every possession was left to Isabella.

The trouble was, there had been so very few of them. And most had been sold already, to keep the girls in shoes and schoolbooks, though Isabella could not have borne to confess it.

Not to a man like Lord Hepplewood, who could have no idea what poverty was.

"Those are lovely portraits by the window," he murmured, taking the chair she offered. "Small, but superbly done. Your parents?"

"Yes, Mother's was commissioned in Liverpool just days before she met Papa," said Isabella wistfully. "It was a frightful luxury for my grandfather, but he lived in the Ottawa Valley—in Canada—where such things weren't easily had."

"And it found its way back to you?"

She shrugged. "It was shipped to Thornhill," she said, "two or three years ago. No one else wanted it, so Everett brought me the pair at Christmas. It was a kindness of sorts, I suppose."

And he had brought with it yet another marriage proposal—an especially obsequious one—though Isabella did not say as much.

"Your father, if you'll pardon my saying, looks a bit older than she."

Isabella smiled. "A dozen years."

"Ah. An arranged marriage?"

"Far from it," Isabella replied. "Her family never really forgave her for staying behind, and they were more or less estranged ever after. But Canada was lonely for her, Mamma said, for they lived much of the year in the wilderness."

"The *wilderness*?"

"Well, perhaps that's an overstatement," said Isabella, "but her father and brother were in the timber trade—simple people, really. Papa said he'd meant to remain a bachelor all his days—that he was too entrenched in his books and his gardens to take a wife—until he saw Mamma standing in the lobby of the Adelphi Hotel in a pair of shabby brown boots."

"Love at first sight, hmm?"

"That's what Papa called it."

"She looks beautiful," said the earl, still gazing at the painting, "and so much like you it steals one's breath."

And in an instant, the awkwardness between them returned. "I beg your pardon," she said a little stiffly. "I am out of the habit of entertaining. May I offer you a glass of sherry?"

His gaze flicked toward her, sharp and knowing. "May I not speak of your beauty, Isabella?"

"I wish you would not," she said honestly.

He studied her for a long moment. "You once said to me that beauty could be a curse," he finally replied, "and that surely I, of all people, must know it."

"I remember," she said.

"What did you mean by it?"

She lifted her gaze from her lap. "I spoke wrongly, I suppose," she said. "It's true of women. Beauty for a woman is often a curse. But for men like yourself, who are both wealthy and beautiful—no, I suppose it does not matter. It's just icing on the cake of life."

He shrugged and looked away. "I've wondered lately if that's entirely true," he mused. "I wonder if it doesn't worsen a man's sense of entitlement and make him more quick to assume what he wants will be his. That he will, in the end, have his way." He stopped for a heartbeat. "But in the end, Isabella, I will not have you, will I? I knew it the minute I laid eyes on you. And I knew, too, that it would be better for both of us if I did not. I should never have allowed Louisa to tempt me with that damned letter."

Isabella drew a deep breath. "I cannot speak to your assumptions, my lord. We must all wrestle with our own conscience."

"I wonder if you ever have to do so." He turned to look at her again, his glittering blue gaze searching her face. "Well,

Isabella, I have asked my question, and you've answered. I can ask nothing more from you." He set his wide, long-fingered hands over his thighs, as if to rise. "Shall I go, then? Shall this be the end of it?"

Did she wish him to leave?

Lord, she didn't know. She didn't understand anything, least of all the feelings that stirred in her treacherous heart as she listened to him. There was something about his deep, beautifully modulated voice that melted over her like butter, warming her to the bone and weakening her resolve.

She dropped her head, her hands twisting in her lap. "I do not know, my lord," she admitted, her voice threading a little. "I no longer know what I wish or think or even feel. Since I returned from Greenwood, I . . . I haven't understood anything. Not myself, and certainly not you."

"Come, Isabella," he gently pressed. "Can we not try and build a friendship between us, at the very least? Have I treated you so ill that I am beyond the pale?"

His letter had, in fact, said precisely that; that he would always feel a fondness for her and be a friend to her should she ever require one. Isabella had assumed the words to be mere platitudes born of guilt and the wish to be rid of her. But there was no denying that, inexplicably, she saw in him much to respect and yes, even to like.

Nonetheless, she was also a little obsessed with him; obsessed in a way that frightened her and had begun to disturb her sleep. Not a fear of him—no, strangely, it was not. It was something far, far worse—an almost dark craving—a fear of herself, perhaps. And it was the reason she would as soon not see him again.

"Yes." She lifted her gaze to his. "Yes, we may part as friends."

"*Part* as friends," he echoed, "but not remain friends?"

Confused, she opened her hands, palms up. "We will not see one another after this. We are not of the same world, you and I—not now, if we ever were." She let her hands fall back into her lap. "I'm sorry. You are kind to come; most men would not have troubled themselves."

"I am not," he said quietly, "most men."

"And this is awkward for us both, I'm sure," she went on. "Perhaps I've been alone and away from society so long I've forgotten what friendship is. Moreover, this cottage . . . it cannot be what you are accustomed to."

He flicked another gaze round the room. "I rather doubt it is what you are accustomed to," he said a little dryly. "You were born at . . . Thornhill, I believe, your father's seat?"

"In Sussex, yes," she said quietly. "But I have not lived there in years."

"Since your father's death?"

"No, before that," she said. "I left when my father remarried. I was . . . nineteen, I think."

"Ah," he said quietly. "And then you became a governess?"

"Because I wished to," she said swiftly. "I love children. My stepmother brought a child to the marriage—my sister, whom I adore—but they were newlyweds. I thought it best I go. So I did."

"So you did," he said in that faintly acerbic tone. "And your father did not forbid it? He should have done. He should have been watching over you."

"You have such charmingly old-fashioned notions," she said.

"Do you really believe, Isabella," he asked very quietly, "that it is old-fashioned for a man to guard what is his?"

She shrugged. "Having never been guarded," she said, "I shall reserve judgment. In any case, Papa could never forbid anyone anything. He was the most lenient and forgiving of men."

"I'm not sure leniency and forgiveness are the best qualities in a man who must steward an estate and a family," Hepplewood replied. "Resolve and discipline are sometimes more useful."

Isabella flashed a wry smile. "Yes, I comprehend your views on resolve," she murmured, "and discipline."

He gave a bark of sarcastic laughter and looked away. "Damned if you can't put a man in his place, Isabella," he said, "for all your quiet ways."

"Do you realize, sir, that a few moments ago you ordered me inside my own home in a most high-handed fashion?" she said. "And called me by my Christian name whilst doing it?"

"No." His mouth twitched into a mordant smile. "I did not realize. That will garner some interest, I daresay, at Tafford's dinner table tonight."

Unease must have shown in her expression.

"Forgive me," he added. "I didn't mean to cause you any embarrassment."

"It is Everett who is the embarrassment," she said tightly. "And I care very little what is said of me at his table. It will be nothing kind, I assure you."

The earl seemed to ponder this a moment, his long, thin index finger tapping lightly upon the arm of his chair. "Is anyone else at home, Isabella?" he said after a time. "May we talk freely? You have young sisters, you said."

She was touched he remembered. But then, he likely remembered each and every time his will was thwarted. "Yes, Jemima and Georgina," she said. "They've gone down to Brighton with Mrs. Barbour, who helps look after them."

"Jemima and Georgina," he echoed softly. "So I'm permitted to know their names?"

"Have I any means, really, of keeping them from you?" she asked a little stridently. "You know where I live. You are already in my home—and you look very much *at* home, if you don't mind my saying. And you have known me in the most intimate of ways. So let us be realistic, my lord. There is nothing I could hold back from you—*nothing*—and I wonder I ever tried."

He surprised her then by jerking from his chair and striding to the window, one hand dragging through his mass of unruly curls—the only thing about the man that did not reek of tightly leashed control.

It was dusk now, the lane empty. She wondered, fleetingly, how he'd managed to appear out of nowhere. He was dressed for driving, in snug charcoal trousers and an elegant frock coat of the finest black merino. But she had seen no carriage.

After a time, he set a hand flat on the low sill and the other at his hip, pushing the fall of his coat back to reveal the lean turn of his waist. "Isabella," he rasped into the glass, "would this have ended differently for us if . . . if I had been a more tender lover?"

"That is a question you must ask yourself, my lord," she whispered, "because *I* did not end it."

He cut a look of surprise over his shoulder, then his hand fell. "Yes, but that's not what I meant," he said, "and I think you know it."

She shook her head. "No. I do not. I very often find I do not understand you."

He turned from the window and crossed the room in two strides, dropping before her on one knee, capturing her hands in his. They were warm, long, and surprisingly gentle. "Could you feel some small affection for me, Isabella," he rasped, "if I were a different man? *Could* you? If I tried?"

"I feel an affection for the man you are," she said. "Or I feel . . . *something*. Something I don't have words for. To myself I would call it an obsession."

"Come back to Greenwood, Isabella," he said. "Forgive me. I made a terrible mistake in sending you away."

"You do not strike me, my lord, as a man who makes mistakes," she said, "or who makes his decisions lightly."

"Anthony," he said. "Or just Tony—could you call me that, Isabella, when we're alone? I don't like this formality between us. It seems . . . cold. It seems not what we are together, you and I."

But they would not be alone again after this evening, she thought to herself. She was not going back to Buckinghamshire. The thought flooded her with an aching sense of loss even as she acknowledged the foolishness of that emotion.

"Come back with me," he said again, "and I will try to temper my ways if that's what you need. I used to be . . . gentler, I suppose. I can try to be that again. Let us get to know one another better before we decide we do not suit."

She shook her head. "No," she said. "I cannot."

Something dark and unhappy passed over his face. "Is there someone else?" he demanded, the pressure on her hands tightening. "Isabella, *is* there?"

She felt her brow furrow. "No," she said sharply.

But Hepplewood's head had bowed, his eyes seemingly locked on their joined hands. "Forgive me," he said. "I find myself unaccountably jealous. And pray do not trouble telling me I've no right. I know that I do not; it makes not a damned bit of difference."

But Isabella remembered Lady Petershaw's taunt. He did have cause, really, to wonder if she was already warming another man's bed. But to be jealous? It seemed not at all like him. Why would a man like the Earl of Hepplewood lose a moment's sleep over someone like her?

"There is no one else," she said. "And there shan't be; I'm not suited to that life. You know it as well as I."

He lifted his gaze then. "Isabella, what are you talking about?"

She shook her head. "You sent me away for a reason," she said. "Don't lose sight of that now. I am . . . just a governess, no matter how pretty you think me. I must find something else I can do with my life."

Those ice-blue eyes drilled into her. "You think you failed to please me."

It was not a question, but she lifted her shoulders all the same.

"Oh, *Isabella*."

His hands slipped away then, both settling instead around her face, lightly cupping it. Words lingered unspoken in his eyes, but he said no more. Instead, he leaned into her, lightly kissing her mouth. He murmured her name again and planted a second kiss on her cheek, and then another at the corner of one eye; kisses tender as the brush of a moth's wing in the night.

"Oh, love," he whispered, "you please me beyond measure."

"Then *why* did you send me away?" she asked a little stridently. "With no explanation, really, save for a letter full of vague inanities? Yes, I left, my lord, and quickly—before you changed your mind. Or worse, before *I* did."

To her shame, her voice wavered a little at the end, and something like sorrow softened his eyes. Then he set one hand to the back of her head and kissed her in earnest, opening his mouth over hers, tasting her deeply.

Isabella felt plunged headlong into a pool of warm, swirling water. It surged all around her, pulling her under, turning her stomach upside down. As if of their own volition, her hands left the chair arms to slide up the front of his coat, then twined about his neck as she gave herself up to the feeling.

When he came away, her hands were tangled in his hair and his breath was rough, his nostrils faintly flared.

"Let me take you to bed once more," he rasped. "Come away with me. Tonight. To Greenwood. To *anywhere*. Let me show you how well you please me."

She shook her head, her eyes widening. "I can't. Not . . . like that."

Gloom had steeped the room now, casting him in shadows. He cupped his hands tenderly around her face again. "Are you afraid of me, Isabella?" he whispered. "Am I too rough? Too demanding? It was wrong of me to be so harsh."

Again, she shook her head. "I am . . . afraid of myself, perhaps," she said. "Afraid of how I feel when I'm with you. Of the things you can make me want."

He kissed her again, and the rush of emotion surged anew. He tasted of wine and of sin, the heat rising from his skin in waves, redolent with his familiar scent; a mingling of soap and chestnut and some kind of spice her mind but dimly recognized—*sandalwood,* she mused—just before he kissed her again, raking her cheek with the dark stubble of his beard.

Isabella kissed him back, twining her tongue with his, returning his thrusts in a way that, a few short weeks ago, she would not have dared. He responded with a deep, almost primitive groan and thrust deeper, fully inside, one hand sliding into the hair at her temple.

Her heartbeat pounding in her ears now, Isabella pushed him a little away. "Take me upstairs," she murmured, her eyes dropping half shut. "Just . . . once more. Please? Will you?"

He kissed her again, swift and hard. "Will you, *Anthony,*" he corrected.

"Will you, Anthony," she whispered, "take me to bed and make me feel . . ."

"Make you feel how?" He swallowed hard, the apple of his throat working beneath the silken knot of his cravat. "Tell me. How shall it be?"

"As it was at Greenwood," she whispered, grateful for the darkness that hid her blushes. "I want to feel as if . . . dear God, don't make me say it. I can't even explain it."

But she was to have no opportunity to explain it; Hepplewood had risen and scooped her up from the chair as if she were weightless.

"Where?" he demanded, starting up the stairs.

"In the back," she said, "the middle door."

He shouldered his way into the narrow room, so small he had to turn to keep her heels from striking the wall. Here, moonlight had begun to spill through the window, casting a shaft of milky light across Isabella's bed.

They undressed one another in a feverish pitch, his hands rough and impatient, and nothing at all as they had been at Greenwood. There, he had been a master of control. Now he seemed different; no less in control of her, but perhaps in far less control of himself.

When she was naked before him, he turned to face her, eyes glittering in the moonlight.

"Isabella." Now stripped to the waist, the band of his trousers hanging off his slender hips, he slid his hand behind her head and kissed her deep, pulling the long length of his body hard against hers.

She could feel the jutting weight of his erection throbbing against her belly and the softness of chest hair teasing her breasts. He let his mouth roam over her face again, infinitely more tender, his hand sliding over and over through her hair.

"How long, love?" he rasped. "How long have we?"

"I've sent everyone away," she admitted, and knew on her next breath that she had done it deliberately—that she had wanted this, wanted *him*—"until tomorrow afternoon."

"Wicked girl," he murmured, nuzzling her face and then her throat. "Did you plan this, Isabella? Did you?"

She shrugged. "I want it now." She tipped back to give him unfettered access as he nibbled his way down her neck. "That's how I think when I'm with you—in the here and now. I want it now, Anthony. In this moment, I want the way you make me feel, and that's all I can ever be sure of."

He pushed her down onto the narrow bed. Holding her gaze, he whipped open the last of his trouser buttons, yanked free the tie of his drawers, and shoved them down at once.

Less anxious this time, Isabella permitted herself the luxury of watching. He was perfectly, beautifully made, well over six feet tall, his body lean and lithe. His shoulders were wide, his upper arms rounded with muscle. Dark hair dusted his chest then quickly thickened, trailing down to the thatch of dark curls from which his manhood jutted, hard and thick-veined.

"Are you frightened, Isabella?"

"No." She swallowed. "Yes. A little."

He stepped to the edge of the bed and caught her chin a little roughly. "Don't be. Tell me what you want this time. I want to please you, love."

She tried to find the words. "I . . . I want you to tell me," she whispered.

Confusion clouded his face. "Tell you what?" he murmured, still holding her chin. "You have to say it this time, Isabella. *You* have to *say*."

She closed her eyes. "I want to be yours," she said. "To feel, for a little while, as if I belong beneath you. I . . . I don't want to make choices."

"You want to submit to me?" he suggested, his voice edged now with something dangerous.

She shrugged feebly. "I want to feel safe," she whispered.

"*Ah*," he said, as if the secret to the universe had just been unveiled. "I begin to comprehend. But it is a little wicked, love, what you seem to be asking for. And I didn't really come prepared."

Her gaze dropped to his jutting erection. "No," she said, her mouth going dry. "No, I think you did."

Something inside him seemed to give way. "God, I want you, Isabella," he whispered. "You rake up something inside me—those old-fashioned notions, I fear—and leave them to burn like hot coals in my gut."

She held his gaze steadily. "Whatever you are," she said, "I cannot deny my desire for you. Not in this moment. If that should alter . . . I will tell you."

"Will you?" he replied. "If you do, Isabella, I will honor it. I will stop. Or leave. Or whatever you require. Do you believe me?"

She did believe him; he held within him great strength of will. But just now, she wished he would stop talking. Her tongue darted out, licking the corner of her mouth a little anxiously.

"Come here, Isabella," he said gruffly, motioning to her. "On your knees, love."

She crawled back to the end of the narrow bed to kneel before him. Slowly, he pulled what was left of the pins from her hair until it cascaded down. When he was finished, he pushed his hands through it, drawing it smooth, all the way down, until Isabella felt it tickle the soles of her feet.

He made a sound of appreciation in the back of his throat. Gathering her hair in his fist, he roped it round his hand once, and then again and again, until he held her fast at the nape of her neck. She breathed out audibly and felt him tighten his grip further.

"Lean down, love," he said, "and take my shaft in your mouth."

She lifted one eyebrow. "And *fellate* you?" she suggested.

"*Hmm,* someone found a dictionary," he murmured, "and a wicked one at that. Yes, love. Suck me. Get on your knees and learn how to do it properly—and then, trust me, I'll return the pleasure in spades."

But Isabella had not needed a dictionary; she'd simply asked the marchioness what the word meant. The lady had laughed and taken from her private library an album of scandalous drawings, along with a beautiful book on sexual positions with a title Isabella could not pronounce.

But she did not need to pronounce it; she'd learned plenty. Now she leaned forward and felt her hair cascade over her shoulders. He gave her head a little push by way of encouragement.

Isabella bent and licked him tentatively with her tongue.

"Put your hands on me," he ordered, tightening his grip. "Put one hand round my shaft—tight, mind you—and slowly slide your lips over me."

Isabella did as she was told, her heart beating fast in her chest. His flesh felt like warm satin to her touch; feverish, really, and drawn tight over the swollen head of his erection.

Gingerly she drew him inside and slicked her hand hard down his length, as she'd once seen him touch himself.

"*Ah . . .*" The word was a sigh that seemed to run through him.

Sinuously, she stroked her tongue around the rim of his head.

He groaned, the sound rising from deep inside his chest. Fisting her hair tightly, he pushed himself deeper, all the way into her throat, then a powerful shudder seemed to rock him. He pulled her back, and obediently she went.

"Again," he choked, urging himself deeper. "And—*aah,* God, Isabella—like that. Just . . . like . . . *that.*"

Over and over, she drew him deep, guided by the pressure of his hand fisted roughly in her hair. He thrust inside her mouth and thrust again, and in time his body became wracked with spasms.

Risking his displeasure, she drew back a fraction to glance up at him. His head was thrown back, his throat corded with tension. "Isabella, *Christ,*" he rasped. "Too fast, love—oh, wicked, wicked—*aahh!*"

She felt his erection spasm hard against her grip, again and again, and in the next instant, he jerked from her mouth, taking himself in hand as his seed gushed forth.

Isabella watched, mesmerized, until the wracking spasms waned.

His hand fell. He was still watching her, the clean blade of moonlight cutting across the flat plane of his belly.

"Good God Almighty, Isabella," he choked.

"Was that good?" she asked a little proudly. "Have I learnt how to *fellate* you?"

"Perfectly, love, and just as I wished," he murmured

After snatching up his drawers to wipe away the evidence of his passion, he crawled fully onto the bed, a shock of hair falling forward to shadow his eyes.

She scooted nearer the pillows.

"So is that how you want it, Isabella?" he asked, still watching her as he approached. "To be told what to do? To be made to please me? And to be given what I think you need?"

"Yes." She licked her lips, desire swamping her. Somehow she managed to hold his gaze. "Tonight, yes. Just . . . tell me. Please?"

"Then lie down," he said, his voice strained.

"Y-yes," she said, scrabbling backward.

He pushed her back onto the pillows and crawled over her. "I could take you now, Isabella," he said, looking down into her eyes, "and oh, love, I will—but I'll need a little time. In the meanwhile, let's play a little game, *hmm*?"

She forced down a knot in her throat, swallowing hard. "Yes," she whispered.

"Yes, *Anthony*," he corrected. "*Yes, love, I will do anything you say.*"

She managed to nod. "Y-yes, Anthony," she whispered, "I will do anything you say."

He stroked one finger down her cheek. "Do you know, Isabella, I half believe that," he murmured. "Now lie back and shut your eyes. And remember to do as I command."

A little anxiously, she did so, watching warily from beneath her lashes.

"I said eyes *shut*," he barked. "You are cheating."

"Only a little," she whispered. " I just wanted to see if—"

In a trice, he had yanked her up round the waist and hauled her across his knee. His hand spread wide, he smacked her hard across the right buttock with his open palm.

"I think you just want to disobey, Isabella," he growled, making warm, soft circles over her hip, soothing the burn. "I think you just want to try me—to see how serious I am."

"I don't know," she managed. "Perhaps. I . . . I don't know."

"I think you just want a firm hand, love." So saying, he struck her again and again, bringing her skin alive and making it burn. "You need this, Isabella. Say it."

"I do," she said. "Oh, I need—I need—"

"To know who's in control?" He smacked her twice more, making her jump. "Is that it, love?"

It was.

God help her, but it was.

And she knew she should be ashamed. She could feel her hips wobble beneath his blows and she closed her eyes, sucking in her breath to steel herself to the burn. Though she lay facedown across him, she could feel him watching her behind. Anticipation went shuddering through her as she awaited the next stroke.

It came, sweet and stinging, her body thrumming to the touch. Hungrily, she wriggled against his thigh.

"Oh, Isabella, you really must come with me to Greenwood," he said, his voice so soft she could barely hear it. "If we were there, my darling, I would open my little toy chest and subdue you properly."

"And how . . . how would you do that?" she whispered.

"Firstly, I would bind your wrists to my bed." His voice was a hoarse rasp in the gloom, his fingers stroking deep into the cleft of her buttocks. "Facedown, of course. And, oh, love, I have something that would make you utterly squirm and beg for more. A little ivory play-pretty." He murmured soothing words, circling his palm over her buttocks. "Yes, love,—I think that you are more adventurous than either of us could dream. By the way, love, *do* you dream?"

"Yes," she whispered.

"Of me, dare I hope?"

She hesitated. "Yes," she admitted, "—of you. Every night. It never stops."

Cupping her cleft, he slipped his hand down and around, between her legs and his thigh, to stroke her intimately with one long finger. Already she dripped with wetness. Heat rushed to her face.

"What do you dream of, Isabella?" He stroked the finger

deeper, grazing her sweet spot. "Do you dream of being beneath me? Being filled with my seed? The sting of my hand? And then, Isabella, do you touch yourself? Like this?"

For a moment, she refused to answer. He withdrew the finger and she felt his palm draw back again, felt the pain and the pleasure thrumming through her buttocks again as if he *had* struck her. She sucked in her breath sharply.

"Isabella?" he asked warningly. "If I ask a question, then you answer. Or I punish you for being disobedient. Or you tell me to get out. Do you understand your choices?"

"Y-yes," she said. "But I forgot the question."

"No, you didn't," he said, the words low in his chest. But he returned his hand to her wetness and stroked deep again. "Oh, so very wet and sweet, love. When I come to you in your dreams, do you touch yourself like this?"

"*Yes,*" she cried. "Yes, a little. Because you've ruined me. I wake in a fever, half-mad and aching for . . . for something. And yes—I put my hand there. But it's not the same. It's *never* the same."

"No, by God, it's not," he said ruefully. "It certainly is not."

"Now let me up." She began to squirm. "I have been good, Tony. I have f-fellated you and pleasured you and—"

He laughed again, more tenderly.

"—and all I tried to do just now was watch what you were doing to me. Don't smack me again. *Please.*"

"Oh, you beg so sweetly." He leaned forward and kissed the swell of her hip. "There, love, you have been—for the most part—a very good girl. Go, and sin no more."

She scrabbled off his thigh—a very large, very hard thigh that left her throbbing—and tucked herself against the bank of pillows.

"Now lie back down, Isabella," he ordered, "and this time do not open your eyes until I tell you that you may do so.

And if you disobey—oh, Isabella, I will have to give that pretty, pink arsehole of yours a good, hard thrust, and trust me, you are not ready for it."

"I am not l-looking," she said, half of her afraid he was not kidding, and the other half of her regretting she'd ever seen the rest of Lady Petershaw's drawings—for she now knew that what he threatened was not impossible.

He was moving around the room, fumbling through the clothing, by the sounds of it.

"Wh-what are you doing?" she asked quietly.

"Surprising you," he said.

"Oh, I know that," she protested, "but in what way?"

"Isabella," he said, snapping something out—his cravat, it had to be. "Do you want me to take care of you, and give you what you need? Do you want to be obedient, and trust me to love you? Or do you want to run the show? Because I can be persuaded to let you, my dear. I just don't think that's what you want."

Isabella did not answer.

It was not what she wanted. She wanted to give herself over to someone strong—to *him*—to feel his hands and the weight of his body on her, heavy and certain. To feel his shaft thrusting deep as he pushed her down and down into the softness of the bed, taking his pleasure of her and giving it back twofold. She was done suffering with guilt for having enjoyed the things he'd done to her.

Good God, what was wrong with her?

The thought flew from her head when she felt something breeze across her face. It smelled of fresh linen and starch. "What is that?" she blurted. "Is—Is that your handkerchief?"

He smacked her hard on the side of her hip. "Not another question from you, Isabella," he ordered, "or I will turn you over and stripe your bottom royally—and I don't mean with the back of my hand."

"You don't have your crop," she pointed out.

"Are you sure?" he asked. "I left my carriage at the coaching inn up the road. Shall I walk back up there and see, love? Or—here's a novel thought—how about I just go cut myself a switch from that birch across the lane?"

"I will be good," she said, stiffening her body like a soldier. "But you are stark staring naked, Tony, and your . . . your thing is getting stiff again. I don't think you're going anywhere."

"My *thing*—?" he said, sounding wounded. "To you, impudent miss, that noble beauty is called a cockstand. Later I'll make you say it. But not another word for now. My hand doesn't sting so badly I can't use it."

And with that, he drew the handkerchief over her face and folded it like a blindfold.

"Turn your head," he ordered.

A little thrill coursing through her at the sound of his command, she did so. He knotted the handkerchief tight behind her head and drew her face back into his, kissing her deeply, thrusting his tongue hard and repeatedly.

Suddenly, Isabella realized her every sense was oddly heightened by her blindness. "*Ohhh,*" she said when he was done.

Suddenly, something caught her fast around the wrist.

She jerked against it instinctively, panic rising in her throat. "What is that?"

"The tie to my drawers," he said, his voice dark. "I'm going to bind you to the bed and take my pleasure very, very slowly—but first, my dear, kindly roll a little to the left."

Uneasily, she did so. He struck her hard across the buttocks again, the sting sizzling through her.

"Ouch!" she said, shocked and yet oddly stimulated. "What did I do?"

"Asked a question," he rasped. "Now will you obey me, Isabella? Because my hand really is starting to burn. And you invited me up here."

She nodded, and gently he rolled her back over onto her stinging hip. In an instant her wrist was wrapped round and round by the tie, the back of her fingers drawn against one of the wrought-iron rods of her bed.

Lord, would she ever be able to lie here again in the dark of a lonely night and not remember this?

But what was he doing, exactly? Certainly he was binding her right wrist—binding it even tighter than the left, and for an instant she felt a little flutter of fear in her heart. He could even walk out now. Leave her like this.

But he did not. He shoved her wrist high above her head, the cold iron rod of the bedstead thrusting between her thumb and index finger as he whipped the cord tight.

"Hold on, my love," he said, his voice dark with satisfaction. "I believe I have you at my mercy."

She swallowed hard. "Are you going to put yourself inside me now?" she whispered.

"Lord, God, Isabella, not another question." He sounded exasperated. "I think you *want* to be punished."

She felt his weight sag onto the bed, and sensed him crawling up the mattress like a predator.

"I will be quiet," she whispered.

He was crawling over her now. "And since my hand stings, love," he said, "I think I will just have to do something that will distract you."

"Y-yes?"

"Isabella," he growled into her ear, "was that a question?"

"N-no, my lord," she whispered.

"No, I thought not," he said, drawing his tongue around the shell of her ear.

Then he proceeded to kiss and bite his way down her jugular vein, down to the turn of her throat. She could hear him drawing in the smell of her skin. Could feel the stubble of his beard raking her and the hardening weight of his erection rubbing its way down her belly.

Everything—every sensation—seemed suddenly intense. Her every nerve ending was heightened by the sting of his hand and the anticipation of what was to come.

"*Ohh,*" she breathed.

He caught her nipple in her mouth and bit—hard. She squeaked, and at once he began to soothe it with his tongue, stroking round and round before sucking her deep into his mouth again.

When her nipples were wet and pebbled hard, he drew back and lightly circled one with his finger. "I would like to bejewel these for you, Isabella," he murmured, "with long, teardrop amethysts."

Her breath hitched, and she recalled the sting of his hand. "I . . . I am not permitted to ask any questions," she whispered weakly.

"*Hmm,*" he said. "And yet you are curious, aren't you?"

"A little," she said breathlessly. "Again, *not* a question."

Delicately, he stroked her again with the very tip of his tongue, the lightest, most teasing stroke imaginable. "To insert a tiny jeweled ring here would bring you great pleasure," he said, rubbing it between his thumb and forefinger, "and cause you but a very brief and minor pain. Afterward, you would find yourself in a constant state of heightened awareness from the weight of the dangling stone—and in a state of constant yearning—for me, if I play my cards well."

"I do not believe such things are done," she said. "That is a statement, not a question."

"Not often done, no. It is a tribal practice in certain lands, and I once met a French lady who favored it." He was still stroking one finger round and round the pebbled nub. "Just think about it. If you wish, I will buy you a pretty chain of weighted platinum to link them. It would be beautiful against your skin."

Isabella tried to remind herself that this was only for tonight—only this one time more—but felt as though she'd entered another world; a world of raw and unrestrained sensuality. His every suggestion seemed to suggest an exquisite sort of control in a world that had so little.

"You would enchain me," she murmured.

"I would," he admitted. "Were it in my power, Isabella, I would enslave you. I would take you back to Greenwood and chain you to my bed this instant. And I do not think, quite frankly, that I would ever let you go."

But she was not going back to Greenwood, and they both knew it.

Tonight was for her; to submit to him one more time and savor that dark and wicked pleasure. To slake that unholy yearning he had unleashed inside her. Good heavens, to compare what he did to her to those few, awkward fumblings Richard had made beneath her nightdress was to compare a pool of flaming oil to a teacup of tepid water.

He was kissing her between her breasts now, slowly working his way lower and lower. When his mouth brushed her belly, she felt her skin shiver. He plunged his tongue into her navel, and she felt that hot draw of pleasure go twisting through her stomach and all the way down until it tugged between her legs, making her cry out for him.

"Patience, my love," he murmured, his lips moving softly

over her flesh. And then he drew the tip of his tongue along her inner thigh, and her body spasmed, fighting against the bindings that held her to the bed.

"*Whoa,*" he whispered, spreading his wide hand over her belly and forcing her against the mattress. "Be still, Isabella. Be a very good girl now—just as you promised, *hmm*?"

She opened her mouth to ask what he was doing, then swiftly shut it. He would only roll her over and spank her bottom with his hand again—or worse.

And to do that, he would have to stop whatever it was he was about to—

"*Oh, God—!*" she choked.

He had thrust his tongue into a most unusual place and set his big hands on her inner thighs, and he was slowly urging them apart. For an instant, she froze, yanking at her bindings in blind confusion.

"Shush, love, shush," he said, kissing his way back up her belly. "Be still now, and let me have my way."

"I—I—I can't see," she choked, tugging against the bed. "What are you doing?"

"Isabella," he said sternly, "I can and will spank you. And I can bind your legs—bind them *open* to me—so cease fighting it and lie very still."

"I—I can't lie still!" she rasped, panting. "Please. *Please.*"

But he had pushed her legs apart again and was lightly probing her most private place with his tongue. The place she had scarcely been aware of until he had brought her to this complete and shocking awareness of what she was. Of what she could *feel*.

Was it normal? Or was she a whore? Was that the word? Had she simply found her true self with him and become what she was destined to be?

He drew his tongue slowly between the folds of her flesh,

and Isabella knew that was precisely the case; knew that no sane and morally upright woman could feel the things she was feeling.

And she was suddenly and quite desperately frightened that she *would* beg—that this would not be the end. That she would never be capable of refusing him this, or anything else he might take from her.

Her breath caught and caught again, and then she was panting in earnest, straining at the ties that bound her in the desperate need to . . . to *what*? She did not know.

"*Anthony,*" she rasped, trying to reach for him.

His hand lashed out, seizing her wrist and forcing it hard against the bed. His rough beard raked the inside of her thigh. He touched her again, and suddenly she was coming apart inside, shattering with a light that began where he touched her and ran stem to stern, like an electrical current unleashed, causing her entire body to spasm and strain against the bindings.

She felt her belly go taut as pure pleasure surged and washed over her, felt his lips warm against her flesh, and then she knew no more.

When she returned to herself, she was still shaking. He was mounting her, shoving her legs wider still with his thigh.

"Draw your knees up," he rasped, his voice demanding. "*Now,* Isabella, for God's sake."

His body settled heavily over her, the hard, hot weight of his shaft rubbing against her belly. He pushed her wider still, until she was utterly and carnally open to him.

His swollen head probed her entrance, slicked through it once, then again. And suddenly he entered her on a deep, triumphant shout.

"Oh, *Isabella,*" he moaned. "Such a good, good girl. So sweet. So open."

He moved inside her with a harsh rhythm, thrusting deep. There was nothing remotely gentle in his movements; he was like a beast atop her. Already the breath was sawing in and out of his chest, the sound rasping in the darkness. Then he shocked her by sliding one arm beneath her right knee and hitching it over his shoulder.

Following suit with the left, he pushed deeper still, her legs hooked high over his wide shoulders, opening her fully to his thrusts.

"Untie me," she whispered.

"No," he barked, pushing and pushing until she felt as if she might shatter again. "Let me take you, Isabella. Come, love. Oh, God, yes. Once more, love. Once more."

She felt her whole body rise to him then, answering his call. She wanted it. Oh, she wanted *him*. And she understood in a blinding flash just why he bound her. To keep her from splintering and flying apart. To keep her bound to him and to the bed; to hold her shattered pieces together until the storm had passed through.

And then the rush was on her again; this time a rush of darkness, her whole being melded with his; forged in the hot fires of passion as they surged and came together.

The storm did pass—eventually. Isabella found herself sobbing. She heard the soft *snick!* of a knife unfolding, and then his mouth near her ear.

"Hold still," he said, his hands going to the bindings. "Oh, love. Don't cry. Oh, just . . . don't."

When both wrists were free, she shoved away his handkerchief, pushing it up and off her forehead. Then, on another soft sniffle, she threw herself against the warm wall of his chest, into his embrace.

He soothed her with crooning and kisses, his hands stroking lightly round her wrists—and then lower, too. Isabella felt thoroughly eviscerated. Exhausted. And too tired even to contemplate the aberrant nature of all she'd just permitted. Somehow he managed to fold half the bedcovers awkwardly over them, and Isabella slept against his chest for a time.

When she stirred to consciousness long moments later, he kissed her again and ordered her back to sleep, his arms bound like iron bands around her, reminding her of the question he'd asked earlier.

Do you really believe, Isabella, that it is old-fashioned for a man to guard what is his?

The words had made her shiver a little, even then. And now Isabella was no longer sure what she believed. She knew only that the restraints with which he'd just bound her had left her more liberated than constrained, and that the viselike embrace about her body made her feel secure and— at least in this moment—beloved.

Oh, it wasn't real, she knew, and it wouldn't last beyond the night. But in that moment, she wriggled deeper into the warmth, savoring it.

Suddenly, one of his hands lifted and gave a playful smack on her hip.

"Isabella," he growled into her ear, "I said lie still, and go to sleep."

Obediently, Isabella returned her head to his shoulder and let Morpheus take her down.

CHAPTER 9

The Earl of Hepplewood woke to a blade of sunlight across his eyes and his arse hanging halfway off the drafty edge of a mattress. For an instant, he wracked his brain.

Isabella's, he dimly realized, and a tide of contentment lifted him fully into the present.

The bed's length being suited to a far shorter man, one of his legs was cramped from being awkwardly bent. On an inward groan, he shifted. Isabella murmured something inaudible and buried her face sweetly against his side.

He pulled her body fully to his, twitched up the covers, and settled back into her warmth, one arm propped behind his head, the other cradling Isabella against him. It was light enough now to look about her bedchamber. Lazily, his gaze wandered over the faded roses on her wallpaper, the clean but shabby curtains, and the window in dire need of glazing.

It was a disheartening assessment, yet there were unmistakable touches of elegance long past in the room; an ormolu clock on the mantelpiece and a delicate figurine of a lady seated at a dressing table, her powdered hair curled high.

Hepplewood bent his head and kissed Isabella's forehead, something about the dichotomy troubling him. Indeed, Isabella's entire circumstance troubled him. But something she had said last night about the portraits downstairs . . .

Then he stretched and yawned, and wondered why he was concerning himself with such matters when she lay beside him, naked as God had made her, and their time together was so terribly short. There would be time later to think about the thing that had been subtly nagging at him these past many hours. And time to deal with that upstart cousin of hers, too.

As to the shabby state of her house, if Isabella could not be persuaded to return to Greenwood Farm—and she couldn't, he feared—then perhaps he might buy her an entirely new house elsewhere, and furnish it to the standard she deserved?

She stirred again then, and turned to him with a drowsy smile. With his fingers, he combed the hair back off her face and kissed her again lingeringly. And then, before she was entirely awake, he rolled her onto her back and wordlessly mounted her, thrusting slowly and rhythmically inside her until she hitched one leg about his waist and lifted herself to him on a sweet and breathless sigh.

It was the most conventional sort of lovemaking imaginable.

It was what he thought of as "married sex"—the bland and furtive sort a couple might have before the servants stirred or the children woke. It was warm and sweet and surprisingly comforting. And when she bowed up to him with a softly keening wail, he swallowed her cries in his mouth, then thrust again, spilling himself deep inside her and finding it glorious in its simplicity.

They slept again, and when next he woke the house was freezing, though the sun was alarmingly high. He glanced at the ormolu clock to find it was a quarter past nine. Quietly throwing on most of his clothing, he went downstairs and built up last night's fire in the kitchen, which ran along the back of the cottage. Then he carried up hot water and set the can by the bed.

When he perched himself on the edge, sinking into the mattress on a ponderous creak, she stirred, looked at him drowsily, and stretched like a sleek, black cat.

"We've slept late," he said, tipping up her chin on one finger. "Have you plans for the rest of the day?"

The languor in her eyes melted and she scooted upright, pulling the covers with her. "Oh, yes." She pushed a shock of inky hair from her face, her brow furrowed as if she struggled to remember. "Yes, good heavens. I have to be somewhere . . . Knightsbridge. At noon."

Disappointment drained through him, but he leaned over the bed and kissed her, gently siding his fingers into the hair at her temple.

When he was finished, he drew away and looked at her. "Isabella, do I need to tell you what last night meant to me?" he said, his voice surprisingly hoarse. "I'm not a man much given to eloquence—and frankly, I'm not sure I could find words sufficient."

She drew a deep, unsteady breath. "Thank you for last night," she said on a rush, her face warming. "It was beyond anything . . . and I don't know how to—" Her words fell away as quickly as they'd tumbled out. "Actually, do you know, I think you're right." She managed a feeble smile. "Some things are best left unsaid, are they not? Thank you. You are magnificent."

He held her gaze for a long moment, certain there was more.

There was not.

Isabella merely looked at him, her gaze steady and earnest, but he was nonetheless struck again with the awful sense that she was waiting for him to leave. Oh, she did not curl up and turn away this time; there was no confusion or fear in her eyes.

Instead she merely looked at him with a gentle expectation, and beneath it, a hint of sadness in her eyes.

He still felt much as he had that morning at Greenwood—struck dumb with it, nearly. "Isabella," he said, "I have to see you again."

"How?" she asked, opening her hands atop the old, worn counterpane. "I have children to care for, Anthony, and a life to live."

"*How*?" he echoed incredulously. "However it must be. Whatever is required. Nothing has changed for me, Isabella. I want you as my mistress. You will not return to Greenwood? Not even for a time?"

She shook her head, the sadness deepening. "Oh, I cannot," she whispered. "I told you that. I'm not cut out for that kind of existence—and you and I, we have very different lives."

"This is not acceptable," he said, seizing her shoulders. "It will not do, Isabella. You need me—you crave what I can give you—and God knows I want you."

"I cannot," she said simply. "Anthony, I said so last night. Didn't you listen?"

"But what has changed?" he demanded, his grip tightening. "Good God, Isabella! This is a hell of a thing for a man to wake up to. You *were* willing. What has changed?"

"The children," she said simply. "I have decided I cannot leave them."

"Why?" he demanded. "Why is this a problem now, when it wasn't a month ago?"

The anxiety returned to her eyes in full measure. "Things have changed," she said quietly. "I was a fool to leave them alone, for they're all I have, and—"

"No, damn it, they are not," he said. "You have *me*, Isabella. You can have me."

She drew a little away from him then, and for the first time, he saw a flash of unease in her eyes. "I may have a piece of you, yes," she said a little warily. "But I am *responsible* for my sisters. I'm all they have—as you are all your daughter has, my lord. We must always put them first."

"Stop *my lord*ing me," he said darkly, "and don't dare suggest that I don't love my daughter."

"Of course you do, and you believe in guarding what is yours, you said," she said.

"You're damned right I do," he retorted. "And you are *mine*, Isabella."

"No, Felicity is yours," she said quietly, "as Georgina and Jemima are mine. Don't you see? It is an awesome duty one must carry out when a child's life and well-being have been placed in one's hands."

He did not see—or at least in that moment did not wish to see.

Moreover, Isabella was raising a mere half sister—and a stepsister with whom she shared not one drop of blood. Indeed, the children's mother, if he'd accurately read the undercurrents, had practically put Isabella out of her own home upon marrying Lord Tafford.

And now Isabella was sacrificing herself to raise that woman's children? But on his next breath, he remembered Diana, and the thought brought a stab of clarity.

How could he *not* understand what Isabella meant?

Didn't he know, perhaps better than anyone living, what a childhood spent being unwanted and unloved could do to the mind? How it could twist and torture a person, turning them into something they would otherwise never have become?

No, perhaps Isabella had no legal obligation to raise the children. To love them. To put them first. But it was morally right. And if they had all done the morally right thing for Diana, however circumspectly, perhaps they might have been spared a terrible tragedy.

He understood, too, that in raising Lissie he had the advantage of a wealth that was probably unimaginable to Isabella—not to mention the luxury of a houseful of servants. Nannies and nurses and footmen, and that governess he had never gotten round to hiring.

And she was right to make him feel guilty.

"I will buy you a house," he said, having barely thought it through. "A large house in Town. Or the country. I can send the girls to the best schools, and generously pension your Mrs. Barbour, and I can—"

"No," she interjected, her hand coming out to encircle his wrist. "Life does not work that way, my lord."

"I will make it work," he gritted, seizing both her hands. "Isabella. I will make it work. It *must*. We are lovers. I will not let that change."

For the first time, he saw true anger sketch across her beautiful face. "You do not rule the world, my lord," she said, her voice deathly quiet. "For all that I think of you—for all that I *burn* for you—you do not get to simply rearrange my life to suit your needs."

"Isabella." He gentled his tone and cupped her face in his hands. "*Please*."

"No," she said, drawing away. "I am not your pawn, sir. I cannot let myself become that, for I had a good glimpse of it, and it lessened me. As to the girls, no, I will not do it. I have decided not to let them from my sight. *I will not*. And that is the end of it."

"It cannot be, Isabella," he choked, "for I—"

But just then, there was a distant sound outside; harnesses and hooves, followed by the racket of what sounded like a door.

"Dear heaven!" Isabella jerked upright in bed just as the front door slammed, echoing through the house. "Can they be early?"

They were.

"Bella, Bella, we saw a monkey on the promenade!" a small voice cried, "and we got taffy! Bella, are you home? We got the first train!"

"*Damn it!*" said Hepplewood under his breath. "It only wanted this."

Eyes wide, her color gone, Isabella turned to leap off the bed, starting for her clothes.

He grabbed her shoulders again. "Isabella, have you a back way out? Anything?"

Lips pressed thin, she shook her head. "Not from upstairs."

He got up, slung his neckcloth around his neck, and snatched up his coat. "I left my hat and gloves downstairs," he said, moving swiftly. "If anyone notices, say they are Tafford's. How high up is your window?"

"High," she said sharply, her hand lashing out to seize his arm. "Tony, you mustn't! You could be hurt."

Hurt?

Fuck it, he was already hurt. And he damned sure wasn't staying here with her guilt-ridden eyes and his unholy temper.

He jerked from her grasp and looked out.

He'd seen worse. He threw up the sash, quieting the

rumble of the weights as best he might, and leaned out. There was a ground-floor roof below—over the kitchen, by the look of it—running all along the back of the house.

Voices were swelling in the rooms below. Children. A female. Much clatter—umbrellas and bags, it sounded. He looked around to see Isabella clutching her shift, staring at him, her face bloodless.

Yes, he'd seen worse falls to be taken after a long night spent in the wrong woman's bed. But he'd never seen anything worse than the ashen look on Isabella's face.

And he knew, too, that on some level, he'd gotten her into this.

That he hadn't taken no for an answer.

Swiftly, he stabbed his arms through his coat sleeves, grabbed Isabella, and kissed her soundly. "This is not over," he said. "It cannot be. I will not let it be, do you understand?"

"How?" she whispered.

He set his lips in a hard line. "I do not know," he said. "But time is on my side, Isabella. You are *mine*. You will always be mine. And I will wait you out, I swear to God."

Her face bloodless, Isabella threw up her hands.

He did not know what else to say.

Perhaps he'd already said too much—and far too demandingly. But this could not end; not now, when he was just beginning to know her heart—to understand Isabella and her needs.

And he knew, by God, where she lived, too.

But there was hot, burning pressure welling in the backs of his eyes; a frightful rush of emotion he scarcely recognized, one he damned sure didn't wish her to see.

He went to the window, cursed beneath his breath again, and swung himself smoothly out.

CHAPTER 10

Isabella was not late for her appointment in Knightsbridge that day; children could not be fed upon heartbreak and tears. After scanning a week's worth of newspaper advertisements, she had found what might prove an acceptable shop a mere stone's throw from Hyde Park.

It was a promising thoroughfare, though hardly a fashionable one, with much of the area still more village than town. But it was affordable, barely. A deal was soon struck with the owner, a lazy, unshaven fellow by the name of Poole, who agreed to defer the lease until April, and to cut her rather a bargain, provided Isabella took the place as-is.

As-is meaning an utter pigsty—if a pigsty was covered in cobwebs and soot.

And so it was that Isabella spent much of that evening, and most of the next week, on her hands and knees scrubbing floors, trying not to think of Lord Hepplewood's iron embrace and high-handed demands. It was exhausting and horrid and precisely what she needed to keep herself from miring up in the misery she felt.

By Lady Day, the maisonette above the shop was habitable, and Isabella found herself counting out a few of her precious coins to pay a carter to haul their furnishings out of the farm cottage and up the steps into the newer, but no larger, space. Mrs. Barbour cheerfully laid out her tools in the kitchen, then they set about washing the shop windows below.

Over the course of the following week, Isabella walked the lanes and alleys from Paternoster Row to Old Fish Street, visiting the printers and stationery wholesalers situated there, then negotiating the best terms she could get.

It was not easy, and more than once she questioned her own sanity. But it was either that or the mire, she reminded herself, and Isabella could not sink. No, she would take too many people down with her.

Slowly, the goods began to arrive in carts and crates, and while Mrs. Barbour watched Georgina, Jemima helped Isabella unpack and sort it, and together they decided where each book or puzzle or card would go. And by mid-April, Glaston & Goodrich Booksellers was open for business, surprisingly busy, and Isabella was all but broke again, having spent nearly everything in rent, refurbishment, and inventory.

It had been a frightful risk, really. A risk that her old self might not have dared to run. But Isabella felt increasingly confident the shop would pay off in the end.

"And *Glaston* is me," said Georgina, pointing at the shop's newly hung wooden placard, "and *Goodrich* is for Jemma."

Ownership was announced, on this particular occasion, to a friend who lived nearby and who had walked with Georgina home from school.

Just then the bell above the door jangled.

"Post's come," said Jemima, swiftly tying on her shop apron.

"Go upstairs, Georgie, to Mrs. Barbour," said Isabella, pointing through the door to the dark staircase that shared their street entrance. "Try to do your sums on your own, all right?"

Her lower lip poking out, Georgina dragged her feet in the direction of the narrow steps.

"Georgie has taken the short end of all this," said Isabella ruefully. "I have neglected her a little with getting the shop started."

"But the shop allows you to stay at home with us, Bella," said Jemima, sorting through the post on the counter, "and that matters more."

"Thank you, Jemma." Isabella tossed her a grateful glance, her heart welling with affection.

Jemima was far more mature than her years would suggest, and had been of inestimable help in getting the shop started. It was in moments like this—moments in which she was so deeply glad to have the girls—that Everett's threats began to haunt Isabella.

Surely no judge would permit him to take them? Jemima had been barely eight when Isabella had taken her from Thornhill, and Georgina could not even remember her parents. Isabella and Mrs. Barbour were the only motherly influences the child had ever known.

But the awful truth was, the law afforded women no rights when it came to children—not even those they had borne. Only a man was thought fit to serve as trustee or guardian, and to make the hard decisions as to how a child would be brought up, educated, or even married off. And technically, Everett was both to Georgina, though he'd never shown the slightest interest in her until now.

So far as poor Jemima was concerned, she was stuck with their pinch-penny uncle, Sir Charlton, who'd never so much as enquired after the girls these last many years. The last time Isabella had written him for help, he had blithely suggested that the best solution for everyone was that Isabella simply accept Everett's marriage proposal, since he was willing to take both children.

Damn it, her father had been such a trusting fool.

Isabella would sooner abscond with both girls into the wilds of Canada than surrender either of them to Everett. She only prayed it never came to that.

But Jemima was opening the mail, and she had paused to frown at something.

"What's that you're glowering at, my dear?" Isabella asked.

Jemima sighed. "A dun from Tallant and Allen. Can we settle the account?"

"Soon, I think," said Isabella. "Sales have been surprisingly good. What else is there?"

Jemima waved a creamy piece of stationery and grinned. "Ooh, another plea from your Mr. Mowbrey in Chesham," she said. "How many is that?"

"None of your business," Isabella said, snatching it.

"Well," murmured Jemima, "one begins to wonder if your scholarly gentleman doesn't want something besides his rocks sorted."

"Do not be impertinent, miss," warned Isabella.

But Jemima's grin had faded. "And here's another from Lady Meredith," she said, pinching it like a soiled rag between two fingertips. "Shall I toss it in the rubbish?"

"No," said Isabella on a sigh. "Hand it here."

Taking both, she left Jemima to watch the shop and went out into what passed for a back garden. This was, in fact, the third letter from Lord Hepplewood, for she'd intercepted the second herself while the girls were walking in the park with Mrs. Barbour.

That one, however, had been hand-carried by a liveried footman from Clarges Street.

Yes, she was very glad the girls had been away for *that* delivery.

Upon returning from Greenwood all those weeks ago, Isabella had lied and told the girls that, having realizing the time required, she'd decided she would miss them too much to be away working for Mr. Mowbrey. That was the trouble when one told an arrant lie; more had to be heaped atop it until, like a dangerous pile of rubble, the whole lot was apt to come crashing back down upon one's head.

When the first letter postmarked Chesham had arrived, the girls had begun to giggle and make jokes about the mysterious Mr. Mowbrey's true interests. Isabella had forced herself to laugh, then gently chide them.

But the letters were no laughing matter. The first had been carefully worded, merely enquiring rather pointedly after her health—a delicate euphemism if ever there was one—and repeating in very firm words his wish that she should visit him at Greenwood Farm.

She had responded by informing him all was well with her, and she had provided her new direction as well. After all, she told herself, if the man wished to find her, he would. Worse, there was always the small chance that her "health" was not all she might hope.

The second letter had been less personal. The delicate enquiry had been repeated, but the invitation had not. He was writing to inform her Lady Felicity had taken up residence with him in Clarges Street, and that he congratulated Isabella on her new business venture.

By then Isabella was quite sure she was not with child and had written in veiled terms to tell him so. And that, she had expected, would be that.

But it was not, she now realized, sitting down on a bench in the sun.

She held the letter in her hands, scarcely able to breathe. Then, in a great rush, she tore it open to find . . . nothing, really.

Hepplewood had decided to return to Greenwood to oversee the spring planting. Lady Felicity was accompanying him. There was no invitation. There was nothing, really, save banalities about the weather, followed by a curious final paragraph.

I should be pleased, I daresay, to hear of your excellent good health. And I am—or so I tell myself. It would be selfish to wish otherwise. I will not be tempted to write again, but I shall remain, ever your devoted servant,

Hepplewood

Good God, what did that mean?

Had he really hoped she was with child? And was he suggesting that, since she was not, and would therefore require nothing of him, he meant to move on?

Had he simply given up?

But given up on what? And what did it matter? A waning of his interest should feel like permission to breathe again. Wasn't that precisely what she wished?

Isabella set a hand to her heart, which had sunk into the pit of her stomach. Apparently, it was not what she wished.

She had not realized until that moment how much she had invested in Lord Hepplewood's promise, or how much she'd come to look forward to his letters, however veiled or stilted or demanding they might be; this, despite the fact that they had not bought her a moment's peace.

They had instead given her an excuse to rekindle a fantasy; a reason to let her mind wander back to the passion that burned between them, and to spin a dream of what could have been. She had saved each and every one—hidden them away amongst her nightgowns and chemises—including his first. The one he'd left for her at Greenwood, sending her away.

No, she did not wish to be forgotten, she realized, her fingertips going to her mouth. And she did not wish to forget him. Because she was in love with the Earl of Hepplewood. The reality of it had been pressing in upon her for some days now.

It was utter folly, of course. His intensity overwhelmed her. His dark edges frightened her. And yet she was in love with him, and his threat to pursue her had allowed her to go on hoping—though hoping for what, she scarcely knew.

And now he had given up his pursuit. He had relinquished, apparently, the claim he'd so boldly laid to her. She was free to relax, to again focus the whole of her emotional energy on the children. So why did she feel so suddenly swamped with grief? What had she imagined would happen?

That he would wait forever? That he had meant all the things he'd said?

Yes, fool that she was, she nearly had.

On a score of occasions—fitful, near-sleepless nights, all of them—she had arisen amidst her feverish dreams of him and gone to the window overlooking the street far below. Through the glass, at the most oblique angle, one could just make out the Brompton Road and the lamppost by the greengrocer's shop.

Three times she'd seen a man standing there in that pool of gauzy, mustard-colored light, simply staring up—or so it had felt—at her windows.

The first time, on an especially rainy night, the man had worn a sweeping greatcoat with a scarf wrapped high against the damp. More recently, he'd been attired in an opera cloak that had swirled low about his calves, its claret-colored lining shimmering in the wind. Always he wore a hat tipped over his face.

And always the same man. Tall and lean, with an aristocratic bearing. And each time, her heart would stop.

Lord Hepplewood, she had imagined.

This is not over, he had said. *I will not let it be. You are mine. And I will wait you out, I swear to God.*

So Isabella had let herself believe, during those dark and quiet nights, that he was keeping his promise. That she was his. And that he, in his harsh and old-fashioned way, was simply guarding what was his.

But she did not belong to anyone. She never had, really.

Despite knowing this, Isabella had twice been obliged to stop herself from hurrying out her own front door, so intent had she been upon tossing on a cloak and hastening down the street.

It meant nothing, she reminded herself now. It was just a man, loitering in the street after midnight. Besides, men made promises lightly and kept them rarely. Not a one of them had ever watched over her, guarded her back, or planned for her best interests—nor was one of them ever apt to. Isabella was on her own, she reminded herself, and always would be.

As to the mysterious man across the street, he was probably some daring fellow waiting to bed the greengrocer's wife, for she was a lively, buxom blonde, and her husband was often away in the wee hours to meet the market carts.

"Bella?" Jemima's sharp voice stirred her to the present. "Are you all right?"

Isabella looked up to see her stepsister framed in the back door, her long, blonde braids swinging over her shoulders, her figure so thin the opening dwarfed her.

"Oh, yes," Isabella said, forcing a smile lest her face betray her. "I was woolgathering. Have you got the shelf dusted?"

Jemima nodded and turned round. Hastily Isabella read her aunt's letter. It was indeed nothing; talk of the goings-on at Thornhill, thoroughly laced with vaguely patronizing remarks followed by an insistent invitation to visit. But the words no longer stung, for they simply did not matter. None of it mattered.

Thornhill was no longer her home.

Lord Hepplewood was no longer her lover.

It felt as if nothing in her life had changed, or was ever apt to.

Ramming both letters deep into her smock's pocket, Isabella inhaled a ragged breath, jerked to her feet, and returned to work.

CHAPTER 11

"His name, my lord, was Mr. George Flynt."

"Flynt?" Lord Hepplewood was closeted with Jervis in the library at Clarges Street on an especially sunny May afternoon, his gaze sweeping down paragraph after paragraph of legalese. "Not a family I know."

"The great-grandfather was called George also," said his secretary, "and possibly another after that. It isn't clear. Certainly there were grandsons called William and James. But I gather the Flynts were in the Canadian provinces at least six generations before them."

"So barely English at all, perhaps?" muttered Hepplewood.

"Indeed, there was a vast amount of French and Red Indian blood in the family, I gather," he said. "It tells a little, I think, in Mrs. Aldridge's dark hair and remarkable face."

It did, thought Hepplewood, though nothing on earth could explain those haunting violet eyes. "What was the Flynt family's origin?" he asked.

"Minor gentry from Shropshire, it's believed," said

Jervis. "You know how it is, sir. A second son of a second son, sent out to the colonies to make his fortune."

"And they seem to have managed," said Hepplewood dryly. He tapped a finger on a line in the document. "So you think this might be the language causing the Flynts so much dyspepsia?"

"It *might* be, sir," said his secretary, "if the thing's worth the paper it's written on. *Per stirpes* is Latin meaning 'by representation.' Legally, it is a way of dividing assets equally amongst the branches of a family."

Hepplewood set the documents aside and pinched hard at the bridge of his nose. He'd begun this fool's errand in some vain attempt to understand Isabella's fears—and to winkle out the motivation behind the bits and pieces of Tafford's threats. But by the time his clever secretary was done unearthing rumors and moldering old paperwork, Hepplewood was beginning to wonder where it would end.

"Well done, Jervis," he said, "though you've raised more questions than you've answered, perhaps."

"Shall I stay at it, sir? Back to Liverpool?"

"By all means," said Hepplewood. "And you suspect that the fellow who drew these documents is on his way to London?"

"Oh, no, he's long dead, I should think."

"But someone from the firm, I mean?" Hepplewood pressed.

"The solicitors I found in Liverpool said the firm threatened as much," reported his secretary, "but as they are no longer affiliated, it's hard to say. I can go up the Ottawa Valley myself, sir, but it will take—"

"—time," Hepplewood supplied. "No. The trouble, I think, is in England—or will be. And England is where I'll need you."

Just then, the library door burst in to admit a whirlwind of blonde ringlets and yellow muslin. "Papa!"

"Whoa," he said, rising from his desk. "What's this? Is the house afire?"

"Papa!" said Lissie again, her expression pleading, "*may* we go to the park with Harry and Bertie? *May* we? *Pleaaase*?"

"Well, miss," said Hepplewood, scooping her up in one arm, "Mr. Jervis and I are just—"

"No, please, please, *please*!" said the child, flinging her arms around his neck.

"Beg pardon, my lord." Mrs. Seawell, her longtime nurse, appeared on the threshold, red-faced and panting. "Got away from me, milady did. Can't think what's got into her lately, sir—begging your pardon again, sir."

Hepplewood waved her back. "It's perfectly all right, Seawell, we are finishing up here," he said, hitching Lissie onto his hip. "Now, what's all this about the park?"

"Lady Keaton sent a note," said Mrs. Seawell, bobbing a belated curtsy. "She means to take Mr. Henry and Mr. Bertram out at four on their ponies."

Hepplewood could feel Lissie quivering with excitement. "*Ponies,* Papa!" she said, setting her lips against his ear. "May we go? May we watch? May Bertie take me up? Please, Papa, *please*?"

For a moment, he hesitated.

Then, as he so often had of late, he relented. "We may go, but first I must finish with Mr. Jervis. He is a very busy man these days."

"May we go as soon as you are done?" she pressed. "I will sit here quietly."

"Somehow, I doubt that," he said, managing to wriggle loose his pocket watch from behind her skirts. "Besides,

Lissie, it is just now three," he said. "We will be waiting a long while."

"I want to go," said the girl, poking out a lip. "I want to go *now*."

"I am so sorry, sir." Mrs. Seawell looked as if she expected to be thrashed.

"Take her back to the schoolroom," he said, coming round the desk to put Lissie down. "Pack up a blanket and enough toys to amuse her, and we will leave in ten minutes."

"And bread crumbs," added Lissie, "for the ducks."

"Yes, poppet." He nodded at the nurse. "Bread crumbs, please. Whatever Cook can spare."

"Yes!" said the child, running to the nurse as soon as she was set down again. "Nanny, I would like to take Pickles, too."

"I will help you find him in the toy chest, Lady Felicity," said the nurse, pulling the door quietly shut.

True to his word, Hepplewood was ready to step out the front door at ten past three, a blanket hooked through one elbow, his top hat in one hand, and a muslin sack stuffed with day-old bread in the other.

Having exchanged her slippers for small, brown boots, Lissie was leading her red-and-blue dog by its string, its wooden head and tail bobbling up and down as it rolled across the glistening marble floor.

On the front steps, Hepplewood put on his hat, and they set off together toward the Stanhope Gate. As his daughter waxed enthusiastically about the ponies, he glanced down at the small, white hand clasped in his, and his heart twisted in his chest a little.

For the merest instant, he considered yielding to the instinct to snatch her up and settle her on his hip again— which he would do had they still been at home. But out in the greater world of London, Lissie had quickly come to associate that tender gesture with being *a big baby*—an aspersion her cousin Bertie, he gathered, had promptly cast upon her.

Hepplewood had complained to Anne about it, of course. But she had snappishly advised him to stay out of it and let the children sort out their own troubles. Oddly, he had listened.

His fatherly instincts thus thoroughly repressed—well, *slightly* repressed—he had stood by in silence when, just a week later, Lissie conked Bertie across the head with a battledore racquet. Anne remained calm and simply took all the racquets away.

Hepplewood had quietly observed, and learnt, perhaps, a little something. That this was how children grew up—and that it was the very reason Anne wanted Lissie here.

It was, after all, precisely how they had grown up, he and Diana with Gwen and Anne—playing and fighting and simply sorting life out with one another. Gwen—older, taller, and far more vicious—had beaten him blue more times than he cared to count. And she had, in some measure, taught him how to go on in life.

No, he did not have this business of parenting down yet, but he felt it possibly within his grasp. After six weeks of steady practice, he no longer felt so thoroughly overwhelmed by it as he once had.

More importantly, it was slowly dawning on him that Lissie was something more than just a fragile miniature of his dead wife; she was her own person—and far more forceful and spirited than Felicity had ever been.

The park was fairly quiet at this time of day, most of the nannies having already pushed their perambulators home in time for tea, and society's horse-and-carriage set not yet out in force for the afternoon gallivant. Still, he looked for a spot well above the Serpentine, and far from the major paths.

"How is Pickles liking his life in London?" Hepplewood asked when the perfect patch of grass had been found not too far from the riding ring. "He is still happy here? He does not miss Loughford?"

"Not very much," said the child, plopping down on the blanket in a *whoosh* of muslin and petticoats. "He misses Grandmamma Heppy. But I told him she is in heaven now, and not coming back."

"No." With one finger, he rolled the little dog back and forth between them. "No, Grandmamma is not coming back. I'm very sorry, Lissie."

"It will be all right," said Lissie, stroking the dog. "Pickles must keep a stiff upper lip. That's what Nanny says."

"Good advice," he remarked.

At that, she looked up at him, her lip drawn thin and tight across her teeth, then she burst into giggles. "See?" she said, falling sideways onto the blanket. "I can do it, too."

"You are silly," he said, tapping the tip of her nose with his finger. "Sit up, Lissie, like a proper lady, and let's talk."

"Yes, sirrrr," she groaned, jerking upright, her curls shimmering in the sunlight.

Hepplewood settled down on one hip beside her and stretched out his legs, propping himself up on his elbow. "Pickles does not miss having his own gardens to romp in?" he asked. "Or his huge toy chest and schoolroom? London is a little dirty, too."

She stared at the blanket and gave a short, swift shake of her head. "No, he likes it *here*," she said. "Loughford is *boorring*."

At that, he laughed. "Is it?" he said doubtfully. "Who told you that? More of Bertie's nonsense?"

She looked up with a wide grin, her cheeks pleasantly pink from her walk. "No, Harry did," she said on a spurting giggle. "He says only mushrooms like living in the country."

"Ah!" said Hepplewood. "Well, I advise you to make your own choices, miss, about what is or isn't boring. You are a bright girl, and you needn't listen to everything Harry and Bertie say."

Her gaze fell to the blanket again. "I just want to stay with you," she said more somberly. "I want to stay where you are."

Hepplewood swallowed down a little knot of shame. "I want that, too," he said. "I'll tell you what, Lissie—if Pickles wants a romp in the country, we'll take him back to Greenwood Farm. Just for a few days at a time. Then we can go up to Loughford for a long stay at Christmas. How would that suit?"

Her smile returned in full force. "I like the farm," she said. "I like Yardley's cow."

He laughed and stretched out on the blanket, tipping his hat forward to shield his eyes. On her first day at Greenwood, Yardley had taken Lissie to help milk the cow—a miracle of nature that still seemed to astound her.

How could she have lived her whole life on a vast, rural estate and not thoroughly grasp where milk came from? It was in part because Lissie had been coddled by his mother, fed a constant diet of *shoulds* and *oughts* regarding how gently bred girls should behave and think.

His mother had been a rigid and overweening woman, full of her own consequence and more concerned with what people thought than with happiness or anything remotely like spontaneity.

She had not always been that way, he did not think. Life— particularly those last miserable years of her marriage to his father—had made the Countess of Hepplewood bitter.

Nonetheless, he was at fault here, too. He had left his

daughter too long in that frigid, judgmental world, telling himself Lissie was just a baby. That she needed a mother's touch—and absent a mother, a grandmother. Which had been true, to a point.

But Bertie, perhaps, had the right of it; Lissie was not a baby any longer.

And Isabella was right, too. His daughter needed him, for he truly was all she had now that her mother and grandmother were dead. Not unless he let her go to her Grandmother Willet, and that he could not bear to do. It would break his heart—and under no circumstances would Lissie be permitted beyond his sphere of protection.

So it was up to him. And in that, Anne had been right.

Isabella. Mrs. Willet. Anne. Perhaps even Bertie . . .

Did everyone see him for the inadequate father he was?

Lissie, apparently, did not. She appeared to love him un-reservedly. It seemed he had only to let her do so; to let down his guard and his guilt and accept that, in someone's eyes, at least, he was neither inadequate nor selfish.

Suddenly, he felt Lissie tugging upon his coat sleeve. "Papa, look at that girl!" she said urgently. "That girl has *ducks*! They are all coming up! May I go?"

He peeked from beneath his hat brim to see a line of ducks marching up the hill from the Serpentine to surround a girl who, seen from this angle, might have been Lissie's twin, save for ringlets a little more gold than cornsilk, and a dress that was, sadly, a good deal shabbier.

He could see, too, a lady's skirts swishing across the stubbled grass beside her as they waded into the surge of ducks. The creatures toddled all about them now, and the crumbs were flying.

"You may go so far as that bench," he said, "where the girl

is standing. If you go farther without first asking, I will have to take you home. That is a firm rule. Do you understand?"

"Yes, sir," she said, leaping up.

"Don't forget your bag," he said, thrusting it at her.

She giggled, grabbed it, and went flying across the grass.

Hepplewood had already learned, from his near-daily forays into Hyde Park, that one little girl loved nothing so well as another—and absent that, a little boy would do.

Out of desperation, Lissie had already tried to coax Bertie into playing dolls. But Bertie, fettered as he was by one of the most pitiless creatures on earth—an elder brother—had wisely declined her every invitation.

Once or twice Lissie had managed to strike up a sort of temporary acquaintance with another girl in the park, but the same girls seemed never to appear two days running, and Hepplewood was never quite sure how to facilitate a proper introduction in any case, for the girls were invariably with nannies or mothers.

But this new girl seemed inordinately friendly and had opened her bag at once so that Lissie might take a handful of crumbs. Lissie flung them wide, and two of the ducks collided with predictably hilarious results; flapping, honking, nipping, and other acts of anatine umbrage.

The girls fell at once into peals of laughter, and soon they had emptied the other girl's bag. Lissie offered up hers, and the pair bent over it, struggling together to unfasten Cook's tight knot. They had an instant camaraderie, it seemed.

This time, he decided, he would simply go and make an introduction, and try to determine what time of day the girl was most apt to be in the park. Oh, perhaps the girl was not quite of Lissie's social standing, but he had been in an oddly egalitarian frame of mind lately. He had begun to wonder if status mattered as much as happiness. His mother was almost certainly spinning in her grave over that one.

This time, however, he did not need to facilitate an introduction.

He realized it the moment the lady knelt down to help the children unfasten the knot and something besides her hems came into view beneath his hat brim.

Suddenly, his heart leapt a little oddly in his chest. His breath caught. And yet he somehow managed to lie perfectly still and let the situation unfold as he observed from beneath his hat.

Isabella was biting her lip as she worked determinedly at the knot. Soon it loosened, then slipped free. The girls ran back into the ducks, now milling about with some impatience, and Isabella stood up again, beyond his line of sight.

Good Lord, but he missed her.

It took every ounce of his determination to restrain himself from simply getting up and going to tell her so. His every instinct still urged him to go and lay claim to her. But he did not, for he now understood that Isabella was struggling to bear up beneath the burdens she already had. She did not need him to add guilt and pressure to the mix.

No, she would either come to love him, or she would not.

He would either resolve her situation, or he would not.

And they would decide, together or apart, the right thing to do for their families.

If these last, lonely weeks had taught him nothing more than the importance of having his own mind—and his own life—straight, then at least he had learned a valuable thing.

She was not carrying his child, she had said.

He told himself he was glad; glad she would not have to make a difficult decision when her life was already awash in difficulty, and glad she would not have to take the awful risk of childbirth. The thought of Isabella wracked with pain and torn quite possibly to pieces struck him with a terror so cold and so deep that he knew it was irrational.

But he was not glad. Not on some dark, primitive level. Not in his heart. And he did not know what that said about him.

That he was still selfish, he supposed.

As selfish as his father had brought him up to be.

As selfish as his mother had always accused him of being.

Almost as selfish as he had been in seducing Felicity, then taking her to Burlingame and throwing her in everyone's faces—no, in *Diana's* face—and setting in motion that awful chain of events that could not now be undone.

He drew a deep breath and realized that all the bread was gone, and that Isabella was looking about the park in some concern, her hand wrapped tight around Lissie's.

Lissie pointed at the blanket, and the three of them started up the slight incline in his direction. He tossed his hat aside and sat up, using his hand to shield his eyes from the sun.

She looked more beautiful than ever today, he thought, as she waded through the grass toward him. And when recognition lit her face—along with a fleeting look of joy—something in his heart seemed to rise and almost go to her.

You are in deep, old boy, he thought to himself. *So deep, there is no turning back.*

No, it was now merely a matter of understanding how best to go forward.

This realization came to him with certainty—and a simple certainty it was, too. Like saying the night sky was black, or that rain was inevitable. That *she* was inevitable.

As they reached the blanket, he stood and held his arm out for Lissie.

"Papa, did you see the ducks?" she cried excitedly. "Did

you see the little one bite the big one? He tried to take his bread."

"I did see that." He drew Lissie companionably to his side and took Isabella's hand, bowing over it. "Mrs. Aldridge, you are a welcome sight indeed. I see you've made my daughter's acquaintance."

But the awkwardness of the situation had clearly caught up with Isabella, and she looked almost desperately uneasy now. The poor woman had not an ounce of dissimulation in her, he realized—and he loved her all the more for it.

Yes, loved her.

The last few weeks had taught him that, too.

"Good afternoon, Lord Hepplewood," she managed. "Yes, Lady Felicity joined us by the ducks—quite of her own accord."

This last was added hastily, as if she feared some other interpretation.

"Yes, I've been watching. Thank you for taking care of her. So, is this Miss Georgina Glaston?" He took the girl's hand and bowed over it. "You are almost as beautiful as your sister—which is quite an accomplishment."

The girl giggled, then turned her face to Isabella's skirts.

"Oh, are you friends?" asked Lissie innocently.

"Yes, friends of some significance, I think," he said, his eyes upon Isabella.

"Oh, good," said Lissie. "Can Georgina play with Pickles, then? We want to walk him along the footpath."

"*Hmm.*" Hepplewood turned and looked. "A spot of exercise would do the old boy good, I daresay. You may go as far as the Ring—but not inside the fence, mind—and then back again. Assuming Mrs. Aldridge agrees?"

Isabella looked a little nonplused, then, after a moment had passed, she nodded and said, "Certainly."

"Shall we walk a little behind them?" he suggested.

She nodded again.

Hepplewood put his hat back on, and they set off at a sedate pace behind the girls.

"Take my arm, Isabella," he gently instructed. "We are friends, remember?"

"Yes, friends of some significance, you said," she murmured in that deep, almost throaty voice that left him shivering inside.

"Aren't we?" He stopped on the path and turned to look at her. "Isabella, aren't we friends—people who care for one another—if no more than that?"

"I do not know what we are," she said, seeming unaccountably shaken.

"Isabella, my dear." He wanted desperately to hold her, but they were in the middle of the park, beneath the watchful eye of at least a hundred people—and half the windows of Park Lane. "What is going on?"

She lifted her gaze to his then, her eyes wide and filled with some nameless emotion. "Have you been watching my house, Lord Hepplewood?"

"Have you, *Anthony*," he softly corrected. "And the answer is no, not very often."

"But . . . *sometimes*?" she pressed.

He nodded, wishing they did not need to have this discussion. Not now. Not just yet.

"Sometimes, yes," he replied, "when my man Jervis—or someone he has employed in his stead—is not available. But they, perhaps, blend in a little better than I? And I dare not stand by your front door, my dear. I am too easily recognized. You don't need more trouble than you already have."

She looked at him a little pleadingly. "What sort of trouble *do* I have?"

"Nothing." He shook his head. "Merely a great many worries, that is all."

"Then why are you watching my house?" she said sharply. "I don't understand."

Isabella had pushed him into a corner, he realized—and she was far from stupid.

"Because I do not trust your cousin," he said bluntly. "No, Isabella, not as far as I could hurl the rotter. Perhaps I overheard a little more of your conversation in Fulham than I might have let on."

"Oh." Some of the pain and indignation went out of her then. "Thank you. You are kind. But Everett is mostly just a nuisance, I think. I am used to him."

"Smallpox is just a nuisance when it first starts to itch," he said grimly. "But once its full evil is revealed, you're already damn near dead."

He heard her sharp intake of breath. "Evil?"

"What would you call it?"

Her lovely brow furrowed. "Yes, evil," she finally said. "Everett is evil. But you seem to be speaking of a different sort of malevolence."

"That is the very problem, Isabella," he said. "I do not know what I'm speaking of—not yet—which is why I should prefer not to speak of it at all."

"Oh." She paused as if to consider it. "Is that why you've stopped writing to me?"

That made him laugh. "Dare I hope, my dear, that you are disappointed?" He leaned dangerously near then; so near he could draw in the clean scent of her hair and a warm hint of perspiration. "Do you wish me to write? Given how we parted, I was not sure. I would love nothing better than to resume my letters at once."

"No, no, I merely meant—"

He cut her off by setting his lips to her ear. "And, if you wish, Isabella," he whispered, "I shall write with far more specificity—and far less restraint—than I have thus far shown. I will tell you how desperately I need to hear your voice, and precisely what dark deeds I long to subject you to. How I burn to touch you and feel you writhing and crying out beneath me. You are, I collect, opening all your own mail?"

Isabella seemed unable to get her breath. "Well—usually."

"Ah, *usually*." He drew away then with a rueful expression. "Alas, you see my conundrum, my dear. The things I would prefer to write to you are things apt to give anyone else great pause—if not heart failure."

She looked at him very steadily. "I still don't know what to make of you," she said. "After all this time . . . I still do not know."

Impulsively, he took her hand and carried it all the way to his lips, pressing them fervently to her glove. "You are in the happy position, my dear, of having time to decide," he said, looking at her very directly. "And I am learning to be a patient man."

She was still staring blankly at him when suddenly, a voice carried from farther down the hill. "*Tony*—?" came a distant shout. "Oh, Tony, that *is* you!"

He pulled away and looked far down the bridle path. "That sounds like my cousin Anne," he murmured, slanting a hand above his eyes to block the sun. "She is bringing ponies. And more children. And at least two grooms. Quite the entourage. Will you stay? I am reliably informed there will be pony rides. Would Georgina like a pony ride?"

Isabella seemed to snap to full awareness of where she was. "Thank you, no," she said breathlessly, looking about in a panic. "We must go. Georgie? *Georgie*! Dear God, where has she got to?"

"Just a few feet behind you," he said, sliding a steadying hand beneath her elbow. "I've had my eye on her the entire time, Isabella, I promise you."

He felt some of the tension go out of her then, and she cast him a grateful glance before turning around to see that Georgina and Lissie were indeed approaching.

"Here I am," said Georgina, drawing up beside her sister. "Must we go now, Bella?"

"Yes," she said, giving a tight nod. "Come, Georgie, and give me your hand. Thank you, my lord, for your many kindnesses. And thank you, Lady Felicity, for playing so nicely with Georgie."

Isabella did not look back. The pair hastened away, Lissie watching them depart, her small face screwed up, as if she might cry. She had spared the approaching ponies not a glance, he noticed.

"I *liked* Georgie," she said on a small, choking sound. "She was *n-nice*."

Hepplewood knelt to look at her. "I thought so, too," he said, kissing the corner of her eye. "Don't cry, sweet. Would you like to play with Georgie again sometime?"

"Yes," said Lissie fervently. "Oh, yes, Papa. May I? Do you know how to find her?"

"I do indeed, poppet," he said, cutting a glance at the lovely sway of Isabella's backside as he stood. "I most certainly do."

Just then, Anne's mount drew up. "Good Lord, wasn't that Richard's widow?" she said, unhooking her knee to dismount. "She's grown so thin I almost didn't recognize her."

Hepplewood lifted her down. "Richard?" he said stupidly. "Richard who?"

Anne landed, then looked at him impatiently. "Richard

Aldridge," she said. "Philip's cousin. Wasn't that Isabella Aldridge?"

But Hepplewood had turned to stare at Isabella's spine, ramrod straight as she continued toward Kensington Gardens, the child tripping along by her side.

"*Aldridge,*" he murmured. "Good Lord! Fenster's son?"

"Yes, the dead poet," said Anne dryly. Then she dropped her voice to a whisper. "Uncle Fenster put it about that she'd poisoned him or some such nonsense, you will remember."

He shook his head. "No, I don't."

"Ah, no, you wouldn't, would you?" she murmured. "That, as I recall, was the winter of your discontent—or one of them."

It had actually been the Season before, he recalled, when he'd learned the truth about Diana, though he'd still been on a dissolute binge many months later. Yes, the truth had sent him on a bitter and ugly journey—one that, some might argue, continued to this day.

Anne had handed her reins to one of the grooms and was giving precise instructions as to how the boys were permitted to go on. "And Bertie may take Lissie up before him," she added, "but only in the Ring, mind—and watch her carefully."

She returned to Hepplewood's side and hitched her arm through his. "Is that your blanket, old thing?" she said, pressing one hand to her lower back as if it ached. "I should very much like to sit on it, if you please."

Like an automaton, he set off back down the slope, Anne waddling a little at his side.

"It was a happy marriage?" he heard himself saying. "The Aldridges'?"

Anne seemed to ponder it as she settled onto the blanket. "Well, it was a love match, certainly," she said, modestly arranging her habit over her belly. "She'd been meant for her cousin—Lord Tafford's heir—but the silly girl came out and fell at once for starry-eyed Richard . . . which one can excuse, I daresay."

"Excuse what?"

"Falling for *Richard*," said Anne impatiently. "Heavens, the year before, I nearly did, and I was already in love with Philip. Fortunately, I knew the family well enough to see the poor boy was a tad loose-hinged."

"Loose-hinged? How?"

She shrugged. "Like his mother," she said. "Buoyed up by these soaring flights of fancy in which he'd write reams of dreadful poetry and dash madly about the world until, eventually, he'd come crashing down into this deep, frightful funk. Except with Lady Fenster, it was torrid affairs with other men. And shopping—sometimes until she literally collapsed."

"Now that, I do recall," he said. "Died of a laudanum overdose, didn't she?"

"Rather like Richard and his drinking," Anne mused, "though it never hurt his appearance. Only you, perhaps, could have rivaled Richard's good looks. But whereas you are merely spoiled, Richard was . . . Richard was *weak*. He could never bear adversity."

Hepplewood snorted. "What kind of adversity did Fenster's lot ever suffer? He owns half the Bank of England."

"Fenster cut Richard off," said Anne. "Cut him off without a penny and told him he hoped he starved to death—which he would have done, had that poor girl's father not taken him in and supported him."

"*Her* father?" said Hepplewood. "Had he any money to speak of?"

"Baron Tafford? Lord, no." Anne's gaze turned inward.

"There was a pretty little estate in Sussex. And she had a little something from her mother, I seem to recall, by way of dowry. But beyond that, almost nothing. It is so common nowadays, you know."

Isabella had finally vanished from view. Hepplewood sighed. "What is so common?"

"Good Lord, Tony, keep up, do," said Anne. "I'm speaking of noblemen who are land-rich and cash-poor."

"Oh, that!" he said dryly. "No, I have firsthand experience with that."

"Well, it's not your fault Uncle Hepplewood let Loughford run to ruin," she conceded. "At least you have turned everything around now—and then some."

"Father let Loughford run to ruin because he let his estate agent get the upper hand and grow lazy," he said quietly. "And Mr. Willet's money turned things around. You know that as well as I, Anne. Felicity paid for it—paid for it with her life, really."

"That is not true," she said. "Felicity made her own choices."

"Did she?" At last he turned to fully face her. "Did she really, Anne?"

"Did you force her, Tony, to do anything?" said Anne impatiently. "Did you? Did you force Felicity into your bed? She was twenty years old, and she was my friend. She was not green, and she was not stupid."

"I know that," he said quietly.

"Furthermore," Anne continued stridently, "there were just as many people who thought *she* was chasing your title, my dear, as believed *you* were chasing her money. Did you never wonder if, perhaps, she might have been?"

He opened his mouth, then closed it again. "No," he finally said. "I didn't."

Anne heaved a great sigh. "I know, Tony, that Mr. Willet settled a ridiculous sum on Felicity, but that was his choice," she went on, gentling her tone. "He wanted an earldom for his grandchildren, and he was willing to pay for it. But you have invested that money, Tony. You have made all the changes and improvements—to all the properties—and made them slowly enough they did not drain the coffers."

"Ah, a great humanitarian now, am I?" he said acerbically.

"No, but you tried to be a decent husband," she said, "and for all your bad habits, you've the makings of a good father. You've tended the earldom's fires with utmost care—well, in between your saturnalia—and when it is time for Lissie to marry, you'll be able to ensure her future. Isn't that, in the end, what Felicity would have wanted?"

"I could hardly say," Hepplewood muttered, "since our entire marriage was spent on opposite ends of Loughford. I didn't really know her, Anne, because after that business with Diana, Felicity was . . . disgusted by me."

"Felicity was traumatized," Anne corrected, "—by *Diana,* who was deranged. Moreover, Felicity was expectant, which brings its own sort of madness, trust me. Given time, she'd have been fine. Tony, I'm the first person to call you out when you bollix things up—you know that—but I hope I'm quick to say so when you are *not* at fault."

Hepplewood stretched out his legs on the blanket and covered Anne's hand with his own, giving it a quick, hard squeeze. "Thank you, my dear, but this is a rutted road, and I don't care to go down it again," he said. "Just finish telling me about the late Lord Tafford—and Richard."

"Well, after Isabella's pittance of a dowry was spent, the poor man beggared himself paying the rest of Richard's bills," she said, "that's all there is to tell. And honestly, it was a frightful thing for Uncle Fenster to do, turn his son off merely for marrying a girl who had no money to speak of. And then to . . . to say such *vile* things. Philip has hardly spoken to him since."

Hepplewood found the entire business vile. Yes, now that Anne had jogged his memory, he had a vague recollection of a tragedy, followed by a bitter row within her husband's family. But having lived those years in a haze of gaming, womanizing, and brandy, he was less sure of the particulars.

"And so what became of Isabella after her husband's death?" he asked as nonchalantly as possible.

Anne shrugged. "It was rumored she was to marry her father's heir," she said, "but that was said during her come-out, too, and it never happened. No, it seems to me, looking back, the poor girl just disappeared. Until today, I hadn't laid eyes on her."

"Yes, I imagine she might prefer to disappear," he mused. "She is a very private person, I think."

"And this is a longer conversation about a respectable female than you and I have had in . . . well, forever," said Anne, looking at him curiously.

"Is she thought respectable?" he asked.

"Does it matter?" asked Anne.

"Not to me," he said quietly, "but to her? Yes, it matters greatly, I think."

"Well, I hope the trouble with Lord Fenster is forgotten," said Anne, "but it did linger, I will admit. But he's bedridden now—an apoplexy, I gather—and past speaking of anything."

Hepplewood was not displeased to hear it. Oh, he didn't wish Fenster ill—the man had had a difficult life, settled as he'd been with an unfaithful wife and an erratic son—but nothing could justify blaming an innocent young girl for one's misery.

No wonder Isabella had chosen to disappear into a life of servitude.

But whatever money Isabella had begun with—precious little, it sounded—she was definitely on thin financial ice now. It told in a hundred little ways: the dreadful cottage in Fulham, the darning on Georgina's gown, and Isabella's rail-thin frame that, as Anne had just pointed out, was not her natural state. Though she had put on a little weight, perhaps, since he'd first met her.

Still, Isabella was struggling. Had it been otherwise, she would never have contemplated selling herself to a man like him.

It made him all the more furious with the present Baron Tafford, who, Hepplewood was increasingly certain, was hiding something. With every little stone Jervis had turned over, Hepplewood's suspicion had deepened.

Tafford, however, hadn't the brains—and likely not the initiative—for such a deception. Yes, he was a nasty piece of work, and not to be trusted. But his mother was more likely at the rotten core of it, and Tafford merely her worm.

"Mrs. Aldridge worked for Lady Petershaw as a governess," he said quietly. "Did you know that?"

"Why, I did not know that," said Anne, clearly intrigued. "But I begin to wonder how you do."

He laughed. "I decline to answer," he said. "I have the right to avoid self-incrimination, don't I?"

Anne looked askance. "Let me guess," she said. "Mrs. Aldridge is the one who finally slapped you, isn't she? Dear God, Tony—tell me you didn't go to one of *La Séductrice*'s orgies and get your hands on the governess by mistake?"

"Don't be ridiculous, Anne," he said. "I met the lady quite by accident. Besides, she hasn't worked for Lady Petershaw in ages. She owns a bookshop off Brompton Road."

"A *bookshop*?" said Anne almost gleefully. "How extraordinary! And how extraordinary that you know all this. Admit it, Tony. You've taken an interest in the lady. But I do not think Mrs. Aldridge is going to play your sort of game."

"No," he said dryly, "I do not think she will."

Anne began to laugh in earnest. "It's about time, old boy, you came up against a woman who isn't willing to tolerate your flirting and philandering."

"No comment," he said again.

"Well, at least the lady is a great beauty," said Anne, looking at him a little oddly, "and most genteel and gracious, as I recall. The bookshop is admittedly unfortunate, but I wonder if life left her much choice. No, in many ways, I cannot imagine you could do better."

"Better at what?" he asked, bemused.

"A wife, perhaps," said Anne, "because that one won't simply bed you, unless she has changed vastly since I knew of her. No, if you want Isabella Aldridge, you *might* have to marry her."

Hepplewood said nothing—which, had he but known it, told his cousin far more than his words might have done.

They simply sat in silence for a time, watching as the horses and carriages began to slowly clog the lower carriageway. After several minutes had passed, Anne gave up her teasing entirely, set her hands flat to the blanket, and sighed.

"Get up, Tony," she ordered, "and heft this poor cow to her feet."

"No, love—merely a heifer," he said, grinning.

She cut him a dark look and thrust up a hand. "Well, whichever I am, I had better hoof these boys home."

He took her hand and drew her to her feet, noticing that she struggled a little. "I cannot believe," he said a little darkly, "that Sir Philip lets you ride in such a state. I would not let you out of the house."

Anne had the audacity to laugh at him. "He does it, Tony, because he knows he cannot stop me," she said, "and because he is wise enough to know what you, apparently, do not."

"Indeed?" he said, offering his arm. "And what is that pearl of wisdom?"

"That the world is both a wondrous and a dangerous place," she said, holding his gaze, "and that if we swaddle those we love in cotton wool, we'll cause them to miss all of it—both the danger and the wonder."

"*Hmm,*" he said, and felt his mouth twitch. "And that is your way of saying . . . what, exactly?"

She beamed up at him. "That you perhaps should stop punishing yourself and blaming yourself for all life's ills," she said, "and stop trying to control everyone and everything around you."

"And . . . ?" he said, lifting one eyebrow—for he knew that there was more. With Anne, there always was.

"And that perhaps you should go to Tattersall's on Monday," she sweetly added, "and buy Lissie her very own pony?"

Just then a squawk rent the air. He looked up to see that, inside the Ring, Lissie was trying to wrest control of Bertram's mount.

With a parting shake of his head and a sidelong look at Anne, Hepplewood yanked up his cuffs and dashed into the fray.

CHAPTER 12

"Ow!" Isabella yanked back her hand to see a pearl of blood welling up on her index finger.

"Did you stick yourself?" Jemima looked up from her darning. "That's three times. I can mend that pillowslip, Bella, if you want to start dinner."

"Mrs. Barbour left a hen in the oven," said Isabella, hastily folding the linen and stuffing it back into her basket. "And the linens can wait. Clearly, my mind is elsewhere. Besides, Jemima, it is Sunday. Why don't you do something enjoyable? Didn't Miss Hokham loan you a book at school?"

"Yes, it was very kind of her," said the girl, drawing her thread through the toe of one of Georgina's stockings. "I read three chapters already—but I'm not wasting candles, Bella, I promise."

"I know you're not, sweet." Isabella had put away her sewing basket and had begun to tidy the sitting room. "What's the book called? Is it good?"

Jemima cut a sidelong look at Georgina, who sat upon

the floor, stacking up her blocks. "It is one of Anne Brontë's works," she said quietly. "*The Tenant of Wildfeld Hall.*"

"Oh." Isabella stopped what she was doing and looked at the girl very pointedly.

Jemima blushed. "Miss Hokham said I mightn't read it if you disapproved," she said. "Do you?"

Isabella pursed her lips. The book was about a mysterious woman believed by her village to be a wealthy man's mistress, and therefore shunned. The fact that, in the end, the woman was proven no such thing did not negate the fact that the book dealt with harsh and indelicate subjects; subjects that hit uncomfortably near home.

"It's a little late to ask now," said Isabella on a sigh, "if you're already on chapter four. No, I suppose you are mature enough to grasp—"

A sudden and very harsh knock on the door downstairs caused Isabella to startle. She exchanged uneasy looks with Jemima. In the last week, Mrs. Barbour had been twice required to send Everett away, once with Lady Meredith in his company.

"I'd better see if there's a carriage," said Isabella uneasily, going at once to the window and leaning into the glass.

"Is it Cousin Everett?" asked Jemima, her face stark.

"Cousin Everett is vile," said Georgina from her pile of blocks, "and creepy."

"Hush, Georgie," said Isabella.

"Jemma says it," replied the child sullenly.

But the carriage that sat in the street below was far too fine to be Everett's; he and Lady Meredith were still tooling around in her father's old rattletraps, and the glossy black landau below was the embodiment of elegance, as was the elderly, well-dressed coachman.

But the occupant, whoever he or she was, already stood too near the door to be seen.

"Well, it's not Everett or Lady Meredith," Isabella murmured, turning from the window.

The anxiety fell from Jemima's posture. "Someone is lost, perhaps?"

"I'll go down and see."

Hastily Isabella went down the narrow stairs that led to the shared entryway. To her shock, a tall man stood framed in the door's window, and just above the frame itself she could see a mop of blonde curls beneath a tiny straw bonnet. Her breath caught, and something twisted a little oddly in her chest.

Another three steps removed all doubt; the Earl of Hepplewood was staring at her through the glass, his face as unsmiling as ever. But there was, she thought, a hint of warmth in his eyes.

A little tentatively, she opened the door. "Good afternoon," she managed. "This is a surprise."

"Yes, isn't it?" he murmured, his gaze taking in the serviceable brown dress she'd worn to church that morning. "How do you do, Mrs. Aldridge?"

"We brought flowers," said Lady Felicity, shoving a mangled bouquet in Isabella's direction. "Askers."

"*Asters,*" said Hepplewood. "Lissie picked them herself."

"Thank you, Lady Felicity." Isabella took them with great solemnity. "They are lovely."

"It was all we had in the garden just now," murmured the earl, his eyes still drifting indolently down Isabella's length, "but even roses could not do you justice, my dear."

"Thank you," Isabella said again, clutching the flowers a little awkwardly.

He lifted his gaze back to hers. "This business of standing in the entrance to your shop is a trifle awkward," he said, his eyes glittering a little dangerously. "It's the height of arrogance, I suppose, but might we invite ourselves in?"

There was no polite way to refuse, and his daughter was still looking up at Isabella with bright-eyed anticipation. The shabby rooms above would mean nothing to a child, Isabella consoled herself, and Lord Hepplewood had already seen how poorly they lived. Indeed, the man was fast stripping her every secret bare.

Moreover, she did not wish to refuse, more was the shame. No, the awful truth was, she wished to do his every bidding—well, the more wicked ones, at any rate.

"I beg your pardon." Isabella threw the door wide. "Please, do come up."

"Marsh," he said, turning to the elderly driver, "kindly await us in the alley round back."

He stepped past her into the small entryway that served as both landing for the floors above and access to the shop, seemingly filling the space with his height and broad shoulders. Curiously, rather than start up the steps, he turned around to study the door that opened onto the shop.

"Take these, Lissie, won't you?" he murmured.

It was then that Isabella realized he held, oddly, a set of small racquets clutched behind his back. The child took them and started up the steps.

For a moment, he bent low, peering at her doorknob. "Hmm," he murmured. "Have you a new lock on both these doors, Mrs. Aldridge?"

"Yes, certainly."

"And another door—with an equally good lock—at the top of the stairs?"

"Yes." She set her head to one side and studied him.

"A solid door like this?" he asked, knocking on the wood with the back of his hand, "or with a window, like the one you're holding open to the street?"

"A solid door," she said, "as any such residence would have. Why?"

"Oh, call me curious." He made an elegant, faintly dismissive gesture. "Besides, one never knows, Mrs. Aldridge, when some wicked man might turn up here with very bad— dare I even say desperate?—intentions."

"*Papa,*" whined Lady Felicity, clutching the racquets to her chest, "you said we'd come to play with Georgie!" She had already climbed half the steps and stood now on the landing above, glowering down at both of them.

Lord Hepplewood flashed a smile in Isabella's direction. "Lissie wonders if Georgina might like to play battledore?"

"She has only played once before," said Isabella, "so she isn't very good."

"Excellent," he murmured under his breath, "an equal match, then."

"Please go ahead, Lady Felicity," said Isabella, who was growing increasingly uncomfortable squeezed into little more than a square yard of space with Lord Hepplewood's tantalizing scent and wide shoulders. "You'll find the door open."

Thus empowered, the girl bolted up the remaining steps as if she were quite at home, calling out loudly for Georgie.

"She's becoming a bit of a wild hoyden, I fear," he said, "under my inept parentage."

"At only age six," Isabella replied, following the child, "she should be a little wild. It is healthy and natural. Do come up, my lord."

But Isabella had just reached the landing when she found herself seized from behind, and spun quite fiercely around

His eyes dark, Lord Hepplewood set her back to the wall, his mouth crushing hers in a kiss as deep and as possessive as it was sudden. His tongue pushed into her mouth, stroking along hers with slow, rhythmic thrusts as he pinned her with his body.

The wall was cold and hard against her back, his weight and his heat unyielding. She could feel his erection hardening as it pressed into her belly, and Isabella realized then how little power she had against him—and how weak was her ability to refuse him.

When at last he came away, Isabella found herself breathless.

In the gloom of the stairwell, his eyes were inscrutable, his breath, too, coming fast and surprisingly rough. He lowered his forehead against hers and caught her wrist hard in his hand. "Now *that*," he whispered, forcing her hand against the wall, "felt both wicked *and* desperate."

"Don't, please," she begged. But her knees already trembled, and she could feel her resolve weakening.

"Come back to me, Isabella," he murmured. "Come back to Greenwood. I need you—and you need what I can give you."

"Anthony . . . I cannot."

He kissed her again, more tenderly, framing her face with one hand in that extraordinary way of his, as if she were his most precious possession. She let him. No, *more* than let him; she kissed him back heatedly. But she clung desperately to her heart's tether all the same and kept one ear attuned to footsteps from above.

He brushed his lips beneath her eye. "Tell me you burn for me," he rasped. "*Say* it, Isabella."

She expelled her breath on a rough, shuddering sigh. "I burn for you," she whispered, the need twisting deep.

"There. Are you pleased? You have had your way with me again."

"Oh, not nearly," he murmured, his voice hoarse. "Oh, Isabella, were I to have my way with you . . . no, it doesn't bear thinking about. Not here. Not now. But tonight, in my empty bed? Oh, love, then you will truly make me suffer."

"You have never suffered a day in your life," she retorted. "Not for the want of a woman in your bed, at any rate."

He drew away on a dark laugh, his eyes somnolent, his mouth turned up in that odd half smile that was at once bitter and inscrutable. "You seem not to grasp your own power, my dear," he said. "I should be thankful—and I should apologize, I daresay."

"*Are* you apologizing?" she asked darkly. "Because somehow, it doesn't feel like it."

He laughed low in his throat and gave her another hard kiss before drawing a little away. "I am not," he admitted. "I want you, Isabella, and I mean to have you. But in the meantime, you may slap me again if you wish."

But Isabella well remembered where that had gotten her— over his knee with his hand to her arse. Suddenly, raw lust went shivering through her, and Isabella knew better than to remain another moment alone with the arrogant devil.

She cast a glance up at the turn of the stairs. "We should go up," she said, setting the heels of her hands to his shoulders, still awkwardly clutching the asters, the stems now nearly crushed.

"*Should,*" he repeated, his lips skating down her throat. "Oh, Isabella. I *should* do so many things. I should bind you to my bed and to my heart and make love to you for days on end. I should carry you away from this life here and now."

"Anthony," she whispered, "this is *my* life. Not yours."

"I know," he said, and for the first time she heard the

faintest hint of regret in his words. "Yes, I do know. I don't mean to be cruel, Isabella. And I don't mean to add to your burdens, but . . ."

"But what—?"

The half smile vanished. "Just don't ever imagine I've stopped wanting you," he said. "I won't. Ever. Fair warning, that's all."

Then, as swiftly as he'd caught her against the wall, he lifted his weight away, seized her hand, and led her up the remaining steps. Her knees were still shaking, her wrist and her mouth still burning. And yet, her every nerve ending had come suddenly alive.

Inside the sitting room, however, the world seemed almost normal, and all was at peace. Lady Felicity had already plopped down onto the shabby carpet beside Georgina, having cast the racquets aside. They were peering at the pile of wooden blocks, turning them this way and that.

Jemima stood by the settle, looking a little flustered, her hands clutched politely in front of her.

Hepplewood bowed. "How do you do, Miss Goodrich?" he said upon being introduced.

Isabella was proud of the girl's deep and graceful curtsy. "Very well, my lord," Jemima said. "Thank you."

"Papa, *look,*" said Lissie from the floor, "Georgie's blocks make arithmetics!"

Hepplewood knelt between the girls. "How very clever," he said, turning one over.

"They are mathematical blocks," Isabella explained, her voice surprisingly normal. "One turns them around to show the various numbers and then moves them about to make examples of addition and subtraction."

"Quite educational," he said, ruffling his daughter's hair. "We must remember those at Christmastime, Lissie."

"We are thinking of stocking them in the shop," said Isabella. "Jemima thinks they might do well. She has had good instincts so far."

Jemima blushed and excused herself to go and read.

"I wish you would not," Lord Hepplewood replied as he rose and smiled at the girl. "I know you're a little old to play with a pair of six-year-olds—well, Lissie will be six in a few weeks—but we have brought three racquets." He turned to look at Isabella. "You've a little garden of some sort round back, I suppose?"

"Well, to call it that is a kindness," Isabella admitted, "but we've a bench, and something that purports to be a pear tree."

A few minutes later, Lissie's asters placed safely in a jar of water and the blocks put away, Lord Hepplewood was pushing open the back door, holding his daughter's hand.

"Take a turn about with me," he murmured when Lissie tore from his grasp, "whilst the girls play."

"A turn?" Isabella gave a sharp laugh. "This is no Mayfair garden, sir. It is a yard—with a clothesline, a shed, and a privy."

He shot her a dry look. "Indulge me."

As the girls ran laughing into the sunlight, Hepplewood turned and, as he had done earlier, examined the door.

"She looks happy," Isabella mused, watching Lissie swishing her racquet wildly about.

"I think she is," he said, sounding almost mystified. "I hope she is. I am trying, Isabella."

"Are you?" she said, still watching the children. "I'm very glad."

"A wise woman once reminded me that I'm all Lissie has now," he admitted, turning around with a faint smile, "so however insufficient to the task I may be, I must try."

Apparently satisfied with his examination of the door, he

offered Isabella his arm, and together they walked around the perimeter, their feet crunching softly in the gravel.

"You do not share this space?" he said, making an expansive gesture.

"No, we have the whole of the building, though it's very narrow."

Suddenly, one of Jemima's swings went a little wild and the shuttlecock struck Lord Hepplewood in the head. Quick as a wink, he caught it, laughed, and tossed it back to her.

Isabella watched, mulling it over. He seemed in many ways a very different man from the one she'd first met in Northumbria. And yet his kiss today—so heated, so demanding . . .

No, he was little changed, she thought. He was still full of his own arrogance and intent upon having his way. But it was clear he had a deep affection for his daughter, and that sort of love redeemed much sin in Isabella's eyes.

"You have high brick walls to either side," he said, casting an eye along the top, "but nothing that couldn't be scaled."

"I appreciate your concern," she said, "but really, what do you imagine is apt to happen? London's petty thieves can have little interest in a shop full of children's books."

"Probably not," he said evenly, "but I wish to see your access onto the alley from this side, if you please."

She showed him the tall, narrow gate, set securely into the brickwork. "You keep this locked at all times, do you not?" he asked, examining it.

"Yes, if anyone needs let in from the alley, either Mrs. Barbour or I come out."

"An inconvenience, to be sure, but a wise one." He turned and set his hand over hers where it rested on his coat sleeve. "The girls seem happily engaged. Why do we not watch them from that little bench?"

The bench he spoke of was scarcely big enough for two, but Isabella acquiesced.

"Again, I appreciate your concern," she said when they were seated, "but I'm afraid I must insist you tell me why you're here."

He cut her a dark, sidelong look. "Other than to kiss you breathless?" he murmured. "Perhaps I'm here, Isabella, because I cannot stay away from you."

"Rubbish," she said. "You've stayed away these last six weeks or better with no trouble."

He looked at her from beneath hooded eyes. "Ah, is that pique I hear in your voice, my love?" he said, his voice dropping suggestively. "How deeply gratifying."

"You will not tease your way out of this one," she said grimly. "Why are you studying my door locks and measuring the height of my garden walls?"

The teasing left his voice. "You are a hard woman, Isabella," he said.

She merely sat, staring at him.

He exhaled audibly. "Very well," he said. "As I believe I've made plain, I don't much care for your cousin, Lord Tafford—and the deeper I dig, the less I find to like. Tell me, what hold does he have over your sisters?"

"Over Jemima, vey little," she said. "Her only relation is a bachelor uncle who is Thornhill's nearest neighbor. But Sir Charlton cares nothing for either girl and would gladly cede their care to Everett. As to Georgina, as Papa left things, Everett is her legal guardian."

Hepplewood shook his head. "An unfortunate choice," he said grimly. "No disrespect, Isabella, but what was your father thinking?"

Isabella threw her hands up. "Well, men ever expect to die, do they?" she said. "I suppose it seemed a mere formality, and the best way to ensure Georgina and her mother might remain at Thornhill should something happen to him. Everett was his heir, and our only male relation."

"More's the pity," muttered Hepplewood.

"Indeed," Isabella agreed. "I'm sure Papa never dreamt a fever would take both him and my stepmother before Georgina's second birthday. But if the worst did happen, Papa probably assumed Everett would welcome Jemima and me, too. That's what true gentlemen do, isn't it? Look after their female relations? Papa just had this naive tendency to believe the best of people."

Hepplewood snorted. "A few simple enquiries could have disabused him of that notion," he said. "And from what I've learnt, it seems common knowledge that Tafford is no gentleman."

Isabella considered it. "You know, I don't think Papa really knew Everett once he went away to school," she mused, "and Papa certainly never traveled in London circles. Aunt Meredith and Mamma were friends, I suppose, after a fashion, both being wed for a time to brothers."

"But your mother died young," he said.

"Yes, when Everett and I were just children," she said. "I think it was Aunt Meredith who, early on, put the notion of our marrying into everyone's heads. She can be very charming when she wishes. She's had four husbands, you may recall."

Lord Hepplewood fell silent a long while, simply staring across the sunlit space at the three girls, who were still shrieking and swinging their racquets wildly in the air. Time and again, Jemima would gently loft the shuttlecock in the direction of the younger girls, but more often than not, they still missed, often falling into peals of laughter and surrendering nothing by way of enthusiasm.

Very discreetly, Hepplewood's hand crept over Isabella's. "You would never willingly leave Tafford alone with the girls, would you?" he said quietly. "You . . . you understand, Isabella, what he is?"

"Yes," she whispered. "I understand. But until a few weeks ago, he had never threatened to actually *take*—"

Her voice broke, and Isabella was unable to continue.

Hepplewood gave her hand a hard squeeze. "I don't think he will try to seize them by legal means," he said, "no matter what he threatens. Moving a case through Chancery might take months, and he won't wish to answer any hard questions. Unfortunately, in his case, possession is nine-tenths of the law."

Suddenly, Isabella understood his concern. "Dear God, you think he might simply *take* them?"

"If he does," said Hepplewood grimly, "he will not get far."

"Oh, Anthony," she whispered, "why would he want these children, when, tragically, young girls can be had for tuppence all over London? Is it just his pride? I can't imagine it. He has never seemed that enamored of me."

"I can understand a man might be obsessed with you to the point of madness," he said without a hint of teasing, "but if you insist Tafford is not, I believe you. So he must mean to use the girls as some sort of leverage. But again, my dear, he will not get far. That I promise you."

"*You* promise *me*?" She turned on the bench to look at him. His face was set in stern, hard lines. "But why has it fallen to you, sir, to deal with my problems?"

"Because it has," he said gruffly, "and that is the end of it."

"My God." Isabella lifted a hand to push back a loose strand of hair. "Oh, Anthony, I am not ungrateful, but people will say that I'm your mistress—whether it's true or not."

"It is remotely possible," he conceded, "that it could

come down to the lesser of two evils. And regrettably, Tafford knows we've some sort of acquaintance. That might even be driving his desperation in some measure. I can't make it out. Not yet."

"Dear heaven," she murmured. "Perhaps he knows you're here this very minute? Perhaps he will . . . he will drag me into Chancery and say I'm unfit, and that I'm just your wh—"

"*Stop*," commanded Hepplewood sternly. "Do not take the counsel of your fears, Isabella. And do not ever use that word in my hearing. Not in regard to yourself, do you hear me? Moreover, Tafford knows nothing of my whereabouts."

"You cannot know that," she said, her tone so sharp that Jemima stopped her swing and cut Isabella an odd glance.

"I can, and I do," he said more soothingly. "Tafford went down to Thornhill yesterday morning with his mother. Otherwise, I would not be here."

"But how can you know—"

"I know because I've made it my business to know," he replied. "Will you please just trust me?"

"I . . . yes, I *do*." She set the back of her hand to her forehead for an instant. "I do trust you, Anthony. But I'm just so scared."

He turned a little and slipped an arm discreetly around her waist, settling his hand at the small of her spine. "Look, Isabella, there isn't much a man can't accomplish with money and ruthlessness," he said. "I've plenty of both, but Tafford has only the latter. Or, more likely, his mother is the ruthless one. And they've gone down, by the way, to ready Thornhill for a house party to be given in a fortnight's time."

"They will be staying in Sussex, then?" she said hopefully.

"No, they are expected back in London on Tuesday," he said, "or so I'm informed."

Isabella paused to consider it, but all she could think of was the warm, comforting weight of Hepplewood's hand on her back and the flood of relief from knowing that, for all of forty-eight hours, Everett would be far from Jemima and Georgina.

"To be on the safe side," he continued, "I shall have someone watching the girls as they go to and from school," he said. "At least until Mr. Jervis discovers Everett's motivations. But I also want to ask you to do something for me."

"If I can, of course," she said reflexively.

"Oh, you can," he said, "but you will not wish to."

"What?" She turned on the bench to fully look at him.

"On Tuesday morning, I wish you to come up to Greenwood Farm—"

"No," she interjected.

"—with the girls. And Lissie. And—hell, my cousin Anne and her brood, too, if it will make you feel any safer in my presence."

Her heart caught then. "Anthony," she said intently, "I do not fear you. *I do not.* I fear myself, and . . . what you do to me. What you make of me. And of how very weak I am when I'm with you."

He took both her hands in his, his grip no longer tender. "Is that what you feel in my bed, Isabella?" he said, his voice low and grim. "*Weak?*"

"Yes," she whispered, "and without a will of my own."

"Well, you are far from either, I do assure you." His glittering eyes drilled into her, into her very soul, it seemed. "But if you feel weak, Isabella, is that wrong? *Is* it? Or mightn't it be, in fact, the very thing you need?"

She shook her head and felt her brow furrow. "How can anyone need that?" she whispered. "What would it say about them?"

"Perhaps it would say that you've had to be strong for so long that you're worn down with it," he suggested, his tone unyielding. "Perhaps it would say, Isabella, that now and again a woman needs to surrender her control. That perhaps it goes against her very nature when her life has become so hard for so long that she cannot let down her reserve. Not to anyone. Not even for her own needs. Did you ever think of that, Isabella? It sounds a hard and miserable existence to me."

"You . . . You are just trying to persuade me," she murmured—and felt herself melting, almost sliding into the warm, sweet abyss his words seemed to offer up. A surrendering—to something stronger than herself.

"I am trying to persuade you, yes, that I am what you need," he said, his voice low with emotion. "I have never lied to you, Isabella. I want you. I want you in my bed, under my control, and under my protection. But if that is not what you want, say so, and I will not lay a hand on you without being explicitly asked. Do you imagine I haven't the resolve to keep my word?"

"No." She shook her head. "No, you have a will of iron."

"If I have, I earned it, dear," he said grimly. "But at least we understand one another—and far better, Isabella, than you might think. Bring the girls to the farm. Let us both let down our guard a little. Let it be a family visit. Anne will come if I ask her to."

Isabella felt she was drowning in uncertainty, swayed by his determination and his strength. "But they have school and I have the shop," she murmured. "I have shipments coming Monday, and accounts to catch up after that, and customers, and . . . oh, all manner of things. I have to earn a living, Anthony. This is my life."

"I understand that, Isabella, but tomorrow *is* Monday," he said logically. "Your account books and the girls' schoolwork you may bring to Greenwood. The village does have mail service, you know. And surely your Mrs. Barbour is capable of waiting on customers whilst you're away?"

"Yes," Isabella admitted. "She often does."

"Then please, Isabella," he urged her. "Just let me keep the three of you away from London for a time. I am . . . uneasy in a way I cannot explain. I will not touch you if that is what you wish."

Isabella swallowed hard and knew that once again Lord Hepplewood would have his way.

Worse, she wanted to lean on him. Her unease over Everett was growing by leaps and bounds, and she did not for one moment imagine that Hepplewood had come here to frighten her or overstate matters.

No, not where her cousin was concerned. Hepplewood was not wrong; something dark and ugly was coming to a head. Isabella had begun to feel it in Everett's desperation— something in him had altered, somehow. There was a sense of urgency that had been waxing since . . . yes, since she'd seen him in the train station.

And had her life not been so fraught with work and caring for the girls and sheer survival, she suddenly realized, she would likely have spared it more thought. Perhaps she was fortunate that Lord Hepplewood *had* thought about it.

"Yes?" He dipped his head to catch her gaze. "Yes, Isabella, you will come?"

"Yes." She nodded. "Yes. If you think it wise. Yes, we will come."

CHAPTER 13

(M)onday afternoon in Park Square, Lady Petershaw's butler bowed politely when Isabella knocked. As she so often did, Isabella asked to see not the marchioness but Lord Petershaw and his brother. Both boys having just returned from school, Isabella was happily received in their private suite, situated in a separate part of the house from the marchioness's salons.

Since Lord Petershaw's departure for Eton almost three years earlier, it had become Isabella's habit to chat with him when he came home from school to ensure his education was progressing as it ought, and she'd followed suit with his brother.

This was a duty Lady Petershaw had expressed an unequivocal disinterest in, and one she had happily ceded to Isabella with a wave of her lace-cuffed hand. But the unspoken truth was that, having no formal education whatever, Lady Petershaw secretly feared herself incapable of assessing her sons' progress, and she did not trust Eton's condescending schoolmasters to tell her the truth.

Isabella knew this, and she knew, too, that despite her blithe declarations, Lady Petershaw cared very deeply for her children.

The boys were as lively and as happy as ever, and Isabella rose half an hour later, her spirits considerably lifted. Before leaving, she gave Petershaw a book on the history of horse racing and Lord John a bound copy of *The Mysteries of London.* They were small gifts, really; samples Isabella had acquired when stocking the shop, but the boys seemed genuinely touched, and kissed her cheek on the way out.

She still missed them, she realized. She had spent more than six years in Lady Petershaw's employ, much of it while trying to support and care for Jemima and Georgina at the same time. And when Isabella looked back on her life and wondered if she had wasted it, those four children were ever in the forefront of her mind.

As she went down the stairs, Isabella could feel something a little like tears warming the backs of her eyes. She blinked rapidly and hastened toward the door, for the next duty called, and she'd not so much as begun her packing.

In the great hall, however, Smithers stopped her and asked that she attend the marchioness in her private sitting room. It was not an unexpected request, and one Isabella had hoped for, despite the press of time. She went up at once to find herself promptly pulled toward a tea tray already set with two cups and a platter of tiny sandwiches.

The marchioness was dressed today in a rich gown of aqua silk, but it was absent her usual flamboyance. Her hair, too, was dressed quite simply. Neither alteration served to diminish her beauty.

"My dear Mrs. Aldridge," she declared, motioning her to a chair. "How wicked you are to try to escape without seeing me when I've been anxiously awaiting news of your new venture. But first, how did you find my lads?"

It was a little ritual they went through, and Isabella began at once. "I believe Lord Petershaw has taken a thorough grasp of his algebraic concepts this term," she reported. "The headmaster's report is quite good. I read it in some detail."

"Did you? How very kind." Lady Petershaw smiled. "That sort of thing bores me excessively."

"Whilst I, on the other hand, perversely enjoy it," said Isabella. "As to Lord John, he excels in his history, as always. And he has become quite the oarsman, as I'm sure you are aware."

"But they will be ready to go up to university when the time comes?" A faint catch in her voice betrayed the marchioness's anxiety. "It was his late lordship's deepest desire that they should both attend—and excel at—Cambridge. I owe it to him, at the very least, to ensure that happens."

"There is no question they will be ready," Isabella reassured her. "Everything comes easily to Lord John, and Petershaw has learnt to work hard. Please set your mind at ease, ma'am."

The marchioness smiled, relaxed almost imperceptibly, and began to pour. "You will visit with them again before term starts?" she asked, dropping in Isabella's one spoonful of sugar. "You will impress upon them how very important it is that they continue to do well?"

"I would be crushed, ma'am, not to see them." Isabella took the outstretched cup.

"Excellent," said the marchioness, as if a plan had just been agreed to. "And now you must tell me about your fascinating little bookshop."

Isabella did so, with little embellishment. Her account

books were still in the red, but only just, and she expected to turn a profit by the end of June.

Lady Petershaw expressed great delight in this advancement, poured a second cup of tea, and said, more coyly, "And what of your other little venture? Have you brought Lord Hepplewood to heel yet?"

Isabella felt her face flush with heat. "I do not think Hepplewood is the sort of man a woman brings to heel, ma'am," she said quietly.

"I shouldn't have thought so, either," the lady confessed, daintily lifting her teacup. "Well, not easily, at any rate. But I saw his face, my dear Mrs. Aldridge, when he sat here angry and bereft all those weeks ago—in that very chair in which you now sit, you may recall. And he was a man stricken, of that I am quite sure."

"He is a man stricken with great arrogance," said Isabella, "of that *I* am quite sure. Moreover, I cannot say he's ever struck me as bereft. And yet . . ."

"Yes?" The marchioness leaned intently forward. "And yet . . . ?"

Isabella looked up from a detailed study of her saucer. "And yet he is a man of great kindness, I've come to believe," she added. "Yes, he has been . . . kind to me."

"Kind!" said Lady Petershaw in a huff. "That is very dull. Tell me, my dear, that he has at least tried to sweep you off your feet?"

Isabella hesitated a moment, her color deepening, she was sure. "He has, yes, in his own way," she admitted. "And he has taken it upon himself to thwart Everett on my behalf."

"Very bold of him," declared the marchioness. "So I'm sure, then, that he has also attempted to lure you back into his bed. Tell me, my dear, has he succeeded?"

"Yes," Isabella confessed, shifting her gaze to the elegant carpet. "Once."

"Only once?" Lady Petershaw's eyes widened. "Hepplewood is slipping. In the old days, no female found herself able to refuse those glittering blue eyes and curling golden locks."

"The truth is, I've seen little of him," said Isabella. "We had some sharp words, I fear, about my duty to my sisters and his duty to his daughter. And shortly thereafter, he brought her down from Loughford. I believe she is taking up a vast amount of his time."

"But that is what governesses are for!" declared Lady Petershaw.

"You may recall, ma'am," said Isabella dryly, "that he has not hired one."

"Still?" The marchioness trilled with laughter. "What does he mean to do with the child, then?"

"That is precisely what I mean to ask him," said Isabella, "and very soon, too. You see, Hepplewood has asked me up to Buckinghamshire, ma'am, with the girls. And with Lady Felicity and some of his cousins. I said that I would go. Have I made a mistake, Lady Petershaw? It seems all so very odd to me."

"Oh, my word!" Lady Petershaw dropped her cup onto its saucer with a discordant clatter. "You cannot mean it?"

"He was most insistent," said Isabella. "He said that since I was uncomfortable going there with him, he would invite others, too. He seems to want to keep the girls far from Everett. I believe he fears Everett is up to something wicked."

"Of course Everett is up to something wicked," said the marchioness brusquely, "for he always is. Fortunately, he is also stupid. And Tony is . . . oh, heavens . . . but surely, I must be right?"

"Right?" Isabella's brow furrowed. "About what?"

"About Tony," the marchioness said, tapping one finger

on her perfectly powdered cheek. "Yes, yes, just so, my dear girl. The earl is going to ask you to marry him. He would not be inviting his daughter and his family were it otherwise."

Isabella drew back, horrified. "Oh, ma'am, I am sure he does not mean to do any such thing."

"I am very sure he does not," agreed the marchioness, "but I am equally sure that he will."

Isabella felt her brow furrow. "I don't know what you mean."

"Well, never mind that," said Lady Petershaw, pushing away the tea. "Men rarely know what they are thinking until it blurts from their lips—or their wives tell them. Tomorrow, did you say? You had better get packing, my dear—and you will, of course, pack those things I sent you to purchase from Madame Foucher's?"

Isabella opened her mouth, then closed it again. "Well, I had not thought on it," she said. "I believe his purpose is more to keep the girls away from Everett's grasp."

"And to get *you* within *his* grasp, you pretty fool," said Lady Petershaw. "Oh, I know that is not what he *said*. It might not even be what he *meant*. But it is what he *wants*, and it is what he will *get*."

"Oh, dear," said Isabella. "Is it?"

But she already knew the answer to that—and knew that, in her heart, it was what she hoped for.

Moreover, the marchioness had already risen. "Well, hurry along, my dear Mrs. Aldridge," she said, waving her hastily toward the door. "Yes, yes, go home at once! And pack your tarty underthings, my girl—or I shall be utterly ashamed of you!"

IT WAS TO prove very difficult, Isabella soon realized, to explain to Mrs. Barbour and Jemima just how she had come to be friends with the Earl of Hepplewood—near enough friends, in fact, to travel alone with the man to his farm in the rural countryside.

In the end, she told Barby something of the truth; that she had become acquainted with the gentleman after having interviewed with him for the position of governess. And that through his friendship with the Marchioness of Petershaw, Hepplewood had come to share her suspicions of Everett and wished to remove the girls from London for a few days.

It did not suffice, of course; the servant merely sniffed disdainfully and said that her mistress must do as she pleased, but that she was very sure no good would come of it. All this said, of course, just before she hugged Isabella and pressed a basket of sandwiches into her hand.

That little exchange had been painless compared to Jemima's puzzled expression the previous evening. The girl had seen, if not quite heard, much of Isabella's anguished conversation with Lord Hepplewood, and Isabella could sense that it had left Jemima troubled.

"Just try to trust me, Jemma, to know what's best," Isabella explained as they packed the last of their things on Tuesday morning. "Lord Hepplewood is a gentleman, and he merely wishes you and Georgina to have a little holiday in the country."

"Don't try to deceive me, Bella," said Jemima softly. "It's more than that, I know. But to travel alone with a man we so recently—"

But they were not to travel alone, for just then, a knock sounded.

Eager to escape Jemima's solemn gaze, Isabella hurried down to find a pretty—and apparently pregnant—blonde on her doorstep. The lady wore a sky-blue gown and a riot of gold curls topped with a wide-brimmed hat turned dramatically up on one side, and pierced with a curling white feather.

"Isabella!" said the lady warmly, offering her gloved hand, "what a pleasure to see you again."

"I beg your pardon," said Isabella, taken aback. "Have we . . . ?"

"Oh, heavens, yes, but I was far thinner!" The lady laughed, showing rows of lovely white teeth. "I'm Anne Tarleton—or was. You came out the year after me. We are cousins, actually, of a fashion."

Isabella was turning the name over in her mind when she realized that children were clambering out of the massive and very luxurious traveling coach parked before her shop.

"Mamma, a book about trains!" said the eldest, practically flinging himself at Isabella's shop window. "Look! Look! That's a Great Western engine on the front!"

"Stand up straight, Harry, and stop smudging the glass," said his mother, snapping her fingers. "Get over here and make your bow to your cousin Isabella."

Harry leapt to it and cut a very pretty bow, his blond curls and sharp blue eyes so familiar to Isabella that her stomach did a little twist. "Pleased to meet you, ma'am."

Cousin Isabella?

"Bertie?" Brow furrowed, the lady was looking about. "Caroline, where has Bertie gone?"

The apparent Caroline, a tall girl who was carrying a much younger one on her hip, turned to look. "Down the street," she said, pointing. "He's seen a dog."

"Bertie!" shouted Anne Tarleton, "get back here this instant."

"May I look at the book now?" said Harry.

"You have a lot of children," uttered Isabella, trying not to stare at her rounding belly.

"Oh, I have another in the carriage asleep," said Anne. "But Caroline—Caroline, darling, bring Deanna here, and go fetch Bertie—Caroline is not mine but another cousin,"

"Actually, I think this is Deborah," said Caroline, handing the girl to her mother. Then she paused and made a quick curtsy to Isabella. "A pleasure, ma'am. I've heard such lovely things about you."

And then the girl was off down the street, chasing after the boy and the dog, who now appeared to be busy sniffing one another's private parts on the corner of Brompton Road.

"In any case," said the lady, shifting Deborah/Deanna to the other hip, "Tony is sending his coach behind me. I thought we might convoy up to Greenwood—all the better to avoid highwaymen, you know."

"Highwaymen?" Isabella was feeling increasingly off balance.

The lady laughed. "Oh, just kidding!" she said. "I see my own toes, I daresay, more often than Buckinghamshire sees highway robbery—neither, of course, occurring with any frequency. Oh, hello? Who is this?"

Isabella realized that Jemima had crept down and was standing in the shadows behind her. "Why, this is my stepsister, Jemima Goodrich," Isabella managed. "'Jemma' for short. Jemma, this is—" She stopped, uncertain how to introduce the lady.

Deanna/Deborah was now chewing off the tip of her mother's feather. Oblivious, the lady turned. "Hoo, Caroline, come back," she shouted. "Here is Miss Goodrich, whom Tony speaks so well of."

"How kind of him," murmured Isabella.

Anne turned her toothy, radiant smile on Jemima. "Hello, Jemma. I'm Lady Keaton, your sister's distant cousin," she said. "We used to know one another a little when we were young."

"And how, precisely, are you related?" asked Jemima, who was no one's fool,

Anne turned her gaze inward. "Well, I'm actually more Lord Hepplewood's cousin," she said, "for we're related by blood. But I married Sir Philip Keaton, who was—now, let me count back—yes, a grandson of the *fourth* Earl of Fenster."

Isabella's gasp must have been audible.

Anne's gaze sharpened, and met hers. "And the fifth earl is your father-in-law, is he not, Isabella?" she said evenly. "He is on his deathbed, in case you weren't aware."

"I . . . no, I was not," Isabella managed.

Anne shrugged. "Well, his life was a tragedy," she said, "some of which he brought upon himself. In any case—where has Caroline got to?"

"Down there, wrestling with Bertie and his dog." Harry had his nose pressed to Isabella's window again and had blown a great cloud of fog upon the glass.

But Isabella was scarcely aware, for her heart was thumping in her chest, the blood draining from her face.

"It is not Bertie's dog," said Anne a little hotly.

"It could be," Jemima interjected. "It's a stray. Mrs. Barbour has been feeding it scraps, but it doesn't belong to anyone."

"Really?" Harry brightened and pulled away from the window. "Bertie," he bellowed, starting down the street, "bring the dog. We can have him, Jemma says."

"Caroline Aldridge, *do not* let Bertie bring that dog up here," commanded Anne.

But Isabella heard all this as if from a great distance. Just then, the jingling of harnesses sounded, and another large coach rumbled in from Brompton Road, driven by Hepplewood's elderly coachman.

"Oh, here is Marsh with Tony's carriage," said Anne, sounding relieved. "Just in time, too. Lissie will be in it—

and Nanny Seawell, of course—and my maid, Nell, whom I sent down with a message." She stopped, and began to count heads. "Oh, dear. Will we fit?"

"I imagine," said Isabella numbly.

Anne was frowning. "I shall put Nell with me," she said, "and Caroline with you. I thought, you see, that she and Jemima might get on. Tony is going up on horseback. He could, perhaps, take Bertie up. Ah, there he is now, on Colossus."

"Shall I fetch Georgie?" asked Jemima, already starting up the stairs.

"I . . . uh, yes, Jemma," Isabella managed, "thank you."

Lord Hepplewood had rounded the corner on the massive bay she'd seen thundering off into the mist during her first visit to Greenwood. The earl wore the same sweeping black duster and knee-high black boots, too. On his head was not his usual top hat but one more soft and broad-brimmed, and better suited for shading the eyes during a long journey on horseback.

As to the horse, Colossus was no misnomer; the creature stood some seventeen hands, by Isabella's estimate, with eyes that glittered as dangerously as his owner's. Isabella watched their approach with trepidation. She had lost track of names, cousins, and children in general—for the word *Fenster* had struck her nearly dumb and sent her thoughts skittering like marbles.

He drew up, the still-fresh horse dancing sideways across the road. After sweeping a faintly heated look down Isabella's length, he reined the creature under control, then flung his leg over his saddle and began to bark out orders.

The street became a hive of activity; coachmen hopping down, footmen fetching luggage, and children clambering back into carriages under the instruction of an elderly woman in a starched white cap.

The boys, Isabella vaguely realized, were busy cramming the dog into the first carriage, and Lady Felicity was hanging half out the second, shouting rather imperiously that Georgina should be brought to her at once.

Jemima led Georgina out at that moment and climbed up into Hepplewood's carriage, but her expression was still uncertain. It was on the tip of Isabella's tongue to order them out again when Caroline Aldridge climbed in, flashing Jemima a shy smile.

It was too late.

To flee now would be as embarrassing as facing the ugliness.

Anne's footman brought down Isabella's last bag, and suddenly Hepplewood was at her side, slipping an arm beneath her elbow.

"Isabella?" He drew off his hat, dipping his gaze to catch hers. "You're pale as a ghost."

"W-we must talk," she said.

He pulled her through the door and into the shadows of her tiny vestibule, pushing the door shut behind. "Is it Anne? Look, I know she can be overwhelming," he said, gently tipping Isabella's chin up with one finger. "Look at me, love. What's happened?"

"*She is married to Sir Philip Keaton,*" said Isabella almost accusingly. "He is—*was*—my husband's cousin." She set her fingertips to her temples. "My God, this is a nightmare."

"Shush, my dear," he said, pulling her into his embrace. "It does not matter."

"It *does* matter," said Isabella harshly, her hands fisting against his chest. "This—this is just one of a hundred reasons I stay out of society. Anthony, that family hates me. They said . . . dear heaven, they said I *murdered Richard*."

He set his chin atop her head and held her close. "*They* said no such thing," he replied. "*Fenster* said it, the poor, half-crazed bastard. But no one believed it then, my dear, and they certainly don't believe it now."

"Well, for a rumor so strongly discounted, it certainly got round pretty thoroughly," said Isabella bitterly. "Moreover—wait, you *knew* of this connection?"

But she should not have been surprised, she realized. Hepplewood seemed to know all her most intimate secrets.

"Anne mentioned it, yes," he said, "and she also mentioned that Sir Philip hasn't spoken to his uncle since. I think it's part of the reason she agreed to come along, my dear. Perhaps she imagines the family owes you something?"

"Those people don't owe me a damned thing," snapped Isabella, "save to be left in peace."

She tried to push away, but Hepplewood held her tight. "Wait," he ordered.

"Let me go," she said hotly, her confusion burning down to righteous indignation. "We will be seen like this."

That seemed to irritate him. "Shush," he said again, his arms banding even more tightly about her. "If we're seen, what of it?"

"I couldn't bear it, that's what," she said into his shirtfront. He smelled of starch and man and sandalwood—of *Anthony*—and suddenly, she wanted to sob.

What of it?

Did he not understand? She was in love with him—desperately, madly so.

Yet could not be his mistress. And she would never be his wife; Lady Petershaw was dead wrong on that score.

Worse, he apparently knew everything about her. Simply everything. It felt as though there was nothing— not one small thing—she would ever be able to hold back from him. And she wondered if she even wished to.

The fight went out of her then, and she let her weight sag against him.

"Let me go," she said more gently. "Just let me go. I have done nothing to be ashamed of."

He set her a little away then and held her gaze very steadily. "No, you have not," he said firmly, "and I beg you will remember it. But if you really do not wish to go with Anne, Isabella, I will not make you."

"Make me?" she said, cutting him a dark look. "You cannot make me."

That dark, familiar smile twisted one side of his mouth. "Technically, I can," he said warningly. "I can throw you over my shoulder and toss you in that carriage, my dear, in an instant."

"You are a brute," Isabella said, only half meaning it. "And that would be kidnapping." She pushed at his shoulders just for good measure.

His eyes going dark, he jerked her to him a little roughly, opening his mouth over hers in one of those deep, all-consuming kisses, thrusting deep until she trembled.

"There," he said when he was finished with her. "Get in my carriage, Isabella. I think I won't give you the choice after all, for that kiss was too tempting. I don't even think you *want* the choice."

And she didn't, she realized, her knees shaking as she turned and opened the door. She *wanted* him to take her back to Greenwood. She wanted him to simply give her what she needed—and to tell her again that it was not wrong to want it.

Moreover, she wanted him to deal with Anne and the whole damned Aldridge family—which, being Hepplewood, he might actually do.

Already her dread had melted away, displaced by a bizarre mix of pride, fury, and a need for him that flowed through her body like a warm river, twisting deep into her belly. Without looking back at him, Isabella held up her head and went out into the brilliant sunshine to climb up into the carriage with the children.

"It is going to be a long drive," said Jemima a little glumly when the carriage jerked into motion.

Oh, you have no idea, thought Isabella. *No idea at all.*

CHAPTER 14

"Oh, my, this is delightful!" As the dog blew past Lady Keaton and up Greenwood's staircase, she twirled about the front hall. "And minuscule! I'm flattered, Tony, that you've finally agreed to visitors, but where shall we all sleep?"

"We've attic rooms for servants, Anne, and four main bedchambers," he said, striding in with Lissie on his hip. "Can we not manage?"

"Well, that's thirty less than Loughford," she said dryly, "but yes, I daresay we can squeeze in somehow."

Out the front door, the luggage was being unloaded, then carried up the steps amidst much thumping and grunting. The mysterious Mrs. Yardley had opened up the house to greet them and was now directing the footmen like a seasoned sergeant major.

"Lady Keaton and the twins will take my bedchamber," Lord Hepplewood told the housekeeper, "with Mrs. Aldridge and Miss Georgina in the connecting room."

"No!" demanded Lissie. "Georgie will be in *my* room."

"You must share yours with Caroline and Jemima," said

her father, kissing her lightly on the nose before putting her down. "Run along, you little tyrant, and show them which room."

"No." Lissie balled up her fists. "I want *Georgie*."

"We can all share," offered Caroline Aldridge. "I do not mind. Jemma, do you?"

Jemima shook her head. "Oh, no. It will be fun," she said enthusiastically. "Georgie, do you wish to be with us? Or with Isabella?"

"With all the girls," said Georgina, her lip coming out to mirror Lissie's.

"Fine," said Lady Keaton, as if it were settled. "One girls' room, and one boys' room, though how four of you will fit in one bed remains to be seen. Tony, you will rack up with Bertie and Harry somehow?"

"No, I shall manage elsewhere," he said evenly.

Lady Keaton grinned, and lifted both eyebrows. "Shall you, indeed?" she said *sotto voce*. "I wouldn't be so sure, old thing."

"I mean to sleep in the valet's room," he said darkly, "opposite *yours*—and if you snore, Anne, I swear to God, I'll come in and smother you with a pillow."

"I only snore in my last month," said Lady Keaton a little woundedly, "which is weeks away. Still, must everyone make an issue of it?"

"Come on, Jemima," said Caroline Aldridge. "Let's go see Lissie's room."

"Papa and Yardley built a dollhouse for me," announced Lissie loudly. "You may all play with it."

"A dollhouse?" said Georgina in a tone of awe. "Do your dolls live in it?"

"Some of them," said Lissie. "Come on!"

The girls started en masse up the stairs, Nanny Seawell

following after them just as the dog came bolting back down, nearly pushing the old woman aside.

"You, sir!" Lady Keaton snapped her fingers at Bertie, who was on hands and knees studying a dead bug on the front steps. "Get up and take that dog out," she ordered, "and give it a bath this minute."

"Yes, ma'am."

"Harry, you will help, since you instigated this," she went on, "and none of you come back in this house until the dog is dry, do you hear? I cannot abide the stench of damp fur."

"We'll need some soap," said Harry, as if this might thwart his mother's plan.

"Yardley will find you some soap," she said. "There must be a trough out back?"

"There's a brook by Yardley's cottage," said Hepplewood, "but nothing deep enough to drown in. Follow the path by the woods, lads."

The boys went out, eyes dangerously alight at the word *brook*.

"Shoes *off*!" shouted their mother. "And cuffs up!"

Mrs. Yardley declared her intent to see what might be done to accommodate the four girls.

"Make the bed up sideways, perhaps?" Lady Keaton called after her.

Then she turned and looked at Hepplewood, thrusting out an elbow. "Now, a tour, sir, if you please, for Mrs. Aldridge and me," she ordered. "We wish to see every corner of your scandalous bachelor's bolt-hole."

With one of his muted smiles, Hepplewood agreed—for he likely had no choice, given his cousin's determination. He escorted both ladies up the pretty central staircase, casting a suggestive smile at Isabella.

"Welcome to Greenwood Farm, Mrs. Aldridge," he murmured, leaning toward her. "I trust you will find much to admire here."

"Stubble it, Tony," said Anne. "Mrs. Aldridge isn't going to fall for your double entendres."

"It does seem unlikely," said Hepplewood mildly.

They wandered through the upper floors, a little of which Isabella had already seen, but she murmured polite remarks and pretended otherwise.

In Lissie's room, the younger girls paid them no mind, entirely absorbed as they were in the dollhouse, while Nanny Seawell and Mrs. Yardley were remaking the massive bed in a sidelong fashion. The room was by no definition a nursery, but a few children's things had been haphazardly added.

"This will do nicely, my lady," said the housekeeper, snapping out a sheet, "once I fetch another bolster."

Caroline Aldridge and Jemima were already tucked up to a little game table, its top painted like a chessboard, and Jemima was setting out the pieces. She cast Isabella a smile but returned at once to her game. She had indeed found a kindred spirit in Caroline, for the girl was near her in both age and quiet temperament.

"Well, that was quick," said Lady Keaton as, ten minutes later, they exited the kitchen. "Really, Tony, you could set this entire house down in Loughford's state dining room."

"Anne, if you fancy Loughford so much, you may go there, and welcome to it," he said evenly. "For my part, I like this farm."

"But Loughford has *eight* farms," she teased as they went out into the sunlight through the back door. "And the *home* farm."

"Yes, well, Yardley will carry you up to Berkhamsted in the morning if you're longing for it," said Hepplewood dryly, turning them through the walled garden's pretty gate—now entirely repaired, Isabella noticed. "The first northbound train leaves at half seven—but don't even think of leaving Bertie and Harry behind."

"And abandon poor Mrs. Aldridge to your wicked devices?" Lady Keaton laughed. "Oh, I think not." She paused and drew a long, deep breath. "Ah, but I do forget how lovely country air smells."

"It is marvelous," said Isabella quietly, "and so very still. I have not enjoyed such peace since my last visit to Sussex."

"Oh, be patient and one of my children will shatter it," said Lady Keaton evenly. "Still, I think, Mrs. Aldridge, we should cavort on Tony's little farm like Marie Antoinette at her Petit Trianon. I therefore declare this a corset-and-crinoline-free week—I can hardly get in mine anyway."

"Good Lord, Anne," said Hepplewood, turning them onto the path toward the trees. "Mrs. Aldridge will think us the most vulgar family on earth."

"Oh, I rather doubt Mrs. Aldridge will be shocked to discover you know all about crinolines and corsets, old thing," said his cousin on a chortle. "And if ever you'd had to wear either—"

Just then a great rattling of bushes arose from the edge of the wood. "Mumma! Mamma!" squawked Bertie, poking his head from the shrubs. "Fluffles dragged Harry in! There's mud everywhere!"

"Oh, dear God," muttered Lady Keaton.

"Well, off you go, Anne!" said Hepplewood rather cheerfully. "It is but a short walk through the wood."

"Oh, *thank* you, Tony!" she said a little darkly, returning her attention to the boy as she marched off down the path. "Dragged—? Or leapt?" she shouted, setting a hand at the small of her spine. "And Bertie, pray do not tell me you pushed him, or I swear, I will stripe your bottom!"

Hepplewood watched her go. "It's enough to shrivel a chap's nether regions, that brood of Anne's," he muttered, "and old Philip has proven more of a man than I first credited."

"Should we go with her?" asked Isabella.

"No," he said firmly. "We should go *away*."

So saying, he took Isabella's hand and led her into the wood in the opposite direction. Here, deep in the shadows, the air was cool and heavy with the scent of damp ferns and moldering leaves. A few yards along, she could hear the babbling of water, and over it, the sound of Anne's scold carrying upstream.

Isabella wore slippers and was hardly dressed for a hike in the wood. Fortunately, the stroll was a short one, and in a few yards, a clearing came into view. Here Hepplewood stopped and turned to face her.

Isabella knew what was going to happen. She did not fight it but instead gave in completely.

His eyes dropping half shut, he set her back to the nearest tree. "I would very much like to finish what I started this morning." He dipped his head and brushed his lips along her cheek. Isabella sighed and turned her face into his.

But when he kissed her, it was with surprising gentleness, first nibbling at her bottom lip, then lightly suckling, as he'd done that first afternoon at Greenwood. There was something at once tender and sensual about it, and Isabella let her hands slide around his waist and up his back, crushing herself against him.

You are mine, he had once demanded.

And he was right.

She was his. Her body was his. Her every fiber answered his touch, and she wanted him with a bone-deep hunger that always simmered just beneath her surface.

He thrust deep inside her mouth, his hand splayed wide

against her lower spine, pulling her to him. She felt her hands curl into the silk of his waistcoat and knew her need for him would never end.

"*Umm,*" he said after a time, slowly kissing his way down her throat. "Yes, I should very much like to finish this—but Anne has a point about crinolines. They are the very devil, and most obstructing to a man's purposes."

Her heart oddly lightening, Isabella laughed. "Perhaps we ought to fall in with her plan?"

"Yes," he murmured, his finger catching deep in her neckline and drawing all the way around it, "perhaps."

With her skin still shivering from his touch, he let his heavily lidded eyes roam over her face, then he kissed her again, long and deep, pulling away with a reluctant smile.

"No, not here, I think," he murmured, "more's the pity."

She felt a crush of disappointment, though she knew it was best. A wry smile curled his mouth, then, clasping her hand in his, he drew her away from the tree and toward the clearing, their feet rustling in what was left of last year's leaves.

Isabella glanced back over her shoulder and told herself she was relieved. That no real lady wished to be taken against a tree with her skirts hiked about her waist.

And yet the hunger for him seemed always to linger and to deepen—just as it had now. Just as it had all throughout the drive up to Greenwood, while, with her lips still bruised by his kiss, she'd watched him through the window of the carriage, sitting so masterfully atop Colossus.

For the first five miles or so, the horse had been a devilish handful, skittering sideways at a signpost one minute, then fighting at the bit the next. But, as it seemed in all things, Hepplewood's mastery of the great beast had been utter and complete in the end—as, she sometimes feared, would be his mastery of her.

At that thought, desire twisted deep and hot in Isabella's belly and her gait hitched.

He hesitated, glancing back. "Isabella?"

"N-nothing," she said, stepping up her pace.

But something dark and knowing had shadowed his too-handsome face, and Isabella wondered if he would come to her bed that night.

She did not, however, wonder what she would say if he did.

She would say *yes*.

Always, she feared, she would say yes to him. It was a perilous and humbling realization.

Soon they reached the other side of the clearing. Here, perched above the water, sat a little folly of sorts—just a hexagon-shaped shed of rough-hewn wood, railed most of the way around and shingled with shake; nothing so elaborate as might have been seen on a gentleman's estate, but with a lovely rustic charm.

The earl led Isabella inside, and they sat down on the bench that ran along the back. In a testament to his rangy length, Hepplewood slid low, then swung his long, booted legs up, propping them on the railing opposite, crossed lazily at the ankles. Then, as she'd seen him do before, he tipped his hat low over his eyes. The pose left him looking, she mused, more like a farmhand than lord of the manor.

Still holding her hand in his, he tipped his head back and closed his eyes. "I think, my dear, we should remain here," he murmured, "until Anne's brood goes to sleep."

Isabella smiled, though he could not see it. "Those boys do seem a handful," she said. "Why did you invite them if they trouble you so?"

His smile twisting, he turned his head to look at her. "Because I feared you would not come otherwise," he said. "And I wanted you here."

"Ah, you wanted *your way*," she said.

"Always," he said agreeably.

"But as I recall, you threatened to throw me in the carriage whether I wished to come or not," she reminded him.

He chuckled low. "And you're not perfectly sure whether I'd have done it, are you?"

Isabella was not sure, though she would be damned before she'd admit it.

"I am sure," she finally said, "that you would not have succeeded had I not wished to go. And I'd suggest you leave it at that."

He laughed again and squeezed her hand, and silence fell around them for a time, broken only by the sound of water trickling over the rocks, for the brook was indeed a small one.

"And I don't dislike the lads," he finally added, casting the hat aside. "Actually, I enjoy them tremendously. I just like to give Anne a bit of hell now and again. Truth be told, we were twice as bad as Harry and Bertie growing up —a regular Mongol Horde, the lot of us."

"Really?" she said. "How many of you were there?"

He hesitated. "There was Gwen, Anne's elder sister—then me, for I fell between Gwen and Anne in age—then Diana, then, eventually, Bea—but she is much younger."

"Diana and Bea are Anne's sisters, too?"

Again, there was a slight hitch in his voice. "Diana was a cousin," he said. "And Bea was a half sister from a late marriage."

"It sounds lovely," Isabella murmured. "Was it a happy childhood?"

"Idyllic, I thought," he said. "Anne would agree, I imagine."

"So you were more or less brought up together?"

"We were," he said. "My father held various government appointments. He traveled. He spent late nights in White hall. So my mother and I passed much of our time at Burlingame Court, her elder brother's estate in Wiltshire."

"Who has not heard of Burlingame?" Isabella said, a little awed. "It's said to be one of the grandest homes in England."

"Yes, but we ran roughshod over it anyway," he said on a laugh. "Anne and her sisters were brought up there. Her father was heir, but he died a few years ago, and the new heir is our cousin."

"I'm afraid I know how that feels," said Isabella. "Is Anne no longer able to go home?"

"Oh, Lord, no, she's there all the time," said Hepplewood. "Lord Duncaster—who is her grandfather and my uncle—is old but very much alive. And our cousin Royden has turned out to be a decent sort of chap. I still have my own private wing in the old pile, unless old Royden routed me out whilst I wasn't paying attention. Mother and Lissie had it, at least."

"Mr. Gossing, your hiring agent, told me your mother recently died."

"Yes," he said, "and then Lissie's governess ran away with our curate."

"That must have been very hard for Lissie," Isabella remarked.

"Very, and I believe—though I'm not perfectly sure—that I'm now letting the child get away with too much." Then he sighed deeply. "But it can be undone, I daresay. Eventually."

"Choose your battles," Isabella advised. "It is hard to lose one's mother—or any maternal influence—as a child. Jemima was barely eight when her mother died. I was just twelve. Yes, it is hard."

"But your father cared for you very much, I hope?"

She lifted her hand in an impotent gesture. "Yes, very much," she said, "but he was lost in his own grief, and he was never very . . . organized."

"*Organized*?" He cut her a curious glance.

"Organized, yes," she mused. "It sounds odd, doesn't it? But a child needs structure and discipline in order to feel secure. It is not just enough to know one is loved. Someone must be at the helm of the ship."

"Ah!" he whispered, closing his eyes again. "And therein much is revealed!"

"What do you mean?" She looked down at him, curious.

He smiled but did not open his eyes. "Another time, love," he said quietly. "But I begin to understand why you think it so important that Lissie be with me."

"Of course it is important," she said sharply. "How can anyone think otherwise?"

"But you do realize, Isabella, that children of the aristocracy are rarely raised by their parents?" he said, opening his eyes. "I never saw my father more than thirty minutes a day until I was grown, I expect, and he was sometimes gone months at a time. Mother had social obligations and a house to run. Was it different for you?"

"Very," she said. "Our household was small and our lives simple. Sometimes I had a governess, but oftentimes there was only my mother. And Papa was always doddering about the house."

"Perhaps you were lucky, then, in some ways," he remarked.

Isabella weighed her next words with care. "I wanted to ask you something else," she finally said. "About Anne. Might I?"

He cut a strange glance up at her. "What about Anne?"

"What does she think of my being here?" Isabella let go of his hand and laced her fingers tightly together in her lap. "Does she think . . . I'm your mistress? I mean, what other conclusion is there?"

"She thinks that I *want* you for my mistress," he said calmly. "Yes, she believes I'm doggedly pursuing you, an allegation I've declined to either admit or deny. And she thinks that I will fail in my pursuit. But I shall not, Isabella. You know that, I trust? I will not give up—*ever.*"

But Isabella saw no use in arguing that point again, and something else was troubling her far more.

"Anthony," she finally said, "did Anne break your heart?"

There was a long, weighty moment of silence. Then Hepplewood's boots fell with a thud, and he came upright on the bench.

"Did Anne break my heart?" he softly echoed, his eyes narrowing as he turned to face her. "Now who the devil told you that?"

Isabella sensed she'd struck a nerve. "It—It's just that the two of you seem quite close," she murmured, "and Lady Petershaw said that . . ."

"Said what?" he gruffly demanded.

"—th-that you were once betrothed to Anne."

"And what else did she say?" he demanded. "What else, Isabella?"

"N-nothing," Isabella lied.

His eyes had grown dangerously dark. "There was an understanding, yes. Much like your family's understanding about Everett, I daresay. But not every understanding results in a marriage, does it?"

"Well, no," she admitted.

"Then leave it be," he said, jerking to his feet.

"Anthony, wait—"

But he had already stepped out of the folly, his spine rigid.

She leapt up and went after him, catching his arm. "Anthony, you do not have to answer my questions," she said, "but you do not get to insult me by simply walking away."

But his expression was not one of anger, or even of pain. It was something worse. Something nameless and cold. His glittering blue eyes had gone flat and black; one hand was fisted at his sides, the other curled so hard into his hat brim that he had crushed it.

"I am going to walk downstream," he said curtly. "I need to speak with Yardley. I beg your pardon, Isabella. Can you see yourself back to the house?"

"Yes, it's five hundred yards," she said irritably. "And I'm sorry if I upset you by speaking of Anne, but my heavens . . ."

His lips had thinned to a hard, almost white, line. "Anne is happily married to Philip—and with my blessing," he finally answered. "And I . . . and I, Isabella, am just about as happy as I deserve to be. May we leave it at that?"

She let her hand fall and stepped away. "Indeed, it seems we must."

He put his hat back on and gave a harsh tug at the front brim. "Then I again beg your pardon," he said curtly. "I will see you at dinner."

"Very well." She nodded stiffly. "At dinner."

Then Isabella turned and walked away, and this time she did not look back. She was, in fact, more furious than she had ever been with the man—which was saying something. But oddly enough, Hepplewood did not move.

He neither followed her nor started downstream, for his feet made not a sound in the leaves, and Isabella could feel his gaze burning into her back all the way through the clearing.

Well, be damned to him, she thought.

She had not wanted to come here in the first place—and now she was of half a mind to walk straight into the village and take three seats on the next mail coach back to London.

She wondered if he would let her go.

No, she wondered if she really *wanted* to go.

Then Isabella stopped just inside the tree line and drew a deep, steadying breath. No, what she now wondered—deep in her heart—was whether Lord Hepplewood was still just a little in love with Anne.

She should have been telling him to go to hell. But she was not.

And Isabella did not know what that said about her.

On a sigh, she marched from the shadows and back onto the sunlit path. The children needed her near, she reminded herself. For all its bucolic beauty, Greenwood Farm was a strange place to them, and they were still amongst people they did not know well.

On her next breath, however, she realized Lissie and Georgina were getting on rather too well. Both girls stood atop the wall that separated the garden from the stable yard, walking as if upon a tightrope, arms outstretched for balance.

"*Georgie*—!"

Despite her slippers, Isabella bolted from the path at a near run, cutting straight across the graveled stable yard. "Lissie! Georgina! Get down this minute!"

Lissie looked back over her shoulder to flash a wicked—and familiar—grin. Suddenly, having almost reached the new gate, the girl lost her balance, tottering precariously.

"Lissie!" Isabella shouted, "look out!"

Suddenly, Lissie tumbled off in a *whuff!* of petticoats, vanishing beneath the wall into the shadows of the garden. Startled, Georgina half leapt and half fell, disappearing after her.

By the time Isabella flew through the back gate, Lissie lay on the lawn, crying, her arm twisted awkwardly beneath her body. Georgie was on her knees, her face screwed up as if she was about to burst into tears.

"Oh, Lissie!" Isabella knelt and lifted her gingerly up from the grass. "Georgie, are you hurt?"

"N-no," Georgina managed, rising.

"*I h-h-hurt my arm!*" wailed Lissie.

"Here, love," said Isabella, sitting on the steps to cradle her. "Let me see."

"N-no," said the girl. "It hurts."

"I'm s-sorry, Bella," snuffled Georgie, looking on anxiously.

Georgina did indeed appear fine. Carefully, Isabella examined Lissie's arm. Her sleeve was torn, but nothing appeared broken.

"Lissie is fine," said Isabella reassuringly, "but the two of you are not permitted on the wall. Here, Lissie, let me feel around your neck, sweet."

Delicately, Isabella examined her collarbone, feeling nothing. Lissie did not wince, and had regained her composure.

Just then, Isabella heard heavy footfalls coming from the direction of the brook, and in an instant Hepplewood had bolted from the trees and past the stable yard.

"What happened?" he demanded, flying around the gate.

Isabella stood, Lissie still clinging to her neck. "They were walking atop the wall," Isabella said, "but they leapt off when I shouted."

"Good God!" he said, scowling darkly.

"I w-want down," Lissie snuffled, refusing to hold her father's gaze.

Soon, both girls were on their feet, grass-stained but no worse for wear. Having squatted to look them directly in the eyes, Hepplewood was scolding them—gently, but firmly—and both girls were nodding, bottom lips thrust out a little tremulously.

Just then, Nanny Seawell appeared on the back steps. After a few sharp words of her own, she led the girls away.

"No harm done, I suppose," said Hepplewood evenly, rising from his crouch.

"I will speak sharply to Georgina," Isabella assured him. "It will not happen again."

"Well, let us not be too harsh," he said, scrubbing a hand around his jaw. "The wall is scarcely over three feet high. One mustn't crush a child's adventurous spirit."

It was on the tip of Isabella's tongue to remark that it was better to crush a spirit than a collarbone. But he was right, to a point.

"Thank you, Isabella," he said, his arm falling. "Lissie is comfortable with you. I am . . . glad."

Isabella did not reply; there was nothing more to say. Almost at once, the awkwardness between them flooded back in to fill the silence.

"Well, then," he said coolly, "to Yardley's."

"Yes," she said a little tightly. "Well. At dinner, then."

Then he turned and set off toward the path again, his long, booted legs eating up the ground.

IN THE END, Isabella did not see Lord Hepplewood at dinner after all. He had been unexpectedly called away, Mrs. Yardley explained, to a gathering of the local landowners at the Carpenter's Arms with Mr. Yardley.

"Oh, that will be nothing but ale and dice and tavern wenches," said Anne as they carried up the food to the dining room. "If they had any honest business, they'd be doing it in the daylight."

Isabella laughed. "You're likely right."

"Aye, she's completely right," grumbled Mrs. Yardley, setting down a huge bowl of mashed parsnips. "They'll be blowing a cloud up there 'til the wee hours, then reeling home reeking o' smoke and hops and that wicked barmaid's lavender water—Millicent, she's been callin' herself, but she was christened Millie, and ever will be."

From the table, Jemima and Caroline giggled.

"Worse still, poor Tony will be missing all the truly elevated conversation we'll be having here," said Anne as she sat down. "Harry wants to tell us how many fleas he drowned in the brook this afternoon. That mangy creature was riddled with them. I am sure Millicent's charms could never compete."

At that moment, however, "that mangy creature" was scooting himself under the table to thump what was left of his tail at Anne's feet, for in the end he'd been shorn bald by Yardley with his sheep sheers, then washed a second time in lye soap.

"I guess we can't call him Fluffles no more," said Bertie glumly, scooping up a big dollop of parsnips, "'cause he's got no fluff and no ruffles."

"And all the better he is for it," said his mother, passing the next bowl. "Lissie, do you need help?"

Mrs. Yardley went at once to help the younger children serve themselves. Save for the twins, the eight of them were dining *en famille*—a circumstance for which Isabella was deeply thankful. She was accustomed to taking her meals with the girls and Mrs. Barbour, and she could not have borne—especially on this night—to be separated from them by cold formality and forced to endure Anne's curious glances alone.

Anne really had given up her crinolines, and tonight she wore a simple gown that, while shapeless, had a flowing sort of elegance that was perfect for her slight figure and rounding belly. The children chattered happily through dinner, Georgie talking of nothing but the dollhouse. Afterward, having finished the meal with an excellent rhubarb fool, they rose as Anne excused herself to put Deborah and Deanna to bed.

By nine it was dark and raining, and there was still no sign of Hepplewood. While the two elder girls began to work on a puzzle in the front parlor, Isabella lingered, alternately standing by the front windows while toying with Hepplewood's brandy stopper on the sideboard, then going to one of the armchairs by the hearth to flip through old issues of *The Field,* which were almost as fascinating as the drizzle running down the windows.

She had returned to stare at it when Anne came back down half an hour later.

"Don't waste your time, my dear," she said, breezing past. "He went galloping off in one of his moods."

Isabella felt her face flush. "One of his moods?" she said, turning from the window.

Anne was picking up some of the children's toys, for they'd been permitted the run of the house. "Oh, it's just how Tony is," she said, bending over to snatch up Pickles, Lissie's wooden dog. "You mustn't mind him, Isabella. He'll come home drunk as a lord round midnight, and tomorrow all will be well again."

"Oh," said Isabella quietly.

She turned back to the window, pondering it. Isabella still had no notion what she had said to make Lord Hepplewood so angry—if he had, in fact, been angry. On further consideration, however, it felt more like an emotion turned inward, rather than directed at her. Nonetheless, it stung to be treated so cavalierly, and to be shut out with no explanation.

Suddenly she felt Anne's warmth hovering beside her.

"Isabella," Anne said softly. "How well do you know my cousin, if I may ask?"

Isabella turned from the window. "Scarcely at all, I begin to think."

Anne flashed a smile of what looked like genuine warmth. "He's a good man, my dear, truly," she murmured, glancing over her shoulder at the girls, who sat at a table in the back of the room. "But he is just . . ." She paused, her brow furrowing.

"What?" asked Isabella coolly. "Just unhappy he cannot get his way in everything?"

"Oh, no, just . . . *unhappy*." Looking truly pained, Anne set a hand on Isabella's arm. "He really is the kindest, least selfish man imaginable—no matter what Aunt Hepplewood used to say."

"His mother?" Isabella looked at her, puzzled.

"Yes." Anne shook her head, as if throwing off some memory. "But never mind that," she went on. "Did you quarrel? If you did, don't worry. Tomorrow it will mean nothing. As I say, Tony is just . . . unhappy sometimes."

"Thank you, you're very kind, I'm sure," said Isabella a little curtly. "But I cannot see he has much to be unhappy about. He has a beautiful daughter and a family who clearly adores him, and so far as I can see, he wants for nothing. So pardon me, Lady Keaton, if I have little sympathy with his so-called moods."

An almost admiring look passed over Anne's face. "Indeed, you would not, would you?" she murmured. "After all, you were married to Richard Aldridge. That, I daresay, would put a little buckram up anyone's spine."

At that, Isabella's spine did stiffen—visibly, apparently—for Anne touched her arm again.

"Oh, good Lord, how thoughtless I am," she said. "Forgive me, Isabella. But trust me when I say that Tony is nothing like Richard. I don't mean *those* kinds of moods."

"That's good to hear," said Isabella weakly.

"Tony used to give the impression of being little more than a charming rake." Anne's gaze had gone a little distant. "But age and life have hardened him, and underneath he possesses an almost ruthless control. People misjudge him at their peril. Yes, he has vices aplenty, but he is not mad, and his life . . . well, perhaps it has not been as easy as you think."

Isabella lifted her gaze to Anne's. "Thank you," she said, more sincerely. "Lord Hepplewood has been very kind to me and to my sisters. I'm glad he has your good opinion. And I'm glad you came up to Greenwood. Thank you for agreeing to do so."

"Agreeing?" Anne lifted one eyebrow. "I cannot think why I need be thanked for attending a pleasant house party in the countryside."

"Lady Keaton, we are not social equals, and I know it."

"It is Anne," she said firmly, "and I don't know what you mean. We're both daughters of the aristocracy—daughters of barons, in point of fact. We came out within a year of one another, and we married into the same family—one of England's oldest and finest."

Isabella shook her head. "Lady Kea—*Anne*—I own a bookshop in Knightsbridge," she said. "Do you know how I met your cousin? I interviewed for the post as Lissie's governess. To be *his servant.* And he would not even hire me. So now I am . . . in trade, I suppose one might say—and I'm lucky it isn't something worse."

"The fact that you were widowed young and thrust into a life that was not what you were brought up for hardly alters the color of your blood," said Anne. "And the fact that Uncle Fenster turned his back on you in your widowhood shames him—actually, it shames us all. Someone should have done *something.*"

"Lord Fenster did not turn his back on me," said Isabella softly, "for he never so much as met me."

"Truly?" Anne set a hand to her heart, something like pain flickering in her eyes. "I had no idea."

Isabella flashed a tight smile. "He cut Richard from his life immediately," she said. "And when Richard died, I asked Lord Fenster for nothing. I buried my husband next to Mamma in our village churchyard and went on with my life. You mean to be kind, Anne, I'm sure. But I do not need your sympathy—or Lord Hepplewood's. I am making my own way now, and while I will not say it is easy, I am at least trying to be master of my own fate."

Anne's smile twisted, much like her cousin's often did. "As young ladies we are taught that the wisest thing we can do is to find a good husband, and entrust to him our fate, aren't we?" she mused. "And I have been blessed in that regard. I do not worry about anything save the health of my children. Philip worries for me. He is wise and good, and I trust him utterly to take care of us. Moreover, I am—and always have been—quite madly in love with him."

"Then you are beyond fortunate," said Isabella, dropping her gaze to the carpet.

"And I'm not fool enough to think otherwise," said Anne fervently. "For all that we are taught to find such a husband, and to surrender ourselves into his care, men worthy of such trust are rare, and we must choose blindly, in many cases. It is easy to find a man to fall in love with—or to lust over, if I may be blunt—but it is hard to find a man worthy of that ultimate devotion."

"You are very wise, Anne," said Isabella, "and your husband is fortunate, too."

"But you were not fortunate, Isabella," Anne said, settling a hand on her arm, "through no fault of your own. And had I suffered through what you have, I'd likely be running a bookshop, too—or at least I hope I would. I hope I would have the courage to do what you have done."

But the topic had grown too intimate—and too painful—for Isabella, and she fell silent. Anne did likewise, as if fearing she had said too much.

After a time, Isabella drew a deep breath. "In any case, thank you again for coming with us," she said. "It is such a treat for my sisters to be here. To have other children to play with. Greenwood is so beautiful, and it feels so safe."

"*Safe*?" Anne smiled. "What an interesting choice of words."

Isabella lifted her gaze to Anne's. "Did your cousin not tell you why he brought us here?"

"Not in great detail, no, but you are beautiful and charming and intelligent, Isabella," she said, "so I think I can guess." Anne gave Isabella's arm another squeeze, then lifted her hand away. "Well. It is late. Shall we put the children to bed and have a sip of Tony's sherry?"

Isabella tried to smile. "I think I will turn in, too," she said, "but thank you."

Nonetheless, for all her declared intentions, three hours later, Isabella still lay sleepless beneath the sheets, mulling over all that Anne had said.

Perhaps she did not know what Lord Hepplewood's life had been like. Perhaps one never knew. Who could have guessed at what her own life had come to, or what she had suffered along the way?

It did not excuse his cold fury—if that's what it had been—but perhaps it explained it.

And perhaps he would relent and come to her bed.

She thumped out a lump in her pillow and rolled over for the twentieth time.

Did she want him in her bed?

Yes, she decided. For good or ill, she still desired him—ached for him in a way she could never have imagined possible. Not just his touch—not just his mastery of her—but the sheer physical release of joining her body to his.

She was so desperately tired of being alone.

But he did not come, and another hour dragged by until at last she heard the longcase clock on the landing strike one. Then, perhaps a quarter hour later, there was a sound—a sort of scrape, as if the front door had opened, followed by the slow thud of heavy boots up the stairs and past her door.

She heard the creak of the door further down the hall—the small room opposite the master's chamber, allotted to his apparently nonexistent valet—and then the house fell again into silence. Isabella held her breath and waited.

And then waited some more. She imagined him undressing. Wedging off his boots. Bathing, perhaps.

He was not coming. Too much time had passed. For an instant, she merely lay in bed, nibbling at her thumbnail, until a sense of urgency overcame her.

Later, she was unable to explain what she did, or why. It had something to do, she feared, with what Anne had said about courage. About being the master of one's fate. Or perhaps it was just the overwhelming ache—the longing for his touch—that had begun to torment her of late. But whatever it was, Isabella got out of bed and went down the passageway.

For discretion's sake, she did not knock but simply let herself in.

Later, when her head was clearer, she realized it had been a foolish thing to do—that Hepplewood might have been drunk enough to drag home Millie the tavern maid, for all she knew. But she went in anyway, and shut the door behind her to see him sitting in the faint, flickering lamplight, stripped bare to the waist but still in his boots and breeches.

Elbows propped on his wide-set knees, he sat on the edge of a narrow bed that was shoved up against the far wall. He lifted his gaze from what seemed a minute examination of his floor and looked at her with eyes both bleary and bereft.

"Isabella," he said flatly. "I'm . . . a trifle sotted, I fear."

He said it as if it was a rationale for something—what, she did not know.

Certainly it was not an apology. Isabella wasn't even sure she wanted one now. Something she'd grasped during her conversation with Anne had brought to her a startling sort of clarity.

That some men were good for one thing; others for quite another. A man that was good for both things was, perhaps, a rare creature indeed. Anne, mayhap, had gotten the last one?

But Hepplewood was good for one thing—of that Isabella was quite certain.

She pushed away from the door and came to stand in front of him. "Is this all there is between us, Anthony?" she whispered, stripping the gown off over her head. "Is it just . . . sex that you want from me? Sex, but not intimacy?"

LOOKING UP FROM his valet's narrow bed, Hepplewood wondered if he'd finally drunk himself to the point of hallucination. Isabella—beautiful, perfect Isabella—stood before him entirely naked, her large, dusky nipples already erect, her eyes almost limpid in the lamplight.

He swallowed hard and wished to heaven he were sober; that he'd not let confusion and self-loathing get a damned grip on him and had instead stayed at home, where he belonged.

Home.

Isabella *was* home.

Isabella was where he belonged. Looking at her now, he knew it, and knew he would not escape it. And he knew, too, that she deserved better. That he had treated her unfairly, and that she was owed . . . something. The truth, he supposed.

He did not have it in him tonight.

"Is this all?" she demanded again.

He drew in a ragged breath and looked up at her with an infinitely weary gaze. "I do not know, Isabella," he said, opening both hands. "If it is, is it enough?"

"For tonight," she whispered, "yes. It is enough."

She stepped nearer; near enough to touch. "Good God in heaven," he uttered, bracketing her slender waist with his hands. He pulled her to him and set his lips to her breastbone on a deep, openmouthed sound of surrender.

But she shoved her fingers through his hair and pushed him away, then knelt between his boots. With slow, precise motions, she slipped loose the buttons of his breeches, her clever fingers working them free with an almost deliberate languor

Soon, however, the buttons were undone. He was undone—or damned near it—for he sucked in his breath when her hand merely brushed his belly.

She grasped his rapidly hardening shaft in her warm hand, her fingers curling around him until raw lust shot deep, his blood surging. He realized her intent.

"Isabella," he choked, "don't—you don't have to do that."

She looked at him, unblinking. "I did not ask," she said, echoing the words he'd once spoken to her. "I have decided, I think, to suit myself tonight."

With her other hand she shoved down the linen of his drawers, bent her head, and took him firmly into her mouth, her full lips sliding inexorably over the swollen head of his cock.

As her black tresses spilled along his thigh, he gave an

almost inhuman groan and shoved his fingers into the hair at her nape, but Isabella wasn't having it. Setting her palm to the flat of his belly, she pushed him back with some force.

Perhaps it was the ale, but he went, falling back against the wall, his elbows sinking into the softness of the narrow cot as he gave himself up to the torment of her mouth.

She rose higher onto her knees and slicked her tongue around the delicate flesh of his head, then down his length, taking him deep. Again and again she stroked him, until his legs shook with it, his hands fisting in the rough wool blanket. Until it was all he could do not to thrust himself upward and shove deep into her throat.

Isabella slid all the way up his length again, and the cold air brushed his heated flesh. Delicately, she drew the pink tip of her tongue around as if willing him to watch it, then drew him deep inside again, slicking him over the hardness of her teeth, all the way down until he begged her for more—for release—for something he wasn't even certain of.

For herself. For her soul, perhaps.

And when at last he was near the edge, fighting for restraint, Isabella released him from the wet warmth of her mouth and left him gasping.

"Christ," he rasped. "Oh, love."

His body ached with the wanting, his groin heavy with it. But tonight Isabella was in control, and he fought for patience, awaiting her next move.

He was rewarded when Isabella simply climbed onto the bed and over him, setting her knees to either side of his hips, one hand flat against the wall just above his shoulders.

"*Isabella*," he rasped, settling both hands at her waist, almost encircling it.

She was putting on weight, he realized, her hips growing almost lush as they curved beneath his palms. Her eyes were closed, her head tipped back with longing. "I need you inside me," she whispered. "Now."

Then she took his shaft in one hand, rose up on her knees, and impaled herself on it.

The sudden intrusion made her gasp, but she took every inch on one sweet, pure stroke, and he had to restrain the urge to beg her for more. To promise her anything. His life-long fidelity. His every last penny. His undying love.

Anything, he thought dimly. *Anything, if she will just forgive me. If she will just love me.*

She did—physically, at least. She drew up his length, rising onto her knees and sliding down again, until his shaft was buried deep inside her welcoming, womanly passage.

"*Aah—*!" he choked, curling his fingers into the blanket. "Good God, woman. I tried—I tried . . . "

Isabella chose that moment to rise up again, stroking him with such exquisite sweetness that he nearly exploded.

"Tried what—?" she whispered.

"To get drunk," he said thickly. "So drunk . . . wouldn't think—oh, *Isabella* . . ."

"Think of what?" she asked, falling forward until her hair cascaded over her arm, spilling like a silken waterfall. "This?"

"Everything," he managed, his eyes squeezed shut. "You. Us. All of it."

She stroked up again, and he exhaled between his teeth. Good God, he was not some grass-green schoolboy. He wouldn't fuck like one. The burning desire to please her so-bered him, and he settled his hands on her hip bones again, holding her down long enough to finally kiss her.

But she was not in a kissing sort of mood—even intoxicated as he was, he could sense it. It stung, perhaps. But the thought flew from his head, for in that moment, Isabella tightened herself around him and sunk slowly down again, her head tipped back in feminine pleasure as a soft moan escaped her.

She soon untwined her hands from his neck and set them flat to the wall again, riding him very deliberately and hungrily, drawing herself up his length. Sensing what she needed, he tightened his grip on her waist and stilled her to his thrusts, pushing himself up inside her, his mouth set to the soft skin between her breasts.

Eagerly she shifted, pressing herself against him, deepening the intimacy. He dragged in his breath, and with it her scent, warm and seductive. So achingly familiar.

With every stroke he felt himself straining for control as his flesh pulled at hers. He let his lips slide higher, up the graceful length of her throat. Through the haze of lust and ale, he felt himself falling. Falling deep and hard as he loved her, falling into something so perfect, so natural, that it was like the drawing of his own breath.

She made a sweet sound, a catch in the back of her throat, and her breath began to come faster. Thrusting up again, he whispered something in her ear, he hardly knew what. Words of love. Words of longing and enslavement. Words he might later regret but in that moment could scarce restrain.

Her body answered if her lips did not; her hands sliding down the wall to curl over his shoulders, her nails digging deep into his muscles as she rose up again. Sweat sheened his forehead and he felt his release near, the tendons of his neck straining. He held it in check ruthlessly and set a steady rhythm. She drew back, and his gaze captured hers.

Those eyes. Those dark and knowing eyes that seemed to drill into his soul. They burned for this now. For *him*. Again and again she urged herself against him, the tempo deepening, until at last Isabella shattered and began to tremble.

He drew her to him, thrust deep, and deeper still, until he was lost to all sanity, his release coming upon him with a powerful certainty. That he had fallen, yes, in a way he'd never known possible.

He had fallen into Isabella's dark, blue-violet gaze, and he would not emerge whole. He was forged to her—she was a part of him—for good or ill. He needed her with a depth and a desperation that frightened him. When at last the spasms of pleasure relented, he opened his mouth to tell her so, but this time, words failed him.

It was as well, perhaps.

Isabella had set the heels of her hands to his shoulders very firmly and was pushing herself a little away. Their mingled scents rose up between them in a sensual cloud. He drew it in and shifted so that they might lie down on the narrow cot together.

But Isabella lifted herself off, still a little unsteady.

"*Ohh*, that felt good." With the back of her hand, she pushed back a teasing tendril of her hair. "Anthony, what you can do—such physical pleasure—oh, I never knew it was possible."

"Isabella." He threaded a hand through the inky black hair at her temple. "I want you to know that I—"

"No," she said, shaking her head. "I don't need your words. I just needed that. What you gave me. Thank you."

She climbed off the bed then, turned around to snatch up her nightgown from the floor, and, in a trice, drew it back on, shimmying the fine white lawn over the perfect, pale globes of her hips with an expert twitch.

Then she turned around, flashed a faintly tremulous smile, and leaned over to kiss him softly. When she drew away, he held out his hand, eager to draw her back into his embrace, but it was as if she did not see it.

Or simply did not want it.

"Thank you," she said again. "You truly have a gift for pleasuring women."

And then she was gone, shutting the door softly behind her.

Hand outstretched into emptiness, he still sat on the bed, his breeches hanging off his hips and his boots still on. He stared at the door, her scent still strong in the air. He had the most sickening sensation of having been . . . *used*.

Yes, that was the right word. She hadn't whispered words of love or longing. She hadn't lost herself. Not as he had done. In fact, it was slowly dawning on his ale-addled mind that Isabella had come in with a purpose—and a very specific one.

One that involved him and his stiff cock—and damned little else.

It was a man's fantasy, that; a beautiful woman who just wanted a good, hard ride and nothing more. He twisted sideways on the little cot, fell into the pillow, and wondered why he wasn't savoring it.

The truth was, it felt unnervingly like the first time they'd made love and she had wanted him to leave her bed afterward. And the second time in her cottage—that awful morning he'd woke with her in his arms, strangely certain that everything in his life was on the cusp of some sort of inexorable change. Then, too, she had simply wanted to say good-bye.

With Isabella, was he forever destined to be left . . . so bloody unsettled? To be left aching for more? But more of what, he was never sure.

Intimacy was the thing he'd been forever hell-bent on avoiding. He stared for a long time at the ceiling, studying the eerie patterns the lamplight cast up. He was not a man much given to self-deception. Yes, he was beginning to fear that it was something like intimacy he wanted from her.

But intimacy meant an ultimate giving and sharing—of oneself, of one's innermost feelings. And failings.

Hadn't he realized from the very first that to touch Isabella might bring him to his knees? Even that day at Loughford— yes, even then, he'd known. He had insulted her and angered her and sent her on her way—far, far away, he'd hoped— because somehow he'd just known.

Now all he could think to do was stride across the hall, tie her to the damn bed, and fuck her until she swore she loved him. He was already up and hitching shut his trousers before he knew what he was about. He sat back down, his hands shaking.

Jesus Christ, man, he told himself, *get a grip on yourself.*

But his usual cold resolve had left him, and he was left with the dreadful sense that this time he just might get precisely what he deserved. There was a dangerously hot pressure welling against the backs of his eyes now and a weight hardening in his chest that he knew was nothing but a knot of shame and regret.

All this weighed upon Hepplewood as he drifted off to sleep. And when he woke somewhere near dawn, it was to find that his bed was still cold and his boots were still on.

That he embraced not Isabella but merely his valet's pillow, the linen damp—with his sweat, he hoped.

CHAPTER 15

Hepplewood spent the next several days determined to get the whip hand on his irrational notions and focus on making the visit enjoyable for his guests. It required no great effort; hospitality came naturally to him. So when Yardley had no need of him—which, given the size of the farm, was most of the time—Hepplewood immersed himself in entertaining the children and dancing attendance on Anne and Isabella, but only in the lightest, most flirtatious of manners.

The party rambled about on wilderness walks with Fluffles, the dog running, snout to the ground, in search of something vile to roll in—and often finding it. This would ultimately result in another wade in the brook, risking Anne's wrath if anyone returned too wet. They also picnicked in the Chilterns and drove out to clamber about the medieval ruins at Totternhoe Knolls.

On fair afternoons, he took Bertie and Harry out for a spot of target shooting—a habit of his when in the country—and, after a little wrangle with Anne, began to let Harry fire his pocket revolver so long as he stuffed the lad's ears with cotton and helped him hold it. And when it rained, he would go up to Lissie's room and read while the girls played dolls.

In fact, within hours of the children's arrival, Georgina's love of Lissie's dollhouse was so profound that Hepplewood had found himself commissioning another. It was that errand, in fact, that he'd used as an excuse to himself—cravenly, to be sure—for abandoning Isabella by the brook.

Fortunately, a second dollhouse was sitting nearly finished in Yardley's shop, meant for a raffle at the village's harvest fair. Hepplewood made a donation well in excess of what any raffle would have brought, and thus the deal was struck.

He also spent a great deal of time simply watching Isabella. It was not easy. Lust stirred in the pit of his belly with every sidelong glance they exchanged. He was still determined to somehow lay claim to the woman. But he found himself oddly intent on viewing her through less heated eyes and getting to know her—getting to know her, that was to say, in the way that ordinary people became acquainted.

Their beginning had not been ordinary; it had exploded in heat the moment they'd met. And he now forced this almost monastic existence on himself because, as much as he cared for her—and burned for her—he was increasingly aware that he still did not *know* her. Not in the way a man should know a woman when he contemplated . . . what?

Befriending her?

He had done that; he had even allowed his daughter to befriend her—which was not something a man did lightly.

Bedding her? He had already done that, too—and in the past, fucking a woman had had, in his eyes, nothing to do with any knowledge of her finer nature. In fact, the darker and more enigmatic a lover was, all the better for his purposes.

Perhaps he contemplated another attempt at making her

his mistress? The notion made him almost laugh out loud. Oh, he would try—of that he'd little doubt. But Isabella would not submit to him. Not in the long run.

Oh, she might—*might,* if he played his cards with the greatest of care—permit him the occasional tumble if it could be discreetly arranged. Clearly she desired that much from him, at the very least.

Perhaps it was all she desired.

But that question more or less mirrored the one she'd asked him a few nights past—right after she'd stripped off her nightdress to stand naked before him.

Was that all there was between them? That gnawing hunger for one another, and no more?

"Your brow is furrowed," she said, suddenly reaching past him. "Give me that. You are merely wiping it over and over again."

They stood now in the narrow scullery, side by side. He passed her the china plate across the sinks, and she took it and set it on the shelf above.

"I cannot believe you are drying dishes again," she said almost to herself, plunging her hands back into the hot water.

He gave a low chuckle. "Do you imagine me emasculated by it, my dear?" he murmured. "I should be pleased to prove otherwise."

She cut him a chiding look and handed him a bowl. "Could anything emasculate you, I wonder?" she muttered, "other than a sharp kitchen knife and a great deal of determination?"

He laughed again and leaned nearer. "Don't do it, my love, for we would both soon regret it," he said. "I'll be of far more use to you as I am."

"Didn't you once promise," she muttered, scrubbing hard at something under the water, "never, ever to flirt with me?"

"Did that sound flirtatious?" He shrugged. "I thought we were negotiating. In any case, dishes must be done, and since I'm the fool who invited a dozen guests to a house with no staff to speak of, it should fall to me once in a while. Besides, Anne helped."

But Anne had slunk off at least a quarter hour ago, casting an odd glance over her shoulder as she went.

"Are you counting Nanny Seawell and Anne's maid in that dozen?" asked Isabella lightly.

He laughed. "Perhaps I'm counting that damned dog of Bertie's," he said, "twice, for he's caused at least that much trouble."

Isabella stopped in the middle of her scrubbing. "Actually, this has been rather pleasant," she said pensively, "to have simple food, and to make our own coffee and wash a few dishes. I can understand why you like it. The solitude and simplicity of it, I mean."

But the truth was, he had not bought Greenwood in order to play Farmer Brown and live in bucolic isolation. He'd bought it for debauchery and bacchanalia—of which there'd been plenty—and the fact that he'd now brought his own family here instead of his usual cadre of sybarites still struck him as very strange indeed. It said something, though, he'd as soon not consider what, exactly.

He could sense, though, that despite her words, Isabella was growing restless. He cut her another glance as she passed him the next plate. Her gaze was fixed on her work, her movements practiced and efficient. He liked that. He liked that she exuded competence and a willingness to work without complaint. It was not something he had appreciated in a woman until now.

They had been here almost a week, and twice she had written letters of instruction to Mrs. Barbour and three times to various wholesalers in the City. She had worked diligently at her ledgers and read through an entire stack of publisher's samples. But a business could not be left untended any more than an estate could.

If he did not soon hear something from Jervis, he realized, he was going to have to take her back to London. Isabella would demand it, and he would be hard-pressed to think of an excuse to refuse her. He had no hard reason not to do so; just suspicions and a grave unease that set his hackles up every time he thought on it.

Nonetheless, he could not bring himself to speculate aloud to her; not when a false hope might hurt Isabella more than the hard truth of her present existence.

A heavy silence had fallen over the little room. Through the high windows, he could hear a spring rain still pattering down as it had for much of the day. The room was small, the lamplight intimate, and it felt suddenly as if the rest of the world were far away. She handed him a glass, their hands accidentally brushing, and in a flash, it was as if his every nerve came to life.

Lust shot through him out of nowhere, straight through his heart, deep into his belly, and lower still. Every muscle hardened with it, his loins pooling with heat. He set the glass in the cold rinse water and debated sticking his head in, too.

"*Isabella*," he rasped, his hands clenching at the edge of the sink.

"What?" She turned halfway around.

He searched for the words to tell her how he felt. His lust and his hopes and his fears for her and the children seemed suddenly tumbled together in a way he couldn't explain. Slowly, he forced his hands to unclench and his lungs to work.

"Anthony?" She crooked her head to look at him.

"I forgot," he said awkwardly, "what I was going to say."

"Oh," she said.

And the silence flooded in again.

"Does Mrs. Yardley always have Sunday evenings off?" she finally asked, breaking the quiet.

He shrugged, jerked the towel from his shoulder, and took the glass she held out, careful not to touch her. "Mrs. Yardley has no set schedule," he said, dunking it in the rinse. "I'm rarely here, and our agreement never required her to attend to the house every day."

"And yet she has done the lion's share of it admirably," Isabella remarked, dredging up a spoon and scrubbing at it. "But you can cook, too, I once heard you boast?"

He grinned at her. "Eggs," he said, "or a slab of beefsteak, perhaps. Be glad, my dear, it hasn't come to that."

She cut another of her odd, sidelong looks at him. They had become more and more frequent, he realized, the last couple of days. His new strategy might have thrown her, but Isabella still desired him. The thought should have been gratifying, and it was. But underneath that gratification lay something aching and uncertain.

He did not like that feeling. He was not a man who tolerated uncertainty. Worse, there was nothing he could do about it.

Damn it all. He would very much like to make Isabella suffer a little for the misery she was putting him through. Perhaps, if he asked nicely, she might permit him to do just that.

"There is a dangerous look in your eyes tonight," she said, reaching into the hot sink to pull the chain.

He watched the water, still steaming, begin to gurgle and swirl down the copper-lined trough as he dried his hands. Isabella's fingertips were set to the rim of the sink, her knuckles red.

"Give me your hands," he ordered without waiting for her to comply.

He took one, holding fast to his emotions, and began to dry it, gently pulling the cloth over each finger in turn.

"Your knuckles are cracked," he gently chided. "What was I thinking? More village girls could have been brought in."

"Anthony," she said, extracting her hand and taking away his cloth, "it doesn't hurt anyone to wash a few plates and glasses after dinner. And my knuckles were cracked long before I got here. You forget that I wash dishes every day—sometimes two or three times a day—and I scrub floors, too, when I must. That is my life now. And I am fine with it."

He lifted his gaze from his study of her hands, which were otherwise long-fingered and elegant. "I do forget," he admitted. "But I'm not so fine with it. You are a lady, Isabella. That sort of life is not for you."

"Then who is it for?" she asked, setting her head to one side as if studying him. "And why not me? Who decides?"

He took the cloth, tossed it over the rim of the sink, and took both her hands in his. "We're not going to debate egalitarianism, are we?" he said, forcing a light tone. "I confess, it bores me excessively. Tell me instead about you."

"About me?"

"About your family, perhaps. We've spoken little of them." He drew her from the scullery into the glow of the kitchen and pulled a chair to the rough-hewn table. "Sit down. I'm going to make you a cup of tea."

"But the others are—"

"Getting ready for bed," he interjected, moving the kettle onto the hob with a harsh, scraping sound. "The twins are already asleep, I expect."

"Well, so far as my family, there's little you don't know."

Isabella half turned in her chair, following him with her gaze as he moved about the kitchen to fetch the teapot and tea chest. "You know about Everett. And my aunt. There really isn't anyone else."

"I meant the other side of your family," he said, lifting down the chest from a shelf.

"Mother's side?" She pushed a damp tendril of hair from her forehead. "Well, I don't know much, honestly. The family was originally from the Midlands; round Shropshire, Mamma always said."

"Have you any relations there?"

"I think not. Mamma's people left generations ago."

"What was the family name?" he asked lightly.

"Flynt, spelled with a *y* instead of an *i* like the stone," she answered, "though it may have been changed at some point."

"Did they leave England for a reason?"

"Yes, criminals, most likely," she said on a spurt of laughter. "Cattle thieves, perhaps. It might even be they were transported. Did they transport thieves to Canada?"

He shot her a muted smile and put the tea chest back. "Petty criminals were perhaps indentured," he said, "but I expect your family was more apt to have been minor gentry."

"Who told you that?" she asked a little sharply.

Unwilling to show his hand just yet, he merely shrugged. "You said they were in the timber trade and lived in the wilderness," he replied. "One doesn't ordinarily mow down a colonial wilderness for profit unless one owns it."

Isabella seemed to accept this. "I believe the original settler was, in fact, a military officer," she said, "who took a liking to the area and decided to remain."

"Ah," he said. "So you know a little of your family history."

"As I said, a very little," she answered. "But why should you care?"

He drew out a chair and sat down to wait for the pot to boil. "Indulge me," he said.

"It is my opinion that you have been too often indulged," she replied, looking at him a little darkly.

He flashed a smile. "Yes, I was indulged pretty thoroughly a few nights past, I seem to recall," he murmured, "—and I hope, my dear, you got what you came for?"

Her face blushed prettily. "Must you remind me of that?"

"Why not?" he said, wondering if he should put his monastic days behind him and send caution straight to hell. "I think of it every night when I thrash about in my little bed, tormented by a cockstand hard enough to drive a rail spike and that vision of your full, bare breasts. Why should I suffer alone?"

"Good Lord," she murmured, the flush running down her throat—but it was not entirely a flush of embarrassment.

He wanted suddenly to reach for her—to jerk her clean across the table and into his embrace. Somehow, he forced himself to stop and return to a more serious tone.

"Ah, but enough of my plain speaking," he said evenly. "Now is not the time. And I truly do wish to hear more about your family. Did they never write? Was your mother completely abandoned?"

She lifted her slender shoulders. "No, I remember occasionally seeing letters posted from Montreal or Bytown," she replied, "and before that—on one of my birthdays—Grandfather Flynt sent three thousand pounds to serve as my dowry."

"Three thousand pounds?" It wasn't much, he realized, by aristocratic standards, but it was something. "Is that what you and Richard lived on?"

Her breath caught a little oddly. "That's a rather personal question," she said. "But no, we lived on my father's largesse—or *small*-esse one might better put it. Grandpapa Flynt's three thousand barely paid off Richard's old debts."

"Ah," Hepplewood said softly.

Her expression stiffened. "It wasn't like that," she said. "For all his faults, Richard wasn't . . . coldly calculating. He never even asked what I would bring to the marriage. And I was too stupid to ask what we would live on."

"Wasn't that more a question your father should have asked?" said Hepplewood, his frustration telling, perhaps, in his tone. "As to cold calculation, I think it an underrated skill."

"How Machiavellian of you," she remarked.

But it was true, Hepplewood inwardly considered. The fact that Isabella's father had not pressed Richard Aldridge for specifics before giving his blessing to the marriage merely spoke again to his ineptitude, however kind he might have been.

Moreover, a husband, to Hepplewood's way of thinking, had damned well better be calculating. He had better be ruthless, were it required of him. The survival of his family might depend on it.

And all of these failings went a long way toward explaining Isabella's need to have someone—how had she phrased it?—yes, *someone at the helm of the ship.*

Neither her father nor her fleeting marriage had brought Isabella the security she so clearly needed. She had learned the hard way, it seemed, that men could not always be depended on.

He shook off his anger and told himself the past was not his concern. "Did your mother have siblings?" he asked, forcing a light tone.

"A brother named George," she said tightly, "but he was some years older."

"*Hmm,*" said Hepplewood, leaning back in his chair.

So far, nothing Isabella said conflicted with any of the

information Jervis had milked from Hepplewood's various sources in Liverpool.

Much of England's timber came up the River Mersey to be offloaded at Liverpool's Brunswick Dock. Because of this, Canada's timber barons sometimes kept agents, solicitors, and even offices situated in that part of town. The Flynt family had not kept an office, but Jervis had found few people on and about the Brunswick Dock to whom the name was not instantly recognizable.

"That portrait of your mother, Isabella, in your parlor," he said musingly, "was it sent to Thornhill upon your grandfather's death?"

"Thereabouts, I think. But I was no longer living there. Why? And why are you asking me these questions?"

Elbow propped on the table, he made a careless motion with his hand. "Merely curious."

"But why is it," she said, "that you get to be *merely curious* by asking me a thousand probing questions about my past, and I'm not allowed to question the slightest thing about yours?"

"I beg your pardon?"

Isabella scooted her chair back and sighed. "Never mind," she said, rising. "Anthony, I don't think I shall have any tea. I feel very tired tonight. And I think we both know that I need to go back to London soon."

He had jerked from his chair as soon as she'd stood. "I beg your pardon," he repeated, this time more harshly. "I did not mean to ask *a thousand probing questions,* Isabella. I assuredly didn't mean to give offense."

"Nor did I," she said tightly, "that day by the brook. I asked a question I thought any woman had a right to ask of her . . . her *lover*—though you were under no obligation to answer it."

"No, and I damned well didn't, did I?" he returned.

"No. You did not." Then she sighed again. "That is my very point, Anthony."

"Your point escapes me," he said a little tightly. "What does our conversation by the brook have to do with anything? And by the way, Isabella, *are* we lovers?"

"I don't know what we are." She gave the faintest lift of her shoulders. "I only know that it's hard for me to invest my heart in this—whatever one calls it—when I haven't the right to even . . ." Her words fell, and she simply shook her head.

He had come around the table, and snared her wrist. "To what?" he demanded. "What, Isabella, do you want of me?"

"Nothing," she said, shaking her head. "Well—pleasure. I can't deny it, for you'd know me for a liar. Yes, I want you. But the pleasure serves only to confuse me, I think."

"Then that makes two of us," he said darkly.

"Then why not leave me alone?" Anger flared in her eyes, deepening their color to blue-black. "Just stop . . . pursuing me, or whatever it is you're doing. Stop asking me questions, spying on my house, and dragging me off like some savage. I can handle Everett—he's nothing but bluster. What I fear I cannot handle, Anthony, is you."

"Damn you, Isabella," he rasped. "You madden me."

He jerked her against him then and kissed her until she shook. He kissed her with his mouth and his hands, plumbing deep as he stroked her.

He kissed her until her knees began to tremble and her hands were sliding beneath his coat. And when her nails curled into the hard flesh of his shoulders, he cupped her buttocks in one hand and lifted her crudely against his erection.

"There," he rasped. "Does that promise pleasure enough for you? Is that truly all you want of me?"

"No, it is all *you* want," she retorted, her breath still fast.

"I'm not good at these lovers' games, Anthony, which you seem to wish to play."

"Oh, no, Isabella, I am not playing games with you," he growled. "I never have done. I have been straight and honest with you from the beginning. And I have told you *exactly* how things are going to be."

She swallowed hard, then nodded. "Well, you've never lied to me, that is true."

"Why is it I suspect you of splitting hairs here, my dear?" he said, refusing to release her. "If you don't wish to answer my questions—if you want sex with no attachment—then by God, Isabella, I am definitely your man. Ask anyone who knows me."

"I don't have to ask." She pushed him firmly away. "I have known it firsthand."

He forced himself to step back, shocked to feel himself shaking with rage . . . or something—not fear, he prayed. And yet there was underneath it all a bone-cold terror that he might lose her entirely.

The kettle was boiling now—blowing steam hard into the room. He went to the hob and jerked it off, almost burning his thumb. He braced his hands wide on the mantelpiece, head hanging.

"*You are mine, Isabella,*" he growled without looking at her. "You are *mine*—and you ever will be. Do you hear me?"

"No, *I* am *mine,*" she said, her voice hard and steady. "You do not own me, *my lord,* and be damned to you."

He turned around then, rage exploding as he stalked toward her. "No, perhaps I do not own you, Isabella, but until I gave it up, I bloody well held the lease, didn't I?"

"You *bastard.*" She slapped him then, a cracking good blow across the face that sent his head snapping back a little.

He stalked toward her, backing her against the kitchen

wall. "Oh, you are going to pay for that, Isabella," he said, catching her chin in his hand. "And you know what I mean, don't you?"

She swallowed hard and nodded, her inky black lashes sweeping down almost modestly.

"Christ, is that what you want?" he growled. "Is that really what this is about? Or are you just hurting me out of spite?"

She drew a deep, shuddering breath. "I . . . I am not spiteful," she said, her eyes tearing a little. "But you are cruel. And I don't know what I want. You—I want *you*. I wish I did not. You confuse me, and I just—"

He kissed her again, hard and swift, forcing her head back against the wall. With one knee, he shoved her legs apart, wedging himself against her as he thrust. Desire pooled red hot and heavy as he pinned one of her wrists to her side.

She maddened him. Good God, this one was going to break him, he feared.

Just then, there was a sound near the top of the stairs. Nanny. Her voice carried, as if she was speaking to someone as she descended.

Shaking, Hepplewood released Isabella and stepped back. "Get upstairs, Isabella," he ordered.

"Up-upstairs?"

"To your bed," he growled. "Take down your hair, take off your clothes, and get that plump, pretty arse of yours between the sheets—and don't you dare lock the door on me. And by the time I've left your bed tonight, you will know with exquisite and unerring certainty *exactly* what it is you want from me."

CHAPTER 16

While waiting for the house to fall silent, Hepplewood spent the next hour praying he'd not overplayed his hand with Isabella.

Upstairs, he kissed Lissie goodnight and read the girls a silly story from her favorite book, grateful that Jemima and Caroline did not roll their eyes at the insult. Then he went down to the parlor, where Anne sat darning, and drank three fingers of brandy while looking out over the carriage drive that encircled the house, wondering if perhaps he should be on it and headed homeward—away from here and what he feared he was about to do to Isabella.

"Penny for your thoughts, old thing," said Anne from behind him.

He threw back the dregs of his brandy. "You would be wasting your money," he said.

She sighed, and after a time, her fabric stopped rustling. "Are the girls asleep?"

"I expect so," he said. "They had quite a romp today despite the rain. Thank you again, by the way, for bringing Caroline. You were right; she's made a good friend for Jemima."

"This has been a pleasant adventure for all of us," said Anne. "They are lovely girls, aren't they? Jemima and Georgina, I mean? And Mrs. Aldridge—her life cannot be easy, can it? Perhaps this has given her a bit of respite. So . . . thank you for that, Tony."

He snorted and poured another brandy. "Yes, ever the altruistic one," he muttered, "that's good old Tony for you."

"Well, you're more altruistic than most men," said Anne evenly, "and a good deal more than you credit yourself. But there—I can barely catch my breath as it is; I shall save it for the staircase."

"A good plan." He watched her reflection in the window as she gathered her sewing. "Going up, then?" he said.

She came to stand alongside him. "Yes, I'm for bed," she said on a yawn, circling a hand affectionately around his arm, "if you don't wish to talk? About . . . *anything?*"

He gave a bark of laughter. "You would be horrified," he said. Then, his gaze distant, he bent to kiss her forehead. "Goodnight, my dear. Sleep well."

"Goodnight, Tony." She started from the room, crossing the front hall with her neat, quick steps. But at the foot of the staircase, Anne turned and looked back at him.

"I think you had better ask Mrs. Aldridge to marry you," she said out of nowhere. "She won't go on like this, Tony. I really don't think she has it in her."

He turned all the way around to face her, harshly lifting one eyebrow. "Go on like what, precisely, Anne?"

Anne had the grace to blush. "Well, being . . . *not* married."

His ire stirring again, he opened his mouth to give Anne the tongue-lashing she deserved, then shut it. There was little use in denying the obvious.

"The lady is not my mistress, Anne," he said grimly, "if that's what you suggest. And to be honest, I don't fancy watching another wife die in childbed. Felicity damn near broke my heart, and I didn't even love—"

He stopped and pinched hard at the bridge of his nose.

Anne came back into the parlor, her expression softening. "Tony, there's but one way to ensure a woman doesn't die in childbed," she said, "and it has nothing to do with a marriage license—or how much you love them."

He dropped his hand, hating how cleanly Anne saw through him. She always had, damn her. It was the reason she'd so cheerfully given up marrying him, no doubt.

He cleared his throat a little roughly. "I know, logically, that you're right," he said. "But you must excuse me if I cannot see my way clear to . . . oh, for pity's sake, Anne. *Go to bed.* We are not having this discussion."

"Fine. We are not having this discussion." Anne took his hand and squeezed it hard. "But childbirth is a risk every woman runs in order to have the one thing she craves as desperately as she craves a good lover—I mean by that a good husband, preferably. And in running that risk, it is best if you let the lady in question choose."

He turned back to the window. "There is no lady in question here, Anne," he said. "Go to bed. You—and that babe you are carrying—need rest."

"Yes, we do," she said. "So I shall plead fatigue and sore feet for the foolishness of what I'm about to say next, Tony."

"What?" he snapped.

Anne sighed. "When Mrs. Aldridge gives you the boot—and she will—I am going to take her under my wing and introduce her to every eligible bachelor I know. And I know every member of the Commons, old boy, and entertain most of them in my drawing room at least once a month."

"Oh, come on, Anne!" he said. "The girl is a beauty. If she wished to be married, she would be."

"She thinks no one will have her," said Anne. "Fenster has cast a constant shadow—no, a constant threat—over her happiness. But Fenster will be dead soon, though what he thinks will scarcely matter if Philip and I embrace her as his cousin's widow. We should have done so years ago; I just never spared it a thought. But when I do, Tony . . . when I put my mind to it . . ."

"No, you never fail at anything, do you, Anne the Almighty?" he said dryly. "I know all about your political maneuverings. Go ahead then. Name your weapons."

"Well, Philip's brother Edward," she suggested. "He's newly widowed, and a—"

"—a dead bore," Hepplewood interjected. "You'll have to do better than that, old girl."

She rattled off six more names, all reasonably wealthy, highly regarded gentlemen—and not a one of them, he inwardly considered, capable of giving Isabella what she craved. They were political dilettantes, mostly, who would merely kowtow to her beauty and put the woman on a pedestal. Or worse, humor her.

Isabella did not need to be humored. She needed a strong man with a strong hand. She needed, at least once in a while, to feel free to yield control to someone she could trust. And unless he missed his guess, she was bloody damned tired of being the only capable person in the room.

She had told Lady Petershaw she would never remarry. He halfway believed that was true. Perhaps her short union with Richard Aldridge had shaken her so badly that she never wished to throw in her lot with another man as long as she lived.

But she damn sure needed one in her bed.

He drank down the rest of his brandy and set the glass on the sideboard with a firm *thunk*.

"Go to bed, Anne," he said again. "I was a fool to throw down the gauntlet. Go ahead and marry off Mrs. Aldridge if you can. I wish her nothing but happy."

"Oh, not *now*," said Anne lightly. "I love you too well to break your heart. I shall wait until she washes her hands of you. That way, I shall feel less guilt."

He returned to his post by the window, but it was too dark to see anything now. After a time, Anne surrendered to his silence and went on her way up the stairs. But she had raised an ugly point, and one that had been nagging at him.

He was selfish. Selfish where his needs and his desires were concerned and unable, it seemed, to stop himself where Isabella was concerned. He had justified dragging her up to Greenwood by telling himself it would be easier to watch over her, but it would have been better for her—and far easier on his heart—to have simply hired another brace of armed guards to watch her and her sisters.

But he had chosen not to do that.

Worse, he had just lied to Anne. He would never let another man touch Isabella. He would do whatever it took. Yes, he would marry her if he had to—if she threw down an ultimatum—and he would do it out of selfishness. Perhaps he could live without her, and survive by merely watching her from afar, but he would never willingly watch her go to another man's bed.

And it was out of selfishness that he waited until the house was still and the moon high, then crossed the dark passageway between their bedchambers in nothing but his drawers. Pushing open her door on faintly creaking hinges, he was assailed by Isabella's scent. He could see her in a shaft of moonlight that cut through the open drapes, sitting half up in bed, her eyes open wide.

Something like joy surged. She was waiting for him.

"Turn up the lamp," he ordered.

He turned to lock the door, then shot the extra bolt he'd added when he'd bought Greenwood. He expected he might need it now.

With Isabella's gaze following him, he crossed the room, unfastening the tie of his drawers as he went. They hung loose about his hips as he settled one knee on her bed and dragged her hard against him, burying his face in the turn of her neck.

"I apologize," he said hoarsely, one hand plunging into the hair at the back of her head. "I apologize for suggesting that I ever owned you. I let my hurt and temper best me, and it was vile."

He felt her swallow hard. "But it was not untrue, was it?" she said. "I sold myself. It is always the truth which most hurts us."

He opened his mouth against her neck and drew in her warm, soapy scent. "No one will ever own you, Isabella," he said. "Your price is so far above rubies, no man could pay it. But you are *mine,* Isabella, and always will be. You were meant for me, God help you."

"I . . . I don't know what that means," she said.

"It means there's something dark and hard and sweet between us," he said, "and I will not give it up. Not ever. Not unless you look me in the eyes and tell me you no longer desire me or what I can give you. Do you understand?"

She shook her head, her hair scrubbing his shoulder. "I don't understand anything," she whispered. "Least of all these . . . these things I want."

He lifted his head to look at her and held her a little away. "That's my job, Isabella," he said. "And I do understand you. I understand what you need."

"And what's my job?" she asked, her gaze falling.

"To submit to me," he whispered, tipping up her chin, "when we're like this. Together, in bed. At least for tonight."

He felt a shudder run through her. "We aren't supposed to be *like this* at all," she said, her voice a strident whisper. "I keep telling myself, Anthony, that I'll give you up. That I'll say no. That I'll stop wanting . . . what you do to me. If I'm so bloody strong, why can't I do those things?"

"Because you are mine," he said again, tightening his grip, "and your heart knows it—as my heart knows what you need. Isabella, do you trust me?"

She almost nodded.

He brushed his lips over hers. "I know, love, that I'm riddled with faults," he said, "but have I ever lied to you? Failed to keep a promise? Failed to make you shudder until you were lost to the pleasure? Or even remotely misled you in any way?"

"No," she said. "But I wish I . . . I understood you—*us*—better."

"That aside, do you trust me to take care of you?" he pressed. "To have your interests—and the girls' interests—at heart?"

This time her nod was stronger. "I do. And I'm sorry I struck you, but . . ."

"But I asked for it?" He smiled. "You need to make it up to me, love."

Her face was growing pink. "How?"

"By telling me what you need," he said, stroking the back

of his hand over her cheek, "and letting me give it to you. And by doing everything I ask."

"I . . . I need you, apparently," she said.

He shook his head, then kissed her deep, pushing her back into the bank of pillows. He thrust slowly inside her mouth, pressing her hands into the bed, forcing her to hold still. After a moment, she sighed into his mouth, lifting herself against him.

Ah, sweet surrender—or the beginnings of it.

He tore his lips from hers and let his grip slide to her wrists. "Tell me," he rasped, "what you need."

"You," she said again, "inside me. *Hard.*"

"And?"

She swallowed and looked away. He released one wrist and forced her face back into his. "Isabella, look at me," he said. "Talk to me. What did you mean in the kitchen just now? When you called me cruel? I'm not, you know."

"Open the chest," she said, closing her eyes. "Just . . . open it. *Please.*"

"There's no going back, love, if I open that secret drawer," he said. "You will be mine to do with as I please. Unless you tell me to *stop.* And if you do, I will. *Completely.* And then I will walk out that door."

Her eyes flew open. "And . . . never come back?"

He shook his head. "I will always come back to you," he rasped, "until you tell me you don't want me. Until you tell me you don't need . . . this. But not tonight. No, I will not come back tonight."

She shut her eyes again and swallowed hard. "You are the devil," she choked. "Open the box."

"No, I have a slightly different plan, my love."

He rose onto his knees, drawers hanging seductively off

his hip bones, and reached high above his head for the hook he kept hidden, tucked into the pleats of the canopy. It fell some eighteen inches, the shiny metal chain dancing a little wickedly in the moonlight.

Her eyes flew open, luminous saucers. "Th-that is *not* the box," she said.

"No, that's payback," he said, swiveling around to sit on the edge of the bed.

He stood and shucked his drawers, his cock already hard. Isabella was watching him, her eyes both greedy and uneasy. He stroked a hand down his length and watched her eyes warm.

"If you are very good, my love, you can have this," he whispered. "Where would you like it?"

"I . . . I don't know," she said, her innocent gaze coming up to catch his.

"Liar, Isabella," he said, turning the chest on its axis without breaking their gaze.

"Between my legs," she whispered, licking her lips.

"Wrong answer," he said, leaning sideways an inch. He clicked the latch and slid out the deep, hidden drawer. He took out the little crop and his length of braided white silk—a rope of sorts, but a gentle one.

"What is the right answer?" she asked, scooting up in bed anxiously.

He tossed the rope into her lap. "Wherever I want it," he said with a muted smile. "Say it, love, please? *I want your cock inside me, Tony—and I'll take it wherever you choose to put it.*"

"And wh-what if I don't?" she said. "Don't want it in . . . a particular place?"

He shrugged. "Then I shall have to punish you," he said evenly, "for being disobedient. Are you disobedient, Isabella? Certainly you are willful—a trait I find wildly erotic, by the way."

"I won't be disobedient," she said, "—I don't *think*."

He laughed and took the matched set of ivory dildos from their velvet slots. "You may choose to be obedient or disobedient," he reminded her, tossing them onto her pillows. "And you may tell me to stop. But what happens then?"

"You . . . stop?" she said.

"And leave," he said firmly. "I won't even let you keep my ivory pretties for comfort. And let me remind you, my love, that I am stone-cold sober. My defenses are not down. You'll not get another easy fuck out of me tonight. Another night? Yes, no doubt. But not this one. Are we in agreement?"

She cast her gaze up at the canopy. "Are you going to . . . to chain me?"

"For a little while," he confessed, "unless you say . . . what, love?"

"*Stop*," she said.

"Good." He managed to smile at her, but this was getting deadly serious. He bent down and stripped the covers back off the bed. She was still in her drawers, he realized.

"Oh, love." He shook his head with a *tsk-tsk*. "That is *not* naked. Quite a blot on your copybook, my girl. A lesser man might crop your arse just for that."

He was nearly certain it was disappointment he saw flicker in her eyes.

He cleared his throat a little roughly. "Actually, I feel suddenly quite . . . *lesser*," he added. "Yes, I'd better make my point right now."

"M-make your point?"

"That this is about you, love, giving in to me," he said. "About remembering who is in charge. Get up, Isabella, and take those off this instant."

She did so, scooting swiftly off the bed and untying them with fingers that were awkward beneath his gaze. The knot caught, and with it her breath, but she worked it loose, and the fine lawn whispered down her legs.

Long, slender legs that made his mouth water, and between them lay heaven's gate.

"Come here," he said gruffly, "and bend over my thighs."

"Are you going to crop me?"

"Unless you say *stop*," he said, "yes, I very much think I must. Because you were disobedient, my love. And I think you did it deliberately. Did you?"

She did not answer but instead bent dutifully over his knees and set her forehead to the coverlet almost submissively. "You *are* cruel," she whispered.

He chuckled and picked up the crop in his right hand. "No, I am *in control*," he said, "and that's precisely what you need."

Then, ever so gently, he drew the length of the black leather through the sweet cleft of her cheeks, drawing it deep enough to make her twitch.

She made a sound, the faintest moan.

"Oh, Isabella." He withdrew the crop and gave her a stinging snap. She jumped and gave a muted cry. He tossed it back on the bed and bent low, pressing his lips to the faint pink stripe. Then he tenderly slipped his finger into her cleft, drew it down and around to give her moist nub a grazing stroke.

"*Ohh,*" she whispered.

Something carnal and untamed surged suddenly through him. "Tonight, love, you are mine," he said, brushing the sweet, sweet spot again. "This is mine. You are mine, to take as I please. Are we agreed?"

"Y-yes," she whispered, writhing a little.

Gently, he pushed her knees apart.

"You will taste so sweet, love," he said, gently easing a finger into her silky passage. "I must have more of that—eventually. But for now, up with you. I need a little something."

She lifted herself up with what felt like reluctance. "You may have whatever you please," she said, her voice thick.

"Good girl," he said. "I think that now I would like . . . yes, that wonderful talent of yours." He took her hand and drew it down his length, now hard as the bedpost, and throbbing. "Yes, on your knees, my girl."

She nodded, then almost sunk into the floor.

"Now that is a lovely sight," he said admiringly, drawing her back up again. "Are you not going to be remotely disobedient, my love? I confess to some slight disappointment. I should very much like to sting those pale, pretty cheeks of yours again. Just enough, perhaps, to make you squirm?"

"Oh," she said throatily.

He smiled and tugged her onto the bed. "Are you squirming, Isabella?" he asked, his voice low. "Certainly you aren't saying *stop* yet."

"I am not saying stop," she agreed, her breasts wobbling seductively as she crawled onto the bed.

"Then between my legs, wench, and on your knees."

He turned and propped himself like some grand pasha against her pillows, one arm behind his head, looking down his chest at her. She came up the mattress on hands and knees, and settled between his legs, her curtain of silken hair teasing over his thigh. Taking him into her warm, capable hands, she sucked his head into her mouth.

His whole body jerked, causing him to hiss between his teeth.

For an instant, she flicked her gaze up, eyes wide.

"Don't stop," he moaned, thrusting his fingers into her hair to still her from pulling back. "Oh, Isabella. So, oh . . . just . . . *don't* stop."

Good it was—and yet still artless. But she didn't stop. For long moments, Isabella stroked him, wrapping her fingers around his shaft and letting her lips slide over his head, gently raking her teeth across his heated flesh.

Dear God, he thought. *It could feel no better than this.*

It was so bloody easy, he knew, for a chap to fancy himself in headlong love when a woman was on her knees with his cock buried deep in her mouth. But Hepplewood was not such a fool as all that; he'd had countless lovers doing precisely this—and nearly all of them better at it.

And yet not as good. No, not nearly. And as Isabella drew him deep with her sweet and unpracticed strokes, and he felt release edging nearer and nearer until it was all but thrumming through him, he *knew* that he was in love. Truly and deeply so.

And he knew it was no misjudgment; that it had nothing to do with gratitude for some fleeting, physical pleasure. No, it was real—desperately so—and he knew, too, that he would take her on whatever terms she laid out. That the moment of cold fear he'd felt in the kitchen was probably going to pale to what would happen to him in the end.

Yes, in the end, he would be the one on his knees.

He would be the one begging. For her. *For this.*

He fisted one hand in the sheets and let Isabella suck the sweet release right through him, his loins jerking with it, his abdomen seizing tight as a washboard as he felt his seed flood forth, his bollocks spasming.

When he returned from the heights of sensual bliss, it was to find her cheek resting on his stomach and her hand set to his heart.

"You feel so strong," she murmured, turning her head to kiss the trail of dark hair down his belly. "You feel so . . . blatantly *male,* Anthony."

He managed to laugh. "I think you like that, Isabella," he said. "Get up, love. I want to look at you—for to my mind, there was never a woman more blatantly female."

She pushed back up onto her knees, her fingers splayed upon his chest. He felt blindly beside him and found the white silk rope. "Yes, let's put you on display, my love," he managed, tossing it to her. "Kindly tie one end of that rope to each of your wrists."

She curled her legs under her and sat up. "I . . . don't think I can," she said.

"Are you saying *stop*?" he asked very quietly. "Or are you being disobedient?"

Something dark glittered in her gaze. "Not stop," she managed, "but I don't know how to tie both . . ."

"Disobedient, then." He rolled onto his knees, his back to the headboard, sending the ivories rolling off the adjacent pillow. He watched her cut a dark look at them.

"You can guess, I daresay, what those are for?"

She paled a little. "One of them, perhaps," she said, the words coming out thick.

"The other one—the smaller one—that is to coax your little rosebud, my love," he murmured. "Isabella, do you trust me?"

She nodded. "But w-what does it do?" she whispered. "Or may I not ask questions?"

"It snugs things up a little, my love," he said. "It creates just a little extra pressure in a very special way. Will you let me use it?"

"I . . . I am not sure," she whispered.

"Ah, the lady reserves judgment," he murmured on a

low chuckle. "Very wise. Now, your wrists, my love, if you please?"

Still up on his knees, he took the little rope, tied one end tight around her left wrist, then looped it gently over her right in a sort of slipknot. Her eyes never left their hands. He could feel the heat of her gaze and the unasked question on her lips.

She was curious. Eager. And yet still a little uncertain of her own needs.

"Isabella?" he asked.

"Y-yes?"

"What are you thinking?" he said. "Talk to me."

Her gaze came up to his, uncertain yet hungry. "I'm thinking," she said, "that there must be something wrong with me."

He shook his head. "You are the most not-wrong woman I've ever met," he said honestly. "You are the most perfect, inside and out."

"But you . . . you are so demanding," she said, "and you make me so angry. And then you tell me what to do . . . and like some little lamb, I just . . . *do it*. And I want it. I want *this*."

He shook his head and looped another knot. "Oh, if you were really doing what I want, love, you'd be on your knees with my cock in your mouth every day," he said softly, refusing to hold her gaze. "Not running a bookshop. Not scrabbling to make a living. You'd be mine to command, in every way. Mine to hold and to care for. But you're not. And so I merely console myself with these few rare moments of bending you to my will."

To this, she said nothing—but he could feel her gaze burning into him as he tied. When he was done, he gave it a little tug, and she jerked instinctively against it.

"Is it overly painful?" he rasped, running his finger underneath the loop.

"N-not yet," she said.

He flicked his gaze up and caught her wide, lovely eyes. "Do you wish it to be?" he asked, his voice dropping suggestively. "I'll give you whatever you need, love. I need only to know."

Swiftly, she shook her head.

"Good, then." He slid a hand beneath her elbow. "All the way up on your knees, my love," he gently ordered, "and put those wicked little hands behind your head."

She hesitated, so he hitched her up himself and smacked her buttocks with the flat of his hand. "Ow!" she said, rolling fully onto her knees and lifting her arms high.

"The answer here, my love, is *Yes, right away, Tony*— unless you're being disobedient? Are you, Isabella? Do you need a little something to help you be good?"

Her eyes shied to the little crop, then she gave a short, swift shake of her head.

On a warm laugh, he kissed her deeply as he pulled the silver chain down to hook it beneath the knot that bound her wrists.

"There," he whispered when her hands were fixed just behind her head. "Oh, Isabella. Those breasts, lifted so high. So perfect and so pretty, with nipples that make my mouth water. I still think the amethysts would adorn them to perfection."

"And I think," she said darkly, "that's a fantasy destined to die unfulfilled."

He grinned. "Ah, well," he said. "I can live with that."

But her eyes had fallen to the burgeoning weight of his erection. She gave a tentative tug on the hook. "What are you doing?"

"Savoring, my dear." He lifted his hand and barely

grazed one nipple, watching, mesmerized, as it hardened again. For a lover so untutored, she was incredibly responsive. He bent his head and sucked her right nipple into the heat of his mouth.

As he'd expected, Isabella drew taut, urging herself into the caress. As he suckled her, teasing at the sweet, hard peak with his tongue, he weighed her left breast in his hand, lightly thumbing its nipple. She made a soft, breathy sound that was not quite a moan, and not quite a plea.

"What do you need, love?" he asked.

"I don't . . . don't know," she managed.

He let his hand drift down between them, making her jump. Returning his mouth to her breast, he slowly let his palm slide down the sweet swell of her belly, reveling in the reflexive shiver of her skin.

"Is it this?" he murmured, easing one finger into her already damp curls.

"*Umm,*" she said.

"Open for me, love," he commanded. "Widen your knees. The chain will give with your weight."

For an instant, she hesitated. He moved away from her then and picked up the little crop. "Isabella, I need you to do what I ask, when I ask, or say *stop,*" he said, keeping his voice low and gentle. "Do you understand? You need to surrender control to me. Can you?"

She shut her eyes tight. "I'm not sure."

She wanted something. He let his gaze drift down her, trying to puzzle out what. Her nipples were pebbled hard, and he knew she was already dripping. He drew the crop through his fingers, letting the end flick audibly.

"I think you want this again, my love," he said, repeating the motion. "Do you? Do you need me to bend you a little to my will?"

Her nipples hardened further, if such a thing were possible, but she turned her head away. He took the little crop and gave her a good stinging snap across her ivory cheeks, making them wobble.

She jerked reflexively, then "*Ohhh,*" she said.

The exhalation was almost a moan. He could practically see the lust thrumming through her. He crawled nearer and held her to him, burying his face against her neck as his cock twitched against her soft thatch.

"What's wrong with me, Tony?" she whispered.

"Nothing," he said again. "You're special, Isabella. Strong. Let me be strong tonight, love. Let me. I have you tied to the bed, after all. You're my prisoner. You might as well surrender yourself."

"But I can say *stop,*" she whispered.

He chuckled "But will I, Isabella?" he murmured. "Will I let you go? Are you sure? Or are you my sexual slave, destined to fulfill my wickedest desires?"

"I . . . I can say *stop,*" she repeated.

"Yes, but *are* you saying that?" He drew a fingertip down her cheek, between her breasts, and down her belly. "Are you unhappy, love? Shall I release you and leave?" So saying, he eased the finger back into her feminine folds again.

"No." The word came swift and certain. "Don't leave. *Don't.*"

"Then tell me what you need," he demanded. "Have you been bad?"

She bit her bottom lip and nodded.

Though the angle was awkward, he switched her buttocks again. She jerked against him and gave a soft moan.

"How bad have you been, Isabella?" he asked, just grazing her clitoris. "Have you, perhaps, missed having me in your bed these past few days?"

She nodded, her hair falling over one shoulder.

"Say it," he ordered, sliding one finger deeper into her curls.

"I have missed it," she whispered. "Terribly. Tony, you . . . you were cruel to stay away each night."

"Did you touch yourself, Isabella?" he asked. "There's no shame in it. Trust me, I know."

She shook her head.

"Liar." He took the crop and lashed her again. Her hips jerked into his. "Tell the truth."

"I . . . I need you inside me," she said breathlessly. "*Now*."

"Hmm," he said. "I think not, my love."

"Please," she said. "Just . . . may we? *Please*?"

"Not yet, love. Be patient."

He moved away and sat back on the edge of the bed to extract the thirty-foot length of black silk from his chest.

"Wh-what are you doing?"

"Binding you," he said. "I want to see you, Isabella, trussed up in this black silk strapping. I will not hurt you, love, I promise—unless you ask me to."

"D-do I have a choice?" she asked, her eyes going to the narrow band of silk as he roped it around his hand.

"Only two," he said, unsmiling. "Give yourself over to me, Isabella, for my pleasure—and, I promise, yours. Or say *stop*."

When he had unfurled half the narrow length, he wrapped it around her waist, cinched it tight, then knotted it above her hip bone. Then he drew it between her breasts, round her neck, and back down again. Two tight circles beneath her breasts, and they were thrust up high. Gently he bound her elbows nearly together at the back of her head, then finished by passing it between her hips, once around each thigh, and knotting it on the other side.

When he was finished, she was an erotic vision with her wrists behind her head, her inky black hair spilling down her back, and the long, black strap thoroughly cinching her. Isabella's nipples were hard, her thighs pulled just a little apart by the tug of the knots. The black silk cut into the plumpness of her flesh so erotically that he felt blood surge into his groin again.

"Good Lord, Isabella, but you are beautiful when bound," he whispered. "How does it feel?"

"Strange," she said.

"Do you wish me to untie it?" he asked, praying she would not say yes.

"No," she whispered.

"Then how does it feel—exactly?"

"Wicked," she said breathlessly. "Tight and wicked and . . . secure."

Secure. Yes, he thought he understood.

He made love to her with his mouth then, fisting his hand in her hair and kissing her deep. He tugged her head gently back and let his teeth rake down her neck. He drew the tip of his tongue underneath the edge of her black silk bindings and drew it down. All the way down to her breast. After that, he suckled each in turn, lightly nipping at each sweet peak until she gave a soft, thready cry.

He touched her intimately and was rewarded with a moan. Good God, his cock felt ready to explode again. For an instant, he debated simply thrusting up inside her and being done with it, but pride would not let him. He hadn't earned his reputation for discipline by surrendering to temptation.

He slid a finger inside her and was rewarded with a tightening throb. "Please," she begged. "Please. Let me loose, Tony. I need your—"

"No," he demanded gruffly. "Isabella, you are mine. You

are mine to fuck tonight—when and how I please—unless you say *stop*. We may renegotiate our terms another night. But not tonight. Tonight it's either *stop*, or you are mine, for my pleasure. Which will you have, my love?"

"I am yours," she said hoarsely. "I am yours. Just . . . *please*."

He took the larger ivory, pushed her legs wide, and slicked it through her folds.

"*Oh, God . . . ,*" she whispered, shivering.

"Are you frightened?" he asked, worried. "This is just a lover's toy, Isabella, scarcely half the size of my cock. Just a plaything."

She managed to give her head a little shake. "No." She licked her lips. "I am . . . *yours*."

"Brave girl." Gently, he slipped it in an inch, causing her to twitch a little at the invasion. "Relax, my love, and let me pleasure you," he said. "Yes, like that."

Another inch, and then another, and after a time, she shut her eyes, let her head fall back, and rode down, almost to his hand. "*Aaahh,*" she breathed, taking the length of it.

"So greedy," he murmured, easing it back and forth. "Oh, Isabella. I worship you."

Still lightly holding the ivory in place, he shifted his weight low onto his elbow and stretched out. Dipping his head, he drew his tongue lightly through her soft folds. Isabella made the sound again—a slow exhalation of pleasure.

Again, he teased lightly, drawing his tongue deeper this time, until he felt her quivering bud. She would not last long, he thought, for she'd not yet learned discipline. Beneath the black silk strapping, her nipples were full and hard, her head already tipped back as if release edged near.

He drew the ivory shaft out a little, and Isabella gave a whimpering sound of disappointment. This time, he let his tongue play over her jewel of a clit and kept it there, slicking the shaft up again and pressing it hard against the front wall of her sheath, in that sweet and perfect spot that almost always maddened a woman.

It maddened her. Isabella began to shake down to her bones, drawing down hard on the silk rope, her whole body straining against it. And then he slicked the rod back and forth again and felt her juices burst forth. She bowed backward, her mouth open on a soft, almost silent cry of release.

He wanted to take her then and there, still bound and tied. He held fast as long as he could, and when her trembling eased, he let the ivory go, rolling up onto his knees, his forehead damp with sweat, his cock already in hand. He lashed an arm about her waist and was already pulling Isabella, still shaking, onto his shaft when some semblance of control returned.

"Good Lord, woman." He let his head fall forward to touch hers, banding her tight to him as he raised his other hand to unhook the chain.

Isabella collapsed against him, almost sobbing. He buried his face against her neck and shoved his fingers into her hair, simply holding her. "Oh, love, you are so beautiful," he murmured.

Her breath was slowly returning to normal. "Oh, God," she whispered. "What did you do with . . . oh, I cannot bring myself to ask . . ."

He kissed her then, deep and sweet, threading his fingers through her hair. "Are you all right, love?" he murmured, against her cheek. "Are you exhausted?"

"No . . . *eviscerated*," she said. "But that is not *stop*, Tony."

He tipped up her chin. "Are you sure?"

She pressed herself closer and kissed him almost aggressively, thrusting her tongue into his mouth, twining it sinuously around his. Against the silken skin of Isabella's thigh, his shaft twitched impatiently.

"Good Lord," he rasped when she was done. "Turn around, my dear."

"Yes," she said in a soft, compliant voice.

His hands went to the knots of the rope and the silk bindings, impatiently unfastening. He wished to the devil he had his sharp knife, he thought grimly. He got them loose, if not completely unwrapped, before he lost all patience.

"Face down, love," he whispered, giving her a little push. "You've been so very good. Just a little more, all right?"

She nodded. "What are you going to do to me?"

"Just give you pleasure, Isabella," he murmured, his lips brushing over her temple. "Or try to. Will you let me? Will you trust me? And if you don't like it, Isabella, we shall never do it again."

She hesitated.

"Isabella," he said a little harshly, "do you trust me? Do you give yourself to me for my pleasure?"

She nodded.

"Then lie down and let me take you," he said, picking up the smaller of the ivories.

"That is odd," she said, "b-but not too large, I suppose?" This last was said almost hopefully.

"Don't look," he suggested. "I won't hurt you, Isabella. Just let me take my fill of you, love. Please. Let me take you to that sweet and exquisite place again."

She gave a short, quick nod and settled herself into the pillows, turning her head away from his chest of trinkets. Stretching, he lifted out his jar of unguent and liberally oiled his toy. Again, his shaft twitched impatiently. Damned if it wasn't taking forever to get himself buried in the girl, but he would sooner die than truly hurt her.

Gingerly, he set his hand to her left buttock, but she flinched at the touch.

"Isabella, do you need the crop?" he asked warningly.

She looked back at him, her thick black lashes fanning down. "Have I been bad?" she murmured.

"A little," he said. "The way you kissed me just now felt very wicked indeed."

Without another word, she pulled a pillow nearer and buried her face in its softness.

Well, he thought wryly, *the lady's needs must be met.*

He set aside the ivory, took the little crop, and drew it deep between her cheeks again. To his shock, Isabella shivered. He did it again, this time slipping his oiled fingers between her legs, lightly circling her clitoris. When she writhed a little against his hand, he struck her a stinging blow.

"Naughty girl," he said. "You need a little something more, don't you?"

"I need you," she rasped. "Touch me again."

He did so, slowly stroking until he felt a fresh pearl of dew. "*Ohhh,*" she whispered.

Again, the stinging blow, just enough to pink her cheeks. She writhed down on his hand, begging for something. "*Tony*—" she whispered, "*please?*"

"Wait," he whispered, laying aside the crop. "Be patient, my darling."

"But what you are doing . . . it seems so wicked. I think perhaps *you* should be cropped."

"We may negotiate that," he said, giving in to the temptation, "another night."

He forgot all about his ivory toys, and she sucked in her

breath as he entered her slick, feminine passage. "Umm," she murmured uncertainly.

Isabella lifted her shoulders, and he bent over her, letting his lips skate down the soft skin between her shoulder blades. Beneath him she felt so small and perfect. He could feel the stubble of his beard rake against her tender flesh, could feel the warmth of her skin and the dampness of her perspiration. He forced himself not to move but merely to hold himself all the way inside her, savoring the almost suspended pleasure.

He felt his cock throb impatiently. She felt it, too, and gasped.

"Love," he whispered. "Oh, Isabella. *So* sweet."

And then he could bear it no longer. He let his hands slide low, stroking the curve of her hips, and then back up, pushing wide the full, fine swells of her rear to fully thrust. On a little moan, she shifted, instinctively—urgently seeking.

In the pale moonlight, her skin seemed to glow with warmth. Her face was turned into the shadows, her mouth open on a sigh. Again and again, she urged herself against him as she rose, and he bit back his urgency, pressing himself into her at that firm, perfect angle.

She shifted, trembling a little, her silken hair fanning over one side of the pillow. He lifted his hand, tenderly stroking it back. Then he cupped her full breast, lightly plucking her hard, sweet nipple until she began to sob. He felt his hard-fought control slip, and he had to will himself not to drive himself up into her too greedily.

On knees and elbows now, Isabella rode back hard, urgently seeking. Her breath came rapidly; soft, needy gasps as her head tipped back. He struggled for control, desperate to hold himself in check; desperate to give her what she needed and bind her to him with that perfect and aching release.

Isabella began to plead with him—begging him for wicked things and using words he was shocked to hear her utter. The erotic vision drove him. He thrust fast and hard, pushing his length inside her as she began to whisper his name like a soft plea.

He lifted her, pressing himself hard against the front of her silken passage as she urged herself back against him with her instinctive grace. And when the head of his cock stroked that deep, sweet spot again, she gave a moan of intense pleasure, her hands fisting great handfuls of the bed linens, her head tipping back.

Good God, how he wanted her.

The need beat in his blood like his own pulse, and his vision began to cloud as he felt Isabella's very essence surround him. He reached out and fisted his hand in her hair, riding her like some stallion mounting a mare. Urgently pushing back to take him, she lifted her upper body, straining, and he sunk his teeth into the tender flesh of her shoulder.

On a soft cry, Isabella jerked hard and bowed back, her nails raking the pillow as he felt her begin to throb around his cock, and then splinter. Maddened by the sight, he thrust again, driving himself dangerously deep.

She cried out again, and it was as if fire and heat exploded in a blinding rush. He thrust once more and the spasms of pleasure seized him, his entire being jerking with it.

Reality dimmed, and he knew only that burning need to claim her; to spill himself deep. To push her past the point of release and bind himself to her, forged as one in the searing heat. Isabella fell into the pillows, sobbing as the pleasure wracked him.

Still pulsing deep inside her, he exhaled on a long, shuddering breath and rolled onto his side, taking her with him and spooning her back against him. "Isabella," he whispered. "Oh, Isabella, my love."

Sinking into the softness of the bed, he marveled at what she had just given him, his gentle, untutored lover. He marveled at how desperately he loved her, and tried not to let the fear choke him.

Countless lovers had come and gone from his life, but this was not the same.

Isabella was not the same.

Isabella was not replaceable. And if she were to go from his life, his life would be over. There would be nothing left for him but to raise his child and try to survive what remained.

This was, of course, hardly a new realization but one that had been growing in intensity these past many weeks. But the magnitude of it still shook him.

They drifted, with her bound in his arms, for a time, then roused to kiss and whisper and stir about before collapsing together again. Much later, in the darkest hours of the night, when the lamp was out and the moonlight pale and clear, they woke to make love again as they had done that morning in Fulham; facing one another, drowning in one another's gaze as they came. He felt himself spill deep again—spilling heart and soul into her—his elbows shaking as the spasms wracked him.

He came back to a hint of dawn on the horizon and to the realization that he was lost. He was lost to Isabella, and there was only one real solution. He knew it even as he turned the possibility over and over in his mind. But even with his need burned down to ash, he now understood that nothing he felt for her would ever change.

He lifted his hand and tucked a long lock of hair back

over her slender shoulder. How many times had he spilled his seed into her womb? Twice tonight. Once earlier in the week. They had escaped catastrophe several times before that.

It was the domination of his unconscious mind, he suspected. It was raw, male instinct—and selfishness—overwhelming his good sense.

He was going to have to make this right.

He only hoped that in doing so, he did not make things worse.

CHAPTER 17

Surrounded in warmth, Isabella stirred near dawn to a lover's touch. After drawing a lock of her hair over her shoulder, Anthony spooned himself about her, one palm settling heavily over her womb. He pressed his lips to the back of her shoulder, and lazily, she lifted her eyelids a fraction.

She could just make out, through the open draperies, a faint glow on the horizon. She stretched, and felt his lips skate up to the curve of her neck.

"*Umm,*" she said, glancing back at him. "What time is it?"

"Five, thereabouts." He moved his lips an inch higher and kissed her again, his hand making soft, almost pensive circles on her belly. "Turn round, love," he murmured against her skin. "We must talk."

She felt her heart skip a beat, but she did as he asked, turning in his embrace. "That sounds ominous," she said, her gaze searching his face in the gloom. "What about?"

He lifted his hand and tenderly tucked a loose curl behind her ear. "Things," he said vaguely. "Questions you asked once before. By the brook. Isabella, I care for you. Very much. You know that, don't you?"

She laid a fingertip to his lips. "I don't expect such words," she said. "They . . . They complicate things."

"Words do not complicate things," he said on a sigh, "but I may have done. I've been careless. Again and again. With you, I seem always to be careless."

Isabella understood then what he was speaking of, and she felt a chill of uncertainty. "It will be all right," she said. "It has to be."

"Life doesn't work that way, Isabella, and if you're carrying my child—" He stopped and shook his head. "—we'll need to marry. Perhaps that horrifies you. I don't know. If it does, I'm sorry."

Her eyes flew wide. "Tony, you cannot marry me," she said, rolling up onto her shoulder. "Think what you suggest. People will gossip. Fenster—he's not dead, nor are his ugly rumors forgotten. And I'm a nobody. By choice. My heavens, I run a bookshop."

"Come, Isabella, do you think I give a damn what people say?" he said harshly. "Do you think Fenster's poison means anything to me? You'll marry me, and I'll give you no choice."

She rolled back into the softness of the bed with a *huff*! "You may have had your wicked way with me tonight, Tony, but beyond the bed, don't dare try to bully me. You'll rue it, I promise."

He reached out and stroked her face tenderly. "Let's not argue, love, over a problem we don't yet have, hmm?" he said, gentling his tone. "But in the future—and don't say, Isabella, we have none—in the future, I promise to take more care. I know better. I do know how *not* to conceive a child. But I have been selfish, and I have not put your well-being first."

Not knowing what else to say, Isabella tucked close and set her cheek against his chest. She could hear his heartbeat, strong and steady. *He* was strong and steady. She had slowly come to understand that he was more than just a tempting—perhaps even tortured—lover. There were devils that drove him to arrogance and anger and self-loathing, but there were better angels, too.

"I will not die, Tony, bearing a child," she reassured him. "Do you think I can't see that's what you fear? I know you don't want that on your conscience. But if the worst happens, I will survive it. I am a survivor. I am not Felicity."

"Indeed, you are not," he said certainly, "for she was delicate, and you are far from it. But the worst, Isabella? What is the worst, I wonder?"

"Sometimes we don't know the answer to that question until we are deep in it," she said.

He seemed to consider her response. "You once said, Isabella, that you thought I must hate myself," he murmured, his lips pressed to the top of her head.

"I meant only that you seemed bitter inside," she said. "Beyond that, I spoke out of turn."

"But you may have spoken rightly," he said. "I'm not sure what I've let myself become. Anne . . . Anne constantly lectures."

"Because she cares for you," said Isabella. "Whatever may have happened between the two of you, Anne cares deeply. I can see that."

He gave a muted laugh. "She warned me last night I should marry you," he said. "She threatened to find a man who *would* marry you if I did not. Would you try to do that, my dear? Marry someone else?"

She did not fail to notice his use of the word *try*. "I don't mean to marry anyone," she said tightly. "I thank Anne for her kindness, but it's not negotiable."

"Still determined to keep your bookshop, *hmm*?" he murmured, brushing his lips across her eyebrow.

"I'm determined to survive," she said, "and to look after my sisters. May we speak of something else? I really don't wish to quarrel, Tony. Not after . . . last night. Not after what we shared."

For a time, he simply lay silently beside her, one arm propped behind his head, his harsh, handsome profile faintly limned by the approaching dawn. Isabella could feel his mind working and the ponderous weight of words left unsaid.

She sat up, lit the lamp, and turned it low, wondering what next to do or to say.

After a time, he stirred, as if from a dream. "May I answer your question, then?" he said, his voice oddly weary. "The one you asked days ago?"

She looked over her shoulder at him. "When we quarreled about Anne?"

He sighed. "Yes, but my reticence wasn't about Anne," he said. "It's about what I am, Isabella. My misjudgments. My mistakes. It . . . It does not cast me in a good light."

"Oh," she said quietly, turning back into the bed.

He cleared his throat. "Still, it does have to do with why Anne and I never married," he admitted. "I owe you that, Isabella. I know I do. I owe you something of myself. But be warned, the tale is vile."

She drew the covers back up to her chin. "Anthony, were you unfaithful to Anne?"

His mouth twisted bitterly. "Define *unfaithful*," he said. "I did not treat Anne as I ought to have done, certainly. But she did not break my heart, Isabella. She did not."

For an instant, she hesitated. "Thank you," she said, letting out her breath on a rush. "Thank you for telling me that."

"Oh, she stung my male pride, mind you," he added, "but my heart has ever remained intact."

"*Are* you prideful? I had not noticed." Then she sobered her words. "Yes, Tony, I should like to hear the truth of what happened."

He let out his breath very slowly. "I don't want to tell you, to be honest. But it's not right to refuse. Not . . . given what you and I have become. But the truth—and my role in it— well, it may disgust you. The sins of omission, Isabella, can sometimes do the worst amount of harm, no matter how we may lie to ourselves."

Isabella said nothing; she neither insisted he speak nor let him off the hook. After last night, she had the strangest feeling they needed to settle this—whatever this was— because something in their relationship had passed the point of no return. Still, before she stepped off so high a ledge, she needed to understand what had made him into that furious, foreboding man she'd met at Loughford.

As a boy, he was a very sweet sort, Lady Petershaw had said. *So very charming and kind—and so unflaggingly devoted to his lovers. . . .*

But what had happened to that sweet and charming boy? What had happened between Anthony and Anne to bring him to such a dark place? Isabella drew a deep breath and tried not to let her imagination run wild.

He kissed her hair again, and she relaxed into his arms. She had the oddest feeling he did not wish to look her in the eye; as if he was already looking back at the past, perhaps.

He finally turned toward her. "Yes, Anne and I had been brought up expecting we'd be betrothed," he said, "and though we rarely spoke of it, we were not unhappy about it. I was older than Anne, but we were close. I looked after her—and after Diana, who was a little older than Anne. I lived many years, Isabella, content that my future was settled and that I was spoken for once Anne had grown up."

"But what happened to change that?"

"Diana," he said. "Diana . . . happened."

"Diana?" Isabella crooked her head to look at him, some snippet of Lady Petershaw's gossip returning to the forefront of her mind. "And she was . . . a cousin, too, yes?"

"On Father's side," he said, "not Mother's. Though they treated her as family, Anne and Gwen and Bea shared no blood with Diana. Diana's father was our estate agent, and they lived in a fine manor house at Loughford. You may have seen it, near the gates leading in from the village?"

She nodded, her hair scrubbing the pillowslip. "I thought at first it *was* Loughford. Not many estate agents have a home so grand."

"He was Father's cousin," Hepplewood repeated. "Edgar Jeffers. Edgar met my governess—more of a nurse, really, for I was honestly too young for a governess—and they married. But she died three years later, and Edgar had little use for Diana. He'd wanted a son, my father said. So when Diana was quite small, she more or less came to live with us."

"Like a little sister?"

"Exactly like that," he said. "But she never seemed entirely happy. I think she felt her father's ambivalence keenly. So with my father's blessing, Mamma took Diana under her wing and more or less raised her."

"How did you feel about that?" Isabella gently probed. "Were you jealous?"

"No, I never felt my parents' love was a finite thing."

He shook his head. "I was glad for Diana. I . . . pitied her, really. We all did—Gwen and Anne and I. I did not grasp until years later how very much she resented that pity, or how very much she had attached herself to me. It was as if Mamma and Father and I were all she had."

"It sounds as if you were," said Isabella grimly. "And her father sounds unpleasant."

"No, just a bitter and chronic inebriate," he replied. "In any case, when Diana was perhaps fourteen, Gwen began to tease her about my marrying Anne. Gwen could always sense a person's vulnerabilities, and the teasing set Diana off somehow. She cried, and hid in our family suite at Burlingame for two days. Then she came to me and said that *she* wished to marry me—that she would die without me—and would I have her in place of Anne?"

"Oh, my God," said Isabella.

"She seemed quite desperate, like someone drowning," he said. "I told her that I was promised to Anne but that she was a part of our family and always would be."

"Did that placate her?"

"A little, perhaps," he said, "but my parents saw what was happening and sent me away to university. I hated it. I loved Loughford and just wanted to learn to manage the estate, for even then I could see it was flagging under Edgar's management and Father's neglect."

"Your father was busy serving the nation."

"Yes, well, that was the excuse we all used at the time," he said a little bitterly. "In any case, I managed to get myself sent down—deliberate mischief, mostly—but Mamma just told me to go spend some time with Father in Clarges Street. But he was always in Whitehall, or at the Palace. And in London, there are all manner of vices to amuse a bored young man."

"I daresay," murmured Isabella. "I wonder what Anne thought?"

"Anne was still in the schoolroom," he said on a harsh laugh, "whilst I was being educated, too—but in places like *La Séductrice*'s salons, or the gaming hells. I think I imagined that Anne's good nature would eventually save me from myself."

"Dear heaven." Apparently everything Lady Petershaw had told Isabella was quite true.

"Anne soon came of age," he went on, "but her mother was frail, so Mamma was asked to bring her out. And thinking Anne's come-out a mere formality before our wedding, Mamma decided to launch Diana, too, though she was probably nineteen by then. My father had settled a dowry of twenty thousand on Diana, but she'd refused to have a Season two years running."

"She was . . . what? Holding out?"

He shrugged. "I suppose," he said, "but this time, Mamma gave her no choice. So there we all were in Clarges Street, with Anne and Diana being dragged from one ball to another, and me hanging on the fringe, trying to look like a dutiful fiancé-in-waiting."

"What was that like?"

"Hell," he said. "Sir Philip Keaton took to snatching all Anne's waltzes and giving me nasty, sidelong looks every time we crossed paths. One night in Pall Mall, he shoved me up against the door of the Athenaeum with his stick across my throat and told me I was nothing but a wastrel and a libertine, and not good enough to kiss Anne's muddied hems—all of which was true, but I bloodied his nose for his insolence, then splintered the damned stick over his head. And Anne, to her credit, kept speaking of our marriage as if it were a done thing."

"But Diana, I expect, did not?"

"No," he murmured. "She played the wallflower and refused every man who approached. She began to . . . to throw herself at me in a way Anne never had. And I was vain and flattered and couldn't bear to hurt her. Then one night Anne came into the salon and saw us kissing—I didn't start it, but I was damned sure in the process of finishing it—and Anne just snapped. She told me to burn in hell, then she rousted Mamma out of bed and told her she was accepting Sir Philip Keaton's suit."

"How did you feel?"

"Devastated," he said. "Ashamed. Like I'd let Anne down. But Anne . . . it was as if she'd got her freedom at last. Freedom from expectations. Freedom to pursue a man who was far more compatible with her than I could ever have been. She was . . . happy."

"And what of Diana?"

"A week later, I said yes," he answered. "Why not? Anne had given me up with scarcely a backward glance, and my young man's pride was scalded."

"Oh, poor you," said Isabella dryly.

"Yes, yes, I know." He rolled his eyes. "I was hot-tempered and used to being pursued by women. But by the time it all blew up—or rather, by the time I managed to blow it up—I just wanted to be settled. I just wanted to be married, and to go home to Loughford. So I went to Mamma and told her it was done."

"That what was done?"

"I told her it was Diana or no one. That Diana needed me, and I loved her and wanted her happy. And why not Diana? An heir has to marry—or so they kept telling me. So after pitching a great row about how Diana wasn't good enough for me, Mamma surrendered and went to my father and said that she was at her wit's end keeping us apart, and permission had to be given."

"But your father refused?"

"Vehemently."

"Why?"

"Father simply said it would not do," he answered. "But Mamma was convinced—rightly—that I meant my ultimatum. She set in on him relentlessly until, one day, there was a great, explosive row. Mamma came out of his study, utterly wild, and after a few short, ugly words to me, she went to her room and just started bawling—which I'd never seen in the whole of my life."

"Good Lord," said Isabella. "Then what happened?"

He shrugged wanly. "Essentially, nothing," he said. "I spent a couple of years whoring, gaming, and steeping myself in dissolution, and Diana was relegated to being Mamma's spinster companion at Burlingame. Diana's father continued to drink. My father continued to politic. Loughford continued to deteriorate. Then one day Father died. And suddenly I was Hepplewood. Philip had to drag me out of a whorehouse in Covent Garden to tell me he was on his deathbed. Apt, I suppose."

"Tragic, I'd have said."

"In any case, Mamma said I'd better marry money quickly or Loughford was done for. I resented being slung about like some matrimonial prize, so to spite her, I settled on the daughter of a Midlands industrialist—a very uncouth man with enough money to buy all of Manchester."

"Felicity," murmured Isabella.

"Yes," he said, "and then I dragged her up to Burlingame, where all the family was gathered to celebrate my cousin Royden's betrothal, and I flung her in everyone's face. Oh, and I seduced her and got her with child. Oh, and did I mention she was Anne's best friend? That's how we met."

The self-loathing was rich in his voice now, along with his sarcasm.

"How did Diana take it?"

He hesitated. "Very badly," he finally whispered. "She tricked Felicity up to the observatory tower and tried to push the poor girl to her death. Until then, we'd all thought Diana merely introspective and a little odd. Turns out she was stark staring mad. A lot of other ugly things came to light that day, too. It was horrific, really."

"Dear God," said Isabella. "Did . . . did they imprison Diana?"

He shook his head. "No, Royden had influence in the Home Office," he said, "and covered it up. Felicity abandoned me, terrified, and ran home to her father. Gwen whisked Diana off to an insane asylum in France, but she withered away until cholera finally took her a couple of years ago."

Isabella lay perfectly still for a long time. "That's an awful story," she finally said. "No wonder you'd no wish to speak of it. You . . . you did not have to tell me all of it, you know."

"I felt I did," he said a little tightly. "But I have not yet done so. I have not told you that it was my fault Diana went mad. That I had within my grasp the means to . . . to help her, and I did not use it. I did not. *I* drove her mad."

"There is no way, Anthony, that Diana's actions are your fault," she said firmly. "You did not lead her on. You were a good son, and when your parents refused permission, you accepted their choice and stayed away from her."

He laughed. "Oh, Isabella, you are so naive," he said. "I was a bad son and a wastrel, and I would have married

Diana to spite them. She was in love with me, and after being chased for damn near a decade, I was in lust with her."

Isabella felt her brow furrow. "But you did not marry her."

"No," he said, "for I could not. Because of the thing Father told Mamma before she locked herself in her room and started crying."

"Yes? What?"

"He admitted to Mamma the truth he'd hidden for nearly twenty years," he said. "That Jane, my old governess, had been his mistress. And that Diana, you see, was actually my half sister."

Something inside Isabella went perfectly still. "I . . . beg your pardon?"

He drew a long, steadying breath. "Father got Jane with child," he said, "and so he manipulated Edgar into marrying her. That's how Edgar won his position and fine house at Loughford. He was a professional cuckold."

Isabella felt suddenly nauseous. It must have told on her face.

"You are disgusted," he whispered.

"I . . . I am not disgusted, Tony," she whispered. "I am . . . sad."

"What could be more abhorrent than a man kissing — and contemplating *bedding*—his own sister?" It was as if he spoke more to himself than to her. "How could one feel that sort of attraction? I ask myself that over and over. How can one not *know*? And what if my father had not stopped me?"

"One *cannot* know," she said stridently, "and that is the very point. You were lied to."

He shook his head. "My father's behavior was reprehensible, but mine was almost as bad. He hid his mistress under his wife's nose, and even after his death, I kept his vile secret to appease my mother. For years she refused to let me tell

Diana the truth, certain it would get out and make a mockery of her marriage."

"But dear God," murmured Isabella, "Diana had a right to know who her father was."

"And she had a right to know why I rejected her," he whispered. "I begged them a thousand times to explain; I could almost feel the blackness growing inside her. Oh, Father looked after Diana, in a backhanded fashion, and deceived Mother into complicity, but worldly goods don't make a child feel loved."

"The dowry did not raise suspicion?"

"It should have done, perhaps," he said quietly. "We weren't awash in cash. Everyone knew Diana was Father's particular favorite—more than Anne or Gwen, I mean—but he was careful, and with damned good reason. Still, it was wrong to hide the truth, and I *knew* it was wrong. But I was weak. I couldn't bear Mother's tears. It was cruel to Diana. It drove her mad—and it very nearly got an innocent person killed."

"Did you love her?" Isabella whispered. "Diana, I mean?"

He hesitated. "How could I not? She was beautiful and fragile, and she needed me. She believed that I was all she had."

"And your mother?"

"My mother loved to ply her *noblesse oblige* where Diana was concerned," he said, "but after she learnt Father's secret, she let Diana know in ways both large and small that she believed Diana her inferior. She was an egregious snob, my mother. But she dared not tell Diana the truth and send her packing."

"Lord, what a coil." Isabella dragged the hair back off her forehead, considering all that he had said. The room had fallen silent, but beyond the window, morning was coming on fast, the birdsong stirring with it.

Just then, there came a faint rumble in the wall behind the headboard.

Isabella jerked upright. "The dining room windows," she whispered. "Mrs. Yardley must have come in."

"Damn it," Hepplewood cursed beneath his breath. "Isabella, this—this awful business—is it going to come between us?"

She let go of the covers, searching her mind for the right words.

There was another scrape; a chair being moved, perhaps.

He sighed. "No, I had better go," he said. "Will you come down to breakfast?"

She looked at him oddly. "Of course," she said. "Why wouldn't I?"

"I don't know." He looked tired and angry as he threw back the bedcovers. He sat for a moment on the edge of the bed, elbows on his knees, the muscles of his broad back knotted with tension. "Perhaps I've given you a thorough disgust of me and my entire family. Isabella, *have* I?"

"No." She shook her head, but suddenly another sash rumbled up in the room below. "Anthony, just *go*," she said, giving him a little push, "before Lissie comes to wake you. You are right; that was a tragic and terrible story. But you were unfairly torn. There's no point now in regret."

"At this particular moment?" he said, bending over to snatch his drawers from the floor. "No, I shall have plenty of time for that later. I shall have the rest of my life."

CHAPTER 18

Unable to put the tragic story of Diana Jeffers entirely from her mind, Isabella bathed and dressed like an automaton, then hastened down the passageway to the girls' room as she did every morning just after six.

But having found herself a little sore from the night's exertions—and in more than a few places—she was slow in her ablutions. She arrived to find that Caroline and Jemima were already putting on their shoes and Lissie was nowhere to be seen. Likely the child had run down to her father's room to wake him, as was her habit.

Nanny Seawell was helping Georgina dress. "Good morning, ma'am."

"Good morning, Mrs. Seawell."

"Bella, look!" said the child, eyes widening. "Pickles slept in the dollhouse last night. Caroline made him a bed."

Isabella bent to look at the wooden dog, swaddled in a stocking and tucked inside the much-admired dollhouse. "How clever!"

Georgina scooted off Nanny's lap, attired for a day in the

out-of-doors. "Thank you, Nanny," said the child, landing lightly on her feet.

It had been a great gift Hepplewood had given her, Isabella inwardly considered: the chance to see the girls romping in the country with friends their own age, away from London's soot and traffic. The chance to relax, far from Everett's prying eyes and annoyances.

The chance to learn the truth. To glimpse, for a mere instant, behind the veil of his family's past and see the young man he'd once been; flawed and arrogant, yes, and yet so desperately, earnestly human.

But she could not long remain at Greenwood and remain afloat, too. And it simply was not possible, she told herself, to consider Hepplewood's mad notion. He had offered it up as a gentlemanly sacrifice; a desperate solution for a desperate situation, and she was not ungrateful. But unless she really was with child . . .

"Mrs. Aldridge? Is anything amiss?"

Isabella realized she had settled her hand over her belly, and Nanny Seawell was looking at her oddly.

"I was just thinking, Mrs. Seawell," said Isabella, dropping her hand, "how very kind you have been to help my sisters, and what a lovely week we've had here."

"My pleasure, ma'am." But she watched Isabella assessingly all the same.

Isabella shook off the worry and knelt to look at her younger sister. "Georgie, do you wish to dine downstairs on your best behavior?" she asked. "Or up here?"

"Here," she said swiftly. "Lissie is coming back. We're having toast soldiers and dippy eggs."

"Ah," said Isabella, winking at Nanny Seawell. "I would never interfere with that. I will go down, then. Jemma?"

The girl glanced at Caroline, and the two of them burst

into giggles. "May we have toast soldiers, too?" she finally managed.

"A good choice," said Isabella, smiling. "I shall take my dull breakfast of ordinary eggs and ordinary toast on my own, then."

But she did not dine alone; Anne was there before her, filling a plate at the sideboard. Hepplewood followed Isabella in a minute later and headed straight for the coffee.

"Good morning, Anne, Mrs. Aldridge," he said, cutting Isabella a telling look as he passed. "I trust you both slept well?"

"Thank you, yes," Isabella murmured, moving a little gingerly.

"Like the dead, and now I'm famished." Oblivious, Anne took a slice of bacon and returned to her place. "Oh, Tony, I've written Gwen. Can you post it for me?"

He turned from the sideboard to set his coffee down. "Of course," he said, drawing out her chair. "What are the two of you conspiring over now?"

Anne smiled up at him as she sat. "Why, not a thing."

"I mean to go into the village later," he said distractedly. "Just set your letter on the hall table."

"Any plans today, Isabella?" asked Anne, poking at her food. "I was thinking we might walk over that steep hill beyond Yardley's cottage, and picnic on the other side. Is it pretty, Tony?"

"Very, but too steep for you to risk." He pulled out Isabella's chair, his hand lingering perhaps a moment too long at her elbow as she sat. "I can drive you out if you wish."

"It should make for a pleasant walk," said Anne. "What do you think, Isabella?"

"It is out of the question," said Hepplewood more firmly. "The slope is too steep, and you are too far along."

"Oh, how dictatorial you are, Tony!" But Anne did look a

little chastened. "Fine. Everyone else may walk, and you may take Yardley's great Shires from the stable to haul me up."

"I think the regular carriage horses can manage, my dear, for another month or so." Hepplewood took the chair opposite Isabella, watching her a little warily.

Isabella drew a deep breath, hating what she needed to say next. "Actually, if you don't mind, Anne, I should begin preparing for the journey back to London," she said, setting her fork on the edge of her plate with an awkward *chink!* "I have begun to feel quite guilty about neglecting the shop. I must write Mrs. Barbour to expect us."

"Oh, no!" said Anne fretfully. "The children are having such fun."

"I'm not saying we must go today," said Isabella, "or even tomorrow." She cut a questioning glance at Hepplewood. "I was thinking Wednesday or Thursday, perhaps? If you would be so kind as to make the arrangements?"

Something dark and unhappy passed over his face. "Certainly, but "

Just then a slight figure appeared in the dining room doorway, one of the village girls who came in to help Mrs. Yardley from time to time.

"Begging your pardon, m'lord," she said, bobbing. "Mr. Cosley at the Arms has sent round your *Times,* sir, and the post?"

"How kind of you to bring it early," he said, motioning her in to put it down.

Blushing, she laid it on the table beside him, bobbed again, and backed her way out as if she'd just had an audience with the Queen.

"Paper, anyone?" he asked, nudging it down the table as he sorted through the letters.

"Yes, I'd like to see what the Commons is up to," Anne

declared. "I wonder they can function without my gentle hands so near the reins of power."

But Hepplewood's attention was suddenly transfixed. As if Anne had not spoken, he extracted something from amongst the post, tossed the remainder onto the newspaper, then tore the letter open almost viciously.

"Heavens, what?" asked Anne, leaning over her plate to look down the table at him. "Is someone dead?"

His eyes were darting over the lines. He seemed unaware Anne had spoken. In one motion, he refolded the letter and shoved back his chair.

"I beg your pardon," he said, his expression severe. "Jervis. An urgent matter. I must get a message to him at once. Anne, can you have your letter down in ten minutes?"

She shrugged. "Oh, never mind," she said. "Get on with your crisis."

But she spoke to her cousin's back, for Hepplewood was already striding from the room.

"Trouble at Loughford, perhaps?" Anne muttered as if to herself. Then she shrugged again, dug into her eggs, and returned to her usual breakfast banter about the children.

Isabella made mechanical responses, but her mind was still elsewhere. After a time, Anne sensed it. She settled back into her chair, her curiosity clearly piqued.

"Now what, I wonder, is going on?" she said musingly. "Have you any idea what was in Tony's letter?"

"None whatever." Isabella felt her eyes widen. "How should I?"

"Well, he left like the house was afire," said Anne a little uneasily. "I know he's a bit obsessed by things at Loughford, but he looked . . . *worried*."

"If he's so worried about Loughford, why does he prefer it here?" said Isabella, staring at the empty chair.

"Sad memories," said Anne evenly. "We all have a few, don't we?"

They do indeed, thought Isabella.

"By sad memories," she said, "you are speaking of his late wife?"

"Well, amongst other people," Anne replied. "After Lissie was born, Loughford became Aunt Hepplewood's domain—and she could be a bitter pill. As to Uncle Hepplewood, he was a great statesman, but I'm not sure he was a great father. Or a good husband."

"Felicity was your friend, I understand?" Isabella murmured.

"So Tony told you that, did he?" Anne said softly. "Yes, she was a dear friend. Her father supported one of Philip's political causes and was very rich. Vulgar, a little, but his heart was in the right place. I invited him to a charity event and met Felicity there."

"May I ask what she was like?" asked Isabella, "if you don't think me too forward?"

"She was lovely," Anne swiftly answered. "Well read and well educated, and she sang beautifully. She was charmed by Tony, of course—women always were in those days— but she did not love him. Still, I do think that if life had not taken such a terrible turn, they might have come to love one another. He meant to try, I know."

Isabella felt herself blushing.

Anne looked at her askance. "Isabella, my dear, are you perfectly all right this morning?" she said. "You seem . . . different, somehow."

"Do I?" said Isabella. "I suppose I am thinking how sad I will be to leave so beautiful and so restful a place."

"Oh, balderdash." Anne's gaze had sharpened. "Whatever is troubling you, I think you should tell me; I have a notion what it is anyway. But I waste my breath, don't I? You are the very soul of discretion."

Isabella smiled wanly. "My troubles are of the most dull and trying sort," she said. "I would not bore so new—and so kind—a friend with them."

"But what are friends for, my dear, be they new or old?" Anne suggested.

For a moment, Isabella played with her food, considering it. According to the unwritten rules of ladies' tittle-tattle, one learned a little something, then shared a little something.

Moreover, this was far from the first time Anne had encouraged her, however subtly, to discuss Lord Hepplewood. Clearly Anne wondered why her cousin had brought Isabella here—or wondered, more correctly, why he'd brought her with an entourage rather than alone, as was apparently his habit with women.

Last night had stirred in Isabella a depth of emotion she had not known she possessed, and a burning curiosity, too. She had fallen so deeply in love with Hepplewood that the very thought of giving him up entirely swamped her with grief.

And if she was choosing to return to London—which she was, for she'd little choice—then her opportunities to learn anything from Anne were fast coming to a close.

But to learn what? And to what end?

"Come, Isabella, out with it," Anne murmured. "Something has happened."

Isabella shook her head and stared at her food, uneaten. "Nothing," she said. "I merely wonder about your cousin's past. He is not precisely charming now, is he? Instead he is . . . I'm not sure how to put it, really."

Anne pursed her lips a moment. "Well, let me ask you this," she said. "What has Tony told you about his past?"

Isabella managed to laugh. "Most of his past, one gathers, is not fit for a lady's ears," she said lightly. "But he has told me what I need to know, certainly."

At that, Anne smiled and toyed for a time with the spoon perched on her saucer. "So has he told you, Isabella, that he and I were once informally betrothed?" she asked. "It was ages ago, of course."

"Actually, Lady Petershaw initially told me," Isabella replied, "not that it was any of my business. It still isn't. But I can see the two of you are very close."

Anne looked a little stricken. "But not like *that*, my dear," she said swiftly. "We are close like cousins. Like brother and sister, almost."

Isabella nodded. "I understand, Anne, truly."

"Good." Anne paused a heartbeat. "In any case, I am glad he invited us here for this little holiday. I'm glad we got to renew our acquaintance, Isabella. And I hope we can remain friends no matter what?"

"No matter what?"

"No matter what happens between you and Tony," Anne clarified. "The Aldridge family failed you, and I'm very sorry for it. I hope that we can remain friends now. You must come to one of my political salons, perhaps?"

Isabella shook her head. "I sell books now, Anne," she said. "I'm sure the kind of people you must entertain would have little interest in a shopkeeper from Knightsbridge."

Anne, to her credit, did not deny this. "Then it is their loss, my dear, but it shan't be mine, for I intend to keep our friendship somehow," she said blithely. "So if I cannot involve you in my life, might I pry into yours? Before leaving London, Tony mentioned you've had some trouble with your cousin, Lord Tafford."

Isabella really did not wish to think about it, let alone discuss it. But Anne meant well. "Yes, my cousin has suggested he wishes Georgina and Jemima to live with him," she said, dropping her gaze to her lap. "Indeed, he has hinted he might try to take them from me."

"Good Lord!" Anne's eyes widened. "How can Tafford expect to get away with such a thing?"

Isabella sighed. "He has guardianship of Georgina," she said, "so technically, he might be able to. But he has never shown the slightest interest in the girls until recently."

"Then there must be money involved," said Anne, narrowing her gaze. "With men like Tafford, there always is—your pardon, I know he is your cousin, but the man is a gazetted scoundrel. Your father must have left the child something you don't know about."

Isabella shook her head. "Father had nothing that wasn't entailed—and that was merely Thornhill, with its leaking roof and crumbling barns."

"Oh," said Anne. "Well, I am sure you'd know better than I."

"In any case," said Isabella, putting her cup down with an awkward clatter, "that was your cousin's reason for bringing us here. Just . . . to give me a little respite and take the girls beyond my cousin's reach. That is all, Anne. There will be nothing more than kindness between us after this."

"And again, my dear, you'd know better than I," Anne repeated. "But I have agitated you, and I never meant to do that. Here, let me refill our coffee."

"Thank you," said Isabella, her gaze following Anne to the sideboard.

Anne lifted the pot and tipped out a graceful stream. "Has my cousin ever told you, Isabella," she said nonchalantly, "why he and I never married?"

"I'm sure it is none of my concern," said Isabella.

Anne laughed and put down Isabella's coffee. "Well done!" she said. "But has he told you?"

"He told me you fell in love with Sir Philip," Isabella prevaricated.

"And—?" Anne settled a little ponderously back into her chair, then smoothed her loose skirts over her belly. "Pray do not tell me he blamed the whole debacle on me and suggested I was inconstant?"

"No." Isabella let her gaze drop to the tablecloth. "No, he said that he was. And he told me about Diana. And the . . . terrible things that happened. I shan't ever repeat it, of course."

Anne gave a dismissive toss of her hand. "I don't give a farthing if you do," she said. "Diana is dead, God rest her soul, and Aunt Hepplewood has gone on to her great reward."

"You did not like her," Isabella blurted. "Diana, I mean. I'm sorry; that did not come out well."

"No, I suppose I did not like Diana," said Anne musingly. "Aunt Hepplewood was just a product of her generation and class, I suppose. But Diana was always . . . *conniving*. I despise sly people. I should far rather a person be outright venal, and in my face with it."

Isabella was shocked by Anne's vehemence. "I beg your pardon," she murmured. "I was of the impression she was . . . shattered, really."

"Well, she was mad as a hatter, if that's what you mean," said Anne with asperity. "But that does not preclude being sly, does it?"

"Well, no," Isabella admitted.

"As to Tony's view, he always did have a blind spot where Diana was concerned—and she played to it, my dear. That wheedling girl nearly ruined his life, and he can feel nothing but guilt and sorrow."

"But it does sound as if her life was hard," said Isabella.

"Yes, well, whose is not, at some point?" Anne had warmed to her topic. "Look at yourself, for example."

"At . . . me?"

"Yes, you," said Anne, tossing a hand in Isabella's direction. "You had a difficult marriage and were left an impoverished widow. You were turned out of your own home and burdened with two children to raise. You have learnt to work for a living, when you were brought up to live an entirely different sort of life. Did you consider murdering anyone over it?"

"Well, yes," Isabella admitted, forcing a smile. "My cousin Everett."

Anne laughed. "Oh, Isabella, you haven't got it in you," she said. "And you certainly have not tried to trick someone who did not love you into marrying you."

Again, Isabella's gaze dropped, and she could feel her face warming. "Is that what Diana did?"

"Yes, and she—"

But Anne's words were cut off by boots thundering back down the main staircase. An instant later, Hepplewood appeared in the doorway, filling it with his height and his shoulders.

"I beg your pardon," he said in some haste. "Isabella, I fear urgent business calls me back to London. And I think . . . yes, I think that you had better go, too."

Isabella pushed back her chair a little awkwardly. Hepplewood looked more than a little distracted. A few moments earlier, he had not wished to let her go. Now, it seemed, he could not wait to be shed of her.

"Well, certainly I shall go," she said, rising. "Thank you for having us. Do we leave at once, then?"

"No, no, in the morning," he said, waving her back into

her chair. "And I do apologize for pressing you. I know ladies require time to—"

"I do not," Isabella calmly interjected. "I came here on no notice, and I'm quite capable of leaving the same way."

He turned his gaze on his cousin. "Anne?" he said. "You are welcome to stay, of course."

"What, with the life of the party leaving?" Anne pushed back her chair. "And taking my new bosom beau with him? Thank you, no. My work here is done."

"You're a good sport, cuz." Then he cut them a little bow. "Well, until dinner then, ladies. I must get a message to Jervis."

And then he was gone, the hems of his elegant frock coat almost flying out behind him.

Anne and Isabella exchanged uneasy glances.

"Well, that bodes ill," said Anne, heaving herself up again. "I supposed we'd better get packing."

CHAPTER 19

Isabella's evening passed no less restlessly than her day had done, and even before going up to bed, she knew she was destined to rise on the occasion of her final day at Greenwood Farm with a heavy heart.

As much as she had hoped he might, Hepplewood said nothing of coming to her bed one last time. Indeed, he scarcely spoke throughout dinner and retired to his study immediately thereafter, pleading letters that needed to be written.

Anne waved him off, and together she and Isabella spent the evening flipping through magazines. It was as if Hepplewood's inexplicable haste to be gone had cast a pall over the ordinarily exuberant crowd, and in the end, Isabella and Anne both went up to bed early.

After tucking the unhappy girls in, and barely forestalling an outright temper tantrum from Lissie over their upcoming departure, Isabella went straight to her room to simply stare at the empty bed and its wicked little night tables. The memories of the previous evening flooded back, making her blush despite the fact there was no one there to see.

She forced the heated memories away, drew on her plainest nightdress and wrapper, then poured herself a glass of wine from the decanter Mrs. Yardley kept filled on the dressing table. Cradling it low, she went to the deep window and stared out into a night so brilliantly moonlit she could see all the way to the wood that spanned the back of the stable yard.

Something Anne had said at breakfast kept nagging at her. *There must be money involved.*

And Anne might be right. Perhaps Isabella had needed some distance from Everett in order to question it. Pretty little girls were tuppence a dozen in London, and pretty little tweeny maids could be virtually imprisoned beneath a man's roof for not much more than that.

Why would Everett go to such lengths over Georgie and Jemma? And why would Lady Meredith keep pressing her to marry him? It had to be more than pride and ruffled feathers.

No, Anne was right, somehow. Isabella's fear of Everett's vices had made her panic and jump to conclusions. She had missed the forest for the trees.

Hepplewood would aid her in thwarting Everett and his mother, she'd come to trust, insofar as he was able. But the law was the law, and she had been chasing the matter around in her head for some time now, always returning to the same terrible conclusion.

If Everett followed through with his threat of Chancery, Isabella could see but two choices left to her. Marry Everett in order to stay with the girls. Or sell what was left of her mother's things and book the first passages to the United States she could get.

Not Ontario, she had decided; the long arm of the British judiciary could too easily reach her there. But the western territories, she'd read, were a lawless wasteland, direly in need of teachers.

It was a sickening thought, leaving England.

Leaving *Anthony*.

On impulse, she downed the rest of her wine and, after listening to be sure the household had settled, went down to see if a light still shone beneath his study door. She was not entirely certain what she meant to say, but she needed desperately to see him alone one last time.

At her light knock, he bade her enter, and she went in to find him at his desk.

He was dressed for the ease of his office, without a coat or neck cloth. His shirt was open at the throat, his burgundy silk waistcoat snug and elegant. Crisply starched shirtsleeves were rolled to the elbow, revealing the corded muscles of his arms, lightly dusted with dark hair.

Before him, in a pool of lamplight, lay a pair of large, rather ominous-looking sidearms, one of them in pieces. The tang of solvent was sharp in the air.

He had risen at once. "My carriage pistols," he said in response to her widening eyes. "I'm just cleaning them."

"Heavens," she said, circling around to better study the impressive weapons. "Expecting those highwaymen after all?"

His smile was muted. "I just didn't think you and the girls would have much use for them tomorrow."

"No. No, I should hope not."

"Isabella?" She lifted her gaze to see him looking quite intently at her. "Was there something you wanted?"

Yes, you, she nearly blurted.

But the sight of the large pistols had thrown her—indeed, Hepplewood's swift change of plans had thrown her, along with his oddly focused mood. And suddenly, she felt hesitant to question his choices.

After all, it was precisely what she'd asked him to do; to take her home to London.

She lifted her eyes to his. "Anthony, may I ask you something?"

"Certainly."

"This haste to return to Town," she said, "has it anything to do with Everett?"

He hesitated. "Yes, in a way," he said. "I've had Jervis poking about. He thinks he may have learnt something—I'm not sure what, or precisely what will come of it."

"But it isn't about the girls, really, is it?" she said pensively. "Anne got me thinking this morning after you left us at breakfast. She's less naive, I think, than I."

He gave a dark laugh. "Anne works with politicians," he said. "Nothing crushes naiveté more thoroughly, my dear. But what did she say to trouble you?"

"She remarked that Everett's behavior must have something to do with money," said Isabella. "Does it?"

He hesitated, a frown tugging at his mouth. "I cannot yet be certain, my dear," he said. "May we leave it at that for now? Can you trust me to uncover the truth? Isabella, *do you* trust me to deal with Tafford?"

"Yes," she said, the word coming swift and certain. "You cannot alter the laws of England, of course, but to the extent it is humanly possible—"

"*Humanly possible,* Isabella, suggests something is *impossible,*" he interjected, his voice lethally soft, "when almost nothing is. It's the sort of thing spineless men say when they don't want to exert enough effort or spend enough money or suffer enough pain to see a thing through."

His certainty made her breath catch. "What are you saying?"

"That I will do what I must," he answered, "to keep your family safe and to keep you happy. Never doubt it."

He'd said similar things before, but for the first time Isabella realized Hepplewood was not just serious but deadly serious. His words were not platitudes or slick reassurances meant merely to land her in his bed. Besides, she'd already been there—and she'd gone easily, too.

She pressed her shoulders back and found a calmer voice. "You are quite right," she said, "and I thank you. I'm not sure what I've done to deserve such devotion, but—"

"You are mine," he interjected, setting the gun down with a heavy *thunk*. "You are mine, Isabella, and those girls, by extension, are mine, too. Just as Lissie is yours. And we look after what is ours."

"Yes, but—"

"But just think how fast you ran to her when she fell off that wall last week," he said, gently cutting her off. "How quickly you snatched her up. Then think, Isabella, what you would have done had she fallen the other way—into the path of some carriage barreling round the drive, for example. You'd have flung yourself over, too, I don't doubt, trying to save her. That's what we do when something is ours to protect."

Isabella could only stare at him and marvel that she had ever thought him shallow. Marveled he could think himself *selfish* in any way at all. He would shoot Everett dead in a dark alley, she suddenly understood, were that, God forbid, what had to be done.

It might even be the reason he was cleaning his pistols. It was at once a chilling and a comforting thought. "Anthony, you are a blessing to me," she said, slowly returning her gaze to his.

"A strange choice of words, love."

"But true." She smiled. "By the way, you asked me something this morning," she quietly continued. "Something important. You asked if Diana changed anything between us."

"I did." After a moment's hesitation, he went on. "Well, Isabella? Does it?"

She shook her head. "No," she said. "No, I don't know, exactly, what there is between us, Anthony, or what will become of it. But I know my feelings will not change. Not ever. And I just . . . I just needed to tell you that. In case it was not obvious."

"Thank you," he said, his voice surprisingly soft.

Then he pulled her into his embrace and kissed her in that deep, soul-encompassing way of his. She loved his touch. Loved the way he banded her against him with arms like iron. The way his fingers speared into her hair to still her to his kiss.

As if she needed stilling.

As if she needed any encouragement whatever.

She was, in fact, kissing him back just as carnally, thrusting her tongue over his teeth to stroke and twine with his. She felt him shudder, then he sat down, pulling her into his lap.

Still kissing him, Isabella straddled him on her knees.

"My love," he said, kissing his way down her throat. He paused to pull free the little tie at her throat, his tongue playing over the V of her collarbone.

She pulled away, bracketing his face between her hands. "I was so afraid," she whispered, brushing her lips over his forehead, "that you would not come to me tonight."

He kissed her again more deeply, his hand fisting in the hem of her nightgown. He gave it a hard jerk, ripping a stitch. Isabella's fingers went to the buttons of his trousers, working furiously.

After pushing a little madly at the layers of his clothing, her breath already rough and a little too fast, Isabella rose up onto her knees. Her need for him was like an instant flame when it flared to life, yet it burned tonight slow and steady.

"Anthony," she softly pleaded.

He entered her gently at first, and then all the way on his second stroke, suppressing his triumphant grunt against the turn of her neck.

They loved one another at a leisurely pace, neither speaking, but instead merely looking deep into one another's eyes, the back of the chair faintly creaking with their rhythm. Isabella stroked his face, dragged her fingers through the thick tangle of his curls, then bent her head to brush her lips round the shell of his ear.

She loved him; loved the way he smelled. The way he felt inside her. The way he measured his every stroke, judging her need and her pleasure.

She loved him.

And when they came together quietly, with no more fanfare than a joyous, bone-deep shudder, Isabella buried her face against the bristle of his neck and told him so.

THEY MADE FOR quite an entourage the following morning, preparing to return to London more or less as they had come, this time with Hepplewood strapping a pair of large, bulging saddlebags onto his beast of a horse, and the boys shoving their now stubble-haired dog into their mother's carriage.

This time, Hepplewood had procured a wagon for the baggage, and his elegant traveling coach stood in the carriageway near Anne's, its black paint and gold crest gleaming, the doors thrown open to reveal the velvet banquettes. The crowning glory, however, was the massive dollhouse carried up from Mr. Yardley's shop in the breaking dawn, strapped carefully atop it.

Yardley tied the last rope, truing the bundle up tight. "There, Miss Georgina!" he said, clambering down via the coachman's box. "That'll hold her 'til you get home to London."

In the carriage drive, Isabella bent to whisper in Georgie's ear. "You must thank Mr. Yardley for his hard work," she said, "and Lord Hepplewood for his great kindness."

Eyes still wide with awe, the child shook Mr. Yardley's large paw when he extended it down to her. "Thank you, sir," she whispered. "It's wonderful."

"Ho, what's this?" said Hepplewood, turning from the saddlebags and Colossus. "I won't be content, Georgie, with a mere handshake for my part in that fine piece of architecture."

He had already knelt down, one knee bent to the ground. Georgina rushed to throw her arms about his neck. "It is the *best thing ever on earth*!" she whispered shyly. "And just like Lissie's! *Thank* you, sir."

It was, perhaps, the most words the child had ever spoken to an adult outside her family. Lissie was hanging out of the carriage, looking on with impatience but not, thank heaven, any apparent jealousy.

"Hurry, Georgie," she scolded. "Climb up with me and Pickles. I've brought checkers."

Hepplewood let the child go, looking up into Isabella's face with some intense yet inscrutable emotion in his eyes. Then slowly he rose and adjusted the hat Georgie had knocked askew.

"Make ready, Marsh," he said to the elderly coachman, who climbed slowly onto the box. "I don't mean us to stop until we see the outskirts of London, God willing."

"Yes, m'lord," said the coachman cheerfully.

On the other side of the drive, Anne was helping Nanny Seawell situate the twins inside the other carriage. Isabella moved to go up the steps, but suddenly Hepplewood caught her arm and drew her toward the back of the carriage, beyond the line of sight.

"Isabella," he rasped, his hands tight on her upper arms,

"tell me you don't regret this. Coming here. Any of this. Tell me you meant what you said last night."

She slowly nodded. "I meant it all."

He kissed her then, swift and hard, releasing her just as swiftly.

"Nothing has changed, Isabella," he said, his voice quiet but grim. "Nothing has changed for me, either. It never will. No matter what happens after today, you are still mine. Do you understand me?"

Her heart wrenching in her chest, Isabella managed to nod again.

Then he strode back around to the still-open door, pausing just long enough to hand her up inside. The carriage jerked into motion, harnesses jingling, and set off at a slow roll.

Isabella looked back to see Hepplewood mounting up, throwing his long, booted leg smoothly across the saddle and setting off behind them.

"Bella," said Georgina, "look at Lissie's tiny checkers!"

Isabella turned around to admire the little rosewood box that opened to reveal a baize game board. Checkers the size of a farthing appeared to have been carved of ebony and ivory, their undersides roughened to stick to the baize.

"How very clever," she said.

"Those might turn a pretty profit," mused Jemima, bending over the board. "And well-read children are often well traveled, too. What do you think, Bella?"

"I think you have a good eye," said Isabella, giving the girl a swift smile.

Soon books and magazines were drawn out, and the children settled happily into travel. It was hardly an arduous journey; the weather was fine and the roads essentially empty. Traveling with children as they were, Hepplewood's wish to travel straight to Town was not granted, but their brief stop at a coaching inn took less than a quarter hour.

Caroline and Jemima read the entire way, pausing sometimes to exchange books and share passages, while the younger girls played with the checkers, or rolled Pickles back and forth on the carriage floor.

Isabella merely stared through the glass at the villages spinning past and tried to focus on the week ahead and her return to normal life—assuming life could ever be normal again. Still, Jemima's remark had returned her mind to the urgency of earning a living. Business was good but not brisk, according to Mrs. Barbour. There were bills to pay and orders to receive and shelve.

On Thursday, the crate of mathematical blocks she had ordered while at Greenwood was due. They would show to good effect, she thought, in the shop's bow window.

But she could not long focus on any of these important matters, for her traitorous mind kept returning to Hepplewood. She felt far more comforted by his hard, passionate kiss in the carriage drive than was wise.

Still, there was a great deal he was not telling her. His unease was about something more than Everett's perfidy. The feeling was growing in intensity as London neared.

Money, Anne had said. But Georgina had none; Isabella was quite, quite sure. And had Jemima landed some strange windfall, the greedy Sir Charlton would have long ago snatched her away.

What else could be going on? She wracked her brain, and slowly a cold fear began to grip her.

Whatever his motivation, could Everett have initiated his case in Chancery? Could her leaving London have pushed him over the edge rather than allow his temper time to cool? And could Hepplewood have learnt of such a thing when she herself knew nothing?

Of course he could. He was a powerful man; a peer of the realm. There was little he could not discover, most likely, if he put his mind to it.

Could that be the business Mr. Jervis was seeing to? It seemed highly unlikely.

Oh, her head was beginning to pound! She felt ashamed of herself. She was doing just what Hepplewood had told her never to do—taking the counsel of her fears. Whatever Everett was up to, Hepplewood would ferret it out and help her get through it. Perhaps she should ask him to loan her one of those massive, freshly polished carriage pistols and simply shoot Everett.

Isabella forced herself to relax and settle back against the banquette, watching the girls play until they tired of their game. Then she opened a book of fairy tales and read aloud until Georgie curled up against her on the seat and drifted off to sleep. Lissie followed suit, tucking against Georgie like a drowsy puppy.

With Jemima and Caroline engaged in their own books, Isabella simply sat threading her fingers over and over through Georgie's curly, baby-fine hair. Though Anne hadn't meant anything unkind by her words, it had stung a little to hear her call Jemma and Georgie burdens.

They were not burdens. Indeed, they had never been anything less than a pure joy to Isabella—and it would be a cold day in hell before she would let them go to a man like Everett, for whatever reason.

"You are nibbling your thumbnail again," Jemima whispered across the carriage.

"I am, Jemma, aren't I?" Isabella twisted her hands together in her lap. "A bad habit."

Jemima's too-old eyes appraised her. "Is everything all right, Bella?"

"Yes, fine, sweet. I just—"

She was jolted from her explanation when Marsh abruptly stopped the carriage. Looking out, she saw they were entering the heavier traffic of London. The girls, stirred by the sudden lack of motion, began to rouse. As Marsh picked up the pace again, Isabella set about tidying Georgina and Lissie's hair as Jemima began to pack up their belongings.

In Brompton Road, they made their turn without Anne's carriage, for it had split off somewhere north of Hyde Park, taking the baggage cart along with it, since it had been decided Isabella's trunk would be brought down last.

By noon, they were drawing up before the bookshop. Isabella saw that the little *Closed* sign hung in the window. Mrs. Barbour had likely gone up for a cup of tea or to put something in the oven.

The girls said their somewhat tearful good-byes and climbed out, Hepplewood handing the two of them down like the grandest of ladies. As Jemima thanked him very prettily for his hospitality, Isabella pawed through her reticule for the key.

"Ah!" She extracted it triumphantly.

"Isabella?" Hepplewood's voice came musingly from the pavement. "Have you a key to the garden gate, by chance?"

She leaned out to see him looking up at the dollhouse a little fretfully.

"Not with me," she said.

"Well, it'll not go through, my lord," said Marsh from atop the carriage. "I can measure with a rope, but I'm telling you, it's too big for that door."

"But it will go in through Mrs. Aldridge's garden," said Hepplewood confidently. "Isabella, we had better take it round. Otherwise we're going to lose Georgie's chimney."

"Jemma," said Isabella, handing out the key, "take Georgina upstairs and ask Barby to come down and let us in through the back, won't you?"

"Yes, ma'am," said her sister.

Hepplewood shut the carriage door, and as soon as Jemima had unlocked the door to the bookshop, the carriage set off around the block. Isabella settled back into her seat with Lissie and Caroline, who looked suddenly bereft.

"I want to go back to Greenwood with Georgie," said Lissie a little petulantly. "London *stinks*."

"It does smell, doesn't it?" Isabella smiled a little dotingly at the girl. "You are a lucky young lady, Lissie, to have Greenwood as one of your homes."

The coach lurched right as they made the corner. Once the coachman had wedged the massive vehicle into the alleyway, it was a simple matter for the men to unfasten Yardley's elaborate ropes.

The garden gate was still shut. Isabella tried it and found it locked.

The dollhouse was cumbersome, Hepplewood assured her, but not heavy. They lifted it gingerly down, with Isabella watching the underside.

"*Umph*," grunted Hepplewood, hefting it upright. "Try the door again, my dear."

"Still locked." This time she knocked hard on the door. "Mrs. Barbour? *Mrs. Barbour*!"

There was no answer. Caroline and Lissie were hanging out the coach window now. Isabella looked at Hepplewood, who, to his credit, did not look remotely impatient.

She banged again, this time with the heel of her hand. Nothing.

"Set it down in the alley," she said. "I had better go round. Jemma misunderstood me."

"We're fine," said Hepplewood.

But the elderly Marsh was not fine; Isabella could see him wincing in discomfort as they maneuvered the cumbersome thing back from the gate.

Isabella turned and dashed back down the alley, round the corner, and to the shop door.

The *Closed* sign still hung in the bow window, but the vestibule door was unlocked. Isabella pushed it open, hiked up her skirts, and hastened up the stairs.

Mrs. Barbour was just coming out the door, a piece of buttered bread still in her hand.

"Have you got it?" said Isabella.

Mrs. Barbour shrieked, flinging the bread high. "Oh, Miss Bella!" she cried, spewing crumbs as she spun about. "Scared the life out o' me, you did! Just nipped in for a bite of nuncheon."

"I'm so sorry," Isabella said, reaching up the steps. "Just give me the key. They are holding the blasted thing in the alley."

Mrs. Barbour's brow furrowed. "Aye, miss? Holding what?"

"Georgina's dollhouse." Suddenly Isabella's knees went weak. "Lord Hepplewood is . . . is holding Georgie's dollhouse."

Mrs. Barbour's furrow deepened.

Suddenly Isabella could not get her breath. "Oh, dear God," she said, setting a hand over her heart. "Barby—the key. *Jemima came up for the key.* Yes?"

But Mrs. Barbour just shook her head. "Why, bless me, no, miss," she said. "I'd no notion any of you was back a'tall."

Isabella's hand clutched at the banister. And then she was screaming for Jemima. Screaming so loud it filled the darkened stairwell as she rushed back into the street.

The next few minutes passed as if in a blur. Her scream

brought Hepplewood round the corner, hooves pounding. Flinging himself from the saddle, he reached Isabella in three strides.

By the time he'd made sense of her panic, the baggage cart had drawn up, and Marsh with the carriage soon after it.

"Mills!" he barked at the footman who climbed off the cart. "Forget the baggage. Get Lissie and Caroline from the coach and take them back to Clarges Street. And don't let them out of your sight, do you hear me?"

He turned back to Isabella. Standing now in the vestibule door, she had bent down to pick up something gold and glittering.

"The front door key!" she sobbed. "Dear God, Jemma got the door open, *then dropped the key!* But she is *so* careful. Anthony, it is Everett! He has taken them! I know it!"

He was looking up and down the street assessingly. "Bloody damned right it's him," he said grimly. "But he cannot have gotten far."

Suddenly, the coachman appeared at the earl's side. "My lord, what can I do?"

"Forget the dollhouse for now, Marsh," he ordered. "Go up and down the street banging on doors until you find someone who saw those girls getting into a carriage. I want a description of it."

Isabella looked about. "On Brompton Road," she said swiftly, pointing. "The greengrocer's wife. She was sweeping the doorstep. Ask her."

"Aye, ma'am," said the coachman, hobbling away.

Isabella tried to think, pressing her fingertips into her temples. "Everett will be driving Papa's old traveling coach," she whispered. "He would not dare use an open carriage. It is dull and black, with mustard-colored wheels. Black and gold livery."

"It is remotely possible he has taken them on foot," he said, "but I doubt it."

"Jemima would never go with Everett," she declared. "He would have to drag her. He could not drag two children through Knightsbridge, Anthony, in broad daylight—*could he*? Oh, dear God! I shall never get my girls back!"

"You will have them back," said Hepplewood grimly, "before this day is out, depend on it. The bastard is taking them down to Thornhill."

"You cannot be sure," Isabella cried. "He . . . He has kidnapped them! He may go into hiding!"

"Sadly, he has not kidnapped them—not Georgina, at any rate," he said. "He has the law—or a bit of it—on his side. But then there is reality."

"Reality?"

"Never mind, my love," he said. "He is taking them to Thornhill. Because he expects and wants you to follow. They are safe enough for now. Likely he has that conniving mother of his with him."

"He wants me to *follow*?" Isabella cried. "Why? What kind of logic is that?"

"Because the bastard has a special license in his pocket this very minute," Hepplewood gritted. "I'd wager half my fortune on it."

"A . . . A *marriage* license?" she said incredulously.

Suddenly, he turned and seized her hands. "Isabella, you will not do it," he ordered her. "Do not panic. You *will not* marry that man. *Promise* me."

She looked up at him through tearing eyes and said nothing.

How could she promise anyone anything? The worst had happened. She had pressed her luck. Misjudged and dawdled. And now even fleeing England was not an option.

"Dear God, what have I done?" she whispered, blinking back the tears.

He squeezed her hands hard. "This is *not* your fault," he said. "Even I did not dream the devil would stoop to something so bold. He is desperate indeed."

"But . . . why?"

"Money," said Hepplewood beneath his breath. "Always, with his sort, it is about money."

"But the girls *haven't* any money," she cried. "Anthony, what is happening?"

"What is happening is that I am going after Jemma and Georgie," he said, releasing her hands and striding off in the direction of the cart.

"Papa!" cried Lissie, who was being carried by the footman, "why is Mills taking us?"

Hepplewood seized his daughter's hands. "Lissie, I need the coach," he said. "And I need you to be extra, extra good for a few hours. Georgie and Jemma are lost, and I must find them. You and Caroline go back to Clarges Street and wait for me, all right?"

The child nodded. "Yes, Papa," she said, eyes suddenly anxious. "Will you bring Georgie home to Clarges Street?"

He cut a swift glance over his shoulder at Isabella. "I might," he said. "We shall see. Go now, and be good, minx."

"I will watch her, sir," said Caroline Aldridge.

"Good girls, both of you," he said, peeling a banknote from a wad he'd drawn from his pocket. "Mills, give me your whip and go and find yourself another. Drive these girls home, and hand them personally into Seawell's care—oh, and find Jervis if he's got home. Tell him what has happened. That Tafford has taken the children. He'll know what to do."

"Aye, sir." The footman tugged at his forelock.

"Should we call the police?" uttered Isabella as the cart drove away.

"No, it is the very last thing we should do." Hepplewood was lashing the whip to his saddle as he spoke over his shoulder. "Isabella, you must let me deal with Tafford. Possession is nine-tenths of the law. Do you trust me?"

She merely wrung her hands. "Yes."

His task finished, Hepplewood turned on his heel and marched back toward her. "Isabella, listen to me," he said. "I know what he is up to. Do you trust me to deal with this? Do you empower me to act on your behalf and get those girls back?"

"Yes, but I am coming with—"

"You are not," he ordered. "You don't want to be a part of this if it turns ugly—which it will. You will go inside the house and pour yourself a brandy. Then *wait*."

"No," she said, gathering herself. "I will not simply sit here whilst my sisters are being carried off by that—that *villain*."

Just then Mrs. Barbour came huffing and puffing her way back up the street. "No one that direction's seen a thing, my lord," she said to Hepplewood, clearly discerning who was in charge. "Couldn't have gone out by Hyde Park, shouldn't think. Shall I take Miss Bella upstairs?"

"In a moment," he said curtly.

The coachman was hastening back from Brompton Road. "Black coach wiv brownish wheels went out that a'way wiv a screaming child in it," he said, "and turned right."

"He is trying to skirt much of Town, but he has to cross the river." Hepplewood seized the coachman's arm and drew him near. "Come here and listen carefully," he said to Marsh. "Now, Isabella, tell us how Tafford will go down to Thornhill from that direction? What is the quickest way? What roads through what villages?"

"Due south, through Croydon," she said. "It is not hard. There aren't too many options if he wishes to make any speed." Swiftly, she told them village by village, the coachman listening.

Hepplewood dropped her hands again. "I'll catch him within the hour on Colossus," he said confidently, going to his saddlebags. "You, Marsh, come on my heels. And take this up on the box with you."

Here, he handed out one of the carriage pistols.

"It's loaded, mind, but not cocked," Hepplewood said. "I've the mate on the other side. On the off chance you find him first, hold the gun to his head—but mind the mother, for she's got the only brain in the family. Tell her if she so much as twitches, you'll kill Tafford."

"Good God, sir," said the coachman.

"Don't actually kill him," said Hepplewood. "Shoot him in the foot first. Now go. I'll pass you shortly."

"Y-yes, sir." The coachman rammed the big gun down the back of his trousers and climbed up on his box.

"And please, *please* don't shoot Brooks!" Isabella cried after him. "He's Papa's former coachman. He's very kind; he will help you if he can."

Marsh tugged his forelock by way of acknowledgement. "Horses are weary, sir," he called down. "But we'll be along, I promise."

"Have a care, sir," Mrs. Barbour said. "He's up to wickedness, that one. Been here three days running with that mother of his in tow."

"Dear God," said Isabella again.

But Mr. Marsh and the coach were already rumbling back toward Brompton Road.

Mrs. Barbour looked back and forth between Isabella and

Hepplewood. "I'd best go put the kettle on," she murmured, turning and going inside to the stairs.

Gently, Hepplewood drew Isabella into the shadows of the vestibule and set the backs of his fingers to her cheek. "Go up and lie down, my dear," he said. "I'll catch Tafford, and he'll have the devil to pay then, I promise you."

"I cannot," she said. "There must be something I can do?"

He hesitated. "There is one thing that might help," he said. "Not the police, but perhaps my cousin Royden."

"Where do I find him?"

Hepplewood gave a short shake of his head. "That's half the problem," he said. "I don't know. Go down to Number Four and tell the duty sergeant you're looking for his new office. They'll know. Say nothing of the children, but just that you're a friend."

"Yes, all right." She nodded.

"He might be at Burlingame," Hepplewood warned. "Just find his office, and if he isn't there, leave a message he's needed urgently at my house. Then hurry back, and wait to hear from me. There is always the chance Jemma might escape Tafford and come home."

"Yes, yes, you are right. Thank you." Swiftly, she rose onto her toes to kiss his cheek, already faintly stubbled. "Thank you, Tony. For God's sake, be careful."

He gave her another of his swift, hard kisses—right there on the pavement—then strode away.

Her heart in her throat, Isabella watched for the second time that day as he threw himself up on the great horse and sprung the beast toward Brompton Road.

CHAPTER 20

Hepplewood made extraordinary time leaving London, passing Marsh and the carriage just beyond Hans Place, then winding his way through the midday clog of carts and carriages to cross the river at Battersea Bridge.

Colossus was by no means fresh, but the stouthearted beast pressed on at the lightest command. It was possible, Hepplewood inwardly acknowledged, that Tafford might have taken another route, but somewhere south of town they would surely merge.

Traffic soon thinned to a trickle, and the outskirts of London gave way to occasional expanses of green broken by places more village than town. Anger churning in his gut, his gaze followed every twist and turn into the distance.

Halfway along Wandsworth Common, he caught a dull, old-fashioned coach lumbering beneath the canopy of trees. Bloodlust surging, he nudged Colossus forward and waited for just the right angle.

In the next turn, however, he caught a flash of red wheels. He cursed beneath his breath and pressed on, overtaking the carriage. An hour later, with Croydon in his wake, Hepplewood began to question his judgment.

After weighing it out, however, he could still see no better plan. Georgina might be placated by sweets and coddling, but Tafford had made the mistake of snatching Jemima, too. She was no one's fool. There would be no putting that girl on a train without kicking and screaming; not unless she was drugged senseless.

No, Tafford might be a mindless brute, but his mother was too sly for that.

Certainly they would not remain in London; Jervis's information had been very clear on that point. The Canadian solicitor was to travel via Liverpool with every expectation of calling upon Isabella at Thornhill Manor in Sussex. So it was to Thornhill, then, that Isabella must be lured.

Hepplewood had kept her from Tafford's grasp just long enough, he thought, to avert true disaster. But he had not managed—unless Jervis was about to greatly surprise him—to have the Canadian gentleman intercepted. And he had not counted on sheer coincidence.

There remained, of course, the possibility that Tafford had been sly enough to bring an unknown carriage to Isabella's shop. But that was unlikely; neither Tafford nor Lady Meredith could have known that Hepplewood and Isabella would return with the children on that particular day at that particular time. And Isabella, for all that she'd been distraught, was a sensible woman. She had been very certain of the coach.

No, this kidnapping had been opportunistic, and driven by desperation. Hepplewood was sure of it. Moreover, it did not escape his understanding that the desperation had been his doing; he had suspected Tafford's motivations and had taken Isabella beyond Tafford's grasp or control.

And because of that, Tafford had panicked, and Isabella's most precious possessions had been taken from her. If he did not get those children back whole and happy, he realized, Isabella's life was over—and his, nearly, with it.

Two miles later he passed a rising, open field and, at the end of it, a small copse of trees from which a pair of farmers was emerging with a large pail, as if from taking a midday meal. A horse hitched to a plow rested in the shade and, with it, a sturdy, low-withered cob.

On impulse, Hepplewood drew up near a little stile and tipped his hat. "Have either of you fellows seen an old, black coach go past?" he enquired across the fence. "With mustard-colored wheels?"

The elder of the two removed his hat and scratched his head. "Nay, but t'was one drew up dahn by that little lane," he said, pointing, "when t'missus brought dinner dahn from the 'ouse."

"Drawn up?" Hepplewood repeated.

"Aye, coachman told our lass thought sommat sheered off in t' wheel."

"The coachman," said Hepplewood urgently, "what color livery did he wear?"

But his rapid-fire questions had unsettled the farmer, who narrowed one eye suspiciously. "Dunt recall," he said, "w' any certainty."

"Ah, well. Thanks all the same." Hepplewood tipped his hat again. "You sound like a Yorkshire man to me," he said more evenly. "I'm from Northumbria myself. What brought you south?"

The old man smiled, showing his crooked bottom teeth. "Oh, that would be t'misssus," he said. "T'was her father's place."

"The land lays beautifully," said Hepplewood sincerely.

Suddenly, the younger man stiffened and set his hand to his ear. "Comes that carriage back again."

Hepplewood spun Colossus about, staring down the hill.

"Black," said the farmer from behind him. "Black as neet, trimmed in gold, t' livery is."

Hepplewood glanced back over his shoulder, crooking an eyebrow. "Then that's the carriage I'm after," he said calmly. "Thank you kindly. What's along the lane, by the way?"

"Smithy," said the farmer, spitting into the grass. "Well, good day t' thee, sir."

Hepplewood shot him a grim smile. "It's not been an especially good one so far," he said. "And now there's going to be a spot of trouble, I'm afraid."

"Aye?" The farmer squinted. "O' what sort?"

"There were two children taken in that coach, and I mean to get them back," Hepplewood said, reaching around to extract his carriage pistol. "I'm in the right of it, just so you know. And the driver's a good sort. But still, there might be a dustup."

"None o' my business," said the farmer, turning and heading back toward the copse. "Ey up, lad, come out t'way now."

The young man followed, the pair observing from the shade as Hepplewood remained on the verge, his carriage pistol low behind the horse's withers. From this angle, Tafford likely could not see him. And the coachman, a stoop-shouldered fellow of middle years, did not know him. But he was watching warily as he rumbled up the slight rise.

When the coach was within range, Hepplewood nudged Colossus into the middle of the road and leveled the large pistol between the coachman's eyes.

"Sir, you will kindly stop," he calmly ordered, "or I will be obliged to shoot."

Eyes wide with alarm, Brooks not only stopped but also threw up both hands with a cry of alarm.

"What the devil?" called a male voice from the carriage.

"H-highwaymen, my l-lord," cried the unfortunate Brooks.

"Nonsense!" Someone was wrenching on the ancient door handle, which seemed stuck.

"Not highwaymen, Mr. Brooks," Hepplewood called up, shifting his aim to the door, "but merely Mrs. Aldridge's emissary. I mean you no harm, but I'm taking those girls Tafford kidnapped."

Brooks's alarm faded to what looked like relief, his shoulders sagging.

"Jemima," Hepplewood shouted at the carriage, "get out, and bring your sister with you."

There came a muffled shriek—followed by a succession of loud thumps, as if someone was kicking at the door. *The bastard had gagged her.*

Suddenly, the handle gave and the door flew wide, almost striking the carriage. Tafford leaped down, a nasty sneer upon his face. "Stand aside, you fool," he shouted up at Hepplewood. "These children are my wards."

Hepplewood drew a bead between Tafford's shifting eyes. "I don't give tuppence, Tafford, if they're your own blood—which, by the way, Jemima is not. I mean to take them regardless."

"Be damned to you!" Tafford flicked a glance into the depths of the carriage.

"Don't even think about it," Hepplewood warned, motioning him away from the door with the pistol's barrel. "Step to the verge, Tafford, or I shall have to shoot you in the knee."

"Stand aside," Tafford ordered, even as he leapt sideways

onto the grass. "This is none of your concern. Georgina Glaston is my ward. As to the other girl, I've her uncle's permission to take her anywhere I please."

"Then he is either callous or ignorant of what you are." Calmly, Hepplewood drew the hammer back. "Now tell the girls to climb out," he said, flicking a glance up at the box. "And you, Brooks, hold your damned horses in case I have to fire this thing."

With a sharp nod, Brooks seized the reins.

Tafford's bravado faded. "Mother, let Jemima go," he said in a tremulous voice. "Put them out, both."

"I shall not!" cried a sharp female voice from the carriage. "Drive on, Brooks, you fool."

"*Mother*!" bellowed Tafford.

Brooks looked at Hepplewood, lifting one eyebrow in silent enquiry.

"Hold those horses, Brooks," he warned again.

Suddenly, there came a short, sharp scream, followed by a flash of blue silk. "Why, you little witch!" shrieked Lady Meredith, who was descending awkwardly without the steps, clutching her hand. "The ungrateful brat bit me!"

Hepplewood chuckled.

"But you certainly shan't have them, Lord Hepplewood," she added, regaining her composure. "Dare to try it, and I'll have *you* up on charges of kidnapping. Georgina is ours, and we'll take her where we please. If Isabella wants her back, we are not unreasonable people. She may come down to Thornhill and negotiate."

"Good afternoon, Lady Meredith," he said calmly. "I'm now negotiating on Isabella's behalf. So take careful note that I'm aiming a gun at Tafford's knee and that I have a horsewhip lashed to my saddle. Then ask yourself if I seem overly concerned with the niceties of the law."

The lady shot a nasty look at her son. "Everett, *do* something!"

"By the way, Tafford," Hepplewood added, "I'm not the best shot, and this gun pulls a tad high. About eighteen inches high, sometimes. Consider where that might put a bullet."

"Mother," said Tafford, "get the girls *out*."

"You sniveling coward!" declared his mother, whirling on him. "I should let you starve to death."

"The two of you may insult one another at your leisure as soon as you reach the next inn," said Hepplewood dryly. "But I'm on a tight schedule. Jemma, get out of the carriage, and bring Georgie with you. *Do it now*."

Jemima poked her head out. "Y-yes, sir." She leapt down into the dust of the road, a man's handkerchief now hanging loosely about her throat. "I'm so sorry, sir. Everett snatched us before I could get Georgie inside our door."

"Jemima Goodrich, you ungrateful little liar!" Lady Meredith declared. "Get back in that carriage this instant!"

Jemima's anxious gaze shot to Hepplewood's.

"It is all right, Jemma," he said softly. With his free hand, he extracted his purse and tossed it toward the stile. "Just hand your sister down, then go across that stile with my purse. Tell those farmers exactly what happened to you in London, and offer them fifty pounds for the cob and its saddle. I'll deal with Cousin Everett. You don't faint at the sight of blood, do you, Jemma?"

Jemima cut a derisive glance over her shoulder. "Not *his*," she said coldly.

Then she reached up for her sister and dashed with her across the road. Georgina's eyes were wide, her cheeks streaked with tears. She snuffled, screwing one fist into her eye. *"I w-w-want Bella!"* she cried.

"Shush, Georgie, and run to those trees," said Jemima, hefting her onto the stile. In an instant, the girls had clambered over and were running toward the copse, purse in hand.

"Now," said Hepplewood, "we are going to settle this business. Mr. Brooks, you have before you two choices. You may come down off that box, go up the hill with those girls, and consider yourself out of Tafford's employment and into mine. Or you may remain on the box and drive this hapless and venal pair back to Sussex."

Brooks started down at once. "I tried to trick 'em, m'lord, into thinking the wheel damaged, but the smithy was no help."

"But—But this is unconscionable!" declared Lady Meredith. "I shall have you before the magistrate, Hepplewood! You cannot come between a man and his ward."

"Lady Meredith," said Hepplewood, dropping his voice, "by no one's definition is your son a man. He is a pervert and a coward. I do not mean him to add incest to his list of sins—which he might well try to do if those girls remain long in his possession."

"And that, sir, is *slander!*" she said, "and I shall tell the law."

"Madam, if you think you can prevail over me," he said, "then by all means find yourself a magistrate. You'll find me at home in Clarges Street."

"Everett, *do* something!" Lady Meredith stamped her foot. "Do you mean to marry Isabella or not?"

"That," said Hepplewood calmly, "will never happen. Brooks, go mount that cob, and take Georgina up before you. Tafford, you will reach into your coat pocket and pull out that special license you're carrying."

Tafford's eyes widened. "But—But—how—"

Hepplewood reached out his hand and snapped his fingers at Tafford. Brooks went hurtling over the stile with nary a backward glance.

"Everett, do not you dare!" gritted his mother, hands fisting.

"Madam, I have never yet shot a woman," said Hepplewood, shifting his aim, "but you sorely tempt me. Kindly get back into the carriage and hush. Tafford, the paper? Or the horsewhip? And don't let me choose."

A flash of white paper appeared, though Tafford's mouth was twisted bitterly.

"Ah, cooperation!" said Hepplewood. "I'll confess to some disappointment. Now, kindly rip that into twenty small pieces—and yes, I am counting."

"Everett, you damned fool!" said his mother, who had dropped the carriage steps and was stomping back up them. "That license is our only hope."

"*Tear it up, Tafford,*" warned Hepplewood, his left hand going to the horsewhip. "You have no hope. Not where Isabella is concerned. You will not enjoy so much as a ha'penny of her inheritance."

"What inheritance?" asked Tafford snidely—but he had torn the paper in two. "Isabella doesn't have two farthings to rub together."

"*Twenty pieces,*" Hepplewood repeated. "Keep ripping, old boy."

When the pieces of the marriage license lay scattering with the wind and Tafford looked thoroughly beaten, Hepplewood motioned him up onto the box.

"Good. Now get up and play John Coachman. I suggest you drive back to Sussex with your tail between your legs. But you won't, I know, for that harpy inside won't allow it."

"You're going to pay for this, Hepplewood!" shouted

Lady Meredith through the open door. "I shall have the magistrates down upon you like all the furies!"

"Have at it, ma'am," he said, watching Tafford scramble onto the coachman's seat. "Now, Tafford, drive on. And if you dare trail me back to Town, by God, stay out of my sight."

THE NEXT HOUR dragged on interminably, and in his outrage, Hepplewood could think of nothing but Isabella and the distress Tafford had caused her. He passed much of the time reassuring the girls that they would soon see their sister, and interrogating Brooks about Tafford's activities.

Though he had clearly held his employer in low esteem, Brooks knew little. But he'd been sufficiently horrified by the snatching of the children to be relieved to escape his post.

By the time the four of them crossed paths with Marsh, Hepplewood's temper had marginally cooled, though he knew their trouble with Tafford was far from over.

They stopped long enough in Croydon to leave the cob at a local livery with instructions to return him to the farmer. After putting Brooks on Colossus, Hepplewood climbed inside the carriage to reassure the girls one more time that nothing would come of Tafford's threats.

"But he said he and Isabella were to marry," said Jemima, picking at a bit of darning on her cuff. "He's giving a ball at Thornhill, he said, to celebrate the wedding. And that we were going to live there again."

"Jemma, what's Thornhill?" snuffled Georgina, her eyes still red.

"Where we used to live with Mamma," said Jemima patiently. "But I don't wish to live there now. Not with Cousin Everett."

"But you would not mind it otherwise?" Hepplewood lightly probed. "You would not, on principal, object to living in the country, I mean?"

Jemima's eyes widened. "Oh, no, sir," she said on a yawn. "We like the country very much."

"*Hmm,*" said Hepplewood. "Well, come over here, Jemma, and lean on me. Georgie, you on the other side. This was a fright, but nothing's come of it, and nothing ever will, I promise. So just close your eyes, and I'll wake you when we reach London."

"Yes, sir," said Jemima on another yawn. Then she sank against him, following his instructions to the letter as he wrapped one arm around her.

Hepplewood tipped his hat over his eyes, threw his boots onto the seat opposite, and tucked Georgie to his other side. And in a twinkling, it felt as if all might—just *might*—be right with the world.

CHAPTER 21

In Clarges Street, the arrival of the earl, accompanied by two young girls that were not his own, required some delicate explanations. To his credit, Fording, Hepplewood's butler, did not so much as crook an eyebrow when his master directed that Jemima and Georgina be taken straight up to Nanny Seawell and be given tea with Lissie in the nursery.

There was no sign of his cousin Royden, not that Hepplewood had held out much hope.

Back out on the street, he ordered Brooks to go up to the mews and get his curricle to fetch Isabella from Knightsbridge in all haste.

"What's to become of that chap?" asked Marsh, watching Brooks go.

"We shall see," said Hepplewood. "For now, train him up as an under-coachman. He'll manage the leathers well enough, but I doubt he has much Town experience."

"Reckon then you can pension me off," suggested Marsh a little sourly.

"You may certainly make that choice," said Hepplewood

evenly, "but I shan't make it for you. If all goes according to plan, I'll soon have need of another driver."

"*Hmph,*" said the coachman as Hepplewood went up the stairs. "Well. I'd best go help with the curricle. Like as not the poor clod'll be hitching up the wagon instead."

"I trust you'll get him straightened out, Marsh." Inside, Hepplewood handed his hat to the butler. "And no word at all from Jervis?"

"No, my lord, still in Liverpool so far as I know," replied Fording. "Shall I fetch your valet?"

"Yes, I want a bath and a sandwich—in that order, and quickly." Hepplewood started up the stairs. "Unless I miss my guess, there'll be a magistrate on the doorstep within the next thirty minutes. Put him in my study."

"Yes, sir." Fording was pinching Hepplewood's favorite— and somewhat travel-worn—hat as if it were infested.

"And Mrs. Aldridge will be arriving shortly," Hepplewood continued, starting up the staircase. "You will remember meeting her at Loughford. She is Miss Caroline's aunt and the mother of the two little girls."

"The governess, my lord?" Fording was clearly intrigued.

"That is no longer the position for which she is being considered," said Hepplewood. "Take her straight to the schoolroom if I'm not down. Oh, and we've taken on an under-coachman by the name of Brooks. Kindly see to replacing his livery at once."

Hepplewood bathed and dressed with remarkable speed, then bolted down half a sandwich with a lack of decorum that would have done Fluffles proud. He was very sure Tafford would turn up; his mother would give him no choice. And when he did, Hepplewood meant to look every inch a peer of the realm—and a rich one, too.

"My best charcoal frock coat," he said to his valet.

There wasn't a chance in hell a London magistrate would take those girls from Isabella, he reassured himself as the valet slipped the elegant garment up his sleeves. And yet it felt just now as though his entire life was riding upon his ability to get this right.

Yes, he had thrown down the gauntlet—and a rather large bluff—all at once. And though a decade of hard gaming and hard living had instilled in him the ability to mask his every emotion, there was still a cold fear gnawing in the pit of his belly.

A fear of losing both Isabella and the girls.

A fear of losing what he'd hardly known he wanted.

But he did want it, by God—and he would have it, he prayed, though it might very much depend on what Jervis had discovered.

Tafford, however, would prove far less a challenge than Isabella would, he felt sure. And as to himself—well, he did not deserve what he wanted. He never did. But he had become selfish again; he needed Isabella with a desperation that was swiftly overcoming his good sense.

Yes, perhaps it was not Tafford who had instilled that gnawing fear after all.

He had no sooner started back down the grand staircase when he heard the knocker drop. He lingered on the landing, one ear attuned to the rising swell of conversation—none of it amiable, and one of the voices instantly recognizable.

"Ah, Tafford, your audacity knows no bounds," said Hepplewood, coming briskly down his stairs. "Have you brought your magistrate, then?"

"This is Mr. Horace Wells, your lordship," sniffed Fording, handing his master a card. "And Lord Tafford, whom I gather you know."

Tucking the card into his pocket, Hepplewood cast an assessing eye over Mr. Horace Wells. If ever there had been a more unhappily disposed bureaucrat, Hepplewood had not met him. The gentleman was slight and balding, with a look of something approaching fear upon his face. Poor devil.

"Mr. Wells, I regret you've been dragged from hearth and home for nothing," said Hepplewood more gently. "The children in question are in my care, and they are well."

"But they are *not* your children," interjected Tafford, leaping forward a good foot, one fist balled. "Georgina is my ward and my cousin. And you have no claim whatever on Jemima."

"Nor have you," Hepplewood calmly countered. "Moreover, the children have been for five years in the care of their elder sister, a well-bred widow who—"

"Well-bred my eye!" interjected Tafford. "Isabella Aldridge is in trade. She owns a bookshop. And now I collect the woman means to become nothing but your wh—"

"My what—?" Hepplewood coldly interjected. "Finish that sentence, Tafford, and you'll have a problem from which only the grave, not the magistrate, will extract you."

"Lord Hepplewood, with all respect," said the magistrate, holding up both hands as if to forestall blows, "this is indeed a curious business. Do you deny this man is the girl's guardian?"

"Technically, he may be," Hepplewood acknowledged, "but that is for the courts to sort out."

Looking apoplectic now, Tafford launched into a rambling explanation of why the children should be given to him forthwith, and how horrifically they were suffering under their sister's care.

When he was done, Hepplewood turned a cold smile on the magistrate. "You understand, Mr. Wells, who I am?" he asked quietly. "You understand that my uncle is the Earl of

Duncaster and that his heir, my cousin, is highly placed in the Home Office?"

"Yes, that's right," snarled Tafford. "Trot out your influential names if you will, Hepplewood, but Wells will not be intimidated."

"I haven't the slightest wish to intimidate him, Tafford," said Hepplewood. "It is my intent to intimidate *you*. And to make plain the full force and authority that will be brought to bear upon you and anyone who inserts himself into my path with regard to those children and their happiness."

"Georgina's welfare is my gravest concern," said Tafford, "and none of yours."

"Your concern?" said Hepplewood pointedly. "Then perhaps you would care to explain to this poor, put-upon magistrate why, for nearly five years, you left the child in a shabby farm cottage in Fulham with a leaking roof, peeling paint, and barely any food on the table?"

"Well . . . she was with Isabella," said Tafford, paling a little.

"Yes, the woman you just accused of being unfit to raise her," said Hepplewood. "And yet you did not see fit, in all your grave concern, to provide a proper governess and a proper education for the child? You did not see fit to provide clothing or shelter befitting her circumstance?"

"I am trying to do precisely that," said Tafford, "but you are interfering."

"No, you are trying to force Mrs. Aldridge to marry you," said Hepplewood.

"Yes, well, because that is what is best for the children," he countered.

"Why?" said Hepplewood sharply. "I fail to see what one has to do with the other, Tafford. Either you want what is best for the children, or you do not. Either you mean to provide it, or you do not. But you've given Georgina not so much as a loaf of bread in all these years and have instead brought more and more pressure to bear on Mrs. Aldridge."

Tafford looked at the magistrate. "*Do* something," he snapped.

"Don't look at Mr. Wells," said Hepplewood, "for he is not about to remove those children from the only loving relation they've known for the past five years—not without an order from Chancery."

"And I shall get one," returned Tafford. "You know, Hepplewood, that I shall."

"But not fast enough," he said quietly, "to keep Isabella from marrying me."

A sudden hush fell over the front hall.

"Yes, pray go on with your argument, Tafford," said Hepplewood. "But trust me when I assure you that your solicitor won't so much as get the proper complaint drawn before Isabella and I are wed and your chance of gaining control of her fortune is at an end."

"You . . . You would not marry her," sputtered Tafford. "She—why, she is a nobody."

"But I make a habit of marrying rich nobodies," said Hepplewood acidly. "Ask anyone. No, Tafford, you have badly misplayed your hand here."

He waited for panic to sketch over Tafford's pasty face, then he laughed.

"No, you were initially uncertain there actually *was* an inheritance, weren't you?" Hepplewood went on. "So you and your gorgon of a mother have been weaseling information—by pretending, I suspect, to be Isabella. Perhaps even pretending you were already married to her. And making her Canadian relations think she never *left*

Thornhill. I can prove none of that as yet, but I am a very patient man, Tafford. Are you?"

"I—I shall see you in Chancery, Hepplewood," said Tafford, but much of the wrath had left him. "Mr. Wells, what do you mean to do about this business?"

"I do not care to be used as a tool for someone else's machinations," said the magistrate darkly. "I wish to see the children, Lord Hepplewood—*privately.* I insist upon it. I will assure myself as to their welfare. And then I will see this mysterious sister."

"As soon as she arrives," said Lord Hepplewood.

"But I am already here." Isabella's voice came from the staircase.

Heart sinking, Hepplewood turned to see her perched on his landing like some delicate bird. She had one hand laid lightly upon the banister, but in her eyes was a look of unholy wrath.

"My dear," he managed smoothly. "I do beg your pardon."

"It is Everett who should be begging my pardon," she said coldly. "And yes, I should very much like Mr. Wells to meet my sisters. Perhaps he might care to examine the bruises Lord Tafford's mother left on Jemima when she gagged her mouth and bound her hands? Or see Georgina's tear-swollen eyes? Then yes, he may indeed decide if Everett wants what's best for them."

"Good Lord!" Wells shot Tafford a thunderous look.

"Might I take Mr. Wells back up to your schoolroom, Lord Hepplewood?" she asked, but there was another, darker question in her eyes. "The girls are tired—and terrified now, Everett, thanks to you. Kindly go away and leave my sisters alone. They hate you, in case you had not noticed."

Tafford said nothing.

She looked again at Hepplewood. "I left word at the Home Office for Lord Saint-Bryce to come here as soon as he returns," she said. "I'm sure your cousin can be depended upon to do so."

Hepplewood bowed. "Thank you, my dear," he said. "Fording, take Mrs. Aldridge and Mr. Wells up to the schoolroom, and arrange for them some private place to speak."

"Isabella, this is madness," Everett finally said. "He— why, he won't marry you! And you would not be fool enough to marry such a vile excuse of a gentleman."

Calmly, Isabella turned around. "And that," she said quietly, "is the pot calling the kettle black if ever I heard it."

"Tafford," said Hepplewood grimly, "I think you'd better await Mr. Wells in the street outside."

With that, he seized Tafford by the arm and propelled him toward the front door. Fording threw it open with a tight smile, and Hepplewood pushed his unwanted houseguest out.

Everett stepped down onto the pavement, still swearing them all to the devil, but he looked beaten, bloated, and a little ill.

"Good day to you, sir," said Hepplewood curtly. "Don't expect a wedding invitation."

After cutting him one last black look, Everett turned and started down the pavement toward the mews on the other side of Curzon Street. Just then, a hackney cab turned up from Piccadilly, but Tafford did not look back.

Hepplewood stood on the last step, merely observing the carriage's approach and scarcely daring to breathe. The denizens of Clarges Street did not generally use cabs. Lower servants took the omnibus. Or simply walked.

But professional men, on the other hand . . .

Yes, the cab was slowing, though it seemingly took forever. As it neared, and he espied Jervis's face staring out the glass, Hepplewood hastened down to fling open the door himself. Relief surged with hope when he saw the rotund, tired fellow seated beside his secretary.

"Mr. Jervis," he said, "welcome home."

"Thank you, my lord," said the secretary, climbing down. "This is Mr. Colfax of Spratt, McCann and Colfax in Montreal. I had the good fortune of finding him yesterday upon his disembarkation in Liverpool."

Hepplewood exhaled at last; whatever Isabella's situation was, it would shortly be made clear—though the fact that Everett had not denied knowledge of an inheritance made Hepplewood all the more certain he had surmised rightly.

He put out his hand. "Hepplewood," he said simply. "Do come inside, Mr. Colfax."

ISABELLA LEFT MR. Wells ensconced with Jemima and a pot of tea in the governess's sitting room. He had scowled upon seeing Georgina's eyes, but he had puffed up with wrath upon examining Jemima's wrists.

When he had asked to speak privately with Jemima, the girl had smiled. "Nothing would please me more," she'd said upon catching Isabella's worried gaze. "I am sure I can set Mr. Wells at ease with regard to Lord Tafford's actions today—and his inactions these many years."

Reluctantly, Isabella had acquiesced and stepped out, leaving the door open to Nanny and the younger girls, who were again playing happily.

"I will be just downstairs, Mr. Wells," she had said.

But Wells had waved her off with the look of a man who was merely going through his bureaucratic motions.

It had been a horrific and trying day, Isabella thought as she went back down the stairs—and if the snippets of conversation she'd overheard earlier meant what she thought they did, then the trials were hardly over. She and Hepplewood were about to have some strong words.

But Isabella did not know the half of it, she realized, as she approached the main staircase. She looked down to see that Lord Hepplewood and his secretary Jervis were entering the front door below, speaking in sharp tones with a wan-looking fellow Isabella had never seen before.

"You represent the business interests of the Flynt family, I take it?" Hepplewood was saying.

Isabella froze in midstep, peering over the balustrade. *What on earth?*

"Yes, yes, but I'm looking for Mrs. Isabella Aldridge," the man replied a little peevishly as he followed up the front steps, "or Lady Tafford, if that is now her name?"

Hepplewood spun about in the entrance hall. "It is certainly not her name, Mr. Colfax," he said tightly. "Isabella Aldridge has not married Lord Tafford, nor does she plan to—though I do not doubt certain steps have been taken to obscure that fact."

"And she is living *here,* then?" The man called Colfax furrowed his brow.

"Certainly not," said Hepplewood. "She is a friend—a very dear friend. And she has not lived at Thornhill since well before her father's death."

"That is *not* what our firm was told," said Mr. Colfax stubbornly.

"Then you were lied to," said Hepplewood.

"But indeed, the lady herself said—"

"The lady herself knows nothing of your existence, Mr. Colfax," said Hepplewood firmly. "I trust my secretary made that plain upon finding you in Liverpool? He has been speaking for some weeks to the businesses and solicitors with whom you and the Flynt family are associated."

Mr. Colfax just shook his head. "Well, that's certainly what he claimed, but I cannot see how such a grave misunderstanding occurred," said the solicitor stridently. "Indeed, I'm not at all sure I should be here. I'm expected at Thornhill. By Lord Tafford."

"Then come into my study and I will press on with my explanations," said Hepplewood.

"Nothing would please me more," said Mr. Colfax with asperity. "My business cannot be put off any longer. The Flynts have made their last and final offer. They will not raise it again. And now I *must* see Lady—er, Mrs. Aldridge—in person."

Isabella's head was starting to spin. She could not fathom what was going on—but she certainly meant to.

"Am I *still* being talked about?" she asked, coming down the stairs.

Hepplewood looked up almost guiltily. "My dear, do please join us," he said, going to meet her. "I am so sorry for all the confusion. You have a caller."

He crossed the marble floor with his hands held out to her.

"I can't think how I could have a caller here when I'm but a visitor," she said, taking them and looking up at him uncertainly. "I have left your Mr. Wells with Jemima," she added, dropping her voice. "I wished him to know without any doubt that the girls spoke freely. He . . . He will not try to take them away, Anthony, will he?"

"He will not," Hepplewood murmured. "But it scarcely matters; I would never let them go. Wells would have to bring half the Metropolitan Police down upon us first, and my cousin Royden will not allow it."

Some of the tension went out of her then, and she cast up a look of gratitude. But there was no time for it, she realized, for the three gentlemen were all looking at her with a strange sense of urgency upon their faces.

Hepplewood herded everyone into his study and sent Fording off for tea. He turned then to Isabella.

"My dear, Mr. Colfax is a solicitor from Montreal," he said. "I've had my man Jervis trying to intercept him for some days now. As I understand it, he represents your cousins, William and James Flynt. Is that correct, Mr. Colfax?"

"My *cousins*—?" said Isabella, sinking into a chair. "Why, I hardly knew I had any. What can they possibly want with me?"

Mr. Colfax's expression darkened. "Mrs. Aldridge, we have been corresponding with you since your grandfather's death in an attempt to settle this business."

"I beg your pardon, Mr. Colfax, but I never heard your name until today," said Isabella, her voice rising. "There is no need to become impatient with me, whatever your business."

Mr. Colfax looked suitably chastised, and he exchanged apologetic looks with Jervis.

"Do sit down, everyone," said Hepplewood charitably. "I think you can now see, Colfax, that everything Mr. Jervis has told you about Mrs. Aldridge is quite true."

"*What* is true?" interjected Isabella irritably. "I only met Mr. Jervis once in my life—at Loughford. I declare, this has been the most frightful day."

"My apologies, ma'am." Jervis hung his head.

"My dear, it is like this," said Hepplewood gently. "I sent Jervis up to Liverpool to attempt to intercept—or at least discover the exact business of—Mr. Colfax. Colfax believes, you see, that he has been corresponding with you at Thornhill."

"At *Thornhill*?" she echoed incredulously.

"Yes, he believes you've been living there all this time—indeed, he thinks you never left, because that is what Lady Meredith has led him to believe. I suspect that's why, when your grandfather died, the portrait he bequeathed you was posted to Thornhill."

Isabella turned her watchful gaze on Colfax, who had flushed faintly. "My father died nearly six years ago, sir," she said, "leaving my sisters and me on our own. We live in Knightsbridge, over our bookshop. I can't think why my aunt would suggest otherwise. On the other hand, I can't think what your business might be with me."

"Why, it is the terms of your grandfather's will, ma'am," he said stridently. "It *must* be settled. This lack of direction is beginning to make strategic investment decisions difficult for the Flynts. They simply wish to know if you are in, or if you are out?"

"In or out of what?" she blurted.

"The family business," said Colfax. "Ma'am, do you not understand you own half the company?"

Isabella felt her eyes widen. "I . . . I beg your pardon?"

"But the cash is piling up," continued Colfax, clearly grateful to finally have his audience, "and capital investments are direly needed. The Flynts have written and waited and written and waited, but you—well, *someone*—kept putting them off."

"I know nothing of this." Isabella sat very rigidly in her chair.

"Well, that is neither here nor there now," said Colfax, waving an obviating hand. "Now I merely need to know if you wish to sell out. The Flynts are poised to buy out a steamship company that will limit the company's liquidity. You need to choose a path, Mrs. Aldridge."

"Anthony." Her voice quavered a little, and she did not

dare turn to look at him. "What is this man talking about? And how do you come to know about it, when I do not?"

Hepplewood considered Isabella's question but a moment, then set his hands firmly on his thighs. It was time, he realized, that they had a very private conversation.

"Gentlemen, I must have some time alone with Mrs. Aldridge," he said, rising. "We have important things to discuss."

Colfax's eyes widened. "But—But I have come all the way from Montre—"

"As I'm well aware, sir." Hepplewood had already thrown up a staying hand. "But the Flynt family has fallen prey to a liar, and that is not Mrs. Aldridge's problem. You should have sent one of your Liverpool associates down here years ago."

"But how were we to know Lord Tafford had died? Or that Mrs. Aldridge had removed from Sussex? Or that someone would have the audacity to pretend to . . . well, to *be* her?"

Hepplewood simply shrugged. "In any case, Mrs. Aldridge now requires time to consult her own solicitors," he insisted. "She cannot depend on you or Jervis to advise her—or even me, come to that. You've brought the financial records, I trust? And the Flynts' offer?"

"Well, yes," said Colfax.

"Leave them with Jervis, then, and Mrs. Aldridge will be in touch," he said, herding both men out the study door. "Jervis, see Mr. Colfax up to Claridge's and arrange a suite of rooms to be billed to me."

"Certainly, my lord."

Just then, Fording approached. "Mr. Wells has taken his leave, sir," he said. "He said he was late for tea, and his wife was expecting him. He leaves Mrs. Aldridge his kind regards."

"Does he indeed?" grunted Hepplewood, glancing back at Isabella. "I daresay Jemma must have told him just how that devil kidnapped her off the street."

Thinly, the butler smiled. "Yes, I gather the young lady likened it to being snatched up by a press gang," he said. "Mr. Wells seemed unamused."

"Sir?" Jervis dipped his head to catch his employer's eyes. "Am I off, then?"

"Yes, yes, thank you." But at the last instant, Hepplewood stepped out the door, too, and caught Jervis's arm. "Wait, just what kind of money is Colfax talking about here?" he murmured. "Any idea?"

"Flynts' has its fingers in timber—cutting, milling, *and* exporting—as well as banking and shipping," said Jervis, arching one eyebrow warningly. "William Flynt sits on the board of the Bank of Montreal. The family has links to trading houses worldwide. Colfax values the entirety at two and a half million pounds. And having merely peeked at the financials, I'd say he's hedging a bit."

"Good Lord," said Hepplewood. "They're offering her over a million pounds?"

"Shocking, is it not?" Jervis murmured.

Shocking did not begin to describe it.

Hepplewood went back in and shut the door, his hands shaking a little.

"Anthony." Isabella had risen from the sofa. "What on earth is going on? Kindly explain."

Hepplewood drew a deep breath and urged her back down, seating himself beside her. "What is going on, my dear, is that you are a very wealthy woman," he said, turning to face her. "It seems that after your mother's marriage, your grandfather never changed his will."

Isabella's mouth fell open. "He never . . . *what*—?"

"Never changed his will," Hepplewood repeated. "George Flynt died leaving his estate to be divided equally between his son and daughter, even though both had predeceased him. His son had two children, your Canadian cousins William and James. But his daughter had only one. *You.* Which leaves you owning half the Flynt empire, with William and James owning a quarter each."

"An *empire*?" she repeated. "How did a Canadian wilderness become an empire? It's preposterous. And why leave anything to me?"

"He was sentimental, perhaps?" Hepplewood shrugged. "Perhaps he simply couldn't bring himself to cut your mother out. Or perhaps he just never got round to the paperwork. He left an old will on file with his former solicitor in Liverpool and never altered it. Jervis found it early on. And at the time that will was drawn, the estate was not likely worth what it is today."

"And what *is* it worth today?"

Slowly, he exhaled. "A lot," he finally said. "A quite shocking amount. Such a shocking amount that I should rather we had an expert run through the financials before I commit to giving you a number. If that is acceptable?"

"*A quite shocking amount,*" Isabella quietly murmured. "That is . . . impossible to fathom, really."

"It is impossible for me to fathom," he admitted, "even though I suspected the truth—or a part of it. But I did not quite expect the full extent of his estate."

Isabella's eyes were wide, and a little hopeful. "So . . . do you think perhaps I shan't have to keep a bookshop after all?"

He gave a shaky laugh. "No, my dear, you definitely will not," he said. "Of that much I can assure you. And you won't need to fear Everett ever again."

"Will I not?" she said, lifting a mystified gaze to him.

"This is all so very strange. Anthony, how could I not have known any of it?"

He took both her hands in his. "Isabella, is it possible your father *did* know?" he asked. "And that perhaps he did not tell you for . . . I don't know—for fear of losing you? Or out of some sort of resentment of your grandfather?"

She shook her head. "He wasn't like that," she said, "though my mother . . . yes, she may have known. Or suspected. But Grandfather was a hurtful subject for Papa, so she never spoke of him. And, as you say, the business was probably worth less at that time."

"Then could your mother at some point have confided your grandfather's plan to Lady Meredith?" he pressed. "Is such a thing possible?"

Isabella's gaze grew distant. "I can't imagine why," she said. "Of course, when Lady Meredith was still married to Father's younger brother, they often visited. She and Mamma were friendly, after a fashion, but never were they close."

"Your grandfather wrote occasionally, you said," he mused. "Perhaps Lady Meredith read a letter that was not intended for her eyes?"

Isabella's eyes rounded. "Anthony, that's *just* the sort of thing she would have done!" she whispered. "In fact, after Mamma died so suddenly, it was she who came to pack up Mamma's things. Papa was so devastated that he could not leave his bed."

"Well, we shall likely never know the whole of it," Hepplewood muttered. "Lady Meredith won't confess. But she has certainly been pretending to be you, and putting Colfax and the Flynts off in her letters. She's likely been trying to coax from them the precise value of the company while ordering Everett to press you into marriage."

"But eventually the Flynts would not be put off." Isabella's voice rose. "That's what's been driving Everett's increasing desperation, isn't it? Why he took such an insane risk today? Lady Meredith knew Colfax was coming—and that he would expect to find me at Thornhill—perhaps married to Everett. Dear God. Is that why you took us all to Greenwood?"

"In part." He flashed a grim smile. "Brooks told you, I suppose, that Tafford had a special license in his pocket today?"

She shook her head. "I have not seen Brooks," she said, mystified. "I was so uneasy I decided to walk here from Whitehall. But I would not have married Everett. Anthony, I *would not*. I would have been afraid for the girls, but I would have trusted you to take care of them. To get them back for me."

For some moments, he simply sat beside her on a narrow sofa, holding her hands in his and drawing in her comfortingly familiar scent. His mind kept turning back to the last time he had made love to her; of the ache he'd felt wrenching at his heart after leaving her bed.

He was tired of leaving her bed. Tired of leaving *her*.

Tired of his worn and empty life.

But Isabella's life—her rich, new life, full of choice and promise—was just beginning.

He drew a deep breath and smiled into her eyes. "Well, you do not really need me now, Isabella," he said, giving her hands a reassuring squeeze. "Not to keep the girls safe; not with the sort of money you'll have."

"W-what do you mean?"

"You can give Jemma and Georgie the world, my dear," he said, "and hire enough solicitors to drag Everett into court and keep him there for the rest of his natural life. But he won't bother now, because he knows the Flynt fortune will never be his. His only hope was to keep you poor and beaten down. To get you to marry him before you learned the truth."

Suddenly, she shivered. "Dear God, Anthony," she said. "I owe you . . . *everything.*"

He lifted her hand to his mouth and pressed his lips to it. "You owe me nothing, my love."

"Oh, I do, but I can still hardly make sense of this," she said. "Indeed, I won't believe it until . . . well, I don't know what would persuade me, honestly. But all I can think of is that I am so grateful it was just the money, Anthony."

He frowned, puzzled. "I'm afraid, my love, that I do not follow."

"I'm relieved it was because of the money that Everett wanted me," she said. "*It was just the money.* It was not . . . something vile and unspeakable. It had nothing to do with Jemma or Georgie."

He understood what went unsaid. "Oh, my poor girl," he murmured, drawing her into his arms. "This has been one of the worst days of your life, I do not doubt. And now this strange twist of fate. Your head must be spinning."

In his embrace, she shrugged wanly. "I don't really care about the money," she said, burying her face against the turn of his neck. "I care only that I am free of Everett, and that you are . . ."

"Yes?" he quietly encouraged.

She held perfectly still for a long moment. "What did you mean, Anthony, by what you said to Everett?"

"Oh, I've said a lot of things to Everett today," he said grimly, "and I meant every damn word."

Slowly, she pushed away from his chest, her hands set

to the front of his silk waistcoat. "What did you mean," she clarified, "when you said . . . that you w-would marry me?"

He held her gaze very steadily then, and carefully considered his words. "I meant just what I said; that I would marry you to keep you safe from him," he whispered. "But more than that, I meant that I *wanted* to marry you. I meant that I love you. Madly. Passionately. My soul, I feel, is so thoroughly subsumed within yours, Isabella, that I cannot envision a life without you."

"Oh," she said quietly, her voice catching. "Oh, my. How utterly . . . romantic you sound, Anthony."

He tipped her chin back up with one finger. "But you do not have to *marry* me, Isabella," he said. "Now that we've found Colfax first, Everett will not be back to trouble you. That's what I meant, my dear, when I said you no longer need me. You don't need me to protect you from Everett. His game is up."

"And what about . . . *your* game?" she murmured, dropping her gaze seductively. "Is it up?"

He drew her hard against him then and kissed her—kissed her for a very long time, with his tongue and his hands and his heart—even as he prayed he would do the right thing by her. He kissed her until she was breathless and her hair was tumbling down. Until she was pressing her breasts fully to his chest, practically crawling in his lap.

It was all he could do to maintain decency; to restrain himself from pushing her back onto the sofa and rutting like some beast. He had the most dreadful fear of losing her, but never would he lie to her.

When at last she broke the kiss, her eyes gone dark with desire, he set her a little away.

"I have *never* played games with you, Isabella," he said hoarsely. "What burns between us—oh, love, it is no game.

It is deadly serious. And it will never be over—*never*—marriage or no."

"But d-do you wish to marry me?" she asked, her voice almost inaudible.

"More than anything," he said fiercely. "I love you, Isabella. I cannot—no, I *will not* live without you. And I will never let another man have you. Yes, I want to make a life with you. A family with you. And yet I'm scared of it all the same."

"And I love you," she said quietly. "Moreover, I am not scared. Not in the way you mean. I will be fine bearing children; I know it with certainty. But I will not be fine without you. That, Anthony, is the thing that might destroy me."

He cupped her face between his hands. "But again, my love, I need you to understand that you do not have to marry me," he said more stridently. "I am yours. And you—God help you—you are mine. *Mine*. I would have throttled Everett with my bare hands before I'd have seen you go to him. Do you understand? As I would throttle any man who dared try to take you from me."

She looked at him almost pleadingly. "Anthony, what are you saying?"

"That you are wealthy, Isabella, and safe. Safe from Everett. Safe from hardship and poverty. Safe from, to a large extent, even the rumor mill, because wealth is society's greatest insulator," he added. "Moreover, my love, you do not have to . . . to run the awful risk that marriage brings."

"The risk of childbed," she said. "That's what you mean, isn't it?"

He squeezed his eyes shut. "Yes," he rasped. "That's exactly what I mean."

"But, oh, Anthony, I want more than anything to have children," she whispered. "*Your* children. Children to play with Lissie and Georgie and Jemma. But I want you more, even, than that." She gave a nervous laugh. "I think I want you on any terms. However I must take you."

He kissed her again, more gently now.

"Yes, *that,*" she said throatily, drawing away and letting her gaze fall to her lap. "I want you, and what you can give me. What *only* you can give me. Do you understand, Anthony?"

"All that," he murmured, brushing his lips over her temple, "and children, too?"

"I am going to be wealthy," she said. "Yes, then. I want it all. Is that not what wealthy people say? Lady Petershaw always did."

He threw back his head and laughed. "Then God help *me,*" he said. "Taking lessons from *La Séductrice,* are you?"

"Actually, I have been taking lessons—or at least advice—from her for some time now," Isabella confessed.

He managed to laugh. "Actually, I had noticed," he confessed. Then he considered what next to say. "Well," he finally added, "I had better do this properly."

Her gaze followed him to his wall safe, hidden within his bookshelf.

"What are you doing?" she asked as he piled the *Encyclopædia Britannica* on his desk.

He made her no answer but instead unlocked the safe behind the books and returned to the sofa.

"Isabella Glaston Aldridge," he said, going down on one knee, "I humble myself before you. I am a bad man, and not worthy of your goodness or your beauty. But will you have me for better or for worse? Will you marry me and live out your days doing my wicked bidding, and bearing my children?"

"It sounds like such a bargain when you put it that way," she said. "Yes, Anthony. I will marry you, with the understanding that sometimes—*sometimes*—the wicked bidding will be mine."

"Yes, that financial independence is going to your head already, I see," he murmured.

With that, he produced a ring of half-carat amethysts mounted around a diamond that looked large enough to span from one knuckle to the next.

"Very well, my love," he said, taking her left hand lightly in his, "I love you more than life itself. And I will marry you—and yes, do your wicked bidding—under one ironclad condition."

Her fingers already outstretched, Isabella drew them back an inch. "What one condition?"

He looked at her, all the teasing gone from his eyes. "That you take every penny of the Flynt fortune, however much it is, and put it in trust for your sisters," he said, "and, if you wish, our children. But I do not want it; not a sou. And Lissie does not need it. Do you understand, Isabella, how important this is to me?"

"Very well, yes," she said on a laugh, "but you act as if it will be millions."

"Regardless of the amount, my love," he said, "you have promised? If you cannot promise me this, I must reconcile myself to nothing but a long and torrid *affaire de coeur* with you."

"Yes, then," she said more solemnly. "I have promised."

He slipped the ring a little awkwardly onto her finger. "Then I promise to be a faithful and devoted husband," he said solemnly, "until death do us part."

Isabella wiggled her finger. "Now that," she said a little breathlessly, "is a beautiful ring—but a trifle too snug, I fear."

"I think you're right," he agreed, "because you were a good deal thinner, Isabella, when I bought it."

"Ah," she said quietly. "At Garrard's, I suppose?"

"Yes."

Then Hepplewood bowed his head, lifted Isabella's hand to his lips, and pressed them lingeringly to her knuckles again.

Epilogue

Hepplewood stirred to the sensation of sun dappling his face, shadow and light shifting above him in a warm breeze. Opening his eyes, he blinked up into a canopy of green, then moved to lift his hand as if he might drag the cobwebs of sleep from his face.

But his hand oddly resisted.

He roused to the sound of soft laughter and rolled his head to see Isabella sitting on the blanket beside him.

"*Umpfh,*" he managed to mutter. "Slept, eh?"

"And *snored,*" she accused. "One might have heard the racket all the way up to Thornhill—well, if anyone were home."

Still drowsy, Hepplewood tried to cut a glance at the manor on the hill to his right. Then realizing his movement was restricted, he finally glanced down at his wrist.

"The devil!" he said.

The witch had bound him.

Trussed him up like some clever little Lilliputian as he slept in the sun, binding him wrist and ankle to the spindles that surrounded the minuscule gazebo—well, those few spindles remaining. The balustrade about them dipped and listed like a drunken sailor in a hurricane. The shingles, too, had long ago flown to the four winds, leaving scarcely a skeleton of rafters above.

Like much of Isabella's old home, it was little more than a lovely ruin.

Tentatively, he twitched at the thin rope that bound his left ankle. "Meaning to have your wicked way with me again, are you?" he said, grinning as he felt the rot give.

"I mean to bend you to my will, yes," she said with an airy wave. "Precisely what form that subjugation will take I am still pondering."

"And the rope?" he asked, amused.

"From the old bothy by the gate." She tilted her head coquettishly toward the garden's once-elegant back entrance. "Papa's gardener always kept it. And now I've made you my prisoner."

He laughed and let his head fall back onto something soft. "Oh, my love, I have long been your prisoner," he said. "By the way, what is my head resting upon?"

"My underthings. I made you a pillow."

"Ah." He glanced at the modest crinoline she'd flung aside. "Most intriguing."

"I took them off," she said, "merely to cradle your head."

"My dear, you are too kind," he replied.

She grinned. "Actually, I'd hoped to stop the snoring."

"Kind *and* plainspoken," he added. "I have indeed married wisely."

"Stop talking," she ordered, rising gracefully onto her knees. "You are my prisoner. I am deciding what use to make of you."

"You already have your drawers off," he pointed out. "Might I offer an immodest proposal?"

"No," said his wife sternly, "—or at least not so willingly."

"Aye," he murmured, narrowing his gaze against the sun. "Sauce for the goose and all that, eh?"

"Indeed, quite." She leaned over him, her gaze running avariciously down his length as her dark, feathery lashes dropped suggestively lower.

And although he lay well sated from an earlier romp in the garden, Hepplewood felt a hot rush of longing go twisting deep. His body stirred to sensual awareness—as it inevitably did when she dropped her gaze in just such a fashion.

"On top," he ordered gruffly.

Isabella drew a finger pensively—tormentingly—down his cheek, and then along his jugular vein. "That sounded dangerously high-handed for a man who's been tied up," she said, her voice husky.

"Isabella," he said more evenly. "Come, love. Just unfasten my—"

"In time, perhaps," she interjected, drawing nearer.

His coat and waistcoat having been cast off somewhere on the hillside that led down from the house, Hepplewood had drifted off in his shirtsleeves. Leaning over him now, Isabella inched one shirttail free with an almost agonizing deliberation. When the second followed, she bent low and drew her tongue lightly through the hair that trailed up his belly.

"*Umm*," he moaned, willing himself to lie perfectly still.

She worked her way up, inching the fabric along as she went. And though he suspected the thin ropes had long ago rotted, he let her have her way. By the time the woman was done with him, his forehead had beaded with perspiration, his trousers were open, and his breath was rasping.

"Come, love," he choked. "Be reasonable."

Isabella took mercy on him then, gathering her skirts about her knees and straddling him. Then, taking him well in hand, she impaled herself upon his erection on a soft sigh of pleasure. And with her small, pale hands set wide upon his chest, her wedding ring glinting in the sun, they rocked and thrust and whispered words of love unending until they found that inexpressible joy once more.

He came in a shuddering explosion of pleasure, then slowly settled back down from the heavens; back to that place of quiet and peace he had enjoyed at such leisure since his marriage. Isabella was splayed across his chest, gasping, her lustrous hair tumbling down. Slowly, he let his hands fall from her slender waist. Only then did he realize he'd ripped the old ropes asunder.

"Madam, you have used your prisoner to exhaustion," he said on a laugh.

"Indeed, no treadwheel for you tonight, I fancy," she agreed, burying her face against the damp of his neck.

"Well, perhaps a lash or two, then?" he said, grinning. "Or another stretch of hard labor?"

They had been ensconced alone together in this lazy little corner of Sussex for some three days now, putting up at the village inn, a pretty, pleasant little place. The visit had felt at times like a second honeymoon, for absent any interruptions from the children, their nights—and even the occasional afternoon—had been torrid and romantic as they'd immersed themselves in one another.

Their days, on the other hand, had been spent being feted like prodigal children as they'd dined and danced and gossiped their way across the countryside with Isabella's old friends and neighbors.

All were agog with Lord Tafford's flight to the Continent some three months earlier. Faced with insurmountable debts, he had sold off what little he could and abandoned both his mother and Thornhill, leaving the staff unpaid and the house empty. Today, after Hepplewood and Isabella had dallied their way about the grounds, Hepplewood had given in to impatience and simply pried up a window.

It was worse than he had hoped. And yet better, too. The place was in utter disrepair, with much of the furniture and artwork gone. But there was not one trace of Tafford left behind.

Isabella had cried a little, then dried her tears and pressed on with her plan. Eventually, it seemed, Thornhill would have to be sold. Even entail, Hepplewood had been advised, could be broken were a man's debts deep enough and his heirs nonexistent. The Crown or the courts or *someone* would eventually have to do something.

Certainly Hepplewood intended to do something. It was the least he could do for her, his hard-won bride. Already he'd had Jervis—along with half the City's solicitors and all his influential relatives—exerting untold pressure on the powers-that-be.

Yes, in the end, Isabella would have her home back. He was determined. And, as Anne was ever fond of pointing out, in the end he always got what he wanted—whether he deserved it or not.

They lay in silence for a time, but despite the lethargy he could sense the questions bubbling up inside her again.

He lifted his head and kissed her hair. "What?" he murmured, sliding a finger beneath her chin.

She lifted her head to look at him, a knowing smile curving her mouth. "Anthony, *have* you married well?"

He laughed, this time at himself. "Oh, I've married far better than I deserve," he said. "If you don't believe me, ask

Anne. I've married up, Isabella. I have married perfection."

"Have you indeed?" She sat up, her lashes lowering again as she drew one finger down the center of his chest. "Then you will not mind so very much then? Taking on this task I have set out for you?"

Hepplewood smiled and tucked a loose curl behind Isabella's ear. "For the merest scrap of a favor, my love, I would be your champion," he said, "and gird my loins to do battle with those indefatigable dragons, Chancery and the Insolvent Debtor's Court."

"Ah," she said, grinning. "Then you are a bold knight indeed."

He grinned. "Actually, I'll first send forth Jervis, my stalwart squire," he said, "along with a quiver of freshly sharpened pencils and a battery of account books. Already he's rattling on about something called a disentailing deed. An estate as lush as this cannot simply be left to lie fallow."

Isabella had begun to fling away the bits and pieces of rope. "It is lovely, isn't it?" she said a little wistfully, picking loose one of the knots. "It is not just me being sentimental?"

"It is certainly you being sentimental," he countered, holding out his right wrist for her ministrations, "which is one of the many things I love about you. But yes, this is good land. What a pity it has been neglected."

"I believe it won't continue so," said Isabella, flinging the last scrap of rope over the rail, "now that Everett has run away to the Continent in shame."

Hepplewood grunted. "With any luck, he'll be snared up in one of their inevitable little wars," he muttered, "and get himself shot. Certainly he won't darken England's door again."

"It was a little sad, wasn't it, how quickly Aunt Meredith

cast him to the wolves once he'd left?" Isabella murmured, rising to gather her things.

Hepplewood gave a bark of laughter. "Oh, she's a survivor, that old cat," he said, handing his wife her petticoat and drawers, "but she has no claim whatever to this land. By the way, I trust you've not returned any of her groveling missives?"

Isabella shook her head. "No, and I pray she never forces my hand," she said. "I should hate to cut anyone in public. But for Jemma and Georgie's sake, I should have to."

"For your husband's sake, you'd have to," he muttered. "But what will you do with this old place, love? Shall we live here? Would that please you?"

She smiled softly. "No, my life is no longer here," she said, stepping back into her crinoline. "My life is with you, Anthony. No, I think it should be Georgina's. It should have been her home. She should have been allowed to grow up here, in her father's house, a carefree and happy child. Instead she doesn't even remember it."

"Fate cheated her," he said, his eyes going to the distant roofline, now dark against the afternoon sky. "But perhaps Thornhill can be her dowry. Shall I arrange that, my love? Would it please you?"

At that, Isabella seemed to brighten down to the tips of her toes. "Oh, above all things!" she declared, extending a hand down to him. "Sometimes, Anthony, you can be the wisest of men—no matter what Anne may say. Now come, up with you. The Misses Greenbittle await, along with their infamous elderflower cordial."

"Damn and blast!" he said, rising. "The parson's sisters?"

"The very same," she said, taking his arm and steering him down the rickety steps. "We're expected there at six sharp. And promise me, my love, that you'll wink and flirt with them outrageously. After all, you have a notorious reputation to uphold—and they have but little excitement here in the village."

"Wink and flirt, eh?" He winced a little. "I confess, Isabella, playing the arrant roué is wearing on me a trifle nowadays."

"Poor Tony!" she said as she pushed through the garden gate. "Your life is so very hard. Now come along, dear. We must find where we shed your coat and cravat—or you shall look one step worse than an arrant roué."

"Hmph!" he said, abruptly snatching her and plunging them both into the shadows of the bothy. "I say the Misses Greenbittle can damned well wait. Now where the devil is the rest of that rope?"

At Avon Books, we know your passion for romance—once you finish one of our novels, you find yourself wanting more.

May we tempt you with . . .

- **Excerpts** from our upcoming releases.

- Entertaining **extras**, including authors' personal photo albums and book lists.

- Behind-the-scenes **scoop** on your favorite characters and series.

- **Sweepstakes** for the chance to win free books, romantic getaways, and other fun prizes.

- Writing **tips** from our authors and editors.

- **Blog** with our authors and find out why they love to write romance.

- **Exclusive content** that's not contained within the pages of our novels.

Join us at
www.avonbooks.com

An Imprint of HarperCollins*Publishers*
www.avonromance.com

Available wherever books are sold or please call 1-800-331-3761 to order.

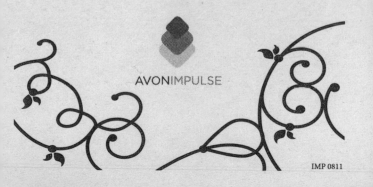